Rob,

Winston Churchill had it right. Writing a book is first an adventure, then an amusement, then a mistress, then a monster, then a tyrant, before being flung upon the public.

Thank you for everything!

Mike

Following a successful 40-year career in the fields of Information Technology, Human Resources Management, and International Trade, Michael MacNeil returned with his wife to his native Nova Scotia to pursue a long-held desire to write.

He and his wife have one grown son, now with his own growing family.

This is his first novel.

To the members of my close family – my wife, my brothers, and my son, whose love and active support have made this book possible.

Michael W. MacNeil

AVENDAÑO'S LEGACY

Austin Macauley Publishers™
LONDON * CAMBRIDGE * NEW YORK * SHARJAH

Copyright © Michael W. MacNeil (2018)

The right of Michael W. MacNeil to be identified as author of this work has been asserted by him in accordance with section 77 and 78 of the Copyright, Designs and Patents Act 1988.

All rights reserved. No part of this publication may be reproduced, stored in a retrieval system, or transmitted in any form or by any means, electronic, mechanical, photocopying, recording, or otherwise, without the prior permission of the publishers.

Any person who commits any unauthorised act in relation to this publication may be liable to criminal prosecution and civil claims for damages.

A CIP catalogue record for this title is available from the British Library.

ISBN 9781786936417 (Paperback)
ISBN 9781786936424 (Hardback)
ISBN 9781786936431 (E-Book)

www.austinmacauley.com

First Published (2018)
Austin Macauley Publishers Ltd.
25 Canada Square
Canary Wharf
London
E14 5LQ

Acknowledgements

To my many friends in Canada, the US, and the UK, my thanks for your valuable observations, comments, suggestions, and insights about the text. You each know who you are.

To the London Silver Vaults, my appreciation for their valuable assistance regarding the pedigree and use of the Royal Presentation Stick Pin, worn by Reginald Binglethorpe, a character in the novel.

Chapter 1

He had to do it. His obligation was to fulfill his promise to Kan 'Ek.

The meetings between the two had been long and often stressful. But gradually the Mayan leader had come around. He said, "If you produce this writing, I will bring my people to you."

Father Andres de Avendaño nodded solemnly. "I will do it."

And now Avendaño had returned to the monastery from his journey to Kan 'Ek's city. His first duty on arriving was to meet with his Father Bishop, to describe his journey and his meetings with Kan 'Ek, and the commitment that he had made. At first Bishop Antonio de Arrigaga y Agüero was scornful, and tried hard to belittle what he was being told. But gradually Avendaño's persuasive arguments of native conversion without additional bloodshed brought him around. He had never seen eye to eye with Avendaño, thinking him far too knowledgeable and worldly for a mere priest. The priest made him uncomfortable.

But one thing the Bishop had learned. As the years had passed since Avendaño had first arrived from Spain, he knew to pay greater attention, albeit somewhat grudgingly, to his junior. He listened now to Avendaño's arguments.

"Kan 'Ek is a powerful leader of more than two thousand. He, his father before him, his father before that, and back through the ages, have all followed their own teachings and customs and practices. Many of his people have heard the horror stories of other tribes of how we have used force to convert, and they want nothing to do with us."

The Bishop scowled. "We must make them," he muttered.

"Yes, we must succeed. And we will succeed. But why continue the forcing, the tortures, the public killings … the terror that turns them all against us, when we can do it much more easily? And bring them willingly to us?"

"You question the authority of the Church?"

"No! I question only the brutality of what we're doing."

The Bishop said nothing, but Avendaño could see the beginning of a gleam in his eye. The Bishop was thinking that this could be a way to curb whispers of criticism that had increasingly been making their way from his superiors about his administration.

"You see, My Lord Bishop, what I have promised Kan 'Ek is to write a book, a simple book that will show the comparisons and relationships between our liturgical Latin and their own sacred language. You know that I have made a considerable study of their language and can speak it. I think that is why you chose me for your sanctified mission to convert his people."

The Bishop nodded, and then decided.

"Go, Father de Avendaño, go and write this book. Make copies. One for me, two for the library here at the monastery, one for His Majesty. It might be something to amuse him, I think. Four copies."

"I must provide Kan 'Ek with two. It's what he requested. I agreed."

"Oh, very well. Six, then."

"My Lord Bishop, I beg to be excused. The fevers are getting worse now, and I need to rest."

"You have my leave. You may go."

Father de Avendaño bowed himself out of the Bishop's hot, airless study and made his way back to his spartan quarters. He dropped exhausted onto his cot, and fell into a deep sleep.

The next day, feeling only partially refreshed, and despite the pains that coursed through his body, he forced himself to begin work. His strength was seeping away. He quailed at the size of the task in front of him. It seemed insurmountable. But his commitment to Kan 'Ek was enough to overcome the pains.

He set to work assembling the materials and the information he'd managed to collect on his long, arduous travels through the jungles to Kan 'Ek's village. He cleared off a space on the small work table in his cubicle.

He began to write.

Chapter 2

Kevin Watts was worried. The worry had been building for months. Only glimmerings of solutions showed: solutions to a large and potentially devastating financial burden.

The family estate was first formed in the seventeenth century. It consisted of three hundred acres of mixed arable, forested and pasture land. A large comfortable house together with its outbuildings occupied the better part of an acre.

The lands were located in Scotland, a comfortable distance away from Edinburgh, but still close enough for its residents to be easily deafened by the large passenger jets that followed the flight path down into that city's airport.

Now the owner, Kevin had been left the property by his father, a man of eccentric disposition. The will stipulated the land be held in the family in perpetuity. This moved the ownership of the property from the realm of accepted but informal family custom to a permanent legal requirement.

The property was heavily mortgaged. It had not always been this way. Initially a royal grant, the family had lived in it and farmed it for more than three hundred years. But with increasingly heavy tax burdens, together with the growing and pressing demands for building maintenance, Kevin had determined that bank financing was the only option. And in recent months Kevin's own precarious financial situation had been laying the groundwork that, if permitted to continue, would put the loans into default.

He was sitting at his desk, staring moodily out over the winter brown fields. 'I can't default on the loans,' he mused. 'Damn the Old Man, he's saddled me with an impossible situation. I can't make the payments, but if I go into default the lawyers'll be all over me for violating the terms of the will.' "Damn it!!" he repeated, this time loud enough for his housekeeper to put her head around the door to see what the noise was.

Despite his outburst, Kevin had for some time been searching for alternate funding options to help him resolve his mortgage problems. So far he had barely managed every month to make the payments, but available funds were beginning to run low and if he did nothing, soon the axe would fall. In no way was he in a mood to allow this to happen.

For some time he had been interested in archeology. Although trained in the field of computer science, that line of work had long since lost all appeal. His interest in archeology had led him into various and occasionally obscure pathways. His extensive library held a number of works on the subject and that, together with the seeming infinite resources of the Internet, afforded him a wealth of knowledge and places to search.

One time, not so long before, he had come across a paragraph in a book about the ancient Mayans of Central America. It had mildly intrigued him at the time, and he marked the passage should he want to come back to it.

Now, with the increasing pressures on him, he remembered that paragraph. He reached up for the book, opened it at the marked page, and read:

"Avendaño wrote a treatise on his studies, but the only known copy has disappeared. Mayan scholars are haunted by the thought that little more than a century divides the death of the old knowledge and the awakening of modern research."[1]

Reading it again, Kevin began to realize it was not only the Mayan scholars who were haunted by the disappearance of that document. It had caught his imagination, and he was, too.

"What would I do," he asked his empty study, "what would I need to do to find this document? If it's the only one of its kind, it must be worth a great deal of money. If only I could find it."

It seemed an impossibility – at first. But as he read, and he dug, and he investigated, and as the weeks passed, he accumulated a body of notes and research materials that led him to believe the search could be a reasonable one.

All the while he had been thinking about what he would do if he found this document. Could he sell it? Possibly, if he could find an auction house that would accept it for sale. But even if not, the search and recovery itself would make interesting reading for others. For this though he would need help. He was no good with words, although he loved to read. One of his weaknesses was fiction, and he tended to read all the works of authors he particularly liked. One such writer happened to be a chap he'd been to

---

[1] *Time Among The Maya*, by Ronald Wright, Viking (Penguin Group), 1989

school with, more than twenty years before. Sam Barnes was the only novelist he'd ever known.

He searched in Barnes's books for a means of contact, but found only information for his publisher. He wrote to the publisher, and was surprised when, a few days later, the publisher provided an email address for Barnes.

That same afternoon Kevin sat down at his computer. 'Dear Sam,' Kevin wrote, 'you will probably think me completely mad with what I am about to suggest, but I want to assure you this is a serious proposal. How would you like to spend a couple of weeks in Mexico?'

Chapter 3

It had been snowing all night. When I opened the curtains first thing this morning, I looked out onto the fourth winter blizzard Toronto had experienced this month.

The smell of fresh coffee coming from the kitchen was warm and seductive. I poured myself a cup, sat down at my desk and opened my email.

The usual mess of junk mail had accumulated in my inbox overnight. I began to delete them all. One message looked like junk, but something stopped me from deleting it. Curiosity took hold. Ever wary of lurking viruses, I nevertheless took the chance and opened it.

'Dear Sam,' it began, 'you will probably think me completely mad with what I am about to suggest, but I want to assure you this is a serious proposal. How would you like to spend a couple of weeks in Mexico?'

"Oh sure," I said to the monitor, "one more crook who wants me to help him."

I get this stuff all the time. Offers to sell me things I didn't want. Unsolicited newsletters filled with information of little value to me. Offers to improve my personal, private life beyond my wildest sensual imaginings. Pleas for my assistance to release millions of suspect dollars trapped in questionable bondage in various countries on the African continent.

I continued reading. The quality of the language was superior to that of the usual Nigerian-style scam letter. I looked again at the name of the sender. Kevin Watts. Did I know that name? It was ringing a distant bell, but I was having trouble placing it.

Then the penny dropped. Kevin Watts. From school, twenty … no, twenty-five years ago.

It was a long message, and I took the time to digest it. But the gist of it was that I should immediately drop everything I was presently doing here in Toronto, join him in Mexico and, with him, search for an ancient document he wasn't sure even existed anymore.

Unicorns?

Staring out at the swirling snow, it was easy for me to agree with Kevin that his proposal was more than far-fetched, but it was also attractive enough for me to want to give it more than passing consideration.

For it *was* attractive. A couple of weeks in Mexico is always agreeable. At this time of year, in the middle of a very snowy February, many considered it a necessity.

I printed the email to take with me to my downtown office, where I usually wrote in the mornings. Then, at noon, I was due to meet my agent, Harry Oliver, for a quick lunch at our favourite watering hole, "The Golden Thumb", thinking I might discuss the notion with him.

Chapter 4

As I entered The Golden Thumb, a six-piece jazz combo was just setting up in a far corner of the room. The players were riffing away, readying to swing into their first set. Live jazz was one of the reasons I liked this place. It was also conveniently located.

I liked the Golden Thumb. Years ago it had started life in a side street just west of Yonge Street, near the Yonge/Bloor intersection. But when the landlords of the area began to recognize the gold mine for what the area was, and rents increased astronomically, the owner of this business decided to move. He shifted the entire operation farther west. It was now housed in one of the many old industrial buildings that lined the western extension of Queen Street in the western core of the city. Originally built as factories for light manufacturing, these old four-story brick buildings had fallen over the years into disuse with the changing economy, and eventually were slated for demolition. Instead, smart developers bought them and converted them into lofts, condos, open plan offices, restaurants, and a few comfortable pubs. The "Golden Thumb" was one of them. It became the regular meeting place for Harry and me.

It is one of those tucked-away places where the drinks are honest, the food plentiful; the prices reasonable; the service friendly, and the music enjoyable but unobtrusive. Along the length of one wall was a long, brightly-polished wooden bar, behind which stood two smiling and very comely young women in matched blue and white uniforms. Those two served an elaborate array of drinks with the efficiency born of long practice. The room was large, yet had an intimate comfortable feel. Across the room from the bar stood the little corner stage where the jazz combo was getting ready to play, the players' little music lights reflecting gently off the beaten copper ceiling. Subdued lighting was artfully placed in the ceiling throughout the room, and was sufficient for the guests sitting at various sized tables to read the daily menus, and to study the stylized art deco posters mounted on several walls, each one describing a different aspect of Toronto's history. The walls were covered in dark paneling, and this added to the overall sense of comfort and persuasive elegance.

Harry Oliver arrived, shaking the snow off his coat and hat. He strode across the dark red carpeting and sat down at my table.

I write novels for a living. Harry is my agent, and a good one at that. He's also my mother's younger brother. Much younger, so at 58 he's more like a friend to my 42, instead of just an uncle. He's been my agent for about ten years now, helping me sell the books that I so painstakingly write.

He took off his rimless glasses to polish the bits of melting snow from them and stared at me. "So? Where's my scotch?"

I had seen him arrive and I quickly waved to one of the waiters, known locally but obscurely as 'thumbs', hovering nearby. "Bring my friend his scotch. Maybe you should make it a double: he looks frozen from the storm."

Putting his glasses back on, Harry acknowledged it appreciatively. "I'm glad my sister taught you manners." He blew on his hands to warm them. "God! It's bloody cold out there. Another storm! This has got to be the third this month."

"Fourth."

Harry nodded, and looked at me accusingly. "You're still drinking beer," he said. "Why don't you switch to scotch, like I'm always telling you? You still drink like a peasant."

"You don't pay me enough of my royalties to afford scotch. Besides, beer's friendlier. Its subtleties are broader than scotch; there's a challenge in treating it just right."

"Don't talk to me about subtleties. Your last book needed an almost complete rewrite. It cost us both a fortune in delayed royalties because of that – me more than you. And you know that delayed royalties are lost royalties. They won't be recouped. I hope the one you're working on won't need so much work."

"Harry, I've told you a dozen times: that was the subtlety. I thought you would have twigged to it by now. I had to be obvious for those readers who always have trouble with the big words. But I used reverse psychology. Being obvious *was* being subtle. The story needed it. Mind you, the reader needed to be subtle to begin with in order to appreciate it." I took a long pull at my beer. "You must be selling to the wrong markets."

"With writers like you in my stable, Sam Barnes," pointing an accusing finger at me, "I'm lucky to have any markets at all. Thank God I don't have to deal with those lit'ry types; I'd never sell anything at all." He heaved a theatrical sigh. "Well, so long as they continue to pay, I suppose I must be thankful. All they want to do is stand around at parties, buttonholing anyone who'll listen, and telling them how wonderful they are!"

"And you've always told me that I wrote literary novels. Just so long as you're happy, Harry, that's what counts. You can keep those big-titted types you meet at your parties. And incidentally, it wasn't a complete rewrite … just a few passages, here and there."

Harry wore a look of satisfaction. His drink had arrived. He lifted it, gave me a quick silent toast which I returned with the glass of dark ale in front of me, and drank. A smile of contentment crossed his face.

Earlier this morning he had called me at my little office to suggest we change our lunch to a different day on account of the storm. But I said, "No, I have something I want to talk to you about."

"What is it?"

"It'll keep till lunch."

Harry hung up the phone without saying goodbye.

Now, here at lunch, he smiled again, and said, "Well, that tastes just right. I'm glad I decided to come after all." He sipped some more of it.

I took another long pull at my own drink. "Besides," I continued, "I say you're wrong. My five successful novels, each one of them pulling in respectable flows of income. And I've got plenty of ideas for more … just as soon as I can get rid of the thing you dumped on me last fall."

"You're not going to let me forget that, are you?"

"Not a chance, Harry. I thought we had an agreement about how we'd work together. You violated it with the ghostwriting project. A 'favour', you said. Just a quick rewrite, you said. But now I've been buried under the damn thing for months when my time could have been better spent working on something that *I* wanted. And all you do is keep prodding me for results. I keep telling you: you'll get the results when I'm good and ready to give them to you."

He grinned at me – we've been having this conversation for months.

"And not a minute before!" I added.

"Hmph!" Then, tiring of the subject, he glanced around him at the crowded room. "I've always liked these saloon-type bars," he said. "They remind me of the old Western movies I was addicted to as a kid. Time was when I couldn't see enough of them. The difficulty I always had with them was that they all were shot in black and white."

"How much did you pay to get in? Ten cents? Or did you slip in when they weren't looking?"

He ignored that. "It wasn't until those movies began to appear in colour that I could get to understand what those saloons really looked like. Then I fell for them. But you know what? Later on, when I was more or less of legal age, and I wanted to go out for a drink, I looked for places like that."

"More or less? Knowing you I'd bet less."

"You know, Sam, your mother always told me that you had little interest in our family history. You really should pay closer attention: you might learn something useful. It would be a fresh beginning for you."

"And she always told me you were the wild one in the family, who had no interest in keeping to the straight and narrow."

He shifted impatiently in his chair and huffed, "I would like to continue my reminiscence – *if* you don't mind! So, anyway … all I could find were those dreadful taverns. They were large, soulless rooms, all concrete floors and little round tables spread all about, each one with its foursome of bent-back hard wooden chairs. Waiters served customers, moving back and forth between the serving counter and the tables. They had little streetcar conductor-style change machines hooked to their belts, and their large tin trays were filled with glasses of 10-cent beer. And the beer!! My God! It wasn't beer at all. A lot of people loved it, but I always thought it was more like liquid air. Just ice-cold fizzy water. Couldn't take more than a glass or two, if that."

"Yeah. I've heard about those places. I'll bet you lived in them."

"Thank God they've all disappeared."

"Have they? I'm not so sure. I heard there were a few of them still around."

"News to me."

The jazz combo was just sliding smoothly into their first number, an old Harold Arlen tune, "Stormy Weather". The long, smooth passages from the rhythm section contrasting nicely with the high, bright notes from the cornet. How appropriate, I thought, glancing out through the windows at the wind-blown whiteout in the street. Thick traffic moved sluggishly, tentatively, warily.

"When I called you this morning you said something about an email. What's all this about Mexico?" He blew on his hands, and rubbed warmth back into them. Instead of trying to explain it all to him, I gave him Kevin's email to read.

"Good God!" he burst out when he saw the size of the message. "I thought emails were supposed to be short."

"They are. Or, they should be. People don't pay as much attention any more to long messages. It's what things like Twitter and Facebook have done. Attention spans have been shortened to 140 characters. How many long, dry novels do you see being written anymore?"

He nodded absently and started to read. I watched him as he read it, his eyes, partially hidden behind rimless spectacles, flicking back and forth. He was a fast reader and I could see him absorbing the message, grimacing now and then when he encountered particularly unusual passages.

Harry was one of those people with an engaging personality, a sharp and ready wit, a searching mind, an encyclopedic memory, and the ability to dredge up the most obscure facts and link them together into valuable knowledge – usually relevant to whatever conversation he was having at the time. This gave him a worldly authority and moral stature far beyond his portly 5' 9" frame. Topping it all was neatly trimmed white hair that formed a semi-circle framing a shiny pate. It reminded me of the caldera of an extinct volcano. Together with a ruddy complexion, and twinkling eyes behind his rimless eyeglasses of the sort that the wearer was obliged to use a finger to hook them over the ears, one arm at a time, I often thought Harry resembled a prosperous gnome.

Dear Sam,

You will probably think me completely mad with what I am about to suggest, but I want to assure you this is a serious proposal. I hope you will forgive this rather long email. I've become quite garrulous over the years. I was able to locate you through your publisher's website. They have agreed to forward this on to you.

I wonder if you remember me? My name is Kevin Watts, and we were at school together about twenty years ago. You studied English and

Spanish... were quite good at them as I recall. I also seem to recall you were a great fan of science fiction. So was I, as it happened, and I was always borrowing your novels. You shared a study– remember those little boxes we all so optimistically referred to as 'studies'– with Jepson Tyler. Mine was just along the passage, and I had Fred Airley in the one right beside me. I was always hammering our common wall to get him to turn down his Dixieland jazz, because I was usually swotting for some exam or other. He loved playing it on that funny little gramophone of his. Much as I enjoyed listening to it, there were far greater pressures on me to study my science lessons!

After you left, I stayed on for another year to complete my A-levels, and then went on to university where I took a degree in Computer Science. It was a dry subject, but one which I hoped would lead to a paying career. During my university years I found bits of time here and there to pursue a personal hobby – that of studying ancient and lost civilizations. I also found time to dip into the rather arcane subject of paleography. You know: the study of old documents."

Harry looked up at me. "Do you remember this guy?" I nodded. Yes, I remembered Kevin. Bright red hair. Full of spark and go. Not a bad scholar. Being about the same age and ability, we were in the same form together. I seem to also remember that he was in the school choir.

Harry returned to his reading.

"I came across many interesting references to those ancient civilizations. Some were in the realm of pure fantasy, yet others had a ring of truth to them. The most popular was the story of Atlantis. You recall the story? How it was supposed to have self-destructed and disappeared beneath the waves of the Mediterranean. Others seemed to believe the ancient site was under the frigid waters of the North Sea.

"I became intrigued with the fact that our planet had known advanced civilizations, (how many?) before ours. The Chaldeans; the Phoenicians; the Egyptians; Babylon; the Aztecs ... all those – a whole, long list of them.

"But upon graduation, I needed to work and earn a living, which meant I could only continue to dabble in my little hobby. It turned out jobs were not as plentiful as I'd imagined and I ended up taking positions in London as an editor of a couple of under-funded science magazines."

"Hmph!" Harry grunted, and began reading the second page.

"Yet times and people change. Last year I found myself in the happy position of having come into a bit of money, which freed me somewhat from the commitment to the 'nine-to-five' routine I've had to follow for too many years. As a result, I left my jobs, and since then I've been able to devote myself almost exclusively to researching my favourite subject.

"In doing so I have come across some rather interesting information. It seems there was a document written in the dying decades of the seventeenth century. It was supposed to have been a rather interesting piece of work, something to do with the Mayan language. It was in Mexico, I think in the Yucatán Peninsula, and seems to have disappeared. No one today has any idea about where it might be. Most of what I've read so far about it suggests that scholars and researchers of those times would be very interested in finding it. And probably the Mexican Government, too.

"From this distance, I've followed your career as a novelist on and off. I've read several of your novels, and enjoyed them very much. Your eclectic choices of subject matter for your books made me think that you might have an interest in wanting to know some more about what I've stumbled across. That story you did about the Mozart manuscript was really quite wonderful. I don't know what you're involved in these days, but I thought I would write and set this idea before you. So, I'm going to take the chance and offer you a rather unique proposition.

"I need to go to Mexico to obtain some additional material, and if possible to launch the search. I have one or two ideas I think could be useful. It has occurred to me that you might be interested to do a book based upon whatever I am able to uncover while there, in addition to what I've managed to glean up to now. We might, possibly, even find some clues leading to where this document might still be."

Harry grumbled again. I knew what he was thinking: he wants me to stay here and finish writing the – his – book.

"As I say I am sure you will by now think I am quite mad. But consider: you are a writer, quite a good one, too. Writers always need good, fresh material ... it is their stock in trade, after all. Also, the subject matter is one with quite good potential. Handled properly, I should think it would sell very well. It would my intention to split any future book sales with you on a contractually agreeable basis. Also, I would want you to be my guest while we are in Mexico. I should think we'd have to be there at least two or three weeks. Keep all your receipts and I'll make certain you are reimbursed. And may I say on a personal note: anyone who would pass up any chance to escape that vile climate of yours would need to be thoroughly examined!"

'Quite a good writer', he'd implied when I'd read his email earlier. Well, Kevin, thank you for that! Another fan. A writer can't have too many of them.

"To conclude, I plan to travel to Mexico in about ten days, and I'd be grateful if you would give all this some thought and let me know your decision. Please let me know soon what you think. Either by email, or you can reach me by phone quite easily. I'm at home most evenings. I'm including my number here.

Your resurrected schoolmate,

Kevin Watts."

Harry finished reading and looked quizzically at me. "So out of the blue after twenty years this guy suddenly has this great idea and needs you to help him."

"Yes."

"You believe him?"

I pointed to the message. "On the strength of this? No. But I knew him years ago; he was alright then. Has he changed much over the years? Who's to tell. But on the available evidence, I'd guess not."

"Evidence?"

"Well, consider. As I recall, the boy I knew at school had certain characteristics, mannerisms, ways of speaking, expressing himself. Some of these are reflected in this message. And after all this time, that suggests a certain stability, wouldn't you say?"

Harry stared at me. "You want to go, don't you?"

"Well, yes."

"Why?"

I shrugged. "Why not? It's an intriguing idea."

"I'll tell you why not," he said – rather forcefully I thought. "You've got a book to write. You signed a contract. Or doesn't that mean anything to you?"

"Come off it, Harry. You know me better than that. I'm curious. I've always been curious. This thing, this message, has piqued my curiosity. I'm intrigued. It's just wacky enough to have a grain of truth in. And who knows? Maybe it does." I stopped, and looked out the window. I jerked a thumb at the roaring snowstorm. "Besides, who wouldn't want the chance for a few weeks in the sun away from all that? Especially if someone else is paying for it."

He could see I was becoming increasingly serious by the minute. He smiled and shrugged good-naturedly. "Sure, Sam. But what about the book?"

"Simple. I can work on it while I'm there. A change of scenery might even give me just the incentive I need to finish this thing you foisted on me. You know it's been boring me to distraction."

"What does Frankie think?"

"I haven't talked to her yet. She's in Vancouver with another of her rich clients. Been there for a week. The last time I talked to her she thought it could be a long assignment."

Frankie! Dear, impetuous, lovable, volatile Frankie. Italian, all brio and intensity, weeping and vulnerability. Thirty-nine year old youngest daughter of a divorced rug merchant father, she had excelled at her MBA studies and parlayed them into becoming the sole owner of Toronto's best-known interior decorating business. She was now out in Vancouver administering to yet another well-heeled client, a man who refused to even consider moving into his new, waterfront, three-story condo without the careful decorating ministrations he knew only 'Signorina Giuffrida could give'. How would she react when I tell her I'm going away for a while? I knew how she'd react. There would be an explosion. Intemperate and unreasonable under the circumstances, but that was Frankie.

I called her by that name, a nickname she'd been given in high school; one she detested. Despite her impassioned objections ever since, and futile attempts to play it down, it had stuck. One day, several months after we'd met, she'd let it slip out, and I discovered it was a lot easier to say than the mouthful of her full name, Francesca Fabiana Giuffrida.

We've known each other for four years. Our relationship has been a varied one, sometimes stormy. At times we had been as close as two lovers ever could hope to be. We delighted in each other's company and bodies. We acknowledged each other's strengths and vulnerabilities. We each did our own part to grow from those strengths, while shielding the other's vulnerabilities. Yet, there were other times when we could barely stand to be in each other's presence, and we would not see each other for weeks … or months. These episodes had become more frequent of late, yet I found I was not quite so concerned about it as I might have been in the earlier years.

"Too bad," said Harry. "Knowing Frankie, she'd enjoy a few weeks in the sun."

"Sure she would. But she's got the consolation prize of being in one of the few places in the country where winter has the least impact. Look out the window! Besides, she's making lots of money doing what she wants to do."

He didn't press me – either about Frankie or the book. He knew me well enough that I wouldn't let him down. It was an article of faith between us that we each could rely on the other's word. I had meant what I told him about finishing it on time. And he knew it.

Our talk gradually drifted off into other directions while we ate the rest of our lunch. At the end of it, quite abruptly, he stopped me in the middle of what I was saying and said, "You still don't seem quite sure about this Mexico thing." He looked at his watch. "I hope you'll let me know what you decide. I must get back. Some other halfwit author is out in the storm today and insists on seeing me."

I ignored the implied insult, and allowed an edge of sarcasm in my voice. "Don't knock it, storm or no storm. You get to see people. I have to go back to my lonely office and work."

But in my mind I was agreeing with him. On the one hand the whole notion of what Kevin had proposed seemed completely absurd. On the other all I need do was look outside into winter's blast. At this stage I just wanted to leave Harry with the impression that I was still only thinking about it. But I have to say that with every passing moment I was edging closer to a positive decision.

We struggled into our coats, and I left to go back to the office I rented on Queen Street West.

Chapter 5

I liked this end of Queen Street. Known locally as West Queen West, it was a more eclectic and welcoming section of Toronto, well west from the financial and entertainment districts. It had lengthened over the years and now stretched beyond Bathurst before returning to the more run-down parts that had for years been the hallmark of the entire street. Now it was coffee bars, restaurants offering an impressive variety of international foods, interesting little shops, and several good pubs with some them having more of a feel of a brasserie than a regular pub. "The Golden Thumb", where Harry and I had just had lunch, was one of them.

Everything I needed was within an easy walk: restaurants from many cultures, comfortable pubs, including the 'Golden Thumb', second-hand furniture and appliance stores. There was a shop that specialized in serious music, where I could browse without being hammered by the wild, discordant cacophony of sounds which pass today for music. I'd heard it once said that they stopped writing music about 1850, and was inclined to agree. And miracle of miracles, not one, but two good quality second-hand book dens attempting to rival those havens of literature which used to line stretches of Charing Cross Road in London.

For years, the debates of what to do about public transit on Queen had grown to fever pitch. The venerable "Queen Car", the streetcar that for decades had run the entire length of Queen, from city end to city end as it drove through the city's central core, had got too expensive to manage any more. Ridership was increasing steadily year over year. Something had to be done. Thank God the city had been sensible in opting for the sort of light-rail transit services so familiar on the streets of European cities. Against a mounting outcry from more conservative traditionalists all demanding expensive subways, city council had for once exercised common sense as well as bowing to the fiscal realities of the times, and gone ahead with these dedicated light rail services. It had made all the difference. It brought prosperity, enhanced energy and increased foot traffic to this end of Queen, as well as doing much for property values.

I'd been fortunate with my office. It was one of a rabbit warren of reconditioned rental offices in a building which, but for a little architectural imagination, would have been torn down long since. I had managed to secure a longish lease at reasonable rate, an arrangement that suited both me and the landlord. Further, I'd managed this just ahead of the gentrification speculators who even then were descending on the area. The building was owned by that most rare of breeds: a wealthy man with a social conscience, an architectural imagination, and an eye firmly fixed on history.

The office was small, yet it met my needs. It was quiet when I needed the quiet, yet its location gave onto a vibrant neighbourhood. I'd furnished it simply but comfortably. Odd pieces of warm-toned old pine furniture I'd picked up here and there. Two slightly worn yet still serviceable woolen area carpets that did little to hide the dark refurbished hardwood flooring. The carpets had been a gift from Frankie, who got them for next to nothing from her rug-merchant father, a man who dealt exclusively in carpets imported from Turkey and Iran. Lighting balance came from one good desk lamp, mismatched with a couple of standing lamps in odd corners of the room. Only the windows clashed with the general air of shabby comfort. Modern double-paned windows, framed floor to ceiling, shrouded and softened by custom-made curtains from the heaviest Italian silk brocade. These, too, had been a gift from Frankie in the first enthusiastic days of our relationship, and at the time when her interior decorating business was showing signs of being successful.

It was now after lunch. After fighting my way back here through the storm, I sat at my desk and stared gloomily out into the flying snow. Kevin Watts' suggestion was tantalizing. A few weeks in Mexico, he said. The search for a lost historical document, he said. The document, he said, supposed to have great historical and commercial value – although I noticed he neglected to say how much. The exclusive rights for me to write it all into a book. He and I to benefit jointly from any future sales.

Sounds good, I thought. I'll run it all through Harry. Let him look after all the business and contractual fiddle-faddle while I concentrated on the research and the writing. And besides, it would be a relief from the book I was working on right now: at least I'd have control over how it was structured and written. Harry's "favour" was turning into a chore.

Harry, I mused. I've always liked him; as well as being relatives, we were friends. And he's a good agent, enjoying a consistently positive reputation in the marketplace. He works by himself, for himself. Like most agents, he is selective about who he chooses as clients. Years ago he chose me at a time when I was still an untested novelist. I was a new risk for him, although my successes since then have proved he was right. One of his strengths is that he won't take no for an answer. He has little patience for those he deems less intelligent, but has the grace to soften it with a brash good humour. His persuasive talents were a minor legend among his peers, and he had little compunction about subjecting me to them, even when he knew I'd make sure he understood any objections I might have.

The phone rang. It was Harry.

"That nitwit never showed up."

I chuckled. "You were stood up?"

"Don't laugh. That idiot demanded that I see him today; something about being unhappy with the editor he'd been working with, and wanting a change. I couldn't find a cab, and had to walk all the way back to my office. Not far, but a pain in this storm. If that idiot hadn't insisted to see me today, I could have spent the afternoon at home by the fire. Better yet, I could have stayed in the Thumb". He paused.

"I've been thinking more about your Mexico thing."

"Good. So have I."

"And?"

"Harry, do you remember that day last September when you came here to see me?"

"Yeah. What about it?"

"It's this damn thing you foisted on me. I'm losing interest in it. It's an obligation I'm still of two minds about. In fact, I'm getting fed up with it."

"You can't," he said flatly.

"'Can't'? I can. I am. I'm getting stale; I need a change. You remember how it was that day? You barged in on me and dumped this whole ghostwriting thing in my lap. It was a fait accompli."

"Your French is improving."

"Yes. Well, let's leave my French out of this, and stick to what I'm telling you."

"Which is?"

"You're my agent, Harry. But more, you're also my uncle. We're family as well as in business together. If you weren't I wouldn't be saying this. But you're the only family I have, and I think you have a right to know."

"Sounds ominous."

"I'm starting to lose confidence in myself. The highs I've been living with recently are taking their toll; they've reached a pinnacle and I can feel the downturn starting. I don't like it. I need out for a while. I need to see different places; be with different people; do different things; be someone else – for a while."

"Oh, come on. You've just got a case of the winter blues. Everybody has. It'll pass."

I continued, "You remember how it was that day? You came barging in here carrying that guy's briefcase? I saw the look on your face: I thought you were going to chide me about something. But you dumped the case on my desk and sat down."

"Oh, sure," he said with a quick laugh. "That was a great day, wasn't it? For you, I mean. Well, me too. You agreed to do it – and it meant we both could make more money."

"You must be rolling in it. What do you need more for?"

For me, it was different. I thought back to that day. It had begun last Fall, on one of those golden mornings in early September, when thoughts of winter's scourge were not even a minor threat. Harry had clumped his way up to my office, burst into the room, settled himself into one of the unmatched guest chairs opposite, and deposited an imposing-looking briefcase on the desk.

The ghostwriting project was his idea. It was at a time when I was more financially vulnerable than was comfortable, and Harry knew it. In that weakened state I paid more attention to what he had to say than I should have. Since then it had evolved into a tedious chore, one I wouldn't be done with for at least another two months.

"Here," he had said waving his cigar airily at me. "It's all in here. His notes, jottings, some finished chapters... and all the rest of it. Man! Have I got something for you?"

I looked warily at the case, then back up at him. I knocked my pipe against the edge of the heavy cut glass ashtray Frankie had given me the previous Christmas. "Whose notes? What is all this?"

"Your new book. It's a terrific deal for you. It'll be a cinch. Most of it's already written: all you have to do is clean it up a bit."

"Harry, has it occurred to you that I'm not a ghostwriter? I don't know anything about it. I do know that some are great at it. Somehow they can get themselves into the head of the other guy. I can't. Besides, I could use some time to myself."

"Oh sure," he waved his cigar at me. "I know all that. But this is just a little filler project for you while you think of something else to write. It's just a small favour I'm asking."

"Favour? What is it?"

The favour? It was for the man's sister. Her brother had died several months earlier. He had been one of Harry's clients, and was a prolific and popular novelist in his time. He'd passed away before completing what was to have been (as he had claimed) his 'final novel in the series'. I had often suspected it was just his way of generating some advance interest at a time when his sales were beginning to show signs of weakening. But then, what did I know?

But Harry was in full flight. "Later, later. I've already told Farnsworth I've got just the right man for this job." Jim Farnsworth, hard-working, demanding publisher of all my novels. "I didn't tell him who I had in mind, you understand, but he sounded keen when I told him you'd already written enough to know your way around a novel, didn't mangle the English language, well – not that much, and that I had complete faith in you. But here! That's not all. I haven't told you yet about the royalty deal I've worked out for you, or the extras ... or about the advance."

Despite Harry's rapid-fire enthusiasm, I couldn't help but look interested. As it happened, I had, in late summer, committed myself to a rather heavy financial burden, the purchase of a summer place on the South Shore of Nova Scotia. I had been wanting to do something like this for a long time. I had found just the right place. So, after finishing my last book, I took the plunge, hoping to take advantage of end-of-season prices. It was an ideal place. Old renovated fishing cottage, just enough land to make one feel private, its own beach, and good swimming when the water wasn't too cold. As a condition of sale, I'd demanded a professional inspection first. But it was only after taking possession that despite the inspection, I'd discovered the true extent of the needed repairs and renovations. My financial vulnerability was increased.

I reached forward, snapped open the two locks on the briefcase and gingerly raised the lid. The case was stuffed with files and bundles of loose pages held together with elastic bands. I riffled through it all. It seemed to be full of the guy's research notes, jottings, thoughts, half-written scenes, and all the rest of it.

I sat back again, still wary. "Tell me about the arrangements."

"Ah, hah! I thought you'd be interested." He puffed contentedly on his cigar and read me chapter and verse of the deal he'd worked out. Despite my initial skepticism, I was impressed. Yes, I could use the extra money.

"Oh, yeah, and I almost forgot. Maybe you could go talk to his sister."

"His sister? Why?"

"He often collaborated with her when he was writing something. She says she knows a lot about his work, his ideas."

"Well, I suppose …"

"Sure, so go talk to her. She's already told me she's really interested. She wants to see her brother's works finished."

"Is that all she wants?" I was wondering why Harry was so keen I should see this woman.

I had a dark thought. "What did you promise her?" I knew Harry.

"Me? Nothing. Well, you know, she *is* interested. And she could use the income. She knows it would sell."

But then I had an even darker thought.

"So, when does Farnsworth want to see it? What have you promised him? I hope you haven't committed me to something I can't agree with."

"Well, I haven't actually promised him anything. I knew you'd want to have a say in the timing – within reason, of course."

I breathed a silent sigh of relief. At least there was something in this that was still within my control. Or so I thought.

Then Harry said, "But he was wondering if Christmas might be a good date to shoot for. I told him I thought it sounded reasonable."

"Christmas. A year from now?"

"No, this Christmas."

"Impossible," I said. "Next spring, summer. Maybe."

Years ago, when Harry and I had first begun to work together as author and agent, he had rather impetuously committed me to an impossible deadline for the first novel I was working on at the time. Because I was still quite new to the writing game, I gulped and said, 'okay' to the deadline he'd imposed on me, meanwhile mentally crossing my fingers and hoping I'd be able to make it. I sweated blood on that book. In the end I had met the agreed deadline. But I also told Harry, 'Never again. You hear me? Never again! You talk to me first!'

He agreed – reluctantly. At least, at the time I thought he'd agreed. And he had, although there have been one or two close calls since then. But while most of them have worked out, it's kept me skeptical about the 'great deals' he's made for me ever since.

However, I'd put my foot down and insisted on the spring time, at the earliest. Even then, it would be tight. But now, in mid-February, that deadline loomed ever larger.

So now, today, on the phone here in this mid-winter afternoon, Harry had listened patiently through this long recital of how it had been. When I'd finished he said, "Yeah, I remember all that. So, what about Mexico?"

"I need to get away for a while. This thing is dragging me down." He knew I meant the book. "It's not working. I'm getting stale. This storm is not helping much, either."

He heaved a sigh. "I recognize what you're saying. I've heard it from others too – about themselves, I mean. They put it differently but it's the same message. But we've got a deadline to meet. It's rooted in the contract both you and I signed. What am I supposed to tell Farnsworth?"

"Nothing. You tell him nothing. You don't even talk to him. Well, not about this, anyway. No point in making him nervous."

"I'll need to talk to him at some point. He shouldn't know his project is at risk?"

"It's not at risk, Harry. Why talk to him? Leave him alone. Let him count his beans. Sleeping dogs and all that. No, it's not at risk. I'll deliver on time. Haven't I always said that? No. I just need a break for a while. It's only February. It's not due until May."

And all the time we were speaking I'd had been making up my mind. I said, "Harry, I'm going."

He sighed again. "Okay. It's on your head," and hung up.

My thoughts then turned to Frankie. I dialed her mobile, thinking she'd want to hear of the Mexico idea, but only got her voicemail. I looked at my watch. It was the noon hour in Vancouver, so maybe she'd turned it off and gone to lunch. She hated phones ringing in restaurants, and she always turns hers off when outside – on account of loud street noises. I shrugged, not surprised. Later, I thought. I'll try again later.

I remembered some other phone conversations I'd had with her. Last September for instance, after Harry had left my office, I phoned her. This time she answered right away. I suggested dinner. Then I told her of the new book project Harry had managed to get for me. Her response was forcefully true to form. "You're writing another book? God! How I hate it when you do that! I can never talk to you. You're always off by yourself, buried in that computer of yours for hours on end."

I said mildly, "That's what writers do."

"But why you? I need you to be with me."

"I'm a writer, Frankie. It's my job, and come to that, it's my life."

"I thought I was your life."

"You told me once you'd take me as I am. You seemed proud – well, pleased anyway, that I was a writer, someone who, you said, could express his thoughts so well on paper." I paused for a minute. "Maybe you didn't mean that."

That dinner got progressively chillier. It made me uneasy about our relationship, which I was even then beginning to wonder whether it would last.

Then, in another conversation, this time much earlier in our relationship, she told me, "I've got a good degree. It was hard for me, harder than you'll ever know. And even though I've got it, or maybe in spite of it, I still feel many times unsure of myself. My older sister is the confident one. And about how I got the business. I'm still surprised I managed it …" her voice trailed off.

Yes, I knew that story, how she'd graduated with respectable educational credentials: a solid training in the history of art, more than a passing interest in domestic architecture, and a hard-earned MBA to put icing on the cake. How she'd joined a local interior decorating firm as customer advisor, and did well. Later, when she learned the owner had fallen seriously ill and decided to sell the business, she persuaded her successful rug-merchant father to lend the money so she could buy the business, and how, after only a few weeks of back and forth negotiations, ended up the sole owner of Toronto's premier interior decorating companies.

I am thoughtful and introspective. I prefer listening to talking. I am quietly self-reliant. I know my capabilities and limits, and have learned not to depend on others.

For Frankie it is different. She is impeccably dressed, has waist-length tumbling black tresses, an olive complexion, and flashing brown eyes that brook no resistance when she demands her own way. Her quick, hot temper lives in a sometimes uneasy truce with an outward serenity. It had been the serenity which first attracted me to her. It wasn't until later I discovered the fires that burned – barely contained – below. I never knew when those fires would suddenly flare out, as they were apt to do at unpredictable moments.

This contrast of our personalities, more than anything else, has made our relationship tumultuous, often leading to disagreements. I might say something perfectly innocent. She would misinterpret it, taking it personally. If I were in the right mood, I would try to explain it. Sometimes it helped. On occasion it did not. She would toss her chestnut tresses, which formed lush waves over her shoulders, and with a careless grace and flashing brown eyes, announce that I had all the tactless gaucheries and degenerate wit of a *cretino ladro*, and stamp angrily out the door.

Since I knew more Spanish than Italian, it took me some time to discover she was calling me a cretinous thief. My imagination would be stretched well beyond its limits if I were to even remotely consider myself 'cretinous'. Also, it was never clear what it was she was accusing me of stealing.

And again, in a different conversation last fall, I'd suggested we take a few days away in Southern Europe before I settled down to work on the new writing project. I thought she'd be pleased. At first she was. She seemed attracted to the idea. An adventure sailing the wine-dark waters of Greece, exploring secluded islands. Or maybe a palm-thatched cottage in Bali. Or, how about the steaming geysers in Iceland? Any one of these. Or is there something else she'd prefer? Momentarily excited with the idea, she mused out loud about shopping in Paris or Athens first. Then, her voice hardened: "Forget it. I have a new client in Vancouver who needs me. Now. He has problems he can't resolve. He wants me out there immediately."

"Well, thanks a lot. You'd already decided to go."

"Yes."

And that was the end of *that* conversation.

So now here I was, entertaining these uncomfortable thoughts on this gloomy afternoon. Visions and sounds of sights and places from previous Mexico visits flirted on the edges of my mind. Here in my office, even with Miles Davis leaking in a minor key from the stereo, in my mind's ear I could easily hear the plaintively upbeat tempos and complex rhythms of mariachi bands.

I sat up straight, breaking out of my reverie. 'Right', I said out loud to the storm raging outside the windows. 'Decision time. Harry doesn't like it, but that's his problem.'

After checking Kevin's email for his phone number, I dialed his home in Western Scotland.

There was the distinctive double-burr ringing tone of the British phone system, then: "Castle Douglas 3223." It was the voice I remembered from when we were at school together.

"Kevin? Sam Barnes. I'm calling from Toronto."

"Sam! Good to hear from you. Did you get my email?"

"Yes, indeed. That's why I'm calling. I'd like to join you."

"Splendid! I'm delighted to hear that. I had been rather hoping that you would agree." He chuckled, then: "It was why I asked you to be my guest while we are in Mexico. When would you be able to get away?"

"I'll see if I can book flights for Thursday. We're in the middle of a major snowstorm here, but the weather forecasters think it should be finished by then, so flights should be able to leave. When are you planning to go there?"

"Excellent. Let me see … today is, what? Tuesday? Yes. I'm due to arrive in Mexico City not until Wednesday, week." He paused, as if thinking. Then, "Now, let me give you some directions. I have incorporated myself into a little business so as to take advantage of the tax laws here, and just in case we make any money from this venture. The company will reimburse you for all your travel costs. Plus any other costs you are put to as a result of this little venture. Do you know Mexico at all?"

"Reasonably well. I've been several times. I thought I'd stay at the Majestic. It's central and I can find my way around from there."

"Oh. Well, yes, splendid. Well, this will be fun. Oh, just give me your telephone number, would you? One never knows when we might need to speak again."

I gave him the number of my mobile.

"Thank you. Now, in terms of your getting ready: we'll be spending a bit of time in the jungles of the Yucatán, so you'll need protection against the mosquitoes and the fierce heat, and so on. Go and see a doctor about malaria prevention, and *'la turista'*."

"That's okay, Kevin, I know how to take care of myself."

"Yes. Right. Well, right, then." Had I embarrassed him?

I knew what he meant. *'La turista'* or 'Montezuma's Revenge' was the scourge of many travelers to Mexico. I'd had it, and it was no fun. But, I'd gotten over it. And along the way, I'd learned a few preventative tricks in the process. I wasn't too worried about it.

I asked him, "Where will you be staying?"

"At the Fiesta Palace. I'll call you when I get in. You wouldn't rather stay in the same hotel?"

"No. I like the Majestic. It suits me, and it's not so far from yours."

As I spoke I scribbled a note. "Anything else? Special equipment? Clothing?"

"No. It will all be taken care of when we're all there."

All?

"Well then, if that's all, I'll say goodbye."

"There is one thing actually," he said, somewhat diffidently. "Perhaps you might like to bring a friend? You know, someone you'd like to travel with?"

"No thanks. I've already made that decision. I'll come alone."

"Right-o then." His voice brightened. "I'll be looking forward to seeing you. You won't regret this." He hung up.

I very slowly and very thoughtfully replaced the receiver. This was, I believed, a different Kevin from the boy I'd known at school. The voice was the same, of course, but he was now more measured in his speaking, more thoughtful, as if he deliberately set out to think through everything he wanted to say before saying it. I had detected something ... I wasn't sure what it was, in his voice. A hesitancy, perhaps. An uncertainty. Perversely there also seemed to be a hint of flamboyancy about him.

I was beginning to feel the niggling sense of a mystery. Nothing definite; nothing I could point to; nothing to cause immediate concern. I gave a mental shrug and turned to my last tasks. Whatever it was, I assumed it would all eventually work itself out.

Two more small tasks. I typed in the address of the airline reservations website and booked flights to Mexico City for two days from now. Then, I opened my email and sent a message to my old friend Pancho in Mexico, asking him if he could meet me at the airport.

I packed up, bundled into my coat and hat, switched off the lights, and went home.

Chapter 6

You arrive in Mexico City with your heart in your mouth. You hold fast to an implicit faith in the skill of the pilots. They lift your plane high over the tops of the towering mountains surrounding the city; their peaks forming the jagged rim of a deep bowl. They plunge your descent, targeting Benito Juarez International Airport. You arrive at the gate, together with your 250 fellow passengers, and are ceremoniously decanted into the stream of humanity flowing through to the baggage claims area. You collect your luggage from the aging carousels, grateful it has all arrived – and safely – have your passport given a welcome stamp, and exit into the swirling maelstrom of humanity. Through the bustling, frenetic crowds of tourists, beggars and taxi drivers, you see a bright red sporty Mercedes parked illegally at the curb. The roof was up against the threat of rain. A luscious brown leg is just emerging from the passenger door. Leaning casually against the car, his black alert eyes flicking back and forth in search of you, is your old friend Pancho, otherwise known as Manuel Garcia y Lopez Bandilero, only son of Luis Victor Bandilero, a leading light in Mexico's oil industry, and possible candidate for high political office.

Even though his real name was Manuel, not Francisco, I still called him "Pancho". When I'd first met him, his dark features and huge black mustache instantly reminded me of pictures I'd seen of the one-time Mexican revolutionary, Pancho Villa. My parents had once had a good friend who'd spent many years in Mexico. It was the nickname they'd given him and it has stuck with me. Manuel didn't like it. He chided me often, but bore it with good humour and considerable grace.

"Sam! Welcome!" as he crushed me into a typically Latin hug, reached for my bags and folded me into the cramped front passenger seat. The luscious brown leg had moved back into the tiny seating space behind, but a slim brown hand extended itself across my shoulder, while Pancho said, "Say hello to Maria, Sam." She crooned a heart-wrenching 'Buenas dias' as I took her hand while twisting around in my seat enough to look into her deep brown eyes. I caught a glimpse of a pair of long, lithe, deliciously tanned legs that disappeared into a short black leather miniskirt. My heart gave a couple of thumps and I said, "Hello, Maria."

Pancho flashed a smile at me that Hollywood would have paid millions for. "Amigo! Sam! It is good to see you once again. It has been too long."

I had first met him seven years earlier, while on my first trip to Mexico. At the time, I was writing 'The Fifth Wave' and found I needed some background material on influential banking circles in this city. Harry Oliver had done some nosing around and had come up with the name of one of the Directors of Pemex, the Mexican oil monopoly. *Señor* Felix Bandilero welcomed me effusively. He wined and dined me; arranged a tour of an oil refinery, and made me privy to some suitably edited material ... the minutes of some high level but rather old meetings. In the midst of all this activity, I had been given the chance to spend a few days at a very private hotel tucked into the magnificent beaches of the Yucatán. "To help me with my researches," they told me, rather tongue-in-cheek. Manuel was staying there too. The first sight I had of him showed him stretched out on the beach one blazing afternoon, eyes closed and seemingly oblivious to the bikini-clad beauty seductively rubbing suntan oil into his back, while another worked on his legs.

"Hi, Pancho. Where did you pick this up?" I think I meant the car. But with Maria shoehorned into the tiny back seat to make room for me I wasn't quite so sure of myself. I had just managed to squeeze my five foot eleven frame into the front passenger seat. She had to share the back seat with my luggage.

"Maria always complains about this car. She says it is too small." (For what? I mused idly). "She thinks I should use a larger one to properly display my station in life."

"You'd find it too small, too, if you were jammed in here like this," Maria countered sharply, her retort zinging directly at Pancho. To me she said, a bit more gently, "I *told* him to bring the other car."

There was throaty roar from the engine as Pancho took off like he was piloting a space ship, and headed towards the city centre. From behind, we could hear the blare of angry horns from the displaced taxi drivers. He wove the car through the crush of late afternoon traffic in the airport's approach roads with a skill born only of those used to fast cars and the arrogant authority that goes with it.

The euphoria that comes with arriving back in the tropics jarred sharply with the mélange of human and mechanical noises, oppressive humidity, exotic sensations assailing the nostrils, and the general sense of unreality that inflicts a northerner suddenly deposited into a Latin culture.

I was exhausted from the flight. Two long jet rides in a row, including a change in Miami, had just about drained me. With Maria's sultry presence less than a foot away, and Pancho's handling of the car, it was some time before I was confident enough to speak.

"Thanks for meeting me," I told him. "I doubt I could have handled a ride in a taxicab with the pollution blowing at me through the open windows. At least you have air conditioning. Although I can't imagine why you don't shut your windows."

As if to prove my point, a local transit bus moved stodgily into the lane in front of us and changed gears down. Pancho braked gently to compensate. An immense cloud of black, smelly diesel exhaust roiled out at us like some fiendish monster from the pits of hell.

Pancho gleamed his teeth at me. "I wanted you to feel welcome in my country; for you to feel as we all do here," he chuckled. "I also wanted to warm those frozen bones of yours."

"Let me wrap my fingers around an ice-cold Carta Blanca and I'll feel right at home, thank you very much," I coughed as I hurriedly touched the control to close my window. A considerable amount of the bus's exhaust had already blown into the car, and I leaned over to turn up the car's fan. Despite the car's air conditioning I was beginning to feel the mid-afternoon heat as the sun's rays penetrated the overcast and poured directly in through the front window of the car.

"Ah, that reminds me ... you are invited to visit my father's house for this evening. At eight o'clock. A small gathering of friends. I will come to pick you up at your hotel. Although why you choose the Majestic after the visits you have made here, I don't know. It is not suitable for a well-known *autor*. Perhaps El Presidente, instead?"

"I may be well-known, but I'm certainly not well-paid. I'm not in that league," I retorted. "No, the Majestic is just fine. They take my money and leave me alone. Besides, it's close enough to everything downtown. But thank you for the invitation. Please give my respects to your parents and tell them I would like to come."

The streets of the capital are wide and busy. The always-congested traffic is typically fast but reasonably well behaved. Tropical foliage lines the streets. Motorists stopping at traffic lights are treated to displays of fire-eaters, sword-swallowers, balloon sellers, and colourfully dressed acrobats walking about like storks on high stilts. Through your car window you can buy flowers, newspapers, lottery tickets and handmade trinkets, or you can have your windshield cleaned on the spot. With consummate skill Pancho waved them all off in a way calculated to say 'no' without offending. Thus we made our way to the city's heart, the huge open expanse of the Zocalo: Mexico's vast central square, framed by the Presidential Palace on one side, and my hotel, opposite.

We drew up in front of the hotel, narrowly missing a taxi that was just pulling away from the curb. I eased myself out of the car, extracted my luggage from beside Maria, slammed the door, said "Thanks and see you later," got a thumbs-up from Pancho and a searching, rather uncertain smile from Maria, and waved goodbye. The car took off in the same way it had left the airport. As I entered the hotel I noted that Maria stayed folded up in the back seat.

Chapter 7

I smiled at the doorman who politely opened the door for me, and walked over the familiar warm marble tiles of the lobby up to the front desk. The man behind the desk was operating a telephone that Alexander Graham Bell might have installed with his own hands. He had his back to me.

The lobby was quiet, except for some loud mouth idiot over by the tour desk insisting that they send someone out to the airport "right now!" to collect his wife's makeup case: a case which she had carelessly forgotten. The tour deskman's English was not up to the intricacies of this request, lending him an air of polite embarrassment. But, with the belligerent manner he was facing, it was quickly giving way to feelings of more than embarrassment.

"Can I help you, sir?" I dragged my attention back to the desk clerk. The telephoning had finished and he was looking at me expectantly.

"I have a reservation … name of Sam Barnes."

He riffled through his reservation slips. There were many. He selected one and waved it aloft with the air of an archaeologist who has just discovered one of the Dead Sea Scrolls.

"Si, *Señor* Barnes. A pleasure to welcome you back again. Your room is just being made up now. Here is the registration card: would you please to complete it?" He pinged the bell beside him on the counter, and a young boy appeared to take my luggage. "Room 516, *Sr*. Barnes. I think you have had this room before, no?"

That's what I liked about the Majestic: service was friendly and fast … so long as you were doing them a favour. The small Indian boy was halfway up the wide marble stairs before I had finished signing in. I was still getting used again to the sibilant pronunciation of my name: 'Barnss', instead of the more usual and harder 'Barnz' I was used to at home.

I took my room key and followed the bellboy up a short flight of stairs to the cramped elevator lobby.

The Majestic is an old hotel. It is housed in a building more than four hundred years old, and as a hotel at least one hundred. Its seven stories fit comfortably and solidly right on the corner of Avenida Madero and the huge open public square of the Zocalo. Despite various misguided attempts at improvement over the years, it has managed to retain its air of a large, cool, comfortable, but with hints of a genteel but slightly shabby hacienda. The floors in the hallways are covered in large red tiles, and if you look down over the heavy wrought iron railing of the staircase that serves all seven floors, straight down into the lobby, you can see a beautiful little stone fountain, which works just fine whenever they remember to turn it on. The tiny elevator is a throwback to the time when all elevators were operated by a dedicated human operator. It's a hotel that is quite happy to let itself slip gracefully into faded elegance: it seemed as though it could continue to operate for centuries. I hoped it would.

Its central location is ideal for people travelling on a budget. I liked it too, not that I was on a budget but because it's so central. Mexico City's principal square, the Zocalo, has the hotel as one of its four sides. The other three are made up from the National Cathedral, The President's Palace, and a vast honeycomb of government offices.

After entering my room, tipping the bellboy, and changing out of my sopping wet shirt into a fresh one, I made my way up to the roof in the creaking elevator, its walls decorated in wonderful blue Pueblo tiles.

The hotel's public rooms are on the roof, seven stories above the street. The restaurant begins inside and flows smoothly outside to the buffet on the al fresco terrace. Off to one side of this floor is an intimate piano bar, which at night will obligingly stay open for as long as you like. From a comfortable table on the terrace you can see in the distance the two snow-capped volcanoes Popocatépetl and Iztaccihuatl.

The sun was still blazing down on the terrace and I sought refuge under one of the terracotta-coloured umbrellas. For Sunday lunches, they bring in one of the mariachi bands which can always be found in nearby Garibaldi Square. Many local families come up to enjoy the music and buffet. Today though, it was quiet, apart from the constant hum of traffic which floated up from the Zocalo below. A few other guests were scattered about the terrace.

A waiter appeared at my elbow and raised an inquiring eyebrow. *"Señor?"*

I assembled my few Spanish phrases, remembering the predilection of people here to shorten the name of my favourite local beer, and gave him one. *"Una Carta, por favor."*

"Si, señor." With a cloth he flicked away a few imaginary crumbs from my table and left to fetch my beer. I lit my pipe.

I stood up so I could lean over to the low stone parapet and looked down into the huge square below. Now an open expanse of flat concrete, it had at one time been an area of grassy knolls and well-tended flowerbeds overflowing with lush tropical plantings. It has since been paved over and can easily hold crowds of more than 100,000 people. And it often did, what with the frequent political rallies that were held there. The same jam-crowded eight lanes of high-speed, noisy traffic still swirled about its perimeter, and in its centre stood the tall flagpole from which a huge Mexican flag proudly flew. Over to the left I looked at the massive bulk of the National Cathedral, and I wasn't sure but it seemed that its eastern wing had sunk even a bit lower since my last visit. What a pity: a huge well-proportioned historical building gradually sinking into the primeval ooze of Mexico's original lake. What did the Bible say about building your house on sand?

It hadn't stopped the squatters, though. A small tent city had sprung up in the Cathedral's forecourt, just inside the gates. These were some of Mexico's homeless: the disadvantaged, or the victims of recent earthquakes.

People milled about the entire area in front of the church. Some were in small groups, others alone. The shoe-shine men had set up their boxes in their favoured places; the souvenir sellers displayed their wares on colourful woven blankets spread out on the bare pavements, and the news vendors did their usual booming trade in newspapers, lottery tickets and comic books.

The "tent people", I didn't know how else to think of them, seemed placid enough. Even at this hour in the afternoon, with the hot sun still blazing from the hazy blue sky, they were lighting up their braziers to begin the interminable process of cooking the evening meal. One man stood in front of his tent, slightly bent over, his feet carefully apart to protect his crisply laundered clothes, as he leisurely brushed his teeth.

Added to the picture were the political slogans, all daubed in red paint on huge off-white sheets strung up on the outside railings of the Cathedral's precincts.

I heard the clink of a glass behind me. I turned to see my waiter setting out my order. I sat down again. He looked at me, his white teeth sharply contrasting against his swarthy skin as he smiled at me. "Here is jore beer, *señor*. And I have also brought jou some peanuts."

I've often wondered why it is so many Spanish-speaking peoples have trouble with their "y's".

"*Gracias,*" I replied. "*¿Que cuesta?*" I had to ask. Prices in Mexico continued to rise with the frequent devaluations of the peso. Years ago they had introduced the Nuevo Peso, a hundred-for-one swap of the old pesos (which were by then almost worthless) for one new one. But that hadn't stopped the devaluing slide. By now it was almost back to where it had been before the re-evaluation, and rumours of another revaluation had occasionally filtered into the popular press. What would they call the next one, I wondered? The New New Peso? The New Old Peso?

When I paid him he thanked me, then said: "It's nice to have jou back again, *señor*," and departed. I thought I had recognized him.

I closed my fingers gratefully around the icy-cold sweating bottle, and gently tipped its contents into the glass.

I leaned back in my chair, propped a foot up on the parapet and took a long satisfying pull at the drink. It tasted wonderful, and I felt terrific! Balm flooded my soul.

For those of you who might be interested, I stand 5' 11" in my bare feet, weigh 160 pounds, and through the good fortune of having selected the right sort of parents, have no need for regular strenuous exercise to keep myself trim and in reasonable shape. I am clean-shaven, never having had the need or desire for facial hair; have blue eyes under healthy eyebrows, wear horn-rimmed glasses only to read, and have neatly trimmed dark brown hair that is beginning to show traces of grey about the edges. My face has been variously described as 'open', 'pleasant', and 'expressive', so I suppose these are all positive indicators of my general attitude and disposition towards the world in general, and my fellow man in particular. I tend to have a 'live and let live' view of life.

I usually dress conservatively. By this I mean I have no need for flamboyant, "look at me" costumes, preferring to buy my clothes in the higher quality shops.

I was raised in a friendly, loving relationship with my parents. For reasons of their own, shared with me on occasion, they chose to have only one child. This left me with the need to assert my independence from quite an early age, while being careful to obey the firmly defined guidelines and strictures they established for my own good and protection. It was a constant balancing act for me, but on the plus side it created in me an easy ability to make – and keep – friends, a trait I still practice to this day.

My schooling, through all the years, was satisfactory, although not outstanding. I've never considered myself a scholar, or been considered one for that matter, although I continue to enjoy learning for its own sake. I am by nature inquisitive, and tend to want to know the "why" and the "how" of things, rather than simply accepting them at face value. It is, I suppose, a characteristic that led me into becoming a novelist. Although I suppose it could just as easily have led me into any number of other fields or professions.

One thing my schooling certainly did for me was to teach me the all-important rules of self-sufficiency and self-discipline. In my early teen years my parents sent me off to a boys' boarding school in Scotland. Why there? That's a story for another time. Suffice to say my three years there implanted in me those two all-important skills (and they *are* skills!), something I've been grateful for ever since.

Women? Of course! I've had my own share of healthy experiences, as any red-blooded male would do. For the past four years, I've been seeing (an odd usage, that) Frankie, a delightful young woman of Italian extraction who, through her own grit and strength of character, survived MBA school and now has her own thriving business. Based in Toronto, it is a business which takes her away frequently to attend to the demanding and sometime bizarre notions of her many loyal national and international clients.

Thinking about her actively enjoying her work in mild Vancouver, I felt little guilt about coming here to Mexico. In fact I felt quite good. She's doing just fine, I mused. As am I. I reached again for my glass and took another long contented pull at it.

I had got barely halfway through it before a small brown hand with well-manicured nails firmly grasped the back of the chair opposite me and pulled it out from the table, its metal legs scraping gently on the tiles. Into the chair slid a man closely resembling an elf with twinkling black eyes.

After settling himself comfortably, he looked over at me and asked, "Aren't you going to offer me a drink?"

I slowly dropped my foot to the tiles and straightened up. "Sure. What'll you have?" I signalled the waiter.

"An Oromocto Punch, with a thin slice of papaya and a squeeze of ginger juice," he said to the waiter while continuing to look straight at me.

The waiter glanced at me. I nodded to my new visitor and then to him, and he departed. My visitor flicked a piece of lint from the sleeve of his immaculately tailored tan tropical suit. From an inner pocket he produced a leather-bound notepad, a razor-thin crocodile skin wallet and a gold Cross pen. He flipped the wallet open and from it extracted a business card, which he snapped down on the table in front of me. It had what appeared to be a pure silver logo embossed on it.

"Dependability Jones," he announced, by way of introduction.

"So I see," I replied, reading the card. 'Dependability Jones – All Things Made Possible'. I looked up at him quizzically. "Are you really that dependable?"

"I am indeed. And my fees are quite reasonable."

"'Dependability Jones'?"

"DJ will do."

"Right. And why would I need things made possible?"

I looked at him more carefully. The resemblance to an elf was not at all accidental. He could not have been more than five foot six, in his light blue seersucker jacket and canary yellow, sharply pressed fitted trousers. Below I noticed white socks, and pure white yachting shoes. His cream coloured Sea Island cotton shirt had obviously been made for him. It all nicely fitted a well-fed and well-proportioned body. When he took off his new Panama hat to wipe the minor droplets of perspiration from his clean-shaven face, I saw a full head of silver hair that seemed to float and bounce in place, while he nodded and fixed his piercing gaze on me. It was those black eyes which I had first noticed, that were deep-set in sockets surrounded by luminescent, slightly crinkly skin, polished to a deep walnut hue by long exposure to desert suns. His age, while not easily determined, suggested early sixties. His mouth and eyes bracketed a prominent nose, and spoke of an ageless wisdom and an unshakeable good humour, suggestive of a happy, well-ordered life. Yet, beneath it, all was a toughness, a hardness that suggested a different and rather darker history. A shudder passed involuntarily through me. I knew instinctively it would be wise to respect this man. As I studied him, he maintained an air of benign calm, occasionally running a careful hand over his magenta silk tie, and casually sipping the drink the waiter had just given him.

Instead of replying, he sat back comfortably in his chair and gazed out over the great expanse of the Zocalo. He was quiet for a few minutes, then in a slightly far-away voice he delivered himself of his version of a travelogue.

"Do you like Mexico? I love Mexico. It is a wonderfully warm, vibrant, remarkably mysterious, and quite violent place. It has a people who enjoy life and want you to enjoy it, too. It has foods that are culinary marvels, if you are prone to enjoying peasant foods, that is. It has scenery to die for. It has a fascinating history – actually several histories, all of which have combined over the years to bring the world to this visitor's mecca. There is a joie de vivre in its music that can be sometimes even more irresistible than the steel bands in the West Indies. The mariachis will play for you for a smile and a handful of pesos."

He turned to look directly at me. "Do you know about Garibaldi Square?"

"Sure. It's where the mariachis gather. It's also been known as a place for rampant crime and drunkenness, although I understand it's been cleaned up in recent years."

"Yes. Well, it is all of those. But it's also part of the Mexican soul. And you must visit the Tequila Museum when you go there. I see it whenever I come here."

"DJ, I'm more than fascinated with your reminiscences about this country, and I'm sure you're the life and soul of all your friends' gatherings. But will you kindly stop all this and tell me what in the hell you want with me?"

Ignoring me, he went on, "Do you know about the Diego Rivera murals in the Palace over there? I do. I like to visit them. You see, I know a great deal about art, and I find the art of Central America quite appealing. It has expressed itself in so many ways over the centuries. Think, for example, of the Mayans, and how they carved their stone stelae. Or imagine their incredibly sophisticated calendar, whose design you now see on so many tourist trinkets and baubles. Of course, I turn up my nose at all that junk; my preference is for serious works, those pieces which attract the highest bidders."

He had been sipping from his glass during this little homily, and I saw that it was now almost empty.

"Do you know anything about artistic artifacts, Mr. Barnes?"

I was on the point of asking him if he wanted another drink, when his question brought me up short, and made me say instead, "You know my name?"

"Oh, yes. I also know that you are meeting an old friend here in Mexico."

I stared at him.

He continued, "You haven't seen him for many years. He is now a man of some independent means: a landowner too, I believe, who has developed more than a passing interest in ancient artifacts."

"You are remarkably well informed, Mr. Jones."

"I told you: DJ will be sufficient. It gets better."

"Okay, then, DJ. But what is all this to you? How on earth do you know my name and what I'm doing here? Why are you telling me these things? And how, exactly, does it get better?"

He put the empty glass down.

He continued, "There have also been suggestions that the man who met you at the airport today is not the friend you remember. I think you should pay attention to this."

"And I think you'd better explain yourself."

"That isn't necessary … right now," DJ said calmly.

I noticed the slight hesitation.

"Well, then, we have nothing more to say."

"All in good time, Mr. Barnes. Oh, yes. I know a good deal about you and your plans while here."

I doubted this. I'd no plans, other than to wait for Kevin to arrive, and then find out more this whole escapade. Since leaving Toronto, I had got more than a little sheepish about how I had made the impulsive decision to come here. Yet, here I was, and so I'd better make the most of it. But I was still rankled by this man's refusal to talk.

"Who are you? What is your business? More specifically, what is your business with me?"

"My business is art. My business with you is your welfare." He drained the last drops from his glass and stood up. Before leaving, he stood there a minute and looked down at me.

"Hold on. Where are you going?"

He stooped to gather his belongings from the table. "I must leave. I meant what I said. Your welfare, your future welfare, I should say, is at the moment my principle motivation. It would be wise for you to cancel your plans to meet Mr. Watts. You should in fact return home at your earliest convenience. Please heed what I say."

He began to move away, then stopped. Turning back, he said one more thing: "You will probably ignore me. You will probably meet with Mr. Watts. However, if you do continue, I must caution you to be most extremely careful." He gave me a sad smile and left.

Chapter 8

Looking about me, I waved at the waiter for another beer. With it fresh in my hand, I sat back and reflected on that extraordinary conversation. How did he know I was going to be here, in this bar, at this time? Why did he leave so suddenly?

How did he know me? Who had he talked to? When did this happen? It must have been within the past day or so. But above all, why? Why would he want to know about me, and what I'm doing here? What possible reason could he have? And why did he choose to contact me here, on this terrace? Why not just telephone?

I am normally a patient man. I'm observant and try to evaluate what I see before reacting to it. I try to analyze what I see against my known experiences and integrate them into some kind of whole picture. Ordinarily, I expect it to fit with my general bias of how I think the world should behave.

It wasn't behaving the way I thought it should.

The questions kept flooding in. Who is this person? Why is he interested in my welfare? How does he get to know so much about me? Is there anything wrong with Kevin? If so, what? What else does this DJ know about me? Or, want to know about me? What else does he know about Watts? What does he want?

Personal privacy is precious. Keeping personal information private is important. It's always been important, for me, at least. With the rise of instant, intrusive communications, right wing politics, and social media, maintaining personal privacy has become almost a full-time occupation.

The questions were there, but no easy answers. No answers at all, in fact. How could there be? I had only just a few days ago read Kevin's long message, and since then had not told many people of my plans. There was Harry, who thinks I'm foolish to have come on what he called a wild goose chase. There was Frankie, who had not yet responded to either my phone or email messages. This was not unusual, and not a worry. She was probably in one of her independent moods. Who else?

No one else.

And what about his speaking style? Slightly stilted ... foreign. Despite his excellent English, I detected slight inflections of what sounded as though Arabic could have been somewhere in his history.

I picked up the business card he had slid to me across the table. The logo stood out: it was quite attractive. It was a small square, done in royal blue. The square was subdivided in to sixteen smaller ones, all of an equal size. Three each evenly spaced horizontal and vertical lines created this effect. Embossed at the centre, in silver was the numeral '16'. Very attractive, I thought. But what does it mean? Beneath the logo was what I took to be his corporate slogan: 'All Things Made Possible'. This was turning into a minor, rather curious mystery to ponder lazily over a glass of beer on a hot, tropical afternoon.

Then I began to connect the two features of the card: the logo, and the slogan. Taken together, I supposed they could make some sense. And this led me to ponder the even deeper mystery of who this DJ was, and why he should seek me out only hours after my arrival.

I put down my glass and the card, and patted my pockets searching for my tobacco pouch. I realized I had left it in my room. I glanced at my watch. Well, it's time I went down anyway. It would soon be time for Pancho to come for me, and I wanted to clean up, first. I also wanted to take a stroll through this marvelous old part of the city, but that would have to wait for another day. I drained the last of my beer and stood up to go. I pulled out a wad of peso notes to leave for the waiter. He smiled his thanks at me as I headed back down to my room.

My room was two floors down: an easy walk down the gently winding staircase. I was once again reminded of the comfortable, slightly worn ambience of this hotel, and how it had been built in an earlier, gentler time. The wide marble steps of the staircase were offset by walls lined with selections of the wonderful, hand-made tiles from Puebla. The handrail was a long continuous one, made from highly polished brass, and supported by an intricate, delicate tracery of wrought iron. The air inside the hotel was cool despite the last of the blazing sun outside.

I reached my floor and walked along the cool, dark corridor to my room. I unlocked the door and stepped inside. The clock by the bed displayed 19:20, time enough to shower and change, and get downstairs to await Pancho.

Slightly more than twenty minutes later I emerged from the elevator into the lobby, showered, changed, and reasonably refreshed. I stepped out onto the busy sidewalk of Avenida Madero. I looked up the street through the rush of the early evening oncoming traffic to see if there was any sign of Pancho, thinking he might possibly be early. There wasn't. I still had about fifteen minutes before he was due to arrive. I decided to take a short stroll around the corner and mingle with the crowds under the shopping arcade on the edge of the vast expanse of the Zocalo.

The traffic hurtled three-abreast along this one-way street, barely braking at the corner as it swung around and flowed into the huge open expanse of the Zocalo. There it fanned out into the 8-lane racetrack that completely encircled the square.

Turning right at the corner I ambled through the covered arcade, feeling the subtle shift from frenetic afternoon to the quickening pace of evening. The arcade was a wide sidewalk lined on both sides with hawkers' stalls. They sold newspapers, cheap jewelry, lottery tickets, freshly squeezed fruit juices, beautifully carved wooden figurines, freshly cooked tacos and brightly coloured frozen popsicles. Right on the corner stood a little knot of policemen in their blue-gray uniforms with very efficient-looking carbines slung across their backs. For a brief moment, in my mind's eye I could see the other Pancho: Pancho Villa and his raiders galloping across the barren, sun-baked plains near Guadalajara. That thought died, only to be replaced by visions of Mexico's teeming poverty-stricken millions finally coming to the conclusion that 'enough was enough'.

I glanced down at my slightly scuffed shoes, and decided to have them cleaned. I stopped at one of the several shoeshine stands and asked the man how much he charged. This was a polite formality: I knew that it would be next to nothing. But I also knew that he was the owner of his business, and that good business dealings involve mutual trust and recognition of the dignity of others. He flashed a quick smile at me and told me how much. I nodded in agreement and carefully placed one shoe on the foot-shaped part of the shoebox that represented his store, his warehouse, and all his corporate assets. He carefully rolled up my trouser leg to keep it free of shoe polish. Then he placed little slips of paper between the shoe and my sock for the same reason, and went to work.

As he worked, I glanced idly around, watching the faces of the masses of people as they hurried home from the day's work, or to an evening's recreation. Young couples, flirting with one another, young men on the prowl, and middle-aged men and women looking preoccupied. There was a man of indeterminate age who was selling pencils from a tin cup, while squatting on a small, wheeled platform raised just a few inches off the pavement. I looked more closely at him, wondering. Then I realized. Of course! That platform was how he got around in this teeming city. If he were to stretch himself to his fullest height, his head would barely reach waist level of the other passers-by.

He had no legs.

I felt a gentle tug on my trouser leg. The shoeshine man had finished one shoe and wanted to do the other. Once again, the same routine with the trouser leg and the bits of paper. Once again, the slow methodical approach to doing a good job. Once again, the application of first a cleansing solution, then polish, then a brisk shining with the brush, and finally an energetic buffing with a soft cloth. He tugged at my trouser leg again. I removed my foot from the shoebox and admired the results. He smiled in response. I paid what he asked for, plus a small tip.

But now it was time, just a few minutes past eight, and leaving the shoe-shine man, I turned the corner back into Madero expecting to see Pancho illegally parked at the curb by the hotel, smoking one of his smelly cheroots while leaning jauntily against the car. He wasn't there. I went back into the hotel.

Well, I thought, perhaps he's been held up by traffic, not surprising in this city. But I also had to admit it was unusual. Pancho was typically punctual, an unusual trait for a millionaire's playboy son.

They were beckoning me from the desk. "*Señor* Barnes ... *Señor* Barnes." It was Antonio, who had just come on duty while I had been out. I walked over to the desk.

"What's up?"

"*Señor*, there is a message," Antonio handed it to me. Behind me, I could hear the tinkling of the lobby fountain.

I opened the message. It was from Pancho. He regretted he could not come for me as promised. Could I kindly take a taxi instead? Sincerest apologies. There was an address, that of his parents' home.

"Can you get me a taxi? I'm in a hurry."

"*Si, señor*, at once." Antonio motioned to the young lad on duty with him, who immediately went outside to flag down a taxi. As luck would have it, an available one was coming down the street.

I followed the boy outside and climbed into the back seat of the cab just as it pulled up at the curb. I nodded my thanks to the boy, and handed him a few pesos through the window. In my best Spanish, I gave the driver the address in Pancho's message.

Chapter 9

On the other side of Chapultapec Park lies an enclave of houses which first saw the light of day early in the nineteenth century; some even before then. They are as far from the slums of this city as you can get, without leaving the city. Many look as though they were patterned after the original designs of the Conquistadors: those well-fed marauders who brought, in the name of God, art, violence and their particular and peculiar form of spiritual guidance to the New World.

My taxi pulled up in the middle of the gently curving drive fronting one of these minor palaces. As I alighted, I could hear through the open front door the sounds of music, merriment and ice tinkling in glasses. Occasional bursts of laughter floated out from through the steady white noise of the party, hung briefly in the soft night air, and shattered in little crystal tinkling pieces onto the front drive.

Pancho's mother, a cool, stately, and well-preserved patrician lady, with skin to match, brushed past the butler who had silently appeared at the door. She clasped me warmly by the hand and welcomed me into the white wall of noise coming from the large patio behind.

The house was built in the traditional square of the ancient haciendas that one often imagines sitting smugly in the midst of a dry, barren, sweltering landscape. In the middle of the square lay what they called the patio, but more closely resembled the tropical splendors of London's Kew Gardens. I stood at the head of a small flight of steps which led down into the gardens. I glanced here and there, looking for familiar faces, but not really expecting to find any.

"Manuel was so sorry he could not come to get you this evening," his mother told me. She always called Pancho by his given name. Before I had a chance to reply, she continued, "Of course, I told him you would not be insulted. You norteamericanos are so much less formal than we." I nodded vaguely, still scanning the throng. "I told him that he must be back here before you arrived, but alas, he is still not here."

I looked squarely at her. "He's not here? Where …?" but she interrupted, "Ah! Here is my husband. Luis! Come and say hello to an old friend."

I turned to look at the big white-haired man slowly threading his way through the throng, his whole face open wide in a large smile that made you feel he was genuinely glad to see you. For me he really was an old friend.

"So Sam, you have come back to us. How long will you be here this time? Look, you don't even have a drink yet."

As if by magic the butler silently materialised at my elbow with a tray of glasses filled with champagne. I took one, thinking, Pancho had told me 'dinner'. My first impression had been of an intimate family get-together. Yet, on observation and reflection, this gathering was more in character. I knew without looking that long trestle tables would be set up at the bottom of the garden, each covered with snowy white cloths and groaning under the combined weight of the assorted dishes of food.

I nodded my thanks at the butler and turned to my host. "It is my pleasure to be here, *Señor*. Thank you for inviting me. What's the occasion? Have you just bought another bank?"

He laughed graciously and waved a deprecating hand. "Oh, just a few friends. Nothing more dramatic, I'm afraid. Come." He took my elbow and led me down the steps and into the crowd. I began to feel I was incapable of moving under my own power. "Here, I want you to meet some of them."

I walked with him. Searching the crowd I had imagined seeing some vaguely familiar faces; familiar in that oddly undefined way that many politicians' faces are familiar: seen occasionally on TV, rarely face to face. Luis and I moved gradually from group to group. By now, I had assumed my party smile, nodding agreeably as I was introduced as 'my friend the writer who had come to his senses and escaped from the frozen North'. Maybe he had something there. It was also what Kevin had mentioned.

On learning I was a writer, I got the standard reply, only it sounded more regretful even to my limited Spanish. They'd not had the opportunity to read anything of mine. It's no wonder. None of my books have been translated into Spanish. Even so, it made me wish I'd brought along a supply so I could autograph them at the door.

Even with the cool evening breeze just beginning to blow in through the sun's afterglow, it was hot down here in the garden, and soon small rivulets of sweat trickled their way down my back. The champagne was making me light-headed, and I looked rather hopefully at those food-laden trestle tables I'd been thinking of. They were just barely visible over the shoulder of the man to whom I was now being introduced, who was saying, "*Si*! Of course I know *Sr*. Barnss!"

I looked more closely at him. A tall erect man, white-haired, and ruddyfaced. Well fed, somewhat portly, with an almost permanently pleased expression on his face. Beautifully tailored in his dark charcoal suit, snowy white shirt and tasteful light blue silk tie. *Señ*or Ranulfo Echeverria, Chairman of the Mexican Reconstruction Board, the organization overseeing the complete reconstruction or renewal of Mexico's entire physical infrastructure. I'd read that it was a monumental task, covering just about every aspect of the country's physical assets. Also generously funded by the central government. It was no wonder he looked pleased.

The Chairman continued, "But only through what you, Luis, have mentioned. And now it is my pleasure to meet you in person. Are you writing another book, *señor*?"

"Well, in a way," I answered. "I'm doing a ghostwriting project for a friend at the moment. But I really want to get started on my next novel. I've been making some notes, but I thought I'd take advantage of my being here to do some research for it."

"And, what will it be about?" he asked me in English.

"Your country. I don't think it's any secret that Mexico has a lot of problems."

"We do, indeed. Earthquakes and the drugs. These are our big problems."

"Also, I think, the uncertain Peso, why it is so many of your people endure their lives mired in poverty, why food prices continue to climb but quality doesn't, why pollution remains a problem, and why the environment is given such short shrift, and whether the people have any hope for any improvements to their lives. There's NAFTA, too … has it been any good for Mexico?"

He gave a rueful laugh, as if to agree with me. He was gracious enough to ignore the implied insult. "You are right, *Sr*. Barnes. These, too, are our big issues. You know much about our country." There was a note of approval in his voice.

"I like Mexico. I have a fondness for the country. I've been here several times. The people are welcoming – open and pleasant. I've always been welcomed wherever I go. I'd like to help my readers see the country and the people as I see them. Not just as a never-ending march of negative headlines across the morning papers. Being able to speak a little Spanish helps."

"Yes, I overheard you talking to some of the other guests. You speak it very well. How did you come to speak it?"

"Would you believe I learned it in Scotland?"

His eyebrows popped up in mild astonishment. "But they do not speak Spanish in Scotland."

"No. It was offered as a language option at the school I attended there."

"Ah, I see. And what drew you to Spanish?"

"Well, I had been taking Latin, and for quite a while, I liked it. But then when the teaching moved on to Cicero, I began to feel I'd had enough. I decided I wanted to change. They offered me Spanish. The two languages were enough related to make it easy for me."

"So ... how long will you be in Mexico?"

"I'm not sure ... I've no definite plans – yet. I'm here because a friend suggested I meet him here to help him find something. He won't be here for another few days. I told him I'd want to do some travelling while here. He said we'd likely be going to the Yucatan."

"Did your friend say what this thing is?"

His engaging manner was attractive, yet I did not know this man, nor where his loyalties lay. True, he was clearly a good friend of my hosts, Pancho's parents. But I was set down in a foreign milieu, and as it behooves any stranger to test the waters carefully before committing oneself too deeply, I decided to be cautious. "No. Not in so many words. He said something about it being of some intrinsic value, but I've no idea what that meant. He'd give me the details when he got here."

More raised eyebrows. "And on the strength of this you came all this way?"

"Not at all. It's been a difficult winter at home – harder than most, and I'd been thinking anyway for some time of getting away. Mexico's always been a favourite destination, especially for this time of year, so Kevin's suggestion was quite timely. Coming here was the logical thing to do."

"Kevin? Your friend?"

"Yes."

He paused a minute. "I think I would like to speak some more with you, *Señor* Barnes. Would you care to call me one day while you're here?"

"I'd be happy to."

"Perhaps I may be of some little assistance." This came as a surprise.

From a card case in his jacket pocket he produced a business card. "Please ... telephone me any day, and we'll arrange an appointment. I hope you will find the time for it. I'd like to tell you of some of our plans to put our country back on its feet. Also, I have a good man in Cancun. If you go there, perhaps you could see him."

"Thanks, I'd like that," I replied, carefully reading the card, before slipping it into my shirt pocket. "It's kind of you. I expect you are a busy person."

"It's true. But I am happy to make time for a friend of our host, *Señor* Bandilero," nodding at our host.

With that he turned away to speak to an attractive young couple standing beside him, patiently waiting to attract his attention.

Señor Luis reached out to take my elbow and steer me away to the buffet tables. "Now I think it is time we found out what the chef has prepared for us this evening." I was only too glad to follow him.

As Luis and I walked away, *Señor* Echeverria turned back to me, "I will look forward to hearing from you, *Señor* Barnes."

"*Gracias, Señor* Echeverria, I will call you soon."

As Luis and I made our way to the buffet, I reflected that perhaps he could start by explaining why his organization had swollen to over 8,000 people only a year and a half after its formation. I was willing to bet that a good percentage of them were there to benefit themselves, and not the country.

Pancho's father invited me to help myself from the buffet. He then left me alone, excusing himself to chat with other guests. Along one wall deep in the garden was a series of alcoves, all with tables and chairs set up for those who wanted to sit while they ate. I heaped my plate at the buffet and gratefully found a seat. Most buffet meals are pretty much the same: this was no different. What it lacked in creativity, it more than made up for in quality and quantity. I finished eating and I chased the last few crumbs around my plate and felt well satisfied with life. But also a little puzzled. I groped in my pocket, extracted my pipe and the black soft leather pouch, which I had stuffed with "Press Club Mixture" before leaving home. It was a tobacco I'd been smoking for years. It had become a favourite a long time ago, and was even more so now. Most tobaccos today taste more like sweet, tinned cherries rather than real tobacco. Too aromatic: too sweet. This blend suited me fine.

I had no sooner finished packing my pipe and put a match to it, than a shadow cast by the discreet garden floodlights fell over my plate. I felt a hand on my shoulder.

"Sam! So here you are. Don't you ever do anything more than eat? Have they been looking after you?"

The voice was familiar. Pancho had finally arrived at his father's party: the party to which he had invited me. I had foolishly expected him to be here when I arrived.

"Well, Pancho, who was she this time?"

He flashed a sheepish smile. "You know me too well, my old friend. Yes, you are right. Maria required me to do something for her, but I thought it would take less time."

I could not imagine what the 'something' was. Instead, I said, "Well, never mind. Your father is his usual excellent host. I knew there had to be a reason for me to come to Mexico."

He laughed. Then his face sobered and his manner became darker. "Sam … there is something I must talk with you about."

"Oh?" I responded. "Sit down. Have a drink."

"No, not here. It would be better if we were alone. Come, we'll go into the library." And he turned away.

I got up and he led me into the house through a different door from the one that I had used to join the party. He closed the door behind us, muffling the sounds of party.

"Actually," he continued, "it's not something, it's someone. There is someone else here. I think you know him. He's waiting for us now in the library."

Now my interest was really piqued. We stopped outside the library door. He opened it and stepped aside to let me pass into the room. I entered, and stopped cold.

Chapter 10

There are times in life when even a double take is not enough. When what you see is what you don't believe. As I walked through the door, I saw the other person Pancho had mentioned. He was standing in front of the bookcases, taking a deep interest in the shelves of Morocco-bound volumes. He had open a copy of Pascal's 'Pensees', and had his back was to us, but I could see by the way he suddenly cocked his head he knew we had arrived. He turned to face us.

I turned and stared at Pancho. "You know this guy?" I hooked my thumb at the figure by the books. For I knew at once who it was. Twenty-five years can erase many memories: others stay with you forever. This one was all too familiar. I had seen this back on the playing fields of our school; had watched him running in that lopsided yet still graceful gait of his in school steeplechases. I had seen it as he processed up the chapel aisle with the rest of the choir in Sunday services. I had seen it bent over his books as he plowed his way through the nightly homework assignments in that cramped, yet homey little study he and I had shared for a year. No. No one need introduce me to Kevin Watts.

"So, Kevin," I began as he turned to face us. "It's been a long time."

He snapped the book closed and approached, his hand outstretched to shake mine. In another part of the house, someone had begun to play the piano. The skill level seemed to indicate more confidence than proficiency, as it picked its way through an unfamiliar tune.

"Yes," he answered, a little soberly I thought. Then his face lit up into a smile. The Spanish have a word for it: "*sonrisa*" – like a sunrise, or so it always seemed to me. It was so this time. Yet, even as he smiled, he was glancing thoughtfully at Pancho over my shoulder. The atmosphere had become suddenly charged. "You are punctual," he continued. "You said you would arrive on the fifth of the month, and here you are."

I shrugged, and walked over to him. "It wasn't difficult. How is it you know Pancho?"

"'Pancho'?" he seemed puzzled. Then his face cleared. "Oh, you mean Manuel! Yes. Well, that's a bit of a story. I think we should all sit down and be comfortable, don't you?"

The piano had broken into the 'Mexican Hat Dance', and there were gales of laughter as the player muddled his way through the difficult syncopated beat. Pancho broke the tension in the room, saying, "My friends! Perhaps we should have a drink? Yes? Come, Sam! What would you like? And, Kevin?" He walked over to the table where bottles, glasses and ice were laid out.

Watts and I made our way to a couple of easy chairs as we told Pancho what we wanted to drink. I sank into the cushions with the uneasy feeling that this could take a while, and even then, I might not hear the entire truth.

As we settled ourselves, and I could hear the drink-making noises that Pancho was making from the other side of the room, Kevin asked me, "Well, Sam, are you working a new novel these days?"

"Making a few sketch notes," I replied. "I'd finished a rather difficult book last Fall. I've been doing a ghostwriting project since then. But, yes, I do have a few ideas for the next one."

"I think I remember telling you in my email, Sam, that I had for some years been interested in obscure, historical documents."

I nodded. "Yes, you did. But I couldn't understand why. What's the point of it?"

"Two things. Pure intellectual interest. Beyond that, money. I don't know if you know just how much money can be made from the discovery and sale of ancient documents. Some of them, anyway. There is a well-established, legitimate market for any document that will add to the body of available human knowledge, or to fill in gaps in specific lines of historical research. The major auction houses are usually ready to handle the sale when the right sort of thing comes along."

Kevin glanced about at the rest of us. "It's what helped turn me into an amateur paleographer. I decided that if I ever came across something that looked as though it had some value to it, I'd want to do some preliminary investigation on my own before going to market with it. A matter of personal pride, you see. I didn't want to be taken for a public fool. Besides, if I could find one document in my searches, why stop there? There IS money to be made. And I could use some right about now."

He looked straight at me and continued, "Over the years I had run into a lot of references, tantalizing ones, to the writings of some ancient civilizations. And yet they seemed to have nothing to do with those civilizations. As I continued my investigations, more and more inconsistencies came to light. Now, one thing I have learned in this field of study is that inconsistencies don't, can't in fact, have any part to play in learning about the lives of the ancients."

I opened my mouth to object, but he stayed me with a raised hand. "No. Hear me out." I settled back in my chair.

"Certainly there are inconsistencies in any field of scientific study. But if you're on the track of anything in particular, a bunch of inconsistencies cannot remain so for very long before a pattern begins to emerge. The pattern may be quite tenuous at first: usually will be, in fact. Nevertheless, it will gradually jell, and as it does the trend-lines gradually emerge. So it was with me. Now, mark you, some years had to pass before my own trends began to make themselves evident. But, no matter. For I knew from almost the start that I was on to something, and that it would be only a matter of time before the whole story would be uncovered. However, it wasn't until just this past year that I was sure I had definitely found something.

"Now, while I may try to be an uncoverer of lost writings, as it were, one who has enjoyed some small successes, I am not very good at telling the world about my findings. Oh yes, I can give all the facts, and announce the statistics of the place names and dates and so forth. But these things, so much like the study of paleography itself, can be rather dusty and dull. And who would really listen? What to do, then? Obviously, I would need to find someone who had a way with words. Not a mere word mechanic, mark you, but somebody with the ability and flair to transmute my knowledge into drama and excitement, and make it accessible to the common man."

I loved that touch about the common man.

"I've read your books and enjoyed them. Your novels are good: very good. They are believable. But what really impressed me were the two biographies. You know, unless you already know something about the person, it is sometimes difficult to get into the work. I suppose it's even more difficult to be attracted enough to the book in the shop to want to buy it in the first place. Yet your two books overcame these barriers, and I went on to read them with pleasure."

I couldn't help an inward glow of satisfaction at this, but I was damned if I'd let him see it.

"And then, one day, it suddenly occurred to me that you might be just the person I needed to do the job. Your books have always been very readable. Lucid and dramatic ... captivating, if you know what I mean."

I did.

"Furthermore, your novels were on, well, sort of related subjects. You know, 'The Fifth Wave' was a masterpiece. Evocative, spellbinding, good characterization ... believable. Whatever did make you hit on the idea of connecting a lost Mozart manuscript to the choppy Mediterranean?"

I had sweated blood over that book. It was probably the toughest thing I'd ever written. That had been three years ago. Funny though: it still didn't feel right. I gave Kevin what I hoped was a reassuring smile. "Well, I'd always liked Mozart's music. Much of it is warm-blooded, even for an Austrian. It all seemed to fit with warmer climes. I suppose it was that year he spent in Italy. Glad you liked it."

"My boy, you write much better than you speak. I think your fingers have the gift of angels."

My boy! Cripes, he and I had been schoolboys together, for God's sake. Had he always been this insufferable? I recalled that he had been a Latin and Greek scholar, while I was still struggling with the *'amo, amas, amat'* of basic Latin. We'd been in the same form together. Yet this didn't mean anything. It was more of an administrative convenience for the School, rather than any attempt at educational parity. If anything, I had the better part of a year in age on him.

"Kevin, I appreciate the rave reviews. Your literary tastes do you proud. Maybe you could write a few and send them to Harry Oliver, my agent. He probably wouldn't believe them, but that's his problem. But, what I'm more interested in right now is how you and Pancho know each other." I shot a quick glance at Pancho who was idly stirring his drink with a finger.

"And another thing. I seem to recall that – if anything – I am several months older than you. So knock off the 'my boy' bit."

A quick look of dismay crossed his face. I think it was genuine. He was immediately contrite. "I'm sorry. I do apologize. It is an unfortunate habit I picked while in Kenya." (He pronounced it 'Ken-ya' instead of 'Keen-ya'. At least he'd been trained properly). "You're quite right. This must come as a surprise for you. Manual – Pancho – and I have known each other for the past four years."

I looked interested, and shifted in my chair to show it. He was about to continue when Pancho broke in, "Ah-h-h, my friends! Such wonderful schoolboy rivalry! I have heard so much about this in the English school system, but unfortunately have never experienced it. Now I am seeing it for the first hand." He had neatly stepped back into the conversation, and had equally neatly deflected it. Why?

Pancho continued, "Here are two old school chums, friends even, perhaps? They have not seen each other for many years, and already they are deep into discussing the artistic merits of one of them. And even a little drama is there for flavour. My father's house is surely fortunate this evening."

I had the distinct feeling that for all his jocularity, Pancho was overplaying his role of "mein host". He had always been a hospitable person, but not perhaps in the same suave patrician way as his father. Mexicans were hospitable anyway, more so than anything I'd known at home. But it seemed Pancho was playing a role, one so subtle that I just couldn't put my finger on any of it.

So I said, "Well I can't speak for your father's house. But his single malt is certainly doing me a lot of good. Harry Oliver wouldn't know me ... he's always berating me for drinking beer. Can I have another?" And without waiting for an answer I got up to mix another drink. But I really needed time to think. I looked pointedly at Kevin and said, "Why don't you go on?"

He had been waiting patiently and rather distantly for Pancho and I to finish our little side-play, rather like a teacher who occasionally lets his students engage in a little healthy horseplay, waiting benignly by for them to settle down again.

"Quite," said Kevin. "If I might continue, then? As I was saying, I met Manuel four years ago, and we quickly became friends. He and his father were in London on business. There was a rather stuffy affair, a reception one evening, given by his hosts. I was there too, though I'm damned if I can remember why. The oil business is of little interest to me. Anyway, we ran into each other at the drinks table and began chatting. Despite my disinterest in oil, we found we had several other interests in common. We've kept in touch ever since."

I wondered what were those other interests they had in common. Why was this all seeming too convenient to me? I was getting more and more skeptical but I didn't know why. All through this evening there had been an undercurrent of something hidden: of something others knew that I didn't, and it was beginning to bother me.

Pancho not showing up to collect me at the hotel, then mysteriously appearing here at the party. Yet, I believed Kevin when he said he'd met Pancho in London. It seemed reasonable. After all, Pancho was the son of *Señor* Luis Victor Bandilero. He was mature. Elegant, in a playboy sort of way, with money to spare, and whose father had enough connections to make any young man's rise a safe and painless affair. And, speaking of affairs, Maria, the sultry presence in the back seat of the car this afternoon, who had cooed in my ear and shaken my hand, wasn't his first by a long shot. Somewhere in the back of my mind she seemed familiar ... as if her name or her face had been mentioned before. Yet I didn't even know her last name. I forced myself to stop speculating. If I was going to remember her, I guessed it would come soon enough. If I didn't, I wouldn't, and that would be that. Yet that touch of her had hand left a tingling on mine, and her features danced in my head.

Kevin continued speaking. "There was a priest, a Franciscan missionary, who had come out to the Yucatán from Spain in the late seventeenth century. His name was Andres de Avendaño. In those days, most members of the clergy were not well educated. Or, if educated, it was with a rather narrow exposure to the world. But occasionally the church would produce, more by accident than design – perhaps permitted to be produced would be more accurate – intellectuals. Avendaño was just such a man. By contrast to the rest of his peers, he was an intellectual giant.

"He was sent there by his Church to help in converting the natives ... the age-old process of forcing Western doctrinaire religion on peoples who had no interest in it; who couldn't care for it, and in fact had their own perfectly good religion, dating back to time immemorial, thank you very much.

"Of course the missionaries would have none of that, and prayed the natives to death. Literally. The conflicts were often horrendous ... battles, bloodshed, sickening torture.

"But while all this was going on, Avendaño, who also knew a thing or two about literature, had stumbled on what he saw was the very essence of the Mayan culture. He took it up as a field of study, and over time his knowledge on the subject grew to be impressive. Eventually he produced a treatise on it."

I asked, "What sort of man was he?"

Chapter 11

It had taken Father Andres de Avendaño several months to become acclimatised to the jungles of the Yucatán. The searing humidity, the dappling of sunlight through the tall palms, the lush, musky denseness of the underbrush, and the cries of unfamiliar exotic birds and animals had bothered him at first. His home in Andalusia was very different from this. It, too, had its hot days, but they were dry and baking, whereas these were heavy, muggy, cloying, and seemingly never-ending. So, too, the nights. At home, they had been cool. The setting sun brought temperate conditions. Here, the cloying heat of the days persisted long into the nights.

The long sea voyage that had brought him here had served to temper the gradually fading influences of his home, to a point where he often thought he could have made a good life as a sailor, sailing his life across the seven seas.

But no, he had work to do. Important work. God's work – the work imbued in him through years of seminary training by the Franciscan friars. And now, here he was, this novice priest, set down in a new land, a troubled land, a land filled with mysteries, one not fully understood.

The day he arrived, on that early March day of 1692, he met first with his Bishop. He stood straight as a lean post in front of his Bishop's desk, and was told in no uncertain terms that he must cut through the superstitions of the natives, their strange, primitive, heathen ways, and make them, "*make them*, do you hear? Make them!" accept the Word of the One, True God.

Avendaño stood an erect six feet two. He was lean, bony almost, wiry in a way that naturally athletic people are slim and wiry. His lean, chiselled face was surmounted with a long, sharply pointed nose, a nose which neatly complemented the dark, almost black piercing eyes, eyes that lived quite comfortably under thin black eyebrows. His clean-shaven olive skin would eventually darken even more under the jungle suns.

By contrast, Bishop Antonio de Arrigaga y Aguëro was quite physically different from this young priest. Aguëro was short, plump of face, portly, also clean-shaven, and gradually growing bald – a condition that caused him constant irritation. He had been appointed Bishop of Yucatán in Merida in 1691, and now was still fresh in his new posting. Before this, he had already been in the Yucatán for years, but gradually grown weary of it. While this new appointment was a welcome honour, he now was grudgingly coming to accept there was little hope of any future appointment – here or elsewhere. His assigned task was to convert all the native tribes in this region of the country. And certainly there would be no further advancement until this had been accomplished – if then.

And now here was this new fellow, newly arrived from Spain, a man with an unconscious but all-too-obvious air of superiority about him, a man who only appeared to be pretending to submit to the authority of the appointed Bishop, the man who rules this particular part of Mexico's vast uncharted kingdoms.

Aguëro's study felt airless, despite the open windows on three walls. There was no breeze at all outside, and it was stuffy in here under the low ceiling. Even with their bare shave-pate heads, the long heavy black robes they each wore were completely unsuited to this climate, and sweat formed on their faces, trickled across their shoulders and down their backs, and contributed to the prickly heat they had learned to live with. Andres once more used a hand to wipe the sweat from his face, and simply said, "Yes, Father".

Thus fully instructed, Avendaño set about on his assigned mission. Together with his fellow monks, he spent the next several years travelling through the dense jungles to distant lands throughout the Petén. The Mayan lands, an area consisting of most of modern Mexico and Guatemala, in which the Mayans had built their extensive and impressive cities, and where they had managed to create a thriving and successful thousand-year civilization.

The years passed. On one such occasion, he had been assigned by Aguëro to lead a small team of monks and native bearers to the tribal lands of Ajaw Kan' Ek, a local king. Avendaño had been told that this one of the last tribes to be converted.

Kan 'Ek himself had on occasion shown signs of wanting to work with the priests. His stated reason was that he had heard of the horrific battles and forced conversions experienced by others and he had no wish to repeat this with his own people. Yet his people were not so enthusiastic. They wanted to keep their old ways, the ways that had served them well for centuries. It was Avendaño's mission to work to persuade them otherwise.

Journeys through the uncharted jungles were arduous and perilous, but eventually the Avendaño team arrived in Ajaw Kan 'Ek's city. They were welcomed, though not effusively. They were accommodated in inadequate quarters; and fed rations that barely sustained.

Weeks of discussions ensued, mostly congenial, often spirited, occasionally acrimonious. Yet all were held in an overall context and continuing spirit of general cooperation that, they all hoped, would lead to an eventual agreement for the tribe to convert.

Eventually, it was resolved. Kan 'Ek was both a skillful negotiator and an accomplished politician. The Avendaño team began preparations to return to Mérida, content in the knowledge their work had been successful. The success was rooted in a simple agreement between Avendaño and Ajaw Kan 'Ek. If Avendaño would produce a formal writing that would document the relationships between the Mayan language and the Latin used by the missionaries in their religious ceremonies, Kan 'Ek would commit bringing his people to the Church.

The idea had come to him one evening. He was sitting out on a bench under a rustling palm tree, the night air just beginning to stir after the setting of the blazing sun. The clouds in the sky were thickly painted with bands of fuchsia, lavender, mauve and purple, their bottoms still aglow with the last rays of the sun. His breviary was open on his lap, and from it he read the evening vespers. His heart was still, his emotions calm, his thoughts serene. But suddenly, out of nothing, it was there. Why not? he asked himself. Why not a dictionary, an encyclopedia, a treatise … a writing to ease the way of future travelers to this land, and to further the glory of the Church?

It was there, crystal clear in his mind. In his imagination, he could *see* the finished product. He had enough material already in his mind and his notes to make a start of it. He would consult with Kan 'Ek and acquire more. His excitement grew at the prospect of making a significant contribution to the Church's work. Excitement tempered only by the ravages of growing ill health brought on by the fevers of the jungle.

The agreement was a demonstration of another side of Andres de Avendaño. During the time of the protracted negotiations, Avendaño and Kan 'Ek had come to know each other quite well. More, they developed a respect for one another. Avendaño, during his years in the Yucatán, dating almost from the time he arrived, had managed to learn how to speak the Mayan language. He was one of the very few of his fellow friars to do this, and he excelled above them.

With Kan 'Ek's help, he had also begun to learn how to decipher, recognize and interpret the language's unique hieroglyphic writing. As much as he was able, he immersed himself in the culture, learning the history and ways of the Mayan people. In doing so, he became more and more impressed with the scope and depth of learning and knowledge these incredible people had developed – on their own – over the course of centuries.

His own intellect was superior to that of the other priests in his enclave. They were, for the most part, a conservative, narrowly focused lot, dedicated more or less exclusively to fulfilling their appointed mission. But while Avendaño was equally dedicated to his assigned duties, he also had the inner need to allow his intellect and native curiosity to expand and seek new knowledge.

The two emerged from Kan 'Ek's ceremonial hut. They stood in the late afternoon sun, looking solemnly at each other, neither speaking. Then Kan 'Ek raised a hand as if to summon someone. His wife appeared at his side and, in a few words, he gave orders for a celebration to be given that evening.

The festivities began. All the people in this local village and all the visiting priests from the monastery attended.

The women wore heavy woven skirts belted at the waist. Their long tresses carefully plaited, the black of their hair contrasting nicely with the light coloured face paint they all wore. Some had tattoos on their arms. The men, by contrast, wore their best cotton breechcloths, surmounted with brightly coloured cotton shirts, all sleeveless. Some men chose white shirts. Both men and women had woven sandals. Dirt was anathema to these people; personal cleanliness their preference.

The foods for the celebration were what they normally ate, consisting mainly of dishes made from beans, corn, rice and bananas. There was usually very little meat, but for ceremonies they cooked the kill from the surrounding jungle, including a small dog that had no bark.

Making up for the limited variety of foods were considerable quantities of drinks fermented from corn, honey or agave. These drinks were very popular among the old Mayan populations, and many's the sore head that woke up to the next morning's sun.

Avendaño enjoyed as much of the celebration as he could manage. But his health was declining. On his journey to Kan 'Ek's village, he had contracted fevers in the jungle and despite the help he was given by his hosts, help rooted in their own medical knowledge about how to cure sickness, it had done little good.

The next day the team of Franciscan priests set out to return to Merida. They retraced their steps, taking the same number of weeks as they had spent on the outward journey.

On arrival back in Merida, the apothecary took note of Avendaño's worsening condition, and provided him with the potions and nostrums he felt would help. But, within himself, Avendaño began to think it might be a losing battle.

Nevertheless, he determined to pursue his project. He sought Bishop Aguëro's approval. Yet despite the positive news that the conversions would take place, it was still only grudgingly given. The two had never gotten along well. The reasons were petty, but real enough to each of them. It was a relationship that was constantly strained as each rubbed the other the wrong way. A clash of personalities – wrong perceptions of the other, together with poor interpretation of each other's motives. But finally the Bishop gave his reluctant approval. It came with the stern injunction to ensure that Avendaño provided copies of the finished work to the Monastery.

Armed with his Bishop's approval, Avendaño began the project. In the ensuing weeks he laboured day and night at it, fighting the fevers until at last, late one night, it was finished.

In the guttering candlelight, he looked at the finished work on his tiny desk. Was there satisfaction in him? He set down his writing tool, rose and lay down in a deep slumber on his cot.

He never woke up.

Chapter 12

Kevin stopped talking. I said to him, with some admiration, "You *have* done your research."

He nodded. "Yes, there is a good deal of information available, but it's all fragmented in many places. It's not all neatly packaged in one nice book. A bit here, a bit there, a public library in one town, university research material in another. Bits and pieces one picks up from conversations with those who have studied the old ways. The Internet, of course. So, there is more to be done to pull it all together into a single picture."

Kevin continued, "Avendaño's book became something of a minor art form in Central America, and eventually back home in Spain. My researches suggest that it caused quite a stir in Europe, and not everybody approved of it. It seems there came a point where the book was banned by the Church for 'writings that were contrary to the Church's true teachings', or some such scurrilous nonsense. At any rate, all existing copies were done away with.

"Except one."

We were all taken up by Kevin's story, fascinated by the fact that literature and thoughtful writings had actually begun to flower so early in this part of the world. The story had been flowing smoothly, until he stopped short. Only one? What happened to it?

Kevin paused.

I asked, "And the document? The treatise? The one copy?"

Kevin said, "No one knows. Six copies were produced. Five have been destroyed over the years. Or lost. No one seems to know which. Only one remained. Again, no one knows what has become of it. But all the evidence I've uncovered so far suggests it still exists."

"So, what happened to it?"

"That's just it," said Kevin. "No one knows."

"But you want to?"

"Yes."

"And you want me to help you."

"Yes."

"Not only that, but you want me to produce what amounts to a written documentary describing the search and triumphant recovery of it."

"Well, I wouldn't put it quite like that, but … yes."

"And eventually, what do you hope to gain from it all?"

Kevin seemed startled by the question. "I thought I'd told you. Money, and lots of it. I thought I'd explained all of that."

"In fact you didn't. You briefly mentioned in an off-hand way that you could use some extra money. But, now what I'm hearing from you, and in your voice, that you're almost desperate to find this document, and unload for the highest price the market will bear."

"Well, yes, it's true. Financial gain is important for me, but for you, too. This document could be worth a lot of money – to each of us, if we play our cards right. Think of its historical value: it's thought to be a missing link in the accumulated research – a link between the end of the Mayan civilization as it has come to be understood, and the beginning of the modern era. The research has a hundred-year gap that desperately needs to be filled.

"Also, there are now something like three hundred thousand Mayans in this country. Many prefer to speak the old language rather than Spanish. This tells me there is a big interest among this community for the preservation of the past, their culture, their language, their customs."

"And you want to fill it."

"Yes, I do!" Kevin's voice and manner were fervent.

"What did you mean by us 'playing our cards right'?"

"Very simple. We don't want our search to become public knowledge, do we? Otherwise, every other budding archeologist and paleographer and their collective brothers, cousins and dogs will be looking for it, too. It's much better we keep the search quiet."

It began to make some sense. So I asked, "Any other reasons?"

"Well, I mentioned the money. I don't mind telling you that I've got a spot of financial bother at home. Finding this document would alleviate a good deal of that. Perhaps all. I also think that the three of us, by joining forces, could make this a success. When I wrote you, Sam, I gave you my reasons. But here's another. Your work on the Mozart book told me that you had developed a valuable insight into older documents. It told me you come already equipped with a body of knowledge not easily found ... at least not in the circles I travel in. And besides, we've known each other a long time. Let's say I'm trading on our previous good relationship while we were at school."

I nodded, although still not entirely convinced. Still, having travelled all this way, I concluded I'd better make the best of it. But just for good measure, I prompted him, "Kevin, it's been more than twenty years since we were at school. We hardly know each other anymore. As much as I appreciate your confidence in me, I can't help wondering why you couldn't have found someone else."

Kevin shrugged. He pointed to Pancho, and said, "And here's Manuel. A good friend to you, and a good one for me, too. He lives in Mexico. He is Mexican. This is his home, his culture, his history, his milieu. Not to be taken lightly, eh?"

Pancho and I looked at him. "Well?" I asked. "So, how do you propose to find it?"

"While I was doing some research in London, I came across other references to it. Indirect ones. Veiled references. Hints. But enough to tell me I was on to something real. I felt that if I could just follow up on each one of them ... track them down ... flesh them out, perhaps I could build enough of a picture to have something solid to go by.

"So that's what I did. One of those pieces being hinted at was the Inquisition, the attempt to stamp out Protestantism throughout Europe, and ensure the One True Faith was extant throughout the land. Or, what passed for the Faith in those days, as seen by the bigots, greedy zealots, and all the rest of them."

We were interrupted by a tentative knocking on the library door, followed by the door being opened. Pancho's mother stood framed in the doorway, looking more than a little uncertain. She said: *"Oh Manuel, lo siento,"* then switching to English, "a telephone call for you." She looked around at all of us, apologizing with her eyes for the interruption.

Pancho muttered under his breath. He looked around at Kevin and me, and said, rather resignedly,

"I'd better take it." He got up and left, brushing not impolitely past his mother as she stayed in the doorway.

Señora Bandilero remained uncertainly in the door, torn between wanting to apologize for the interruption and the need to attend to her other guests. She turned to return to her guests just as Maria burst into the room, filled with feminine anger and passionately proclaiming high dudgeon at Pancho. Unbidden, images of Frankie's twisted features when angry at me flashed through my mind, and I was quite happy not to be the target of Maria's emotions.

She was wearing a simple off-the-shoulder floor-length sheath dress, emerald green, cut from shantung silk. There were simple black pumps on her feet. Around her neck was a beaten silver choker necklace, and her ears had matching silver earrings, all of the same simple ancient design. Set against her soft brown skin and chestnut hair, the overall effect was magical. Stunning.

I looked at Kevin. The mood was broken. He felt it, too. The atmosphere had been building nicely during his story telling now evaporated with the sudden small dramas of Pancho's departure, his mother's obvious concern, and Maria's explosive arrival.

We stood as she entered. I approached her. "Maria, hi, come, sit down. Here, let me get you something. What would you like to drink?" I was trying to step her down, talk her down, hoping to give her a chance to recover.

She stopped in mid-sentence, and with quick, flashing eyes, but also the hint of a gentle smile, looked gratefully at me. *"Si. Un scotch. Gracias."* And with that, she took the chair I'd offered. I gave her the drink and she took a large gulp from it, gradually settling into the depths of her chair.

Gently, tentatively, I asked, "What's the problem?"

She flared up, sitting forward again. "Oh-h-h! That Manuel! He makes me so angry. He said he would meet me at my office and bring me here this evening. But no … no sign of him. I waited and waited, and finally decided to come here on my own. He's always doing this. And I wanted to tell him what I thought of him. But now I discover he's not here."

"Not here? You mean he's left? But he was here just a few minutes ago. We were together here in the library, and he had to go to the phone."

"Well, he's not here now."

Kevin and I looked at each other, puzzled.

"Well," I said, "if he's not here, he's not here. I think I've had enough for today. I'd like to go someplace for a quiet drink, then back to my hotel. Why don't you both join me? I'm going to say goodnight to our hosts and call a taxi." In the back of my mind, prompted by I'm not sure what… chivalry, maybe? … was the thought that I'd like to find out a bit more about Pancho's seeming errant ways, and helping Maria cool down a bit more might be a way to achieve this. This day had raised some questions about Pancho.

Kevin looked up. "Yes, I'd like that. I'll come with you, if I may."

Maria chimed in, "So will I."

I said, "Sure," and went in search of Pancho's parents.

While I was saying goodnight and thank you to Pancho's mother, she told me that Luis would find me a taxi.

Luis said, "*Si*. But Sam, please remember to call *Sr*. Echeverría. He told me again he would you to visit him. He's interested in this book project of yours."

"Thanks … I'll call him. I'd like to see him, too." But I was puzzled. I hardly knew the man, only having met him this evening. Why was he interested in me, and what I wanted to write?

"*Bueno*. I will call for your taxi." Shortly after, the taxi arrived, and Maria, Kevin and I climbed wearily into it, and we drove off.

Chapter 13

In the taxi Kevin asked, "Is anyone hungry?"

I groaned inwardly. I doubted I could eat another thing. "Not really."

Maria also sounded doubtful.

Kevin continued, "Alright. But I am. I'd like to stop someplace for a bite. And Sam, I'd like to talk to you some more about Avendaño." He paused, then, "Maria, you might as well come, too."

Maria asked, "*¿Quien es Avendaño?*"

I said, "A man who lived a long time ago. His writings are what we would like to find." Then, to Kevin, "You've told us something about him already. What else is there? About him, I mean?"

He didn't answer. Instead, he tried again to encourage us to join him for food. He looked at us, expecting us to agree.

"Kevin, no. Thanks. I'm just about done in. Can't it wait until tomorrow?"

Maria said nothing.

Kevin sounded grumpy, as if he was not used to having his ideas thwarted. "Well, alright. But look, we'd better get together to prepare for the trip."

I glanced over at him across Maria's head. "How about lunch tomorrow? But not too early."

"Fine then. Lunch it is. We can pick up what's necessary afterwards."

"Sounds good. Where?"

"There's a steak place in the Zona Rosa I'm quite partial to. Any taxi will take you there." He named the restaurant.

"Sure, that's fine. What time?"

"Say one o'clock? That should be enough for you to get rested," he added rather impishly.

"Hmph! Speak for yourself! But sure, one's fine."

"What are you boys up to?" again from Maria.

By his reaction, I had the impression Kevin seemed somewhat miffed at Maria's question, although it wasn't clear why. "We're planning to go to the Yucatán for a few days," he said, rather shortly. "Need to get some gear together."

It puzzled me. What's bugging him? He's been diffident and rather secretive all evening. Once again I had the distinct impression he's hiding something; keeping information closely guarded. I was about to say something when Kevin leaned forward to speak to the driver, and in impeccable Spanish gave instructions to his hotel. He looked over at me, "Well, that's it then. You can drop me at my hotel; it's not far from here."

Shortly, the taxi pulled up in front of Kevin's hotel. A doorman hurried to open the door for him, saluting as he Kevin got out. The doorman closed the door and stepped aside. Kevin, leaning through the open window, reminded me, "One o'clock sharp," and disappeared into the hotel.

We drove off. I turned to Maria. She had moved over into the space vacated by Kevin. I asked her, "Do you still want to stop for a drink, or would you prefer to go home? Do you have very far to go?"

She pondered this for a minute. "Where is your hotel? Is it close? If so, you are much closer. I could keep the taxi to get home."

"Yes, I am. I always stay at the Majestic. Yes, of course, keep the taxi. I will make sure he is fully paid."

"Thank you. It's kind of you. I do have a distance to go." I was mildly disappointed she'd decided to go home.

We drove on towards my hotel in the Avenida Madero in amicable silence. The late-night traffic still swirled and hooted, carrying its multitude of evening revelers, late-night diners, home-coming shift workers, and all the rest of combined humanity to all its appointed destinations. Maria had calmed somewhat, the fires that had earlier sparked in her had abated, and I felt her presence not only calming, but comforting. Perhaps it was my own drooping fatigue, the result of a long day travelling and then the inevitable strain that came from meeting a press of well-heeled strangers at this evening's party, but I felt this welcoming calm creeping over me from being in her presence. It was enough to enervate me.

Our taxi pulled up in front of the main entrance. The driver turned around in his seat and looked enquiringly at me.

She noticed this, hesitated briefly, then turned to me and put a hand on my arm. "I've changed my mind. Do you mind very much if we stop here for a while? I know you're tired from your journey, but I'd like to speak with you."

I was startled; this took me by surprise. But then this thought came to me. Have you ever heard of the second wind? That moment when you realize, despite all the pressures you've endured, all that's happened, the wilting fatigue, that you know you can keep going indefinitely? In the few short minutes we'd been in the taxi together, I'd got mine back, and I felt brighter now than I had earlier today. Suddenly the prospect of spending more time with this gorgeous creature was very appealing.

I said, "Yes, I'd like that."

"*Bueno!* Do you like music? This place has a piano bar that specializes in many jazz favourites. It stays open until quite late. It's quiet and very pleasant, overlooking the Zocalo."

"You mean you know this place? I do, too. I like jazz very much."

In my younger years, I'd experimented with the saxophone, thinking that I'd like to become a professional musician. I'd been captivated by the "sound" made by such masters as Ben Webster, Lucky Thompson, Sonny Rollins, Ike Quebec, Red Norvo, and Coleman Hawkins. And yes, even by John Coltrane… although his style was quite radically different from the others. I had imagined a life as a professional musician would be ideal for me; on the road all the time, in the company of people I admired, playing with small groups in all the best clubs all over the country. Maybe even cut a few discs on my own.

I said to her. "Do you know that at one time I'd even hoped I'd be able to play some professionally, Hah! It was a naïve ambition."

But youth is ill served without adequate exposure to naiveté. Try as I might, I could never get it quite right. It was either clumsy fingering or a predilection to breathe in through the horn when I should be blowing out. Or, maybe I just didn't want that life enough. Well, never mind! One can't be perfect in all things, and I came to realize soon enough that I'd never make it. It just meant I'd have to try something else to earn a living. I would always enjoy the music.

But I did spend many of those same years just listening – soaking up the recordings of the 20th century's jazz greats. The Miles Davises', the Peterson's, the Ellington's, the Brubeck's, the Koffman's, and yes, the incomparable Ella and the irrepressible Satchmo. As a result, my ear had become attuned to many of the nuances of jazz, and when I finally moved to Toronto, I felt as if I had suddenly come home.

I've often thought that most major cities have their own unique sound. Sunday mornings in London bring the discordant clash of bells from countless church steeples, countered by Big Ben tolling sonorously the hour across the city. In Mexico, it's an all-day, all-night frenetic rush of traffic. Ottawa and Washington share the same sounds, each exhaling a steady susurration of hot air and misplaced dreams. And Toronto has its own unique sound. For me, it's the sound of jazz. I first felt it when I moved there fifteen years ago, and the feeling has stuck with me ever since. It seemed the sound of this music was everywhere: in the shops, in small coffee bars, in restaurants, where you could see small combos setting up to play for the customers, out on the streets, and in the many clubs scattered about the downtown core and elsewhere throughout the city. It was like this all year around. But it was even more noticeable during the warmer months, reaching crescendo proportions during the several annual international jazz festivals. For me, jazz was Toronto's sound track.

While all these thoughts were tumbling around in my head, Maria said, "Oh, *si*. I know this place well. When my friends and I go out together, we often stop here at the end of the evening."

"Alright, then. Let's go in."

I paid the driver, helped Maria out of the car, closed the door, and we stepped into the lobby.

The lobby was quiet, with only the gentle tinkling of the little water found in the back to break the quiet. We rode up alone in the elevator, And in the slowly rising lift she stood close to me. I could look down onto the glinting copper tones in her chestnut hair and smelled her gentle scent as it drifted up. She looked up at me and smiled shyly. I felt my pulse rising, but knew I'd be wise to control the impulses.

Alarm bells sounded faintly in my head. I had to remind myself: this was Pancho's girl. As attractive as she was; as empathetic as I felt she wanted to be with me; as bizarre as Pancho's behaviour was – Maria was still Pancho's girl. Pancho was a good friend. Over the years, he and I had developed a strong, mutually respectful friendship. He had introduced me to his home and his family. He was an integral part of, and was my entrée to, aspects of Mexican society I could never have managed on my own. But to top it all, he was Latin, with an inbuilt Latin temperament; and if I had even an ounce of wisdom left in me, I would do well to remember it.

Yet, as we stood close to each other, just barely touching, I was acutely aware of her perfume and the warmth of her closeness, and for just a brief heady moment I was reminded of that curious condition the Japanese call the 'floating world'. A serene, dreamlike world. It was that wonderful, unique condition where one is lifted out of oneself, and given over to a whole other world of willows, reeds, butterflies and flowers. It was a sort of temporary sweet madness that made all yesterdays forgotten and all tomorrows possible. For a mad, brief moment, I imagined Maria and I transported off to this magical world, with nothing to do but enjoy the moment and the pleasures of each other, giving not a care to consequence. I even supposed that, somewhere in the back of my mind, it could be made possible. She would look up longingly at me, and I would disappear into those luminous black pools of eyes, and we'd drift off together into a daydream. Somehow – how could it be possible? I knew instinctively that she could be a great deal of fun. Somehow, she must have felt what I was thinking, for she leaned even closer. But then the elevator jerked to a stop jerking me back into reality. The door slid open and we were in a different ambience; a soft one, with lowered lighting casting a warm glow across the room, the tables and the remaining drinkers. From the small corner lounge drifted out the melodic chords of professional but well-modulated renditions of George Shearing's better-known piano pieces. It was just the sort of atmosphere I needed at this end-of-evening hour; relaxing, graceful, welcoming.

Several tables were still taken with late-evening couples, who had dined earlier and were now relaxing their way through their late evening with coffee and liqueurs, all seeming intent on forgetting the events of their own days; or building, each in their own way, a slow climb to a night of love and impassioned companionship. Looking through the open archway to the outside terrace, I could see many of the tables still filled with late-evening diners, who were working their own ways through their evenings' revels.

We were shown a small table in a corner of the piano lounge. Maria took the bench seat, while I found a comfortable chair opposite. She pulled a cigarette from the package in her purse. I stopped lighting my pipe while I held a match for her to light it. She steadied my hand. her eyes thanking me. She waved a bit of smoke away from her face and asked, "Do you think I could have a martini?"

"Of course." I signaled the waiter, and gave both our orders.

"Do you always drink beer?"

"Most of the time. It's only Harry who can afford scotch. I tell him he doesn't pay me enough from the contracts he gets for me. So I have to settle for beer."

"Harry?"

"My agent in Toronto. I've used him for about ten years. He's also my uncle, my mother's younger brother. We get along quite well."

"Are your parents still living?"

She saw the shadow that crossed my face. A sudden surge of grief and irretrievable loss came flooding back. I managed, "No. They're not."

She reached and laid a gentle hand on my arm. "I'm sorry. I think you are very sad to say this."

I smiled, tightly. "Yes. It's still a painful memory. It's not easy to talk about it."

"I think you were very close to them."

"Yes. We were close. I was their only child. They wanted more, but, well, it wasn't possible. They treated me with kindness, love, and I always had the sense we were more friends than parents and son. We always suspect, don't we, that someday we'll lose our parents. But we think it will be a 'someday' far off in the future. Some distant, uncharted future. But when it does happen, your world is turned upside down. Instant numbness. Total unreality."

She said, "It sounded like a beautiful relationship."

I nodded. "It was."

I paused, thinking back

"It was a car accident. One of those freak things that aren't supposed to happen, but do. All too often. They liked to travel by car. See different places. It's not that they didn't like planes; it's just that the car gave them so much more flexibility. It was a bright summer day. They were on a four-lane freeway. It was in Ontario. Traffic was quite heavy. Then suddenly, out of the blue, there was a car coming towards them, on their side of the road. At high speed. My father tried to get out of the way, but as luck would have it, just then they were boxed in at that point by other cars on their side of the road. Both lanes. The accident was terrible. All the cars were either horribly damaged or destroyed, and some people were killed. Including the rogue driver. The police told me afterwards the autopsy revealed that both drugs and alcohol were in him. He was way over the limit." I paused for a moment, and my hands tightened around the base of my glass. I could feel the ends of my fingers grow numb with the pressure. "It's a good thing he was killed," I said tightly. "I'm not sure what I would have done to him if I'd ever met him later. Even after seven years, I …" I had to stop talking. I could feel the emotion welling up in me. I had to suppress it.

Her voice was gentle and quiet. I could hear the tremor in her voice. "Sam, I am so sorry to hear this. I cannot imagine how painful it must be for you."

I held her eyes for a few moments, nodded, looked down.

She sensed it was too painful for me to talk about, so she asked, "Have you always been a writer?"

I pulled a face. "In my mind, I have. But when I was fresh out of university I realized I had to earn a living. From all the stories I'd heard, writing would not do it for me. Even as a young boy, I'd had the itch to write, but after getting my arts degree and accepting the reality that writing in Canada is often a recipe to ensuring a life of continuously scratching for pennies, I opted instead for employment that had the potential of paying a living wage. Consulting, especially management consulting, was all the rage in those days, now more than twenty years ago. I managed to join one of the big consulting firms and over time worked on a number of interesting assignments, usually as a member of a team. I became quite good at it, and enjoyed a certain respect from my colleagues. But it grew stale. I grew stale. As time passed, I felt there was a plodding sameness about the work, even though each client was new, and each assignment different. The fun and challenge of it began to drain away, and I knew I had to stop. Otherwise my life would become an endless flow of an increasingly depressing sameness. I eventually decided it was not for me."

"But," she prompted, "you're a writer now."

"Well, yes. During the later consulting years, I once again felt I had to scratch that boyhood itch that I'd had to write. By then, I'd saved some money, so I quit my job, and took six months to produce a novel. Was it any good? I could not tell. I liked it, but my instincts told me it was filled with flaws. So I asked myself who I might know who could help set me straight. By chance, one day I was talking to my uncle Harry. I knew he was something in publishing, but had never paid much attention to it. In fact, he was a literary agent; had been for several years. He said, 'Sure, I'll look at it.' And he did. We spent another month going through it, line by line, until he pronounced himself satisfied with it. Then he told me, 'Let me show it to a couple of publishers. Let's see what they have to say about it.' Of course, I agreed. I was delighted, beyond what I had dared imagine.

"Two months later, he called me. 'They've bought it', he yelled. 'They've actually bought it!' He was as excited as me. Anyway, that's how it happened ... how I became a writer. That company published my first novel. There have been four more since then."

She squeezed my hand. "It's a nice story; I'm glad it worked out for you." She paused, then said, "I think you met my father this evening."

I looked up at her. "Oh?"

"Yes. He told me afterwards. Ranulfo Echeverria. The Chairman. You were talking with him."

"He's your father?"

"*Sí*. I'm his youngest daughter. My sister still lives with him. But I prefer to be independent."

"But your name is different."

"Yes. I decided to take my mother's name."

"Why?"

Her eyes were downcast, and she demurred. "Perhaps another time," she said quietly.

I changed the subject. "You live alone?"

"I know what you're thinking. This is a big, dangerous city for a single young woman. But I know how to take care of myself. I have taken professional self-defense classes. Believe me, I know how to use the skill. And I am not foolish about taking unnecessary risks. Yes, I live alone."

I was impressed. For her well-built petite size, I would not have expected this. But then again, maybe that was part of her defense. Potential attackers would be lulled into assuming she'd be an easy target. But I also said, "Despite your assurance, I hope it is in a safe place."

"Of course! I am not stupid. The building is well kept, well lit, with security guards and equipment everywhere. My apartment cannot be entered easily."

"Your father invited me to meet with him. He said something about lunch one day."

"I know. He told me. You will enjoy it. He's a good man, doing an impossible work."

"Impossible?"

"*Si*; he was appointed by the President. The President has no interest in the Reconstruction Board; it was just a political move only to keep the opposition quiet."

"Yet, from his manner, I saw your father as a contented man. Not overly burdened with his work. I wonder why the President has no interest in the Board?"

"Oh, yes! It's true. But who would not be? He is well paid. His organization is well funded. His staff is large. He has pleasant offices in one of the best buildings here. His scope of operation is across all of Mexico. His life style is pleasant. And, to tell you the truth, his ambitions have diminished over the years."

"I wonder why that is?"

"I don't know. He's very quiet about that. But still, he is my father, and I respect him for the man he has always been."

"Do you love him?"

She paused again. "Yes! ... I think so. Sometimes it's hard to get through to his inner person. Since my mother died, he's closed himself off a lot more than he used to be."

It was my turn to show her some empathy. She saw it right away, and seemed grateful for it. We smiled gently at each other, and self-consciously paid great attention to our drinks. The music played gently in the corner, and the soft old tunes seemed to fit so well with the mood of this conversation.

Then she said, "But there is one other thing about him; it's something I wanted you to know."

"Oh?"

"Yes. You spoke of him being contented. Well, yes, in a way, he is. But he's also a person who can be devious at times. I do not know why you agreed to see him. But I think you need to know that you should watch what you say to him or agree to."

"Why?"

"He is a subtle man: much more so than many others. Some have called him Machiavellian. I have seen him manipulate people beyond what they imagined to be their capabilities; yet in the end they have always excelled above what they believed possible in themselves."

"And you think he might try to manipulate me? If that's his motivation, I could even agree."

"It's possible. I do not know why it is you agreed to see him. I don't even know why you are here."

"It's no mystery. A friend invited me to join him. You met him this evening – Kevin, at the party. He was in the taxi. He wants to find an old document."

"This afternoon, you and Manuel mentioned this Avendaño. And then again in the taxi. Does he have anything to do with this document?"

"Not 'does', did. It was many years ago. So I understand… yes."

"Who was he?"

"He was a priest, a Spanish priest. He lived a long time ago, and spent a lot of his time in the Yucatán."

"So?"

"Well, he was also a scholar. He is supposed to have written some sort of treatise about the Mayan language. I'm told it was a kind of dictionary, that allowed for the translation of Mayan into Latin."

"Alright. But what's your interest?"

"This document, if found, could be very valuable."

"'If found'? You mean it's missing?"

"So I understand. This Avendaño made several copies. Most were destroyed, or lost. One remains, apparently … somewhere. But no one seems to know where."

"Interesting. So, you have a mystery on your hands. But, you haven't answered me … what is *your* interest?"

"Yes, I suppose … we do. It was Kevin that told me about it. He wants my help to find it."

"And can you?"

"God knows! I've no idea where to begin."

"Then, why?"

"Kevin seems to have some idea that I could write about the search and discovery of it. When he first told me, it seemed like a reasonable idea. I was intrigued by the notion. I've been working on a new book for the last few months, but it isn't going as well as I'd like. I was thinking I needed something different for a while. So, I thought, why not? But, I also came for another reason. You've never experienced a Canadian winter. This year's has been particularly difficult. This book I've been working on – it's been dragging. But the short answer is I needed a break."

"Actually, I have. I was in Toronto last year… it was unbelievably cold. It was January. But, why here? Apart from the document, I mean."

"I've been here before. I've come to like Mexico very much, for all sorts of reasons. And besides, the climate's a good deal more congenial than Toronto's. I needed to get away for a while." Then I asked her, "What were you doing in Toronto?"

She gave a little laugh. "Oh! That was no holiday. I was there with my father. He was in meetings with some government and business people in Ottawa and Toronto. I came along see what it was like."

"Did you like it? What did you do?"

"I liked it very much. But the cold bothered me. I wasn't as prepared for it as I had planned."

"You told me the President appointed him; that it was a political appointment. And… why him? Why your father? Why not someone else?"

"It was a reward for campaign contributions. But, you know, he is very good at what he does. My father is very wealthy, and has always been supportive of the President's party, and the President. Still, the appointment was five years ago. Now there will be a new election. Next year. New candidates will be considered."

"And *Señor* Bandilero is seeking contributions for his own campaign?"

"You saw that, did you? Yes. Exactly. It was the reason for the party this evening. And for my father being there. *Señor* Bandilero is hoping to raise enough money to launch a campaign to be the Mayor of Mexico City in next year's elections. But they are also old friends. So there are now two connections."

"Why doesn't he make a run for the Presidency?"

"The candidates have already been chosen by their parties. Besides, *Señor* Bandilero knows that the Mayor's job is sometimes a stepping-stone to the Presidency. He wants to be President, but he knows that he needs to approach it the right way."

I nodded my understanding. Then I asked her, "Why do you think Pancho did not meet you this evening? Won't he be worried that he doesn't know where you are now?"

"Oh-h-h! That Manuel! I could crucify him! He makes me so mad sometimes. Besides, he can always call me."

Her manner had changed dramatically. One moment she was a sweet, empathetic and warm companion, out for a late-evening drink with a new friend; a situation that held subtle overtones of becoming romantic. Now, she was a raging lioness. Although, to her credit, she kept her head, remained still, and smiled. But looking around the corners of her smile, the dark eyes blazing fire, I was again glad not to be the target of those volatile emotions.

"You're not happy with him."

"Absolutely not!"

"Acting strangely, differently, perhaps? I noticed something earlier. He said he would collect me, here at the hotel, and take me to the party. Then he phoned to say he couldn't make it. That's not like the Pancho I remember."

I looked at her. "Tell me about it." I hoped it would give her a chance to cool down.

"I'm worried, Sam. I'm worried about him. I'm worried about some of the things he's involved in. He's not the person I thought I knew."

With this, she launched into an impassioned reading of the failings of Pancho, whom she preferred to call by his given name, Manuel. Much of it came as a complete surprise; I'd no idea of some of the things she talked about. I listened in silence as she unfolded her feelings to me.

"I know you call him Pancho, but I've never liked that nickname. It's too reminiscent of so many things that are not Mexican. For me, he is Manuel. He is the Manuel I met two years ago in London. And it is he, Manuel, who has been since then – a rock, friend, protector, and lover, too. But he has worried me. Now, much more often.

"When we met in London, it was because my father had to go there on business and he had asked me to go with him. It was some sort of diplomatic mission. The President wanted him to go. I think it seemed appropriate for my father to be chosen. I wasn't doing anything at the time, so I agreed. I'd been there before, and had some mixed feelings about the city. Still, I needed a change. I decided to go.

"It turned out that I had a wonderful time there. On that visit I did all the things a first-time tourist would do. It was springtime: all the flowering trees in the parks were in full blossom; the flowerbeds were a riot of colour, and the people seemed to have come alive from what I'd learned had been a difficult winter."

She was right. I knew from own experience what some London winters could be like. I was just able to remember those now long-ago days when London had still been afflicted by thick, blinding, sickly green fogs, commonly known as 'pea-soupers'. Damp, green, mist-covered streets, yellow electric street lamps shining thinly though the swirling dank mists; pedestrians with noses and mouths muffled against the chill and the fog. Straight out of Sherlock Holmes. And the chill! My God, the chill! Even with adequate protection, it was still enough to seep directly into the marrow and remain lodged there all winter long. It's no wonder gin had been so popular in earlier times when central heating did not exist for most. It's always amazed me how people who did not have the means to clothe or heat themselves adequately managed to survive those long desperately cold and damp months.

Many didn't.

Maria was still speaking. "My father and I were having lunch in a restaurant. Manuel was with some friends at another table. From where I was sitting I could see him directly … and he, me. I recognized him at once. We'd run into each other from time to at home. We kept looking at one another during the meal, and though his bright smile and black mustache were beginning to annoy me, I couldn't help myself. I kept looking back at him. Despite my resolve, I knew somehow that we would be spending time together.

"My father was helping me into my coat as we prepared to leave the restaurant. Suddenly, Manuel was there beside me, apologizing profusely for the interruption, but asking me if he could call on me. I was startled, but agreed."

She paused, thinking back to that day.

"Of course we recognized him. He was the son of one of my father's friends, and we'd often attended the same social functions. He politely asked how it was we were in London, and how long we'd be staying. My father said he was there on business and I'd come with him – and I chimed in to say we'd be there another week. I told him the name of our hotel. I said he could call when he wanted. His face brightened, his smile widened. He gave a funny little bow in acknowledgement, shook our hands, and returned to join his friends."

She stubbed out her cigarette, and took out another. I lit it for her and asked,

"And then?"

"Then? We left. He called me later that day. We arranged for dinner. From then until our return to Mexico, we were inseparable… with each other every day… and some nights. I learned more about London and Manuel in those few days than I think I've managed ever since. It was a glorious time. He told me all about himself, his interests, his passions, his hates, his dislike of excessive authority, his need to prove himself, to become more independent from his father. He showed me a London he'd just learned about, but being a fast learner was able to give it all to me. Money? Not a problem. His parents are well placed, and his own trust was enough to make it unnecessary for him ever to seek employment. I asked him why he was in London, but all he said was that a friend had invited him, and it had become an attractive idea. It wasn't until much later that I found out what sort of person this 'friend' was." Her mouth twitched into an ugly shape when she said 'friend'.

"And your father?"

"Oh, he just carried on with his meetings, and the only times I saw him during the rest of that week was when I returned to our hotel to change, or have a quick meal with him."

"But now? You're not so sure of Pancho?"

"No. I'm not. He's not the same person. Well, superficially, he is. But I know this man, and he is changing… has changed." She was troubled.

"How?"

She paused. "How? He's more distant now. Less giving of himself – to me, at any rate. He seems more distracted. And he doesn't spend as much time with me as he used to. He disappears at odd moments, and is gone for a long time. And when he returns, there is no explanation."

"Another woman?"

"No!" She was emphatic.

"What then?"

She looked up at me, a puzzled, concerned expression on her lovely face, a glint of concern in her eye.

"I – I'm not sure. But I think he has money problems, and he's trying to fix them. I see this from the way he's been behaving in recent months. But what he's trying to do to fix them is dangerous. He's been seeing some very unusual people lately. They phone him at strange hours, and he's nervous when he talks to them. Sometimes they want him to go to them right away… no matter what time of day or night it is. Sometimes he disappears for days at a time. This evening was such a time, even though it was just a few hours. Didn't he tell you he could not pick you up, even though he'd promised to? He's now telling me he wants to get rid of his mobile phone, but that he's afraid to. It's very puzzling. I'm worried for him. And it's getting too much for me."

I nodded sympathetically.

"Yes," I said. "That's true. That message he left me here, and how quickly he disappeared from the party." You say he's been meeting some strange people. What sort of people are they? Do you know who they are? Have you met any of them?"

"No, I haven't. He always goes out to meet them. But, once, I did overhear a part of a phone conversation he was having. I could just hear the man's voice on the other end. It was ugly, and silky. Smooth. And, angry. I've never heard anything like that. I went cold when I heard it, and I was suddenly much more afraid for Manuel."

"Did he ever say, hint even, about who they were… are?"

"No. But underneath it all, I can't help thinking he's somehow mixed up with the dr…"

Just then my own mobile rang. It was Pancho, calling to apologize for his behaviour earlier this evening. He asked me what he can do to make amends. But by this time I'd about had enough of Pancho, at least for today. I told him I was with Maria, and that he should come to collect her and take her home. He sounded a bit startled, but recovered quickly to ask where we were. I told him, and he said he'd be there in twenty minutes.

I looked at Maria. She seemed somewhat miffed by this sudden turn of events, and gave me a strange look, which I countered by telling her Pancho is my friend, and I've no intention of doing anything to damage the relationship. I was there as a courtesy to a beautiful girl who had been abandoned for the evening, and such things went against my nature.

She sighed, got up and left for a few minutes. I settled back and contented myself with my pipe while she was gone. It wasn't long before she came back and sat down again. She had now an air of someone expecting to depart. She said, "I'm sorry he's coming. I had been hoping you'd take me home." Shortly afterwards, Pancho came puffing up to our table. I looked at the time. It was well into the early hours of a new day. He'd been quicker than the promised thirty minutes.

"But even at this hour, the traffic's a madness," he said by way of a greeting. He dropped onto an empty space on the banquette beside Maria, and looked at us both.

"So! You are having a nice drink together."

Now he was looking quizzically at me. I could see a dangerous glint in his eye, and I held up my hand to stop him from speaking any further.

"Pancho, I'm dead tired. You abandoned Maria. It's far too late. For God's sake, don't start anything and just take your girl home!"

His face relaxed. He looked at Maria, who nodded solemnly. They rose, wished me goodnight, and left.

The waiters were wilting. One was sagging against a door jamb. The other looked expectantly at me. I paid the bill, descended to my room, and collapsed into a deep sleep.

Chapter 14

To the untrained ear, morning comes much too early in the heart of Mexico City. With the sun barely showing its first rays over the eastern horizon, a daily ritual is played out in the centre of the huge open Zocalo. Even at this early hour, enough people are about on the vast concrete expanse to witness a small contingent of sleepy soldiers assemble at the base of the towering flagpole for the daily ritual of raising Mexico's huge national flag.

This little ceremony is accompanied by an enthusiastic, though not necessarily professional, playing of a solitary trumpet, whose squeaky high piercing tones are sharp enough to make their way directly through the open windows into my room, penetrating my deep sleep.

Shaken reluctantly awake, I groped my way into the shower to stand under the tepid stream, and gradually prepared myself to face the day. On my way up the elevator to the open air restaurant where I'd been yesterday, I remembered that I was supposed to meet Kevin for lunch. But, coffee first.

Despite the ever-frenetic pulsing rhythm in the city below, breakfast on the rooftop is a leisurely affair. I welcomed the chance to enjoy at my own pace the fresh fruit, *huevos rancheros*, and a pot of excellent coffee.

Lighting my pipe to accompany a final cup, I thought again about the little scene I'd witnessed in the small hours of this morning, not so many steps away from where I was sitting, here in the morning sunshine.

What concerned me most about it was what Pancho may be wondering why I was alone with Maria up here so late at night. I did not want to alienate him; he was too good a friend for that. Besides, truth be told, he also was a very useful entrée into those parts of Mexican society that otherwise would have been closed to me. Last evening's party at his parents' home was a case in point. Without him, I would never have met the Chairman of the Mexican Reconstruction Board, who was generous enough to suggest that I call on him while I was here. Although, as I had pointed out to Maria last night, I'm not sure why he wants to see me. When he issued the invitation, my immediate reaction was that he was simply being polite; offering a courtesy to a guest of one of his friends. But, after Maria's description of him, and her revelation he is her father, I was now thinking better of it. Yet I was rather perplexed about it. Still, I mused, there was only one way to find out.

I finished my coffee, signed the check, left a handful of pesos tucked under the saucer, and went down to my room. I fished out the Chairman's business card that I'd stuffed into the breast pocket of the shirt I'd worn yesterday, and dialed his number.

Even with my schoolboy Spanish at its best, and the several secretarial layers I had to navigate, it was the better part of half an hour before I heard his voice.

"*Sr*. Echeverria, it's Sam Barnes calling."

"*Ah, si, Señor* Barnes. Yes. I am glad to hear from you. Did you enjoy yourself last evening? *Señor* Bandilero is a fine host, is he not?"

"Yes, thanks. Indeed he is. His son is a friend of mine."

"He is a fine young man, although a little wild sometimes, I think."

I decided to ignore that. "I was wondering if you still would like to meet with me."

"But of course! I invited you. Are you free today? Can you come for lunch?"

"Unfortunately, I have another commitment at lunch time. But could you possibly suggest another time?"

"Ah. A pity. Well, let me see." I could hear the rustling of paper at his end. I guessed he was consulting a diary. He spoke again. "Yes! Three days from now … Monday. Monday morning. Would 11 o'clock be alright? It will give us time to talk before lunch."

"That'll do very nicely." As I said this, I knew that Kevin and I should be leaving the city sooner, yet I seem to have recalled him saying something last evening about his need to spend some more time here. It was okay with me. I'd double-check it with him at lunch today, but in the meantime, I'd let it stand with Echeverria.

"¡*Bueno*! The address is the same as on my business card. Come straight up to my office… It's on the top floor. I will inform the guards in the lobby."

I jotted down the details, said goodbye, and hung up.

I looked at the time. It was barely 9.30; more than three hours before I was to meet Kevin for lunch.

The heat was already building, together with the clouds of smog the city's administration had laboured valiantly but so far in vain to erase. But never mind! I wanted to be part of it. I dressed for the day by putting on lightweight tan coloured cotton trousers, off white short-sleeved shirt, no tie, and my light blue cotton jacket. I filled my pockets with fresh wads of pesos, the slim mobile phone Frankie had given me last Christmas, my credit card and other IDs, pipe, tobacco and matches, and set off out into the city to explore.

I like walking, especially in big cities. The simple act of strolling along busy sidewalks offers constant novelties, kaleidoscopes of new experiences. The city had come fully alive – of course, it never really slept. The morning traffic had reached its peak, and would remain so well into the late night hours. Shops open for business were in full operation; the bourse had opened, trading its financial wares across the world. The museums, libraries, coffee shops, auction houses, and art galleries were gradually coming to, readying themselves to greet the day's flood of visitors.

I hadn't told Kevin last night, but I knew the restaurant he'd suggested for lunch, and so I set off in that general direction, but being quite open to be seduced into sidetracking the moment something interesting or unusual caught my eye.

It wasn't hard to be distracted. No sooner had I crossed the Zocalo to the other side, paying passing respect to the huge national flag I'd heard, rather than seen, being raised a few hours earlier, and a short way down a side street, than I came across, as I suspected, the diggings of one of the earliest Aztec temples. There, in the middle of this busy street, being gradually exposed from spending centuries below ground level, the variegated ruins of a huge, square pyramid installation, 80 meters to a side. Here, in the Sacred Precinct of the Temple, I could watch below me, workmen digging cautiously, carefully, cautiously, painstakingly scraping away the dust of five centuries to expose the steep stone stair cases, each one rooted in an intricate but random design of stones. Bystanders, observers, passers-by, all were protected from falling into the diggings by a narrow barrier at the top of the digging. Street hawkers hovered nearby, each offering genuine historical models of the tomb, all manufactured last week in some cut-rate, back alley shop on the outskirts of the city, and trucked into this place under cover of darkness.

This was the ancient sacred temple of the original settlement, the Aztec city of Tenochtitlan, now better known as Mexico City. The original temple was thought to have been built about 1325, from earth and wood, but as it is now below the waterline of the ancient lake, is largely inaccessible to archeologists. Subsequent centuries had seen progressive constructions of enlarged versions of the temple, built layer on layer atop the original, each fitting neatly over its predecessor like a stack of Russian dolls.

In the centuries prior to the Spanish Conquest, six more layers were subsequently added. But then, in 1521, came proud, marauding Cortes, and the Spaniards systematically destroyed the Aztec Tenochitlan and built over the rubble this massive modern Mediterranean-style city. As the new construction had progressed, the ancient Aztec Templo Mayor was gradually buried beneath the new city, remaining hidden until the mid-20th century.

I thought back to what I knew of how it had been used during the centuries when it had been the centre of power of those Aztec priests. Even now, on this sunny, bright, warm, modern morning, my blood ran cold at those thoughts and the images they conjured up.

As I continued strolling, I was reminded that just around the corner, in the Presidential Palace, were the wonderful Diego Rivera murals. They were a favourite, and I tried to visit them each time I came here. I determined that I would visit them again before I left.

It was closing in on the noon hour, and there would be just enough time to walk to the restaurant. I chose not to take a taxi, as Kevin had suggested. Traffic in this town is notorious.

Slightly out of breath, and in need of a cooling drink, I arrived at the restaurant just in time to see Kevin stepping out of his taxi. We greeted each other and entered. A table had been reserved. We sat, organized ourselves, ordered drinks, studied menus, gave our orders, and the waiter departed to fill them. For a moment we looked silently at one another. I opened the conversation.

"Kevin, it's been a long time."

"Yes."

"I thought you weren't arriving until next week."

"My plans changed at the last minute, and I decided to come early." It was the same voice I'd heard on the phone, and again last evening, a sort of long, plummy drawl that was quintessentially British; in some quarters attractive. I found it a bit grating.

"Well, it's good to see you. I recognized you immediately last night in the library, even with your back turned."

He smiled. "Well, I don't suppose it's too surprising. I've tried to keep myself fit over the years."

"Yes. I didn't know you knew Pancho."

"Pancho? Oh, you mean Manuel. Well, yes, we've known each other for a while."

"How?"

He looked at me curiously. "Why does this interest you?"

"Simple. Pancho's been a good friend for several years. I knew you at school, but that was a long time ago. It's logical I'd be interested to want to know how two people I know, know each other."

He nodded slowly. "Well, yes, putting it that way, I see what you mean."

"What other way is there to put it?" This was stupid. "Kevin, this is stupid. I don't understand why you'd be so defensive about a simple question."

"Defensive? Not at all! No. It just took me by surprise, that's all."

I didn't believe him, but I let it go. I didn't want a confrontation so early in this venture. I didn't want a confrontation at all. So, I clamped down the rising irritation and instead asked him, "Alright. So tell me how you think this whole thing is going to work. How do you see it playing out, and where I can be of help in it."

"I thought I explained all of that in my email." He sighed. "Well, then: do you remember one time at school …?" and he launched into a lengthy description about how he and I had once become involved in a harmless schoolboy prank, a scheme that I'd largely forgotten about. It involved the large and very primitive coal-fired boiler that supplied hot water to our residence. It was designed to provide enough for sixty boys, all taking showers at about the same time. Keeping the fire burning was a duty shared on a weekly rotational basis among the junior boys, in teams of two. Large amounts of hot water were especially required in the late afternoons to shower the accumulated mud from the skins of the senior boys and prefects arriving back from spirited games of rugby football out on the muddy grass fields. Woe betide any junior derelict in his duty charged to keep the water hot!!

Kevin and I had the duty that week. One morning he'd had the idea to drain off all but the top level of hot water. The idea was to leave just enough for the senior boys to shower first, giving the prefects gathered about time to talk shop, as was typical for them. While doing this, they anticipated good, hot showers for themselves.

"Yes," he continued. "And I brought in that Hungarian chap, Tibor Something-or-other ... I can't remember his last name. And do you know why I wanted him? Because he was Hungarian. Even at that early age, I somehow knew that Hungarians are adept at survival; past masters at smelling the winds of change. And if ever was needed protection when going up against the prefects, that's where Tibor could help us."

And the scheme worked. No sooner had they begun to wash than the water ran cold. And in those unheated shower rooms, cold water was anathema. There were howls of outrage. Tibor was instantly front and centre, explaining excitedly and volubly there had been a fault with the coal in the flue, and the draft had taken the fires the wrong way, and he insisted we were working diligently to correct it because we knew how much they wanted their hot showers, and he was there speaking for us because we were down in the basement stressing away to fix the problem.

Tibor speaking that way, in his fractured, flamboyant English, was persuasive enough to still even the most aggressive prefect. The aggrieved ones gradually calmed, and eventually took it all good-naturedly in stride. They washed their hands, brushed as best they could the mud from their soiled games uniforms, and muttered off for their tea.

I smiled, remembering. "Yes, I remember that now. Tibor was helpful. And it seems to me we actually pulled it off."

"We certainly did! We ran back to our little study rooms, laughing all the way." Then his face darkened slightly. "Of course, in the end the whole thing backfired on us. That Latin master, Partington, had been on to us all the while. It was less than a week later that he sprang his trap on the three of us. He had us all up on the carpet in his study, and slowly and maliciously I thought, spelled out in excruciating detail, the errors of our individual ways. He had overheard us hatching the plot. We stood there silently, in a row on his carpet, while he sipped his tea in front of the coal fire, and languidly laid it all out. Then he gave us two hundred and fifty lines each, imposed an impossible deadline for their return, and dismissed us."

Yes, I remembered those 'lines'. A convenient form of punishment, liberally handed out by teachers and prefects alike. Infractions of minor but annoying school rules frequently attracted assignments of lines ranging from the minor to the severe. The number of lines assigned corresponded roughly to the nature and seriousness of the offense, but the assignments were sometimes modified by how the assignor was feeling that day. A minor, one-time infraction resulted in a 25-line assignment. At the other end of the scale might be the imposition of several hundred. I had once heard about an assignment of one thousand.

The punishments were to be written only on prescribed sheets of foolscap, a legal-sized piece of paper, pre-ruled with 25 lines to a side. They must be neatly written in the schoolboy's own hand, with material copied only from approved texts. The Bible was a popular source of material. To add insult to injury, the miscreant was obliged to buy the sheets of lined paper, at a penny a sheet. They were available only at the school "tuck shop", a small confectionery on the school grounds, open only at certain hours. In those long-ago days, frequent assignments of lines, even at a penny a sheet, rapidly ate up significant percentages of one's weekly pocket allowance. They also represented substantial income for the little shop. It was an effective way for the school to teach self-discipline.

I said, "It's a nice story, Kevin, but I still don't quite see why you selected me for this caper."

"But don't you see? You were prepared to take the risk. You were always 'up' for a prank, regardless of the danger."

"There is danger in looking for a document?"

"No, no! Not danger exactly; at least not physical danger."

"What, then?"

"Well, I suppose it could affect your reputation … if we find it, and you write about it."

"Meaning…?" Why did I have to drag everything out of him?

"Well, we haven't found it yet, have we? Although, I've a few ideas about where I suppose it might be. But I want to do some more research here first."

"Here? You mean here in Mexico City? I thought you'd done it all."

"Yes."

I set down my fork with a clatter. People at tables nearby turned around to look at us. "Kevin, are you telling me we're not going there right away? I thought that was the whole idea… that we'd go to the Yucatán shortly after we got here."

"Well, yes, it was. But before I left I came across some additional information, something I'd not read about before."

"And it was …?"

"Do you know what Tayasal is?"

"No."

"Tayasal was the last holdout for the Maya Itza. It was their village, and encampment and home, all on an island in the middle of a big lake. That lake is in the Peten."

"In Guatemala?"

"Yes. In Guatemala. It seems that it was one of the last places Avendaño visited before he died."

"And so you think …?"

"The only thing I think is that more research needs to be done. Everything I've read so far about Avendaño's movements include only the vaguest of references to his document. He could have produced it first, and taken it to Tayasal to give a copy to Kan 'Ek. Or on the other hand, he could have gone first to help do a final pacification of Kan 'Ek and his people, learning something more about the Mayan hieroglyphics while there, then returned to Merida to produce his treatise. The record is far too vague. Not clear at all. It's open to too many interpretations. It's no good us chasing all over Mexico and Guatemala on a wild-goose chase now, is there?"

I conceded the point. Which was just as well: I had no intention of going to Guatemala.

He went on, "There are lots of records about those times in the late seventeenth century. But they're all in fragments, a bit here, a bit there. It all has to be pieced together. It takes a long time to make anything of it."

Yes, he made sense. But it still rankled. He'd made no mention of including me in his searches. What was I supposed to be doing while he holed himself up in dusty libraries digging for golden nuggets of information? Especially ones that might not exist? "And what makes you think you'll find it there?"

"Well, it stands to reason, doesn't it? The information is more likely to be here than anywhere else. This is the centre of all Mexican culture and history. The museums and libraries and universities are supposed to be brimming with information about it all. Besides, the last bit I read in London was only just enough to point me in the right direction."

"But it will still take time though, won't it?"

"Yes. But not as much you might think. I've already arranged an appointment with the leading Mayan hieroglyphic expert here, and I'm due there after lunch for a preliminary meeting."

"Well, Kevin. That's great. It's a good thing I like Mexico. I can find plenty to do here."

He looked up at me sharply. I could see that he could tell from my tone that I wasn't particularly pleased with his news. Then I asked him, "Why do you want to find this document? Why come all this way on what could be a wild-goose chase? What's in it for you?"

"I told you; I found out about it in my researches at home. I was intrigued. The whole thing seemed implausible enough that it might just be true."

"Come on, Kevin! I wasn't born yesterday. A bit of intriguing knowledge sends you across the Atlantic, at considerable expense, and my expenses too I might add, to chase down something that might not be there? We've hardly talked in more than twenty years? I don't buy it."

"Well, of course, there's the money angle, too." He looked a bit sheepish. "It's the chance of some really good money that's the main incentive. As it happens, I've a bit of bother at home, something that's been hanging over me for a while and could be coming to a head quite shortly."

"And that would be …?"

He shifted uncomfortably in his chair. I could see that he had been reluctant to talk about it. He poured some more wine and drank. Then, as if he had been struggling with himself, he came to a decision.

"My family has owned property in Scotland for centuries. It dates back to the time of Rob Roy and the English Conquest. There's quite a bit of it, about two hundred and fifty acres, and we've done well to keep it more or less intact over the years. I'm the present owner – at least I am in name. As distances go in the UK, it's not far from Edinburgh, and as the city grew, the land's value has appreciated enormously, and there is already pressure from land speculators on me to sell. It's also supporting a rather heavy mortgage, one I've been trying hard to pay down. But, despite the money I came into a couple of years ago – what I mentioned to you – and it was substantial, expenses have also been heavy, and if I don't look sharp, the loan may go into default. I can't let that happen."

"Apart from the obvious reasons, why not?"

"My father was somewhat eccentric. A kindly man, but an athletically eccentric one. He was the previous owner, and he passed it to me in his will. When he died and we opened the will, we discovered he had insisted the land be kept intact in the family in perpetuity. He'd always had romantic notions about establishing a new Scottish royal seat. He wanted it to become the centre of Scotland's soul if separation from the rest of the United Kingdom ever happened. It was all nonsense, of course. The powers that be at Holyrood House would never have dreamed of agreeing to such a romantic notion; never mind Westminster. But if I let the loan go into even early default, the lawyers'll be all over me. What I actually inherited was nothing but an ongoing nightmare."

Yes, I vaguely remembered Kevin's father. I remembered those occasional weekends during school term when parents were encouraged to visit their sons in boarding school. Kevin's parents had come once or twice during term, and one time they invited me to go along on one of their outings. Even at that young age, I thought I saw signs of eccentricities. And yes, it's quite possible some of them could also have rubbed off on Kevin. A case in point was his quixotic quest for an ancient document that might not even exist. And here I was, more or less committed to helping him. Was I equally eccentric? Or, just plain out of my mind. Ah, well! I was here now, so I may as well make the best of it. I asked him:

"Because of simple default? What could it do to you?"

"Not so simple. Far from it. They'd insist I sell everything I own, or go and get a second job, or rob a bank, play the shares market, pimp for the girl trade, gamble… anything to obtain enough funding to keep the mortgage current."

"But that's unreasonable!"

"Of course it is. But they're lawyers, and like most of them, they can't see beyond the pages of their overstuffed briefs. And they would have the upper hand, as usual. So, rather than doing battle with them, one I knew I'd lose, I decided instead to take a different route to try and find some funding. All my researches and some rather discreet enquiries have all told me that Avendaño's document could bring a very pretty price if put up at auction."

"Have you contacted an auction house?"

"Only peripherally. Can't give the game away too soon, now can we?"

"No. No, I suppose you're right."

"You sound doubtful."

"No. It's just that I was thinking if you had been more open with them you might have had a better understanding of the real value of this thing."

"Sam, you know I couldn't do that."

"Yes," I said, somewhat ruefully. "Yes, I know that. But it does leave us at something of a disadvantage, though."

"Well, yes, I suppose it does." Then he straightened up, with, "Well! We'll just have to make the best of it."

"But," I objected, "surely you must have at least some idea of its potential value. I mean, if it's as rare as you've been suggesting, and is of such interest to Mayan scholars, again as you suggested, then I should it would command a lot."

He frowned over this for a short time. Then nodding, as if he'd come to some sort of conclusion, "You're right, of course. Those are certainly arguments in favour of a high value. But how much? I've really no idea. Maybe hundreds of thousands, maybe millions. The market will eventually decide it."

There didn't seem to be much else to say after that. Our talk drifted off into reminiscences of school life: the boys we'd known; the lessons we'd learned, or not learned; the teachers, who had done their best to instill hard facts and some of life's lessons in us. We shared our memories of the school's elaborate, private language, much of it consisting of words that brought expressions of puzzlement to the faces of outsiders. We talked about, and gently scoffed at the whole range of petty rules and attendant punishments inflicted on all of us who'd had the good fortune to attend that Spartan school.

During this, he asked me, "What about you? Why would you, a raw youth from the equally raw Canadian snows, be sent to that school? Aren't there any schools in Canada?"

I couldn't help but smile. What else could I do? His description of Canada rankled, but I was determined not to let it show. I also felt irritation at the implicit ignorance. Nevertheless, I told him:

"Of course there are schools in Canada; many excellent ones. But you spoke of your father being a romantic. In a way, my parents were, too. Both their surnames were historically linked to Scotland, although in rather roundabout ways. They'd also spent many happy summers in Nova Scotia, and if you remember any of your Latin, you'll know the name of that place translates as New Scotland. They'd come to love the province and over time, for reasons I'm not sure I can adequately explain, they'd also come to relate one Scotland to the other. As I was just then growing into my teens, they had this great idea to turn their vicarious experiences of Scotland into real ones for me."

"What did you think of the idea?"

"Hmph! I was quite happy where I was. I liked my school; all my friends were there, or close by. I was beginning to know myself, or thought I was anyway, and I discovered that I liked myself. But this was in the context of being among my friends and all things familiar. I had little desire to be uprooted and sent four thousand miles away to a strange place, no matter how much I loved my parents."

I smiled, somewhat ruefully. "But, families being the somewhat autocratic institutions they often can be, I had little say in the matter. The next thing I knew, come the next term time, I was packed off to Scotland and committed to durance vile. The rest, as they say, is history."

"Yes. I suppose it took a while to adjust."

"Indeed it did! My first year was a purgatory. I don't know which was worse: the never-ending cold in those unheated stone gothic buildings, or dodging the unremitting gauntlet of petty rules."

Kevin nodded knowingly; he'd been subjected to the same strictures. And with that, we reminisced our way through the remainder of lunch. But I remained puzzled by the apparent shift in Kevin's mood during our meal – his proclaimed enthusiasm for our venture, contrasted by what seemed a creeping indifference. He had signalled during lunch his interest in doing his own researches, and I was quite happy to let him. I had little interest in cooping myself up in dusty libraries. He at once had seemed more committed, yet more distant. I could not fathom either, but in the absence of any proof of the latter, I chose not to quiz him about them.

We parted on the sidewalk outside the restaurant, and he left me with one final thought: "Don't bother too much just yet about the special clothing arrangements and all that. We'll take care of it in the next few days." We shook hands and he strode off to meet his hieroglyphic specialist.

Chapter 15

With Kevin's abrupt change in plans, I found myself at loose ends for the afternoon. It came unplanned, but not unwelcome. As I'd told him, it was fortunate I liked this city, and could find plenty to do. In other words, 'screw you, Kevin'. Standing there on the sidewalk, an unbidden memory came over me. It was from that snowy afternoon in my office, just a few short days ago. I had been sitting in the gathering gloom of late afternoon, puffing morosely on my pipe and idly contemplating the swirling storm outside the windows. I was recalling the siren attractions of the mariachis, and how, on previous visits, I'd enjoyed listening to their brilliant, effervescent and compellingly soulful music. Their playing was at once inspirational, heart wrenching, memorable and completely irresistible. It was the thought of that attraction that was strong enough to help me frame the shape of this afternoon.

In my mind I visualized a map of the city, focusing on where I was, and tried to estimate how far it was to Garibaldi Square, the traditional gathering place of the mariachi bands. It felt like about a kilometer and, since it was not too hot, I opted to walk.

I made my way over to Reforma, the main thoroughfare connecting the countless vast reaches of this impossibly large city. In its own way, it was Mexico's answer to Toronto's Yonge Street. Paseo de la Reforma is a multi-lane, divided, tree-lined and in places, very pleasant main avenue that runs through the heart of Mexico City. It stretches across this vast city, joining the many outer communities on its way from one corner of the city to the diagonally opposite one. It is lined in the main with restaurants, shops, businesses, office skyscrapers and prosperous apartment blocks. Its bustling wheeled and pedestrian traffic is non-stop from midnight to midnight. With many of its sections tree-lined, it seemed more a boulevard than a busy thoroughfare. The trees provided ample and often welcome shade to pedestrians, welcome against the day's noon-time sun.

It gave me time to think. My conversation with Kevin had proven nothing. If anything, I'd come away from it more puzzled than before. I could see right away that he wasn't being straight with me, but I had no idea why. His behaviour was odd and not what I would have expected. He was the one who had suggested this trip. He was the one who had indicated my expenses would be paid. He was the one who had encouraged me to leave the snow-frigid winter behind and enjoy a few weeks in the sun. He was playing an odd sort of game, but for the life of me I could see no reason for it. He had talked about his money problems. And yes, I could see they were real and pressingly urgent. He had made no secret of his intention to do all he could to secure funding to extricate himself from the mess he was in at home. In that, I told myself with some honesty, it was a noble objective. I'd felt, was now feeling, some of the same pressure myself, but nowhere near the degree that he was. But his manner, his selection of words, his very actions so far, convinced me there was something else behind it all – something he wasn't sharing it with me.

I mentally shrugged, and turned my thoughts to something much more pleasant: my late-night conversation with Maria.

Now there was a pleasant thought if ever I'd had one! She was delicious. A petite bundle so appealing it made me want to package her all up and take her home with me. My senses quickened even at the thought of her. That she was attracted to me was not in question. Nor, if I was to be honest with myself, could I claim I was not attracted to her. It's one of those instant truisms of life: an instant, fleeting attraction of someone who catches your eye. It's happened before. Walking down a crowded street. Riding on the subway, to catch a glimpse of someone through the windows of the train opposite when both were standing still in the station. A fleeting glance. Eyes searching then locking for an instant. Perhaps the ghost of a smile. Pretty, gently upturned corners of a mouth. You might have been thinking about something entirely different – how much money you still had remaining in your bank account before the next royalty payment arrived, for instance. But suddenly, all your senses are engaged, and you felt an urgent need to make contact. But it was not to be.

Not then.

But now here, almost as though the fates had decreed it, dropped into my lap was this gorgeous creature who seemed to think that she liked me – in spite of her long-term relationship with Pancho. And Pancho! And just what do you think he might have to say about this? Hmmm? I had immediately seen the warning glint in his eye when he came to the bar last night to collect Maria. It was almost enough to make me pack my bags and head right back to Toronto – snow or no snow.

But not quite. I've never been averse to risk. If I had been, I'd have taken a safe government job at a young age, and stuck with it until pensioned off. I wanted to know more about why Maria was showing this side of herself to me. And I couldn't very well do that while hibernating three thousand miles away in the frozen north. So, let's face it, Sam. She intrigues you. And not just because she's an attractive, warm, intuitive, welcoming woman. Attractive, hell! She's drop-dead gorgeous, as so many Latin women can be. She has eyes you can melt right into, deep glistening pools of welcoming intelligence that actively invite you in to immerse yourself and to stay – forever. A sense of returning to the cocooning comfort of the womb – safe from all threat; all-systems nourishing; grateful for the chance to help and succor. But not, I knew instinctively, as if I didn't already know it, at the risk of losing my own independence or sense of who I was.

Her face danced before me, and I had to be careful not to jostle others as I walked along the crowded, shaded sidewalk. I'd passed the Angel, that other 'heart' of Mexico City, that tall monument to Mexico's independence, topped by its glistening, golden Angel, with busy traffic swirling around it. "Other heart?" Well, the Zocalo was the real centre, a gathering place, the logical place right in front of the National Palace and the National Cathedral. And I could hear her voice … unusual for me. I'm musical, as I've already told you. Jazz is my favourite listening. But oddly enough, I often have trouble recalling how people's voices sound.

But not Maria's.

I knew I wanted to see her again. But somehow I had to square it all with my relationship with Pancho. I didn't want to put that in jeopardy. He was too good a friend: he and his family, both. If anything were to develop between Maria and myself, it would have to be she who would need to confront Pancho's machismo, to quell any angers, to comfort his feelings, to smooth it all over. But even so he would blame me.

A seemingly hopeless task!

Who was I trying to kid?

And yet, and yet. There she was, now firmly planted in my mind. More: I was startled to realise she was beginning to occupy that small, dark, secret place inside where only the favoured few are ever permitted to dwell. The very few.

I was approaching Garibaldi Square. Even before I got there, I could hear the bright, brassy, brilliant music cutting through the constant din of traffic and people's cell phone conversations.

And then there it was – the open expanse of the plaza, paved in London-style paving stones and bordered by a mix of shops, bars, restaurants and, off to one side, the new, blue-sided Tequila Museum. I should go in there and have a look around.

Despite the pleasant walk I'd had up tree-shaded Reforma, I was hot by the time I arrived, and I searched out one of the many bars. I found a likely looking one and took an empty table, one that was shaded by the large awning that stretched the entire front of the building. It had now become unbearably hot under the mid-afternoon sun. In the distance towards the mountains, I could hear the faint rumblings of thunder. Sure enough, the sky was starting to take on that slight haze that was not the heat constantly rising from the city's countless square kilometers of asphalt and concrete, nor the ever-present smog – despite the City's determined efforts to clean the air. No, this was the haze that presaged a storm. The clouds would gradually thicken and darken until the sky had become quite black, making way for the clouds to open and release a torrential downpour.

For the moment it was still reasonably sunny and clear. There would be time enough to seek proper shelter.

The beer the waiter brought was icy cold, the condensation trickling down the outside of the dark brown bottle. I poured, and emptied half the glass in that deep, satisfying way that left an indescribable feeling of 'bite satisfied' at the back of my throat. I emptied the bottle, and waved at the waiter for another.

The usual crowd of tourists and sightseers milled around the square, aimlessly strolling about here and there, taking countless selfies and pictures of the many statues in the Square, including the one to Cirilio Marmolejo, the musician who had been responsible for popularizing mariachi music. They poked about in the tiny gift shops, sought quiet places to sit and rest, or did as I was doing, collapsing into chairs to cool off with an ice-cold drink. Others clustered around the groups of bands whose wonderful, irresistible music steadily filled the air.

There were several bands, each playing its own tune. Instead of an unbearable cacophony, the various melodies seemed to mesh and blend, making it all much easier on the ear. I noticed a young couple talking to what appeared to be the leader of one of the bands. Perhaps they were negotiating for the band to come and play for them at an event they were planning.

There was a constant stream of visitors entering and leaving the museum. Through a break in that crush of people, I saw three men leaving the building. Two were instantly familiar. One was Pancho, another Kevin. The third I'd never seen before. The three were deep in conversation, contriving to be inconspicuous, intent on walking away without attracting any attention. They might have succeeded, but I had the distinct impression that Pancho had seen me sitting at my table across the square and looking directly at him.

Chapter 16

Even after having been here in Mexico for three days I found that it was not yet enough to shake off the rigours of the northern winter. Sometimes I felt that three years might not be enough. It had only been Thursday that I'd arrived, decanted into a land so different and welcoming, and even while still on the plane, I felt I wanted to see as much of it, and experience all of it that I could while here.

After having lunch with Kevin, I spent the intervening days on my own. The weekend had passed; a new week had begun. Over the weekend I wrote in the mornings, valiantly chipping my way through the book reconstruction that Harry had foisted on me.

In the afternoons I played tourist. On Saturday, I spent the afternoon in Chapultapec Park, Mexico's enormous 700-acre response to New York's Central Park, or those great green expanses of gardens and trees in central London that had once been jealously protected royal preserves. I strolled among the ancient, centuries-old trees, marveled at the startling variety of migratory birds that chose this place in the City's centre to rest. I meandered along the Avenue of the Poets, and resisted the urge to feed the animals in the Zoo. Before closing time, I climbed the Hill and spent a pleasant hour in the halls of the old Chapultapec Castle, the one-time home of Emperor Maximillian. The building is better known today as the Museum of History.

On Sunday, I took myself out to Xochimilco, to paddle idly along the canals among the floating islands. The extensive inland waterways in this huge borough on the City's southern fringes were a mecca for residents and tourists alike, eager to escape, even for an afternoon, the persistent weight of heat, humidity and smog in the city. I'd been here before, but wanted to see the place again. I rented a *trajinera*, one of those brightly decorated gondola style boats, each named by its owner for a girlfriend, a wife or, should the owner not be so blissfully attached, a favourite flower. Travelling with me was a young couple from France, and an American family of four, the parents keeping careful watch on two bright eight-year-olds, each bubbling over with laughter and questions and eager to see how far they could lean overboard without falling in.

I made only casual conversation with the French honeymoon couple, who were understandably more interested in themselves than in a slightly jaded bachelor. The American parents were more open, giving me the opportunity to share careers and travel experiences, and the chance to give a rueful mental shrug when I learned neither had ever read anything I'd written.

For all that, it was a welcome respite from the puzzles of Kevin and Pancho, and I returned later that afternoon with the smiling sultry image of Maria's face still dancing in my mind.

The puzzles were still with me the next day as I prepared for my meeting with Chairman Echeverria. The minor mysteries I'd been encountering since I arrived had begun to take on the outlines of some shape. It was increasingly clear that Kevin was obviously in no hurry for he and I to set off into the jungles, despite all his enthusiasm for it when we had spoken on the phone. To tell you the truth, this was fine with me. His reasons, or were they excuses, were that he needed to do more research while still here in the city, but vague about how much more time he needed.

Pancho, the great friend I'd first met on the Yucatán sands, was showing me a side I'd not known before. That Maria was a part of the mystery made it all the more intriguing.

******

The entrance lobby of the gleaming tower that housed the Mexican Reconstruction Board was a modern wonder of shining glass, gold trim, softened daylight and lush tropical gardens. For a moment I thought I'd mistakenly taken a wrong turn and returned to Xochimilco, with its lush floating islands and canopies of overhanging trees. The lobby glowed with prosperity. Huge floor-to-ceiling windows in front, through which carefully filtered noonday sunshine splashed down over the throngs of office workers lusting for their lunch. I pushed my way through them to the elevators at the back of the lobby. It was like walking through a tropical rainforest. Off to one side, in a clearing, was an impressive reception desk at which sat three identical, scrupulously groomed and polished young men staring intently at video monitors or scanning the departing crowd.

At one of the banks of elevators I made my way into one which had just arrived at the ground floor, decanting its own load of lunch-bound workers.

Riding up with me were only two young women, both of whom gave the impression that they'd rather be heading the other way. They got off, each on her own floor, while I continued alone up to the 25th floor penthouse at the top of the building.

The doors slid open onto a lobby any potentate would have been proud to call his own. From the glimpses of the other floors I'd caught on my way up, they shouted that no expense had been spared on this central city monument that addressed the ever-pressing needs of Mexico's burgeoning population of wretched, under-nourished, unemployed, and impoverished peoples.

Another young man, polished and shined as if newly unpacked from the shoebox, presented himself to me.

"*Señor* Barnes? Please to come this way. The Chairman is expecting you."

I followed him down a long carpeted corridor that ended in a pair of heavy, polished teak doors, one of which opened silently to reveal an office the size of an Olympic-scaled tennis court. In one far corner, across an acre of hushed carpeting, sat an ornate antique desk, from which the Chairman was just rising to come over and greet me. He was wearing a well-practiced smile on his ruddy face. I imagined it was the same sort of smile he used for the TV cameras.

Shaking one hand and clutching an elbow, he said over my shoulder to the young man, "Thank you, Roberto. That'll be all. Please see we are not disturbed. I'll ring when we're ready for lunch."

Roberto left the room, and one of the big doors closed silently behind him. *Sr.* Echeverria waved a hand at a place on the far wall. There was a whirring sound. Still clutching my arm, he conducted me over to the drinks cabinet that was just now being revealed from behind heavy louvered doors. "A drink, *Sr.* Barnes? What will you have?"

He saw the look on my face. "A neat trick, is it not?" and he went on to explain about the motion detector embedded in the wall beside the cabinet, which controlled the cabinet's doors.

As he poured our drinks, I had the chance to study him. He was powerfully built, slightly shorter than me. I thought he might have been a long-distance runner when younger. Now, in what appeared to be his early sixties, he stood straight in his beautifully tailored dark blue suit, white shirt and discreetly checked white and dark blue tie. His full head of white hair surmounted a slightly ruddy complexion in a face that was gradually filling out.

His handshake was firm, his smile ready, his laugh jovial and spontaneous, his English impeccable, and it all added to up to a man secure in his own skin, glowing with good health, comfortable in his life, and with all of life's worries long since banished.

He turned, and handing me my drink, led me over to a set of comfortable chairs. I chose one with its back to the window. Even with the shielding of the window blinds, the filtered noonday sun blazing in through the windows was hard on the eyes.

He opened the conversation. "You told me a little about the book you are writing. Two books I think you said. It sounds quite a challenge. Can you tell me more?"

"The one where my greatest interest lies is a new novel I'm thinking about. I'm still in the note-taking, idea-gathering stage, but do want to get it moving. The other one an obligation … I promised a friend I'd do it, at first I thought it would go smoothly, but it's fast turning into a chore. I want to get it finished as soon as I can, so I can concentrate on the novel. Perhaps I'll be done within a few weeks – I hope so, anyhow."

"You are generous with your time."

"I suppose, although this is something I promised a relative, so …" I shrugged, "I must do it."

"And your new novel?"

"I think I mentioned something about it when we spoke at *Sr*. Luis's party. I want to tell the story – as fiction – about how Mexico is dealing with its problems. You know, I am reading about them all the time in the daily press, although I imagine that many such stories are highly coloured."

He gave a rueful smile. "Yes, the newspapers are a two-edged sword, are they not? We need them as much as they need us – self-fulfilling cannibalism. But many of their writers do often demonstrate considerable enthusiasm."

I nodded. "Then there's the drug problem. The world's press tends to sensationalize this. And no, I don't discount for a minute that it's a serious problem. But I want to understand it better, understand it as it viewed from here. Plus the recent earthquakes, two of them I understand. Devastating. So serious they made headlines around the world."

Señor Echeverria grimaced at this. "Yes, they were terrible, with many tragic consequences. Have you ever felt an earthquake?"

"Of sorts. Several years ago. It was in Ottawa, a place not known for earthquakes. But very disconcerting. I felt the ground shift under my feet, just a little bit, but for just those few seconds it was heart-stopping. Fortunately no damage was done. So, yes, I have some small understanding of their impact. But those two that you had! Thousands killed, serious and widespread property damage, infrastructure seriously out of commission."

"You may be interested to know that my Department has many teams working right now who are busy helping with the aftermath. It will take a long time."

"I can imagine! I've seen the news films on TV."

I went on. "Then there is the Peso. Another revaluation, the second in what … twenty years? What impact can it be having on your economy? How is the country managing? How have the international markets reacted? Will react? And with the still rampant and extensive poverty, what are the continuing impacts that a devalued Peso must be having on peoples' ability to feed and clothe themselves."

I leaned forward.

"You see, *Señor* Echeverria, you are well placed to know so much better than I how difficult these things are. I had read, I think it was only last year, that your organization had been created to address these and so many other similar problems. So, if you don't mind, I'd like to talk about these things."

He flashed me his big smile. "Of course! I am very glad to talk about these things. The President has placed great trust in me, and this organization, to get Mexico moving ahead again. Yes, we have serious problems. But as you see, I have a very large and well-equipped staff to manage them. This building you are in. It is only the headquarters. We have branch offices in every State around the country. And that's not all. There are many field outposts actually working closely with the people at … how do you say? Ground level. It is a massive undertaking."

I couldn't keep the irony out of my voice. "Yes, I can imagine."

Either he didn't notice, or he ignored it. "And more – the resources we've been given to do all of this. It's truly wonderful! Our funding is largely unlimited. We've hired the very best engineers, sociologists, computer technicians, lawyers, accountants … all, all of them deployed daily on addressing the nation's ills. They have access to the finest equipment in their offices, they are in constant contact with one another; they are sent on missions abroad to study how other countries have recovered from their own misfortunes. We have opened training facilities so that new recruits out of the universities can be focused on helping our country grow. And we have our own press and communications offices, so that the general public is kept regularly informed of our plans and progress."

He stopped for breath.

"But what is it you're actually doing?" I asked. By now I wasn't expecting very much. He surprised me.

Getting up from his chair he walked over to his massive desk to operate some controls. "Look at this."

On the opposite wall a huge video display lit up. It showed a map of Mexico, with the borders of each state delineated in bright yellow. The cities glowed red and green; red for the larger ones. Outlined in pink were the locations of the most recent earthquakes. Both covered wide areas. The ancient Mayan sites pulsed a deep purple in the jungles; the seaports, a mix of red and black; the small villages destined for tourist development, a soft magenta. All in all, it told the story of where and how extensive were Mexico's slate of problems. Walking from his desk to the display, Echeverria used the electronic pointer he'd picked up, and began to talk.

"You see this?" aiming the pointer's little green dot at the larger of the pink earthquakes. "Three medium-sized towns and one large one, all hit. Roads, bridges, power grids, water pipelines... everything effectively destroyed. People living in tents, the fortunate ones... those not so fortunate living under sheets of plastic, and scrabbling in the dirt for whatever water and food they can find."

The pointer light moved to the smaller, green-coloured cities. There were many of them. "In these places we have chronic shortages of fresh water supplies and efficient sewage treatment plants." The pointer touched on the big red one. "Mexico City itself. You know how big this city is... and it keeps growing. Huge numbers of people moving here every week, thousands possibly, all off a land that can barely feed a small family, never mind even the smallest of communities. More coming because they feel a greater sense of protection against the drug gangs. Not true of course, but that's what they tell us. The population's exploding, and the city's infrastructure is creaking and in danger of collapsing under the weight.

What are we doing? Drive through the streets. See the constant traffic interruptions! Interruptions caused by construction. Huge holes dug in the roads to make way for repairing of ancient water supply pipes, or installing new power supplies, or building additional subway lines. Everywhere traffic chaos. It's bad, no?"

"Yes."

"Yes. But I tell you this: it would be even worse, with no hope, if we were not doing these things. This way there is hope. This way we have a chance to make a better city. This way we have a chance to make a better Mexico."

Despite my earlier skepticism, I was impressed. The passion in his voice and manner was real. He was clearly committed to this monumental task, despite the evident trappings of wealth and good living so evident here in himself, in his office and in this building.

"And drugs. It is the curse of the modern world, and we are in the middle of it. What you read in the newspapers is only the most sensational. It is a cancer eating away at the very essence of our society, our nation. But it is a very large priority for the President. He is determined to get it under control."

"How?"

"He proposes using methods not thought important by previous administrations. Under control? More!! He wants to destroy it…completely. But, to be sure, he must control it first."

"Has he explained how he proposes to do this?"

"The root problem is money. The gigantic sums generated by the cartels, fueled by the incessant need so many people have to buy such poisons. There will be new legislation he tells me. It will place all the main drug products under government control. These will be readily available through specific, controlled outlets…shops…throughout the country. There will also be other important controls and approaches, but so far I am not permitted to speak of such things."

Trying hard, but barely succeeding to keep the skepticism out of my voice, "And he thinks such measures will be sufficient?"

"Ah! You are doubtful, my friend. Of course! I see this. Most people will be … but only for a time. Eventually these measures will take hold, and gradually the tide will turn in our favour. The President, you see, is a man who plans for the long term – not just the next election. It is his nature to think for the long term. I believe Mexico is fortunate to have him."

"I certainly hope he is right. But I keep reading of the horrible acts of violence caused by those in the drug business. Surely these will continue ... get worse, maybe."

"Yes, he is planning for this, too. But now let me continue."

The pointer moved again, this time to the glowing purple areas. "Our cultural history is fast eroding. We are proud of our history and what it has given the world, and the wonderful temples built a thousand years ago. But have you seen them lately?"

"Not for years. I was hoping to see some this trip."

"When you do, you will cry. You will bewail the erosion causing the effacing and disfigurement caused by weather. Of course, it began when they were built. But the pace has been accelerating in more recent decades. Pollution and climate change, mainly. But that's not all. Vandalism and artifact theft, too. How to protect those marvelous, massive constructions against fortune hunters and willful damage? Impossible!" A slow smile spread across his face. "But maybe not so impossible. We are planning for how to make it less impossible."

"But how can you do this, and still make them available for tourists? Surely that's an important source of income. The tourist trade. People come from all over the world to see the temples... to climb them, to take the pictures they'll remember all their lives. Just to experience them."

"Yes. You are right. How to protect them for this purpose. Well, we are trying we can accomplish this, too."

He stared at the glowing display, deep in thought. For a moment, I had the impression he'd forgotten I was there. Then he turned back to me, a bigger smile on his face.

"But come! We speak too seriously. Lunch be will ready; it's time to eat." Back at his desk, he lifted a phone, and said tersely, "*Horita.*"

Roberto appeared immediately at the door. "Lunch is ready, *Señor*."

I placed my empty glass on the little table beside my chair, and followed my host into a beautifully appointed small dining room adjoining his office. The table was large enough to seat eight comfortably, but today places were set for only two. He waved me to a chair. Seated, I looked around the room. In contrast to the stark modernism of his office, this room was paneled in mahogany, with beautifully handcrafted trims around each panel. On one wall a set of four framed watercolours, each representing one of Mexico's principal trouble areas – infrastructure, drugs, the peso, and archeology.

He saw me looking at them. "You like them? We have them there on purpose, as a permanent reminder of the reason for our existence."

I nodded.

"Wine." He was filling my glass. "You think fine wines come only from Europe and California? Here. Try this."

I drank. It was wonderful. "Where is it from?"

"Right here in Mexico. Baja California. The Guadalupe Valley. A long tradition of wine-making. Not in large amounts, and yes, it is true, there has been a history of inferior qualities. But it's changing. This is an example. It stands up well against many of the better-known vintages you're possibly more familiar with."

I drank again. It was a deep, rich ruby colour and the lights from the overhead shaded lamps sparkled enticingly through it. It had a tangy, spicy bite, leaving a pleasant afterglow on the back of the throat. He filled my glass again.

Lunch was wheeled in. Not Roberto; a tall lean man, dressed in impeccable whites, with a large white chef's hat perched on top of a long, bony head.

"Ah, Jasper! What are you giving us today?"

I was introduced to Jasper Sauvage, Echeverria's personal chef. I nodded and smiled. As Jasper quietly explained what he had prepared, he deftly served us, glanced professionally over the table to satisfy himself that all was in order, and discreetly withdrew, silently closing the door behind him.

I said, "He's very discreet."

"Jasper? He has to be."

"Has to? Why?"

"Interesting story. He's English. He was born in England. Trained in one of those very demanding culinary schools in Switzerland. Changed his name from Savage to Sauvage, to make himself seem more European. He was able to get himself hired on as an under chef in one the few remaining

European royal houses. He'd be there still, except he got mixed up with one of the princesses of the house he was serving. They didn't like that at all! Then a friend told me about him, and I brought him over here. He didn't know a word of Spanish when he arrived, but his credentials were impeccable. Apart from that little peccadillo. This was three years ago, and he's improving. He's proven himself time and again here. The President and his Cabinet have praised him several times. So, discreet? Yes, he has to be."

I nodded.

"But come! We can't let Jasper's wonderful food grow cold. Here, have some more wine. Enjoy!"

And enjoy I did. The meal was everything my host had said, and more. We chatted our way through lunch, and afterwards we took our coffee back into his office. The sun's rays were slanting more sharply into the room, but the air conditioning made short work of any extra heat they brought. He stirred his coffee, and asked:

"Would it help your researches if you saw some of the things we are doing?"

I sat up, "Indeed it would. What do you have in mind?"

By way of answering he got up and walked back over to the still-glowing video display. He ran his hand over the Atlantic coastline of the Yucatán Peninsula. "Here," pointing at the Tulum monuments. "And here," a small seaside village. And, "here": farther south along the coast at what looked like a tourist attraction. He turned to face me.

"The Mayan Gold Coast. All these places have one thing in common. They are all tourist destinations. They are under our purview. We have people in each one of these places repairing, expanding, installing ... Doing whatever is needed to make them more attractive and desirable for visitors to Mexico. And of course, there is Cancun."

By coincidence, he was discussing the very part of the country where Kevin and I were planning to go.

"Oddly enough, I'd been thinking of going that way anyway."

" Excellent! I will write you a letter of introduction to my senior man in Cancun. He will show you what you want to see."

As if by magic, Roberto appeared at the door. Echeverria unleashed a flood of Spanish at him, telling him to have my letter prepared and have it returned immediately for his signature. The door closed.

He came back to his chair. Sitting down, he looked at me.

"You will be well taken care of. I also told Roberto to book you into our hotel. Our man will meet you there. You'll have all the arrangements before you leave. When do you propose to go?"

I thought for a minute. I was supposed to see Kevin this evening. But I was suspecting, rather sourly, that he would tell me he'd still need more time here. Other than the planning with him, there was nothing else for me to do here. I was beginning to read Kevin more clearly.

"Tomorrow. I thought I'd drive."

"It's a long way."

"Yes, I know. But I've done it before. I might stop in Merida."

"A good choice. A lovely town."

"Yes. And there's a pretty hotel there. The Casa San Angel. I like it."

"Good. It's settled."

Roberto came silently back into the office. "Ah! Here is your letter."

Echeverria stepped to his desk, uncapped an elaborate fountain pen, and with a flourish signed the letter in deep mauve ink. He handed it to me along with the hotel reservation and other information that Roberto had brought with him. Escorting me to the door, he said, "*Sr*. Barnes, it has been a great pleasure for me to speak with you. I hope you will benefit from your trip to the Yucatán. Juan Carlo will meet you."

I thanked him for his time, his courtesies and his hospitality. With his firm handshake still tingling my hand, Roberto escorted me to the elevator. He pushed the button, and while we waited for it to arrive, he told me, "You will see some interesting things, *Señor*. I hope you will not be disappointed."

Chapter 17

Outside on the street, I glanced up at the sky. It was clouding over, pressing the day's accumulated heat down onto the scurrying ant heap that characterizes most of this city's public spaces. People glanced up nervously expecting the storm to begin any minute. I whistled for a cab and climbed in just as the first raindrops splashed dark spots on the pavements.

By the time I reached the hotel, the rain was a teeming, torrential downpour. Thunder growled ominously among the occasional flashes of brilliant lightning. The rain was so thick it was almost impossible to see through the cab's windows. Traffic had slowed to a crawl, except for the taxis, which maintained top speed through it all while doing their best to drive through every large puddle they could find, splashing pedestrians on the sidewalks and people riding bicycles in the curb lanes. Pedestrians lucky enough to find shelter had long since done so, while those less fortunate, including the many lottery ticket sellers and street buskers withstood the sluicing sheets of pouring water, knowing this was part of their daily lives.

By seven, the rain had stopped, the clouds rolled away, and the setting sun painted its brilliant yellow, magenta, and indigo colours across the clear, washed sky. I was still in the glow from the Chairman's excellent lunch as I made my way back to the Zona Rosa. On Saturday, Kevin had phoned to suggest we get together this evening to continue work on developing our plans for our trip, and I was on my way to meet him at the restaurant he'd suggested.

He was there when I arrived, looking both energetic and somewhat perplexed. This was a different Kevin from the man I'd met at lunch just a few days ago.

"Are you alright?"

He smiled wanly, "Yes, of course I am."

"You don't look it. Something bothering you?"

"Well, I'm glad you're here. I need to talk to you. Do you recall from our lunch the other day when we talked about Tayasal …?" I nodded. "….and how we both agreed the information we needed would most likely be found here … In Mexico City?" He paused, thinking. "It seems I spoke too soon. My conversation with the hieroglyphic specialist that afternoon was very interesting. When I started talking with him, I was under the impression that all of what we needed would be answered here. It seems this is not so."

"How so?"

"You recall me telling you about how the hieroglyphs told not a complete story? About how they had to be pieced together from available fragments? It was an almost vain attempt to recreate a record – even an incomplete one."

I nodded.

"He told me that he had seen writings that suggested, no, stronger, made it almost a certainty that Avendaño had indeed gone to Tayasal after writing his treatise. The way the record tells it is that he went to see Kan Ek to get him to give up and convert to Christianity."

"Is there any information about Kan 'Ek's reaction to all this?"

"Well, it seems that Avendaño had taken a copy of his document with him, as a gift to Kan Ek; but more…as evidence and proof of what a Christian education can do, and how such an education would be used to benefit his people." Kevin sat forward, as if to emphasize his next point. "You must remember! These were a people who honoured learning; who knew the value of an education. Think of how they might have seen his argument: as a whole new world which could be opened up to them if only they agreed to 'come over' to the Christian side and embrace all its teachings and learnings."

I listened carefully to him. He said the words. But underneath I heard a fervour in his voice that had not been there before. His eyes were brighter, his manner more definite, his attitude more positive. I had the sudden image of a quivering cat at the mouse hole. He seemed to have the scent of Avendaño in his nostrils, and he wanted nothing more than to be on his way. I could read it all over him – or so it seemed.

"And you want to go there." I said it flatly.

"Yes."

"When?"

"Tomorrow. I've already booked us on the flight to Flores. It's the closest airport to Tayasal. I thought we might look in on Tikal while we're there."

He saw me shaking my head: slowly, emphatically, brooking no nonsense.

"What?" He seemed genuinely puzzled.

"Kevin, I know you want to find this thing. I'm rather curious about it, too. You told me on the phone when I called you that your researches had pointed you here, that you felt sure you'd find the rest of what you needed here … in Mexico City. Once done, we'd head off to the Yucatán, the most likely place to discover its whereabouts … or even if it ever existed. Now we're here, and now you tell me you want to go chasing off to Guatemala. Fine! For you. For me, it's a little different. I'm persona non grata in Guatemala. Never mind why – just take it as fact. I can't go there if I want the assurance I can ever return to Toronto. Which I do. So, no. I'm not going to Guatemala, no matter how much your hieroglyphic man may have told you about it."

His face fell. "I was counting on you to help me. I'm disappointed you didn't tell me this before."

"Why should I? The subject of us going to Guatemala has never come up, not in any serious way. And all through this I've been led to believe that our search would be confined to the Yucatán. I'm sorry; it can't be helped."

We fell silent, staring at each other across the table.

It was at that point that Pancho walked in. His face lit up, "Ah, my friends! How good to see you again!" He pulled out a chair and joined us.

I looked over at him. "Hi, Pancho. What brings you here?"

"Sam, it was arranged that I would join you here for drinks. And then maybe a little something afterwards? You did not know?"

It would be an understatement to say I was surprised to see him.

Kevin said, "He and I were talking the other day. I suggested he join us this evening. I hope you don't mind."

"Mind? Of course not. Just … surprised."

"Surprised?"

"Sure. It was my impression we'd be doing some more planning for our trip to the Yucatán. I wasn't aware that Pancho was int …" My words were suddenly drowned out by four men talking loudly at a nearby table. I had the impression, from all the glasses and bottles on their table, they'd already been there a while. It also seemed they knew each other well. Their accents could have been from anywhere between the Rio Grande and the Arctic Circle.

"Yeah," said one, "that Billings. He's a real prick. I'd just finished the pile of work he'd dumped on me then he came with another load. 'Hey', I said to him. 'It's quitting time. I'm supposed to be at my son's birthday party tonight. He's seven'."

"Billings? You mean that little guy in Accounting? The one who's always got all the little coloured pens stuck in his shirt pocket?"

"Yeah. That's the one. I'm in Shipping; along with Jake, here." Jake nodded solemnly. Then Jake said, "I don't know why the Old Man doesn't tell Billings to back off."

"Back off?" shouted the first man. "Never! Billings runs the place. The Old Man's happy as a pig in …"

"Oh, I wouldn't be so sure about that. I've sometimes heard the Old Man take Billings down a peg or two."

I twisted around to see them better, they were getting more garrulous. They waved for the waiter to bring another round. Just a few guys on holiday, I thought, bitching about their workplace.

Shipping was saying, "That Billings, and his sidekick Robbins, they swan around like they own the place. It's 'Do this', or 'Take this to Purchasing', or 'I'll send you an email about it so you'll know what to do.'"

"Email!" snorted Jake. "I've had enough with emails and inboxes. I've seen enough inboxes for a lifetime. The only inbox I want to see right now is between my girlfriend's legs!" His voice had risen as he spoke. There was a noticeable drop in the buzz of conversation throughout the restaurant.

A look of dismay crossed Kevin's patrician features. I wasn't too happy either. And before I knew it, Pancho was on his feet, a black scowl darkening his face. He crossed to their table to stand beside Jake. Jake had seen Pancho coming, and half risen to meet him. Pancho stood over him in quivering ferocious passion, like an avenging angel. He put a firm bear-like grip on Jake's shoulder and gently but firmly forced him back into his chair.

"I think those tamales you had for breakfast were too hot and are still troubling you, *Señor*." Pancho's voice was low, clear, with more than a hint of menace in it. "I ask you remember there are ladies present and that you sit among gentlemen. You do dishonour to the other guests here, to this place, and lastly to yourself. I think also you are a recent visitor to my country, and have not yet learned the value of manners or polite talk." And with that, he rejoined us.

I glanced over to Jake and his companions. He was visibly shaken; they were all subdued, the passion of their complaints about their work drained away. They muttered quietly to one another, and less than ten minutes later, they called for payment, got up and left.

Pancho leaned over to me and asked, "How did it go today, your meeting with *Señor* Echeverria?"

The question startled me. How did he know I was meeting with the Chairman? Then I realized that Maria must have told him; I had mentioned it to her when we were in the Majestic bar the other evening. "Very well. He's a good host, and sets a fine table."

"Yes, he is. And were you able to get something for your book?"

"Indeed I was. He was most helpful."

"Chairman? What Chairman?" Now it was Kevin's turn to ask.

I looked at him. "At the party the other evening; the one you weren't supposed to be at because you weren't planning to come to Mexico until this Friday."

"I told you; my plans changed."

With an ironic edge in my voice, I said, "Yes." Then, "He was gracious enough to ask me about what I'm doing, what I'm writing. More, he invited me to meet him in his office. I was there today."

I turned to Pancho. "What's your interest in this old document?"

He and Kevin looked at each other. Kevin gestured to Pancho, and said, "I happened to mention it at his father's party. He told me had an interest in the history of Mexico and offered to help. I suggested he join us this evening. I also invited him to join us for lunch the other day, but he told me he was busy."

Yes, I thought, preparing to meet Kevin and that guy I'd seen, and trying hard not to let me know about it, or see him.

Pancho said, "*Señor* Echeverria is a very close friend of my father's. He is also Maria's father, so I do not think it unusual that I should ask you about your lunch today. And Kevin is right: I do have an interest in my country's history. You'll remember I once told you I'd studied it at university."

Yes, he had told me. But even so I couldn't help wondering whether his interest was merely casual – a friend just helping a friend. Or, did he have a deeper interest in what I still considered to be a wild-goose chase, based on nothing more than Kevin's apocryphal evidence?

They were both looking at me. They could see the doubt on my face, and as I spoke they could hear the mounting irritation in my voice. "Well, that's just fine. Pancho, your help is welcome. Whatever you can think of." I turned to Kevin. "Kevin, I see you are keen to head down to Tayasal. Perhaps Pancho would like to go with you. As for me, I told you I can't go, and since I am here in Mexico on what can be considered something of a busman's holiday, I'm going to go to the Mayan Gold Coast, Cancun maybe, or Isla Mujeres, and enjoy the wonderful sunshine and substantial pleasures this country has to offer. I have a letter in my pocket from Ranulfo Echeverria, who has offered to help me in researching for my book. I'm leaving tomorrow morning."

I emptied my glass, dropped some pesos on the table to cover it, and walked out.

Pancho followed me out. I turned to look at him, waiting for him to say something. Finally, I said, "Pancho, what are you up to?"

"What do you mean?"

"You know very well what I mean. You're not the friend I thought I knew from before. There's something strange going on; you seem to be acting strangely."

"Sam, there is nothing. There is nothing strange with wanting to spend time with old friends."

"No, there isn't. But there is something strange when an old friend keeps disappearing like a magician. There is something strange when more people seem to know what I'm doing here in Mexico than I do. There is something strange when those close to you, Pancho – Maria, for instance – are very and publicly worried about you. There is something strange when friends who know me well don't want me to see them. And there is certainly something strange when I begin to feel that I'm being taking for a ride."

He was silent for a time. I think my outburst must have startled him. Then, slowly, as though he was thinking his way through his reply, his thoughts came out. "Sam, my friend, and yes, you are still my friend and have been since we first met. But these things you speak of are only normal to me ... normal as I must live my life these days. It is perhaps, not the same type of life that I was leading when we last met, but it is important to me that I do some things that may appear strange to you, but are necessary for me. I hope you can ... will understand."

Did I want to pursue this? I felt suddenly deflated, not used so much as if the interest in Kevin's wild goose chase – for I still mainly thought of it as such – had drained away. If he – and Pancho – wanted to chase rainbows, fine! Let them!

"No, Pancho, it's okay. If you and Kevin want to chase unicorns, it's fine with me. He told me about wanting to go to Tayasal, down in Guatemala. Maybe you could go with him. But for me, I've got some researches to do of my own – I think that time spent will be more profitable for me."

"Researches? What researches?"

"Pancho, I'm a writer, remember? I'm working on developing material for a new novel."

"Oh."

"Yes. You thought it was something else?"

"Well, no ... sort of."

"Pancho, stop. Just stop this." I looked at the time. "I've got to go. I've several things I need to do before I leave in the morning. He reached out and shook my hand in farewell. I don't know if he was mollified by what I'd told him, but at this point I did not really care. I turned and walked away.

Chapter 18

The next morning was sparkling fresh. The road was open, the car a dream to drive, and I was finally on my own, in pursuit of my own pleasures. Already the mysteries of recent days were dimming, and certainly less pressing. I had mariachis on the stereo and the car's open top gave me a clearer view of the mysteries of this mysterious land.

Despite my original intentions, I had changed my mind after leaving Kevin and Pancho in the restaurant. I decided instead to fly to Merida, and from there drive on to Cancun. It meant some last-minute work by my hotel concierge who was better equipped to deal with intricacies of navigating through the maze of booking flights and changing car reservations. I told him I already had a booking for the San Angel Hotel in Merida, and he needed only to bring that forward a day to fit my revised plans.

On an earlier visit to Merida, I'd found I'd liked the city very much, but had had very little time to see anything of it. Now that I was here again, I decided to take advantage of this time. On the morning after my arrival I phoned the desk and asked them to book me a second night in this room. After preparing myself for the day, I walked downstairs into a lobby not unlike the one in the Majestic. On my way into breakfast, I stopped by the concierge desk and discussed with him the sights of the city and how I might profitably use my time by seeing some of them.

After a leisurely breakfast, and armed with a map and the brochures the concierge had given me, I set off into the city to see as much of it as time would allow.

Now, another day. With Merida behind me, I was on the 'free' road. It was slower than the higher-speed toll road, but much more interesting. Flying in Mexico can sometimes be a purgatory, as I had seen when I witnessed the concierge making my changes, and so this drive became a pleasure. I was passing through a kaleidoscope of cornfields, thatched adobe cottages, dense vegetation sometimes verging on jungle, and the occasional mangrove swamp. The heavy persistent scent of burning brush and rubbish was a constant companion, and I frequently had to go slow to avoid chickens, dogs, bicycles, small children, donkey-driven carts and other slow moving vehicles. For all that, the only other motor traffic on the road at this early hour was the huge Coca Cola truck that I'd been following for several kilometers. Finally, it turned off onto a side road to make a delivery, and I had the road to myself.

It's an easy drive to Cancun, about 300 kilometers. I'm usually a fast driver, but was in no rush today. I had enjoyed my stop in Merida. It's a pleasant, bustling city, with its air of commercial activity through the thoroughfares of its diminished colonial grandeur. The hotel had been the relaxed oasis I'd remembered, the large fountain splashing musically in the tiled forecourt.

The morning had grown increasingly hot and humid under the prevailing influences of the Gulf of Mexico. Towards noon, thirsty and somewhat tense from the drive, I stopped in Valladolid. After some searching, I came across an attractive little restaurant from which the tantalizing aromas of *lomitos* were wafting out. A tall thin saturnine waiter escorted me to a table in the busy dining room. He perfunctorily dusted the spotted table cloth of the bread crumbs left by a previous guest, took my order and left me to ponder tomorrow's plans. I would then be under the watchful eye of the Chairman's man in Cancun. But here was the waiter setting before me the plate of *lomitos*, this wonderful local specialty of pork in chicken broth and tomato sauce. It was even better than the aromas I had smelled outside, and I finished the meal with a dish of soursop and cups of hot, sweet coffee.

I paid the waiter, thanked him, and got back in my car. It was much hotter now. High cumulus clouds were gathering determinedly about the high peaks of the distant mountains. Some were beginning to show signs of descending to cast their shadows across this sunny landscape. The afternoon wore on and as I drove I kept a wary eye on the sky. I was no stranger to Mexico's torrential afternoon downpours. If it began to rain, I'd be drenched to the skin before I'd finished putting up the car's top.

Cancun was now coming into view. Shortly afterwards, the towers of the many hotels that had sprouted like mushrooms on the Caribbean's edge loomed large. Privately, I viewed them as a blight on the landscape, but acknowledged they regularly brought important tourist dollars to this coast. From a distance, they exuded a certain crass attractiveness, but I foreswore them in favour of the boutique lodgings I'd mentioned to the Chairman in his office, and where he had subsequently requested be booked for me. It was there I was to meet his 'man in Cancun'.

I parked the car where directed, checked in, and dumped my bag in my room I had an early dinner in the half-deserted dining room, drank a nightcap in the bar, and fell exhausted into bed for an early night, to ready myself to meet *Señor* Echeverria's man in Cancun.

Chapter 19

Juan Carlo Arturo Lopez clasped my hand, welcomed me to Cancun, enquired after my health and well-being, asked if my lodgings were comfortable, and assured me of his utmost desire to assist me in whatever way I deemed needful. His greeting was voluble, bordering on the effusive. He had received the command from his Chairman, and as he said, would do all he could, and more, to make my visit to his city a filled, fruitful, and memorable one.

We were meeting in the lobby of my hotel. I showed him the Chairman's letter. He read it over, paying close attention to the distinctive signature in mauve ink. In response to my question, he thanked me but told me he had already had his breakfast, but would take me to a 'fascinating place' later that morning for coffee. He asked if I preferred this sort of hotel. I told him it was very comfortable. He agreed that it was, and said he – like me – preferred these smaller hotels to the great glittering plastic and glass *palacios* that littered the shoreline.

He asked me what I wanted to see this day. I mentioned the research I was doing for my book. He nodded, as if in enthusiastic agreement with my wishes, and launched into a description of a range of places and sights in the city that he felt would admirably suit my purposes.

And with that, he swept me out through the door and into his car. We drove off into the swirling maelstrom of cars, bicycles, buskers, and tourists that were the principle features of life in this seaside mecca for visitors from all over the world.

I had the chance to read him more closely as he navigated his way deftly through the busy streets. He was as polished and groomed as the legions of other young men I'd seen in the headquarters of the Mexican Reconstruction Board. Slightly shorter than me, but with a muscular build, he was dressed in what I thought of as 'business casual', with open necked, crisp white shirt, sharply-pressed black trousers, gray socks, and mirror-polished black shoes. His black hair was cut short, which did little to hide the typically flat facial features hinting at his Mayan ancestry. His car was fast, modern, spotless, and filled with every accessory the parts manufacturers of the car industry could imagine. Bright fire engine red on the outside, the tan leather upholstery we sat on bore not a speck of dust. The ashtray remained unused, and the interior still carried the unmistakable smell of factory-freshness. Despite his effusive greeting, he wore a slightly twisted smirk that immediately flashed into a brilliant smile whenever he turned to speak to me. As we drove it became increasingly clear he viewed this assignment as a professional obligation, one that stood distractingly in the way of more attractive personal pursuits.

"Are you married, *Señor* Barnes?" he asked, apropos of nothing.

"No."

"You are travelling alone, then?"

"Yes." I began to wonder where this was leading.

"It is a beautiful day, so let us begin your visit with a look at the beaches."

"I am in your hands, *Señor* Lopez..."

"Please! You must call me Juan Carlo."

"Yes. So, Juan Carlo, I am in your hands."

"Excellent! We shall first see all the improvements that our Board (as we like to call it) has been making to the beach conditions. I think you will be mightily impressed."

I waved an agreeable hand at the front window, and invited him to 'drive on'.

It was now mid-morning. The sun was hot, the humidity rising, but both mercifully tempered by the trade winds blowing in off the water. Winter guests had long since left their breakfast tables in favour of the virgin white sandy beaches, where they had painted themselves lavishly with sunscreen lotions and prepared to languish their day on deck chairs thoughtfully put out by hotel staff. Only the call to lunch would rouse them.

We drove into the parking area of a large hotel. I recognized its name as one of a major international chain of hotels. I got out and looked around me.

Emerging from the main entrance was a group of elderly men made prominent by their paunches, dressed in flamboyant multi-coloured short-sleeved shirts, coral coloured shorts and floppy straw hats. Accompanying them were equally elderly women, all dressed just as flamboyantly in pink or blue halters, and skirts that would have better suited younger women. The women's hair had been carefully styled, but looked as though it would have been more at home on Fifth Avenue than here in this holiday setting. They all climbed carefully into the minibus waiting at the curb to take them off for the day.

We walked around the building to the beach side. In the distance, I watched some late-morning risers, taking a first cautious dip in the placid ocean in an attempt to shake off the vestiges of excessive time spent in last night's bars. Some swam gingerly dog-paddle style through the gentle waves. Others were somewhat more athletic, taking turns at tiptoeing into the water, then dashing out again. Somewhat closer to me, a group of four young women, all in bikinis, were standing knee-deep in the water and tossing a beach ball back and forth. One of them, in a bright canary-yellow bikini, seemed somehow oddly familiar. But that couldn't be right. I didn't know anyone here. A group of bronzed young men were performing athletic handstands nearby, doing all they could to attract the girls' attention. One took a huge spangled black sombrero, and sailed it frisbee-style towards the girls. The wind caught it before it reached them and blew it back into the face of the boy who had thrown it. The girls burst out laughing, but continued with their game.

Juan Carlo nodded at them. "They are lovely, no?"

I agreed they were. "But what is it we are here to see?" I asked him.

He shrugged. "Water. Come," and he led me through a service entrance door, and down into the basement of the hotel. We entered a clean, well-lit room vibrating with the humming of large modern equipment in full operation. I looked at it, not quite sure what I was seeing.

"You are looking at the water filtration and purification systems for this hotel," Juan Carlo told me. "This may look like an ordinary filtration system. On the outside, this would be true. But it's on the inside where the real difference can be found. This system, and many others just like it, are going to transform Mexico from a place that many people are afraid to come to because of the potential for water-borne diseases, to one where just about everyone will *want* to come to … because the threat of disease will be banished forever."

"How does it work?"

"I am neither a chemical engineer nor microbiologist. So I am not able to describe the internal intricacies of this system. But the general idea is that no organism, no matter how small or virulent, can escape alive after entering the system. It is built on the principle of using a series of multi-stage particulate sediment filters, each stage filter more detailed in entrapment than the previous, coupled with the most powerful ultraviolet purification systems available. Chemicals too, I believe."

"An important claim." I was remembering my phone conversation with Kevin while I was still in Toronto, and the experiences I'd had with *'la turista'* from previous visits to Mexico. So far on this trip I'd been lucky.

"Yes. But also verifiable. No virus, no bacteria, no parasite, nothing that can adversely affect the human digestive system, can survive. The secret is in the increased efficiencies of these systems. More rigorous examination and testing of input water to remove all physical foreign bodies greater in size than a third of a micron. Enhanced killing procedures internally to destroy – please note the word – all bacteria and other parasites. Some consideration is being given to installing pristine pure holding tanks to hold all treated water held for consumption."

I nodded, then asked, "But what about all the other infrastructure? All the collection systems, and delivery pipes and so on?"

"Yes, and all that, too. The Board has a major upgrade and expansion program ... it will take years. But the President has decreed that he wishes to be remembered for having given Mexico, all Mexicans, clean safe drinking water."

"It's a huge undertaking."

"*Si!*" emphatically. "But I believe it will work. Cities, towns, villages all over the country are targeted for work. But here, in this hotel, it is a true manifestation of the desire, the plan, and the work. Not one guest here has suffered an ailment due to bad water. This, in the past five years. And so it is for all the other hotels in this city, and all up and down the Riviera Maya."

As he spoke, we were walking back outside to the car. The four young women were still playing beach ball. The sun was hot, and I was full of questions. Before I could ask them, he said,

"We will now have some coffee, and I will show you something interesting."

"Interesting? What?"

"The coffee. A particular favourite."

"How so?"

"It wonderful mixture of fresh hot coffee, rum, Grand Marnier, lemon, sugar and whipped cream, and they set the whole mixture alight with a candle … right at the table."

I groaned at the prospect, but in all good conscience had to go along with it.

Fifteen minutes later, after navigating streets cluttered with construction signs and legions of workmen shoveling in deep holes below street level, we stopped at an attractive little restaurant that bore no resemblance to any of the coffee chain outlets I knew in Toronto. We went inside. It was comfortably cool and the light was dimmed to contrast with conditions outside. Along one wall was a full-length bar, with stools for seats. Behind the bar the wall was covered in blue and red handmade tiles, each with its own distinctive design. The main part of the room was filled with little tables and chairs, most of them occupied. A waiter stood at a push serving-table and was doing something spectacular with hot coffee and various alcohols. A small, lighted candle nestled in its own stand on the table. Coffee percolating machines sent heavy tantalizing aromas of fresh coffee through the room.

We took one of the empty tables. I pulled out my notebook to make a few notes while the information he'd given me was still fresh.

Juan Carlo saw me and said, "and while you're doing that, you should also know that the Board is replacing all of the sewage collection systems throughout the country. Continued construction over many years, especially in the cities, has caused significant degradation of the land in many places. Continual excavation has impacted huge pipes already there, often causing them to split or crack or even break. Sewage has leeched into the aquifers, some of the main sources of our water. It's one of the reasons so much water has been contaminated. Now we're going to fix it – permanently."

I looked up at him from my notebook, "But the cost? My God, the cost! How can the country afford this?"

"Ah, *Señor* Barnes. That is not the question. The real question should be, how can the country *not* afford to do this? The very reputation internationally of our country is at stake. Over sixty percent of our national GDP is based in services, and tourism represents a very high proportion of that. But it's been slipping in recent years, and the country can't afford to let that happen without doing something about it."

"And so you see it as a necessity to invest huge amounts of capital to do these things. But where does the money come from?"

"Mexico has a relatively low debt-to-GDP ratio. We can afford to borrow internationally, as well as use our own resources, both private and government, for that. We get favourable rates as well, and that is also beneficial."

And with that he ordered his coffee and pastries from the waiter who was hovering over our table.

The waiter trundled over the push-table he had been standing at when we came in, and as we watched him with his magic, made the coffee. It was delicious.

We sat and chatted for a while. He asked me about the book I'm working on, as well as the one I'm now researching. I asked him about his job, the work he did, and was he content in the service of the Mexican Reconstruction Board.

"Content? No, not content. Not at all. Rather, I should say it is wonderful! This is the sort of work I do on many days ... showing visitors what we are doing. I am well-paid, the benefits are beyond reproach, I live in a very comfortable home in a better part of Cancun, you have seen what sort of car I drive, and I have the direct ear of *Señor* Echeverria should ever I need anything beyond the scope of my usual duties. Content! If this is what you mean by 'content', well then yes, by all means, I am content. But," and he shrugged with a broad smile, "I prefer to think of myself as being incredibly lucky."

"Lucky?"

"Oh, *si*. I come from a poor family. They managed to find the money and help for me to do university studies. I graduated five years ago with a good business administration degree, and got a job at the Board's headquarters – where you were the other day – immediately. As time passed, they liked me. They thought the work I did for them was acceptable, and asked if I would like to move here to take this posting. I moved here two years ago."

"Are you married?" I was trying to be polite, but even now he was beginning to wear a bit thin on me. There was something about him that grated.

He flashed a bright toothy smile. It echoed how I've seen Pancho smile. A feral glint shone in his eye. "Oh no, *Señor* Barnes, no, I am not married. I have, how shall you say it, a friend ... actually several friends, who keep me company when it's convenient."

More than anything else, his response reinforced an earlier conviction that this guy was just a playboy taking advantage of an ideal situation. I kept hoping he would use the rest of our day together to show me something more substantive than he'd done so far.

It was not to be. Shortly after coffee, we went for lunch. It lasted much longer than I would have preferred. Later, in the heat of the mid-afternoon, he took me to one of the Mayan tombs within the city's perimeter. It was of passing interest only in how I saw a few languid workmen trudging about with wheelbarrows looking as though they were attempting to shore up some massive stones that were in danger of toppling over.

As we walked the long way back to the car I pleaded heat and fatigue, and told him I was still becoming acclimatized to local conditions, and would Juan Carlo mind very much if we called it a day?

He did not mind. He politely showed regret on his face, but his body language spoke of other, more private plans. He brought me back to my hotel in record time, climbed out of the car as I did, shook my hand, told how great a pleasure it was to meet me and have the opportunity to show me 'his city', returned to the car and drove off with a cheery wave as he looked at me receding through his rear-view mirror.

I shrugged, turned and walked up the steps into the hotel. The day had been less than fruitful, despite Echeverria's promise and all of Juan Carlo's effusiveness when we'd met here this morning. I was glad it was over, but nettled it had not given me very much in the way of material for my book. Some, maybe.

I went up to my room. It was clean and airy and large enough to house a maharaja and his entire retinue. It opened onto a wide balcony overlooking the Caribbean. I stripped off and stepped into the shower. It was lukewarm and comforting, and while toweling down afterwards, I opened the room's mini bar to find out what it held. It was liberally supplied, and I discovered in it several bottles of Harry's favourite Scotch. 'Later', I thought. I'll save them for later, but right now I wanted a reviving glass of beer. I took it out onto the balcony and flopped contentedly into one of several comfortable wicker chairs.

Putting my feet up on the railing, I sipped beer and gazed out onto the beach below and the ocean beyond. The fluffy clouds floating on the horizon were even now being painted with streaks of pink, and families on the beach were making the unmistakable motions of gathering their belongings and children, preparing to head inside for whatever the evening might bring.

Suddenly I was lonely. It was an odd feeling. It was the feeling that can unexpectedly afflict the solitary traveler; an empty feeling that can overwhelm one. As a rule, I enjoyed my own company, and had no trouble finding things to do. But now I wanted company – not the company of bright young men from the Mexican Reconstruction Board, but the company of a warm, cheerful, intelligent woman. I wanted light conversation and laughter, and the chance to talk of things other than Kevin's wretched document or the travails of Mexico trying to find itself again.

It was clear I'd find no such company in my room. I must go out. To that end, I dressed in clothes that I considered flexible enough to suit most evening occasions in a tropical holiday setting, and made my way back downstairs to the public bar.

Like my room, the large bar area faced out onto the water. This public space consisted of a main room with several alcoves or nooks off to various sides, each with its own set of table and chairs. The room was gradually sinking into a semi gloom, but yet too soon to turn on the lights.

I chose an empty table. The waitress took my order. I sipped it, and looked casually about me. There was the usual mix of holidaying families with half-grown children, and groups of singles, none of whom seemed very interesting. Far across the room, in one of the alcoves, was a group of four young women, all animatedly deep in conversation. They were in semi darkness. As casually as I could, I studied them with somewhat greater care than I'd given anyone else in the bar. One of them, the chestnut-haired beauty, seemed like the girl in the yellow bikini I'd seen earlier today on the beach playing ball with her friends. But her face was turned away from me, and common courtesy made it difficult to see more of her.

Their conversation continued, but appeared increasingly agitated. First one then another would toss her head as if to refute what had just been said. Their voices were rising. It was easier to hear them now, although I still could not make out what they were saying. Suddenly, the girl I'd noticed twisted in her chair to face away from her companions, and towards me. I could see her quietly plainly now.

It was Maria.

Chapter 20

She was as surprised to see me as I was of her. I smiled and waved tentatively. She smiled, a bit shyly I thought, and then turned back to rejoin the conversation with the other women.

I had half-risen with the thought of going over to greet her, but sank back down when she turned away from me. The waitress asked if I'd like another beer. When she brought it, I took it outside with me on to the open deck to watch the evening sky grow ever darker. Streaks of magenta, pink, and varying shades of blues slashed across the sky, and high in the east an almost full moon was beginning to rise. The steady buzz of conversation from inside made a counterpoint to the emptiness I was feeling. I patted my pockets, looking for my pipe and tobacco, and realized I'd left them in my room. It was a measure of this uncomfortable feeling of being adrift. Usually they were with me wherever I go.

Why had I taken up the pipe so many years ago? My father had smoked a pipe. I suppose I had wanted to emulate him. He had a big wooden bowl filled with them on the desk in his study, a room I'd often associated with peace, contentment, and infused with the lingering aroma of his special-blend tobacco. His tobacco arrived regularly, once each month, neatly packaged from a shop in London. He was such a long-standing customer that the shop had begun paying the shipping and the import duty. As a young man, he'd lived in London, at a time when just about everyone still smoked, and he'd stumbled across the shop on one of his many walking trips about the city. He always said that London was a "walker's paradise", and it made one of his favourite pastimes. He said there was always something new and unexpected to be discovered, no matter how many times one might have passed by that way. He'd come across this little hole-in-the-wall tobacconist's shop, run by a wizened gnome with an encyclopedic knowledge of the world's tobaccos, and which particular pipes were best suited for each. It was a time of great austerity in England, retail prices were still low, when even people on modest incomes could manage to indulge occasionally in their little luxuries. As the old tobacconist had trained my father, so had he – in later years – passed his knowledge on to me, doing so on the several trips I've managed to make to that fabled city. I savoured it then, as I do today, because even though the old gnome and his shop have passed into history, it was the connection with my father that made it all seem so special.

My father had been a special person – I'd loved him. We'd always been very close. He shaped me, scolded me, set me straight on the ethics of money and learning, and women, and knew more than a thing or two about how to treat vulnerable people. He included women in this category. Despite all the formal learning crammed into me by various educational institutions, it was he who gave me my solid grounding in life.

Odd how the memories take hold of one. Here I was in this tropical setting, some would call it the holiday place of a lifetime, and perhaps they might be right, while I was standing in the middle of it all, sipping a lonely glass of beer, thinking of the years-ago with my father, and wondering idly how I would disport myself during these immediate evening hours.

I heard loud voices coming from inside. Angry voices. Female voices. Speaking the rapid-fire, liquid Spanish that only the native born can manage. The voices rose and fell, but seemed to be getting increasingly more agitated and angry. I turned to look inside, to see where it was all coming from. Other people in the bar were stopping their own conversations to turn and stare.

It was the group of women with Maria. Looking more closely, it seemed to me that she was the butt of the anger of the other three. Their voices had the shrill fiery tones that Latin women are so good at mustering. She was sitting back in her chair, well back, as if trying to fend off, avoid the attacks coming at her from three directions at once – almost as if they were physical, not verbal. Then the three women rose as one, purses and shopping bags clutched to their bosoms, and flounced out of the bar. Maria sat, stunned, dejected. She seemed about to burst into tears, but did not. I admired her for that.

I couldn't let her just sit there – alone. I went over, and gently eased myself into a chair at her table. I said nothing. She saw me, but kept quiet. I gave her the clean handkerchief I'd stuffed in a pocket before coming down here. She nodded, and smiled wanly.

A waitress appeared at my elbow. I gave her my empty glass, ordered a refill and another of what it was Maria had been drinking. I asked her to tidy the table and clean away all the empty glasses and dirty ashtrays. It seemed a small gesture, but Maria seemed grateful for the small attention.

The drinks came. I asked her, "Do you want to talk about it?" She shook her head. She was still morose from the incident and needed to time to compose herself. I sat quietly. I just wanted her to know I could be quietly companionable, not intruding where I might not be welcome. We sipped our drinks. She took out a cigarette, and I lit it. Again, she gently smiled.

A few more minutes passed, giving her time she needed to compose herself. She lifted her glass to her lips and looked at me over the rim. She seemed genuinely glad to see me.

"What can I say?" she said at last. "They were friends. We've been friends for a long time. We decided to come to Cancun for a little 'girl-away'. It was just us girls. Yesterday. We flew. It was supposed to be just a break from our regular lives."

I nodded sympathetically, and then remembered the girl in the yellow swimsuit from this morning. "Were you on the beach this morning? All of you? Playing with a ball?"

She dimpled. "I looked; I thought it was you, but couldn't be certain. Yes, we were there. They are staying in that hotel. They like it, but I prefer something more relaxed ... less like a tourist resort. It's why I am staying here. I've stayed here before. What were you doing there?"

"Oh, that! One of your father's protégés was showing me all the wonderful things the Mexican Reconstruction Board is doing here. I could have learned more from a guide book."

"You must be disappointed."

"Not really. I wasn't expecting very much. But I do appreciate your father's hospitality and his willingness to make introductions for me. I've already written him a quick thank you note."

"You *are* a gentleman," she answered with a gentle smile.

"Not at all. It's the way I was trained. My father was a man who understood, almost instinctively I often imagined, how the relations between people should be conducted. He trained me well."

"So, I suppose your day was a wasted one. You might say mine was, too. We started this morning as all good friends. I went over there to join them for an early breakfast. Well, not too early. I had my bathing suit with me. Afterwards, we went to the beach to relax, get some sun, see who else might be there. Yes, I saw the college students and thought it very funny when the sombrero was blown back into their faces. Later we went back inside for lunch ... it was getting too hot on the sand. We decided to go shopping in the afternoon. Isabel had rented a car; it was big enough for us four. Antonia said, come up to my room ... you can shower and change there. I knew it wouldn't take me very long. I'm not one of those women who spend hours primping in front of the mirror."

I looked at her shoulder length copper-streaked hair. It was clean, shining clean, the sort you just want to run your hands through. If she noticed, she didn't say anything.

"We all climbed into the car and drove off into town. There isn't much to buy ... nothing of any real value, that is. The shops here cater to the tourists, which is fine for them, I suppose. But, I haven't been here for a long time, so I thought it would be fun just to browse and window shop and look at people ... you know."

I nodded.

"We came back here after that. I invited them for a drink, and we could decide where to go for dinner. We were sitting here, enjoying each others' company, when somehow, I don't know how, the conversation turned to talk of Silvia's new boyfriend. Antonia and Isabel both said they liked him, even admired him. Silvia was happy. But I, I wasn't so certain. I'd met him, too, several times. Every time I had this uncomfortable feeling, as if he was deliberately trying to show me how wonderful he was. I don't like that in a man, and I told them. They just laughed and said I was being silly. This annoyed me, but I tried not to show it. They're my friends, after all. But it still upset me.

"Anyway, we ordered again and the conversation shifted again to something else ... I don't remember what. But, half an hour later, it was back to Umberto again ... Silvia's friend. I didn't like it. To be honest, I don't like him, and I just didn't want to talk about him. We were on our holiday; what we thought of as our little girl-away. It's a silly word, but it meant something sort of special to us."

She stopped. A frown furrowed her brow. "That was the start of it. I couldn't help it; the others couldn't help. For a stupid reason we all were arguing with one another; more so the three of them with me. It was getting so I couldn't take it anymore. The whole feeling of our break was broken. I was on the point of getting up and leaving, when they got up and left. I was relieved. But sad, too. They're still my friends – I think. I hope."

"I'm sorry this happened to you. It's too bad when friends fall out. You know, I'm beginning to have similar thoughts about Kevin Watts."

"Who?"

"Kevin Watts. You know, the man at the party at Pancho's parents' home. He was in the taxi with us afterwards."

"Oh, yes. Of course. He's a strange one, that one."

"Strange?"

"He kept looking at me in the taxi. I wasn't sure why. All I know is that I didn't like it."

"Did he do anything?"

"You were sitting beside us. Did you see anything?"

"No. But I was thinking perhaps something secretive … hidden, so I wouldn't notice it."

"Nothing like that. No. But even while you two were talking, he looked at me, then at you, then back again at me."

"Well, I should think that's a normal part of being in a conversation, wouldn't you?"

"Ordinarily, yes. But this was different. He was different. I felt these strange nudges, almost if he was wanting to take me, devour me, use me … somehow."

"Ummm." I wasn't sure how to respond. Then, "Well, he's certainly been giving me some odd signals since I got here."

"Oh?"

"Yes. When I was still in Toronto, out of the blue came this email from him inviting me to come here – at his expense – and help him look for this old document. It seemed a crazy idea. But it had been a bad day for me, and Toronto was in the middle of a major snowstorm, the fourth this month. I'd just about had enough of winter, and the prospect of a few weeks in the sun suddenly was very attractive. I phoned him. We spoke. And we agreed to meet in Mexico City – tomorrow, actually. He said he would fly from England tomorrow. Yet, when I got here the other day, I discovered he'd already arrived. His plans had changed, he told me. I accepted it, but it seemed odd. It still does. Then there have been a few other things, small things since then. Each one of them is insignificant, by itself. But they're all beginning to pile up, and they all point to something strange. But I can't think what it could be."

"But that was in Mexico City. You're here. Why are you here?"

"He was delaying. He kept saying he needed to do more research. And he told me that Mexico City, with its universities and museums was an ideal place to do it. Well, fine, I can understand the need for good information. But at the same time, I'm not in Mexico just for this reason ... looking for an old document. I'm also on holiday. And I'm doing my own research into another book I'm planning. So I told him I was going to go off on my own for a few days. This all happened the same day I met your father for lunch, and gave me his introduction to Juan Carlo Arturo Lopez, his man in Cancun. It all seemed to fit together nicely. So here I am. But Juan Carlo was not as helpful as I'd been hoping, so I'll do some nosing around on my own."

"I'm in no hurry to go home yet."

I acknowledged this. "I also wanted to go back to Tulum, and Akumal, and see the caves at Xel-Ha again. I was there a few years ago, and wanted to pay them another visit."

"I've never been there. Every time I've come to this coast, it's always been just to Cancun."

I had the feeling she said it rather wistfully.

She asked, "How do you know this Kevin?"

"We were at school together."

"Were you great friends?"

"No. Well, sort of. We both lived in the same place, so naturally we saw a lot of each other. He had his group of friends; I had mine. Every now and then, our interests would coincide. On those occasions we did some things together."

"And you've been friends ever since? Where did you go to school?"

"Well, no. Not really. It's been more than twenty-five years. We haven't really stayed in touch. It was in Edinburgh."

"But ... I mean, now you're working together on this document? I don't understand."

I looked her right in the eye. "Maria, to tell you the truth, neither do I. A lot of it just doesn't add up. Sure, I agreed to meet him here. But, frankly, I was more interested in just getting away from what had become horrible winter weather. I'm a writer. Last fall, I'd just recently finished a book, and the publishers had it and I had little more to do with it. After a few weeks, I was beginning to think about starting something new. And then there was the project my agent had dumped on me. But, I'd almost lost interest in it. I know it's hard for you to understand, living here in this tropical climate all the time. But come sometimes and try a Canadian winter, and then you'll see what I mean."

"I have."

"You have? Oh! Yes, of course you have. You told me."

"Yes, it was three years ago. My father needed to visit some government officials in Ottawa. It was January. I have very little interest in dry bureaucratic talk, but I was curious to see that country of yours. It seemed a good opportunity to see something new."

"Did you like it?"

"Yes ... and no. I liked the cities, and yes, I was in Toronto, and the people were very friendly and welcoming. But not as open as I am used to. But cold! It was so cold! I've never felt anything like that. Grey skies all the time. And the wind. They had told me before I went that it would be cold, but I had no idea that it would be like that. Some days it snowed. Heavy snowfalls. How quickly the streets filled up with it."

She stopped, thinking, remembering. A lovely smile spread across her face.

"But after the worst of the snow had passed, it was like being born again, walking through the fresh snow. Some people I had met suggested one evening that we go for a walk in one of the city parks. It was a sensation I'd never known possible. A few snowflakes still drifting down, forming haloes around the streetlights. The whole world muffled, almost silent, even with the busy traffic nearby. They had a camera and we all took pictures of each other. I still have them, somewhere."

She paused. "I once heard a piece of music. I think it was called, 'Skating in Central Park'. While I was walking through the soft snow, I remembered this tune, and felt it was just exactly right. I could imagine myself skating in the open air, on clear flat ice, with the snow gently drifting down. Skating in long, slow glides, and languid circles, while the snowflakes fell softly on my nose." She sat up, a flash of excitement on her face. "Sam! I'd love to do that someday."

"Yes," I said. "It is a special feeling. Too bad it's not like that all the time."

"You told me Edinburgh. Why there?"

"It's a long story."

"I've got time."

"My father had this romantic notion about his son being educated in the environment of the great Scottish clans. I don't know where he got that from, but there it was. My mother liked the idea, too. He knew the UK pretty well from other years, and he had been told I wasn't doing very well in the school I was in at the time. He knew some people over there who he thought could help get me enrolled. He had some money that he had set aside years before for my education. His friends helped, and he released the money, and I landed in Edinburgh. It was deep in December. It was late afternoon, a steady drizzling mist was falling. The streetlights were just being turned on, what the British used to call 'lighting-up time'. My taxi arrived at the heavy wrought iron front gates, and I looked through the gloom across the expanse of emerald green lawns all glistening in the early evening mist to this huge imposing Gothic building. It was something straight out of a Frankenstein movie."

I stopped talking, thinking back to that long-ago evening. I shivered. She looked at me. "Did you like it?"

"Not really. I endured it. Life was different there, rough, nothing like I'd ever known before. But the education was sound. In balance, I suppose I came out of the experience in profit."

"I'd like to hear more about it."

"Sure. Another time maybe." I looked at my watch. She saw it. "Do you have to go somewhere?" she asked.

"No. Do you?"

"No. Not now. We were going to have dinner, but ... well, not now."

"Would you like to have dinner with me?"

Her eyes brightened. "Yes. Very much."

"Good. Wonderful, in fact. I was hoping you'd want to."

"Do you want to stay here?"

I thought this was not a good idea. This was the scene of recent unhappiness for her, so I suggested, "No. Let's go someplace else. I have a car. Is there any place you'd like?"

It was the right decision. I could see it in her eyes. She said, "Give me a few minutes. I want to go up and repair some damage."

I could see no damage; she looked terrific, every hair in place, and not a trace of smudged makeup. But I shrugged mentally, and said, "Sure. I'll take care of the bill."

She got up and left. She was wearing the same short black leather skirt she had worn the day I arrived.

I signalled the waitress, and settled the bill.

In less than five minutes Maria came back. I was pleased.

"That was quick."

"I told you before," she said pertly. "I don't need a lot of time." I thought of Frankie. She took ages in the bathroom preparing herself. I had no idea what it was she did in there. She always kept me waiting.

I said, "Let's go."

*****

We drove to a pleasant little spot she knew.. It was mercifully free of tourists and noisy students. We settled ourselves comfortably, and I asked her, "Would you like some wine?"

She nodded. "*Si, favor*. Red, please."

It was ceremoniously delivered, poured, tasted, and we were enjoying our first glasses. She put down her glass. "Do you like writing?"

"Well, yes, I do. Most of the time, anyway."

"You must be very good."

I shrugged. "I try. Actually, I try very hard. It doesn't come easily. But it's something I wanted to do from the time I was very young. I've been lucky; five novels still on the market, and I want to do more. Harry has helped. He's the one who's very good – at what he does, I mean. He knows how to talk to publishers. I don't. I'd only make a mess of it if I tried."

"Harry? Oh, yes. Your agent. Your relative."

"That's right. We have a good working relationship." I paused. "Do you like to read?"

"Very much. My apartment is filled with books. More than I need. How do you work? Do you make yourself write a specific number of words each day? Do you use a computer, or a typewriter?"

"Hah! A typewriter! I haven't used one in years. I did when I first started. I was using my grandfather's ancient machine, one he'd used 'way back in the 1930s, would you believe. He was a dentist, and he had his dental office in his home. My grandmother had given it to him as a good luck present when he first set up in practice. He used it all the years that he practiced. When I got it, it was old but it still worked fine, and in those days ribbons for it were still available. It could print in either black or red, if you had a ribbon made with the two coloured strips. But no, I don't use a typewriter any more. It's a computer now. Much easier, more flexible, and I can correct mistakes more quickly.

"Words? It's a happy accident if I produce the same number of words each day. Every writer is different. There was writer, a Canadian, dead now, very prolific. Richler, his name was. Some days he could produce thousands of words. Other days, he'd sit in his book-filled office, and just smoke cigarettes all day long and stare at the walls. Wouldn't write a word. I suppose in that way I'm more like him."

"I've often wondered what it would be like to be a writer. Someone who makes their living with words. It seems a romantic life."

"I wouldn't go quite that far. It can be enjoyable, yes, but it's also a lonely life. When I'm writing, I need to be alone. I can't stand interruptions. Even someone coming to me and saying something, anything … relevant or not. It's not a matter of being rude. Not at all. No, it's on account of the fact that when I'm writing, I'm building whole scenes and characters and bits of dialogue and images in my head. Relationships between people, events, and situations. It takes time and hard work, especially when I want to get it just right. Sometimes the pieces just won't fit together. They just don't feel right. It's not working the way I wanted, and I have to find ways to re-arrange them, like this, like that, until they do seem right. But it's all in my head. If someone interrupts or something unexpected happens, like the phone ringing, or someone knocking at the door, there's a very good chance the whole delicate crystal structures I've mentally built up will collapse and fall shattering down into tiny little pieces. Like Prospero's cloud-capp'd towers. It's almost impossible to explain how frustrating and angry that makes me. Think of an architect. He draws and he draws, and the measurements and the lines are finally just so, the way they need to be. He's done it all by hand, with ruler and pen and ink. And then someone comes along and spills coffee all over his drawings. It's ruined! He has to start all over again."

"Yes, yes ... I see what you mean. You explain it very well." She paused, and said quietly. "I wouldn't interrupt you. I'd respect your privacy."

I looked at her. She'd dropped her gaze so I couldn't see into her eyes.

We'd ordered. The waiter brought the food, and with flourishes and good humour, served it, refilled our glasses. He examined the level remaining in the wine bottle and looked meaningfully at me. I nodded. His smile broadened and he went to fetch another. I'd made him happy.

I asked her, "Didn't Pancho want to come with you?" I didn't want to break the developing mood, but I needed to know.

She shook her head angrily. "That man! I don't ever want to see him again!"

"Oh?"

"We went out for dinner on Monday night. At first it was pleasant. He told me he had met with you earlier, and that you had decided to go to Cancun for a few days. He even mentioned where you would be staying. We sat; we ordered; we ate. He was talking about some of the business dealings he's involved with. He was enthusiastic about them, trying to get me to agree with him. I couldn't. I've known about them for a long time, and I just couldn't. They felt so wrong. I tried to get him to see what he was doing could be dangerous for him. And for me, too. He told me I was being silly. It was the wrong thing to say. Our nice dinner quickly collapsed into a white-hot argument. These things had been festering with me for a long time. It was like Popocatepetl, simmering quietly away, gradually building up pressure, and then suddenly releasing and exploding all at once, the way that huge mountain volcano can do. I was so angry with him I couldn't stop shouting. People were looking at us, and he kept waving his hands at me trying to get me to shut up. I couldn't. I got up, threw the rest of my wine in his face, flung down my napkin, and walked out. I didn't even look back. I found a taxi and went home."

"I'm sorry. I like Pancho. And I like you. And I'm sorry this happened. Don't you think you could try to talk to him again?"

"No! At least, not now. Perhaps not ever. I'm glad I'm not in Mexico City right now. It's easier. I'm content here."

"But you've talked with him about it before."

"Yes."

"At least, I think you told me that."

"Yes."

"What made it different this time?"

"Sam, it was getting to be too much. It's the same thing, every time. He says he knows what he's doing. He says it's all safe, that it's just an easy way to make some extra money, so he can 'stand on his own feet', is the way he says it."

"Extra money? I would have thought he'd be okay that way. His family is doing quite well. And if his father is politically successful, it'll be even better for Pancho."

"You don't understand. Manuel has some serious money problems, and he doesn't want his father to know. He owes a lot of money – to people who are not very nice."

"Oh."

"Yes. And what's worse is that he is involved in some things that are also not very nice. I've seen what people like them can do to those who cross them, and Manuel just doesn't seem to understand. Or he refuses to see it. I'm frightened for him. I don't want to be connected with any of it."

I nodded sympathetically. There wasn't much I could say. As an outlander from a different culture, I had little experience with the milieu of this one, and my own background and lifestyle hardly gave me the context to enable me to even begin to relate to what she was telling me. I could only guess at it. But I also knew I had to do something, say something, to help her keep her fears under control. Perhaps even allay them.

"Maria, I've known Pancho on and off for several years. I like him. I'm glad to count him among my friends, and I think he feels the same way. Do you think it would help if I were to talk with him?"

"About this?"

"What else?"

"But you can't. He doesn't want people to know. Not even his friends. He wants to keep it quiet. He's afraid it would damage his father's election hopes. He's also afraid for himself. He won't admit this, but I know him well enough to see it."

"I see. Well, let me say this, then. If you can see him again, and talk to him again …"

"I just told you."

"…if you can, I said, then please let him know that I'm good at listening."

"Just that?"

"Yes."

"That's all? It doesn't seem very much."

"You see, it's what I believe. It's what friends are for. Sometimes the best thing a friend can do is just listen. I think he needs someone to let him know he's navigating in dangerous waters. From what you're telling me it sounds like he's in over his head, and getting deeper all the time."

She nodded. Maybe she agreed. I decided to change the subject, and asked her, "You know, up to now, most of our talk has been about me. What about you? I'd be interested to know."

It was not easy to read her. I thought I saw a hesitancy. Despite her earlier hints of warming to me, I felt a reserve. Her face had shown a whole series of emotions. From shy warmth, to outright anger; through concern, then puzzlement, and now a mask of almost non-emotion.

"For instance," I continued, "do you work? You see, I don't even know that."

"My father has always been very generous. Many years ago, when I was still a little girl, he established a trust fund in my name. My mother had just died, and he was concerned that if ever anything happened to him, that there would be enough for me live on. It was easy for him to do this. While I was still growing up, he managed it for me, so that by the time I became of age, it had grown to … well, a lot."

"But that's not working. How do you spend your time?"

"No. I have worked. My university studies were heavily influenced by my interest in the world of arts. I began with a general course in art appreciation, which later evolved into a program of the history of art. Then came some travel, to give realistic meanings to the things I had studied in class. Rome, Paris, Florence, Moscow, Athens, Sydney, Bangkok, New York, and eventually London. I stayed several weeks in each city. A few days' stay would have been pointless. I immersed myself in the local cultures, learning the foods, their local histories, the music, and gradually, finding ways to communicate in each local language. I found it all came naturally. English, Russian, Greek, Italian, Thai. Am I fluent in them? Not at all. But I can manage easily enough. It's funny though, with you my English comes very easily and naturally. It's very nice."

"Thank you. You're helping me with my Spanish, too." I had been trying out bits of my schoolboy Spanish with her, and she had gently suggested better ways of saying what I wanted. "After your travels, did you come back to Mexico?"

"I stayed in London. While I was there, I met a man whom I thought I would like very much. We fell in love, desperately so. A few weeks later, we got married. My father was furious when I told him about it. He demanded to know why I'd done this. It was an unhappy time for me with him, and we didn't speak for a long time. My husband and I moved to a town outside London. It's called York. Do you know it?"

"No. I've never been there, but I've wanted to. The cathedral is supposed to be worth the visit."

"It is. I was in it several times. It was one of the few things I enjoyed about living there. There wasn't much else."

"Oh?"

"No. Our relationship soured quickly. Peter was … is … a dress designer. In business by himself. He could have been a good one, but he was unsure of himself. He was so filled with anger. I don't know where that came from, but I think it was frustration that he couldn't convince the fashion world that he was 'the next great thing'. He took it out on me. More than once. He drank, much more than he needed to; much more than he should have. It got worse. Whatever money he made disappeared into the pubs. I had to use some of my own money to keep a roof over our heads, pay the bills, and help support his business. Little thanks I got for it."

"He never asked where the money came from?"

"No. He never seemed interested; just glad he didn't have to worry about it. In the beginning, I had thought of telling him about my trust fund – share and share alike. But I kept putting it off. And then it was getting increasingly clear that it would more be more prudent for me to say nothing about it. So I never did." She paused for me to light another cigarette for her.

"Thanks – I like it when you do that. He'd often come home late at night, more drunk than sober, mumbling and angry. I was convenient and he'd take out his anger on me. There were times when it was more than unbearable. I am strong, as you can see, but Peter was built like a bull. No matter what I did – I knew what to do! – I couldn't always fend him off, and I'd end each time very sore. Black eyes, bruises, a broken finger and one time, a sprained wrist at another. I endured it for two years, thinking it might get better. I was a fool. Finally, one day, I'd decided I'd had enough. I called my father in Mexico City. I asked him to send me some extra money for the airfare. He agreed, but told me he wanted me to come directly to him when I arrived. My passport was still in order. I walked out of the apartment, took the next train to London, and booked into a hotel. I had the concierge make air reservations for me to Mexico. I was lucky. It was mid-week, and I got a flight for the following day. When I knocked on my father's front door, he drew me into his arms. He told me was overjoyed and very relieved to see me."

I sat silently for a while. Then I took her hand, and told her she'd managed very well. She left her hand in mine. I asked her:

"How long ago was it?"

"It's been ten years. A nightmare I've learned to put behind me. At the beginning it was not so easy after I returned to Mexico. The day after I returned, I visited a lawyer and started divorce proceedings. No amount of entreaties from any authority was enough to prevent me from getting one. It took two years, two very long and stressful years, but finally it was over. I was granted the divorce I so desperately wanted. I didn't want alimony. I didn't want any kind of compensation at all. I only wanted to be free of that man. And I was successful."

"It must have been a trial for you."

"It was! And it's made me wary of marriage ever since."

"What's it been like for you since then?"

"Life has been good. I took up my art studies again. I used the knowledge I'd accumulated while abroad to secure a junior restorer's position at the museum. I'm still working there, but more as a freelance now. My time is precious to me. Sometimes I travel alone. Sometimes I travel with my father, as I told you about our trip to London when I met Pancho two years ago. Sometimes I travel with friends, like with this trip. I found a nice place to live, where I can be myself, be safe, and enjoy life."

The coffee had been served, and the restaurant was gradually emptying. I asked her: "Do you know of any jazz clubs in Cancun? I feel like hearing some, and it's not very late."

"Yes," and she named a place. "It has several live groups – jazz, mariachi, flamenco. Sometimes they play alone, just their own music. Sometimes some of them will join and play together as one. It's unusual, but a wonderful mix of the cultures. A different kind of musical fusion. They should be open this evening. Would you like to try it?"

"Yes. It sounds perfect. If you're ready, let's go."

"I'm ready."

I followed her out of the restaurant. She was small and brown and delicious, and against my better judgment, my attraction for her was growing. Both men and women, late diners all, looked up at her as she passed their tables. It was impossible not to notice her.

The jazz club was filling up quickly, but we managed to find a table close enough to hear the players but not so close that they inhibited conversation. We were growing more relaxed with one another. I filled and lit my pipe, and she lit a cigarette with my match, taking my hand that still held the match. It burned down quickly and I had to drop it before it singed the end of my finger too much.

"Sorry," she said.

"Okay. Pipes sometimes take a long time to light."

She settled back in her chair, stretched languidly, and blew a cloud of smoke at the ceiling. "Why do I like you?" she asked, still looking up at the ceiling.

I looked at her. The graceful tension between us had been slowly mounting all evening. I chuckled, and replied, "It's on account of my pipe. You like the smell."

She leaned forward, rested her elbow on the table, cupped her chin in her hand, and said, "You're a good listener."

"Well, I am. I like listening to what people have to say. It helps me decide how I should respond to them. At least, it does sometimes. Maria…"

"Yes?" She leaned closer to me.

"I've no right to ask, but do you think you'd like to come with me tomorrow? I want to head down to Akumal and see how the place has changed in the past few years."

She took no time to answer. "Yes, Sam, I'd like that very much." She sat up, thinking. "We could ask the hotel to pack a lunch for us. We could make a picnic of it. Maybe we can find a nice place to swim."

"I'm sure we can. There's a wonderful beach at Tulum. Right beside the ruins."

For another half-hour or so, we listened to the music, with its varying rhythms and soothing piano and sax combination. It was just the right sort of relaxing environment for a late-night envelope of companionship. She was sitting closer to me now, sometimes with her hand on my shoulder or arm, and it was all I could do to keep from putting my arm around her waist and pulling her closer to me. But the image of Pancho kept recurring in my head, and I still had this now uncomfortable notion that I didn't want to do anything that would damage our friendship.

I looked at her more closely, not a hard thing to do. She was different now, different from the rather uncertain girl left behind when her girlfriends abandoned her earlier this evening. She seemed content; at one with herself, responding to the music, gently beating time with a hand, glancing at me occasionally to share a pleasing passage in the music, smiling at the way the pianist managed his chord changes, waving energetically at the waiter to order more drinks for us. This was no shrinking vine. She was her own woman, and even within the constraints of this male-dominated society, she has the strength to rebel against the often overbearing blanket of protection Pancho believes he needs to impose on her. She displayed the self-confidence I admired in people, women especially. She had told me of the freedom to be herself her father had given her as she was growing up, and this confidence was reinforced when he informed her of the trust fund he'd set up in her name. I could agree. Financial independence was always a confidence booster.

The club was packed now, even standing room at the back was at a premium. The air was filling up with heat, tobacco smoke, odours from drinks carelessly poured, and the soft but unmistakable aroma of marijuana that wove tendrils of its own smoke among the accumulated smells. There was a gradual rising of talk and chatter from around the room, and this was beginning to challenge the music for sound supremacy.

Now with midnight well behind us, I was beginning to feel the weight of the day: the arrival in Merida, the pleasure of running into Maria and the disappointment I'd felt for her after the argument with her friends, and our evening together. I nudged her to see if she felt the same way. She did. She telegraphed clearly her thought about wanting to leave.

After leaving the club, we walked back to where I'd parked the car. More accurately, where I thought I'd parked the car. It wasn't where it was supposed to be. I'd left it at what I'd imagined was a legal parking area, but it turned out the local police had a different idea. We stopped a passing taxi, and Maria quizzed him on where impounded cars would be taken. The driver knew where it was and he drove us to the city's pound for towed cars. I was thankful I had plenty of room on my credit card. I paid the fine, the towing fee, the storage fee, and a gratuity to the operator of the pound. He handed me the device to unlock my car, and while doing so, I paid off the taxi and sent him on his way.

As I climbed into the car I saw that she was already seated. She was looking at me mischievously, laughing eyes in a face aglow with the absurdity of it all. At first we said nothing, but then each of us burst out laughing. "It's an adventure!" I spluttered between breaths, to which she cheerfully agreed, and planted a feather-light kiss on my lips.

It was as sudden as it was unexpected. My head swam.

We got back to the hotel. We stopped at the front desk to collect our room keys, and rode up in the elevator, first to Maria's floor. We stopped at her door. She gave me her key to open it. It swung open. She took her key back, gave me a quick peck on the cheek, and …

Chapter 21

And nothing. I awoke the next morning still stiff with desire. The empty space beside me in the bed did little to help. I had spent the night tossing about in splendid isolation, troubled by dreams I'd not had for a long time. She featured prominently in them.

When I came down for breakfast, she was already in the middle of hers. She gave a brilliant, welcoming smile. She was perky, alive, filled with good humour. She looked good and smelled good, and she knew it.

"Good morning. I was starving. Did you sleep well? I did. It's a beautiful day. I've been up for more than an hour. That was great fun last night. Imagine losing a car. Sit down. I've asked the kitchen to make us a lunch. It should be ready soon. I hope you like what I asked for. Shall we take some wine? Or beer? Or both?" she was bubbling with high spirits.

"Both."

I hesitated. "I had a dangerous dream about you last night."

"What was it?"

"I was standing off to one side of the room. It was a party. The others were in a different part of the room and could not see me. You joined me. You were wearing attractive shorts and a full halter, and the copper highlights in your hair shone in the reflected light in the room. You stood in front of me, close but not touching. I looked at you. Somehow, our hands touched. Gradually our fingers slowly intertwined. My pulse quickened. I could feel yours, too. You drew me closer. I could sense your scent in my nostrils. I could feel your breath. I bent my head to touch your lips … and then I woke up, disappointed."

"You're right, it was a dangerous dream. I wonder why you'd be dreaming about me."

It was an opening I'd been secretly hoping for, but it also opened dangerous traps. "Because you've been on my mind since the day you and

Pancho met me at the airport. I thought you were the most beautiful girl I'd ever met."

She took it gracefully. She knew herself and was aware of the impact she had on people. She could have been angry. Or offended. Instead, she smiled, gave a mock bow and said, "Thank you, Sir."

My mood brightened. It was hard not to be cheerful with her around. I greeted her with a smile, and sat down with the waiter at my elbow offering coffee. I drank it hungrily. He poured more.

I looked at her. She could see the remains of disappointment in my eyes, but said brightly, "We'll have a wonderful day today. I'm so much looking forward to it."

"Have you ever been to Isla Mujeres? I thought we might have a quick look around it first. It's not far."

Her eyes told me she'd go along with any plan I suggested.

"I have. It was a long time ago. My father took me there. He wanted to see the Underwater Museum, but it wasn't open yet. They were still building it."

"Odd ... that's what I wanted to see. I'm sure it's open by now."

We talked our way happily through breakfast and, as we were about to finish, our waiter brought out a huge wicker basket filled with the picnic Maria had ordered. I lifted the cover and glanced inside. There was more than enough for us. We could have doubled our party and still had leftovers. Tortillas, fresh cooked; cold fried chicken breasts; little dishes filled with various coloured sauces; seared strips of succulent beef; four bottles of local amber-coloured lager; a chilled bottle of chardonnay-style wine from the vineyards of Baja California, and all accompanied by plates, glasses, napkins, good quality metal cutlery, and openers for the bottles. It was more than a picnic lunch. I looked up at Maria. She was smiling impishly at me.

"You said you liked lots of good food."

I smiled back. "Indeed I did. Hey! This is great!! Thanks for ordering it."

She looked at the time. "Come on; it's getting late. Let's go."

It's a short ferry ride from the north end of Cancun to Isla Mujeres. We'd left the car parked on the mainland, hoping to find easy transportation on the island. We had debated about whether to leave the food in the car, but decided it would be fun to find a pleasant beach for lunch after seeing the Underwater Museum. There was a lot but I found I could manage to carry most of it.

We were standing on the deck, leaning over the rail of the ferry, looking down through the crystal clear waters. Although they were deep here, we could see all the way through bright turquoise depths, down to the sandy bottom. Brilliant coloured schools of fish darted and flashed about. This, more than most sights I'd seen since arriving in Mexico, brought home to me the vindication of my deciding to make this trip. I sometimes have thought I must have lived an earlier life in a tropical climate – where the breezes were always warm, the sun always bright, and the people always smiling.

Isla Mujeres is not big. On landing, we opted for one of the many mopeds available for rent at the ferry dock. I'd never driven one, but Maria said, "Hop on. I used to own one of these. They're great fun. We'll each have one. I'll show you how. There's enough room for the basket."

I looked dubiously at the mopeds, but agreed that they seemed easy enough to manage. After a short lesson from Maria, I climbed on mine, and started it. Before driving off, we gave a quick study to the map the man had given us, and discovered the Underwater Museum was not very far.

Maria had told the truth. She knew these little scooters very well, and showed she was an excellent driver. I was a bit wobbly at first, but soon got the hang of it, and in tandem we zoomed past a lush variety of sights and sounds. There were whitewashed churches with blue roofs; rows of brightly coloured skirts and dresses for sale hanging from lines stretched between coconut palms; piles of freshly-cut coconuts for sale; trays filled with costume jewelry of many designs; glass-bottomed boats with their sun awnings, moored in rows in the harbours, ready for hire. There were cemeteries filled with brilliant white block-shaped tombs of varying sizes, looking for all the world like a freshly-built, closely-packed housing development. The streets and roads were teeming with life, and music. I glanced over at Maria from time to time and enjoyed the sight of her smiling face, her pert breasts, and the copper highlights in her hair shining in the sun.

Before long, we came upon *el Museo Subacuático de Arte*, the proper name for the Underwater Museum. We parked and locked the mopeds. A man approached us with an offer to take us in his glass-bottomed boat to see the underwater sculptures. As we hadn't planned to swim just yet, we agreed, and off we putted through the lagoon. His Spanish was rapid-fire, and I had some trouble following it, but Maria slowed him down periodically to translate for me.

He told us the history of the Museum, and how it had come about. He spoke of the Englishman, Jason Taylor, who was the force behind the Museum and the sculptures. He explained that the reason for the Museum was an attempt to protect the natural coral reefs at other parts of the island from erosion brought on by too much tourism. He went on to tell us about how the sculptures were made of materials designed to enable the eventual growth of new coral on them, and in so doing attract more marine life. He described at length the various designs that we could see through the bottom of the boat into the clear, shimmering waters.

The glass-bottomed boat is the best way to see the sculptures, and soon we were gliding over one of the three underwater galleries that had already been built. We saw a forest of concrete structures. We had only our guide to explain it all, and he told us the life size figures of men and women were designed to resemble members of the local community. As we rode over them, I tried to count them, but water refraction and the times when the boat turned so the sun was in my eyes made it difficult. Our guide saw me, and said, "The last time I heard, there were over four hundred of them in this gallery alone. More are being added all the time."

After more than an hour of skimming back and forth above the sculpture galleries, we'd had our fill of them, and were getting hungry. We asked the boatman to take us back to shore. He accepted our payment, and a tip to sweeten his own lunch to compensate for the extra time we'd used. We told him we were looking for a beach where we could swim and have our lunch. I pointed to the picnic basket. He told us about one just a few kilometers away, towards the northern part of the island. "Less crowded than the *Playa Norte* at the North End," he said. It sounded fine, and we bid him goodbye.

The beach was all he said it would be. Now past the noon hour, and very hot. We had just enough time to cool off in the water, and then open the basket to enjoy all our hotel had packed for us. It was wonderful, and made us feel quite lazy. But I was determined to get down to Akumal today, and so I pulled a gently dozing Maria up on her feet, and she helped me pack away all the things we'd have to return later.

It was another short trip back across the water to Cancun. We'd left our mopeds with the man who had rented them to us, collected the deposits, and just caught the ferry as it was getting ready to sail.

Back on the mainland, we dumped our few things into the car, opened all the windows to vent the buildup of stifling heat from inside, and took off down the coast to Akumal.

She said, "You like music. Let's see what we can find." She turned on the car radio. They were playing mariachi music. It was tantalizingly irresistible. I was reminded inadvertently of the mariachi opera I'd seen on television a few months earlier, not to mention when, just a few days earlier, Kevin had tried to avoid me seeing him in Garibaldi Square.

After a while, the music changed to several of the softer and more melodic traditional songs of Mexico. Some of them I recognized, including the one that was playing right now – *"Cuando Caliente el Sol"*. She began to sing along, and I discovered she had a lovely soprano singing voice. Actually, not really discovered. Liking music myself, I'd suspected it when I'd first heard her speak. She knew the words to this coincidentally appropriate song about when the sun gets hot. It was a pleasure listening to her, and after a while, I quietly joined in with my baritone. She looked over at me, startled, then pleased, and smiled the sort of smile that only a woman who approves of you can do.

Then it was *"Cielito Lindo"*, the beautiful sky (it was), but more poetically about the pretty sweetheart; the song about the swallow, *"La Golondrina"*; then the companion, plaintive one about the dove, *"La Paloma"*. We had great fun with that one, stretching out the choruses that each began with the *"Cu-cu-ru-cu paloma ..."*, and each time we sang it I could hear in my inner ear the long, soaring plaintive cries of the male chorus on the recording I have at home.

The afternoon had reached that stage of the day when all the world seemed to stand still. It was that magical moment separating the earlier growth of the day from the point where the slide into late afternoon begins. It was as if the day had temporarily stopped.

And the music played on. Now there were some of the softer tunes, as if they were readying their audience for the romantic evening ahead. There was *"Adios Marquita Linda"*, and *"Besame Mucho"*, and the achingly beautiful *"Solamente Una Vez"*, with the man proclaiming softly that his beloved belongs in his heart.

Thus we made our happy way south down the coast road to Akumal. We were in no hurry, stopping periodically along the way for the views, and so made it a two-hour drive. If I'd had my way, it would have been a forever drive. We were growing comfortable together, and I could feel rather than see how Maria saw me as someone she'd like to spend more time with.

Years earlier, I had spent a few days there when it was just awakening from being a sleepy fishing village. I was curious to see what had become of it. Since I was in the Yucatán anyway, it seemed a shame not to go the extra distance to satisfy an idle curiosity. It *was* my holiday after all, Kevin Watts and Harry Oliver notwithstanding.

And now it was becoming even more of a holiday for me. This whole business about the Avendaño document was becoming so unreal and tenuous as to be almost absurd. I still couldn't fully understand why Kevin had approached me in the first place. It made very little sense. And sense, to me, was something I needed. As a novelist, I needed to see all the pieces fit neatly together, and the mishmash of stories I'd been fed so far were nowhere near the point of fitting into a cohesive, understandable pattern.

And yet, and yet ... I am, at bottom, a curious soul, and despite my misgivings I needed to see this thing through. I couldn't go back to Toronto with an unfinished story. It would do my pride no good to have Harry crow over me that I'd flown off into the tropics on a flight of fancy, chasing a rainbow at whose end no pot of gold was ever to be found.

We took the exit for Akumal. I saw at once it completely transformed from what I had been imagining. It was now all expensive hotels, shops, bars, restaurants, roadside stalls ... the whole assemblage catering to visitors who decided that Cancun was too much for them and wanted a quieter pace of life for their holidays. The town even boasted an artists' colony, where painters and other artists could, for reasonable cost, spend a quiet month pursuing their craft in the company of their fellow spirits.

I guided the car through the crowded, narrow streets, and eventually found the hotel I remembered from the last time. Even it had grown, now including a third story to the main building as well as a few small villas scattered about the property. But the coconut palm grove was still on the beach, and the hammocks for guests were still suspended from some of them.

Maria looked at me. "I'm ready for a swim. Can we find a place to change?"

"Sure."

We looked about, and spotted a kind of cabana *cum* changing rooms on the edge of the coconut grove. I parked the car, we got out, and she said, "I'll be in the water first."

"That's what you think."

She proved me wrong. I could see flashes of her yellow bikini as she stroked through the water, heading straight out. I stood on the edge of the water for a moment, admiring her until she ducked out of sight by diving straight down. The next I saw of her was when she surfaced in front of me near where I was standing on the beach.

"Come on, slowpoke. What are you waiting for?"

"Admiring the view."

She dimpled, and swam away again.

I waded into the water. It was a wonderful feeling after driving in the sun, and especially after having had only a taste of the salt water where we'd had lunch. The sun was still strong, but it seemed more welcoming now I had the water to act as a sort of counterbalance. The water sparkled and shimmered, and tiny wavelets lapped at the warm white sand. I swam out, away from the beach, heading more or less to where I'd last seen Maria. Couldn't find her, but didn't worry. I had seen that she was a strong swimmer, and knew instinctively she'd be alright.

I like to swim under water, and had been able to do it since I was a little boy. At first my parents were petrified, my mother especially as she had never really liked to swim. My father was okay with it, and soon they'd came to accept it as me just being me when they saw more than once how I'd surface splashing and laughing from a longish pull under the surface. I would take several deep gulps of air, then a huge breath and then dive sharply towards the bottom, kicking my feet up in the air as I sank below the surface.

I swam about like this for a bit while looking again for Maria. I spotted her floating on the water a little distance away. She was facedown. This alarmed me, and I swam over in her direction. I looked again, and saw her lift her head to take another breath. I breathed a silent sigh of relief. She's just enjoying the gentle womb-like warmth of the water, I thought. It's a nice feeling – a feeling of almost complete release.

I don't think she was aware I was watching her. She seemed oblivious of everything around her. Then I had an impish idea. I took a few more deep gulps of air and ducked down under the surface again. After I reached the level I wanted, I chose my direction and started swimming that way.

I swam over towards Maria, and awkwardly positioned myself below her. Everything was crystal clear, with the sun shining down through the womb-like water. I still don't think she knew I was there. I rolled over on my back, a difficult maneuver when you're under water, trying to keep at the same level. Then I took quick aim, rose up and kissed her squarely on the yellow bulge at the point where her legs met.

She started, surprised, and folded herself involuntarily. I erupted out of the water, and she grabbed me, and we rolled round and round, mock fighting, thrashing, each trying to gain the upper hand (she was strong!), laughing, gasping for air and trying to breathe. Finally, we'd had enough of this and came out of the water, laughing, blowing and wiping the salt water from our eyes.

"Why did you do that?" she demanded, laughing and spluttering. "You shouldn't do that."

"I did it because I wanted to. Besides, you enjoyed it. You know you did. So, why not say so?"

She didn't say anything to that, but I had the feeling she wanted to agree with me. And I could see the start of a twinkle in her eyes.

We flopped down on the sand to dry off, not so easy to do without towels. I was feeling drowsy. We dozed.

Somewhat later I was awakened by the sounds of children. They were laughing, playing, shouting. I shook Maria's shoulder. I was beginning to feel tightening of the skin across my shoulders. We both sat up and looked over to where the children were playing. They were in the palm grove. We got to our feet, and tacitly agreed we should prepare to leave. We walked back to the change rooms; I was keen to get into some shade.

When I emerged fully clothed Maria was waiting for me. She was looking over at the children. She said, "Let's go over."

As we drew closer to the group, we saw the children were accompanied by an older man. He seemed to be supervising their game. He wore an air of quiet dignity, of inner strength. His skin had the consistency of tanned leather; his face a deep mahogany, with thick white hair on his head. All this, together with his smiling dark brown eyes and strong only slightly yellowed teeth told me this was a man content with his well-lived life, with much still to live. He was shorter than me but well built; seemed closer to seventy than sixty, and stood straight and solid. He had a high forehead, and wide flat nose. His face had classically broad features that typically were set in somber repose. Yet, when he smiled, which he did often, his high cheekbones lifted higher, making his smile as wide as his face – and as warm and welcoming as one could wish. His clothes were simple but spotless. He wore a plain white cotton guayabera shirt with its simple twin embroideries down the front, and short sleeves revealing his powerful brown arms. Plain black ankle length trousers and sandals protecting his bare feet made the rest of his dress. He spotted us and with a smile beckoned us over. He pointed to one of the children, a little boy, and told us it was his birthday, and the children were playing a game with a piñata.

It was a wonderful piñata. Large, and about a meter long, it was made in the shape of a very full and very friendly elephant. It had a long gray trunk, which matched the colour of the rest of its body, but its big wide white eyes seemed to have a look of astonished surprise as the children took turns batting it with their long sticks.

They had trouble hitting it, because the old man (I was beginning to think of him as *El Viejo*) had attached the elephant to a long rope which he'd slung over a wooden bar set high up between two trees. He held the other end of the rope and pulled on it making the elephant rise and fall, rise and fall, making it rise each time he saw a child trying to hit the piñata with his stick. Eventually, one of the children was lucky, smacking the bottom of the elephant's belly just as it was rising out of reach. There was a loud cheer from all the children as a small trickle of candies fell to the sand.

El Viejo pointed to us and then to a pile of spare sticks lying nearby. He gestured and nodded emphatically. We each got a stick. I took a swing at the elephant, and then another, and missed each time. The children laughed delightedly. It was enough for me, and I retired from the field of play. Maria tried, and on her second attempt opened the elephant's belly a little more, and a few more candies trickled out. Again a loud cheer. But she didn't want to spoil the climax of the fun for the children, so she stepped back and suggested to the man that the children should finish the game.

We smiled at each other, and I was about to speak when there were shrieks of laughter and joy as the full shower of candies and party favours poured down from the now fully opened piñata. There was a great scrambling on the ground as all the children tried to fill all their pockets, leaving nothing but the shredded shattered papier-mâché elephant dangling mournfully from the end of its rope.

The children drifted away to play their own games on the beach. Maria, *El Viejo* and I remained behind as we watched them. It was getting on for late afternoon, the sun still strong but now showing signs of preparing to set. Sunset comes early in the tropics.

He asked us if we were guests at the hotel. We told him no, but I was already thinking it might not be a bad idea. Dusk was approaching, and I didn't relish the thought of the drive back to Cancun. I wondered what Maria might think of the idea.

They were busy talking away in Spanish, and I tried to follow the conversation. Since returning to Mexico a lot of my Spanish had come back to me, but there were still times when even clearly spoken conversations eluded me. Maria was sensitive to this; I'd discovered she had wonderful empathy. I looked at her; she seemed quite content to be here on this beach, in this palm grove, with me and the older man, whose name he told us, after we'd introduced ourselves, was Nelson Zengotita.

He was an engaging man, this Zengotita. He told us the event was a tenth birthday party celebration for the hotel owner's son. The other children were friends from the town. Their parents had brought them out to the hotel for the day, and left them in Nelson's care. They all knew him and trusted him. He was a fixture in the area, and had been for many years. He did many small tasks and jobs for the hotel, and had proven himself invaluable in many small ways. He told us that he also acted as a guide for tourists. He said he knew the Mayan ruins in this part of Mexico very well, and had become well known among tour operators who periodically engaged his services. If the tour groups were very large, he'd share some of the work with his friend, Poquito.

I listened to the conversation, most of which was between Nelson and Maria, with me offering the occasional question or comment. But I also watched Maria, and again I felt that inescapable feeling of knowing that we were each becoming increasingly comfortable with one another.

And then I had a fugitive thought. It was at once a comfortable and a faintly disagreeable one ... like the pebble in your shoe that you can't shake loose. This pebble came from the joint concerns I had about Maria's relationship with Pancho, and my own with Frankie. From the way I was seeing things right now, neither of these was on very solid ground. Maria had said that she wanted some distance between herself and Pancho: he was becoming too protective, she said. He was increasingly showing more of the typical macho arrogance towards women, women whom they thought they 'owned'. 'I will never be owned,' she had told me tartly, and I believed her. I just hoped she had said the same thing to Pancho. But then, I concluded that she had. She was capable of saying just about anything when her temper was aroused.

And so it was with Frankie, as I knew to my rueful experience. More than once. We'd sometimes talked around the thought of making our relationship more permanent. At times, it had been an attractive idea, yet it never seemed to last for long enough to gain much substance. We were each strong people, each with an inherent wish, no … need, to maintain an independence, with a blanket of privacy we could wrap around our individual lives whenever we felt the need. She had her career, and loved it. It gave her the physical, spatial, psychological and financial independence that was at the centre of her being. So, too, it was with me. I was an adventurous person. I needed the flexibility to be able to drop everything and go whenever the urge took me. This trip was an example. Adventure dies in domesticity, so goes the old saying, but I had no burning desire to put it to the test.

Which brought me, by a round turn, to standing here in this palm grove, half-listening to the conversation, but increasingly falling under the spell of someone I barely knew. It was the floating world all over again; a concept I'm told the Japanese knew well. It was born of a desire to immerse oneself, for however long, in a world not quite real, characterized by gently waving willows and floating flowers on still ponds, under zephyr breezes, giving the illusion of an escape from reality, but hiding the very real possibility of emotional tragedy when it all ended. A gossamer world. Yet, however small, and however briefly it might last, it was an escape, or at least a temporary reprieve from the unnecessary uncertainties caused by both Kevin and Pancho. It was an escape from them. But it was also an escape to something: to a magical time with an agreeable companion. She had, perhaps without knowing, cast a spell about us both, and it had made us the happy couple that now stood on this increasingly darkening beach.

I looked at her, and said, "Perhaps we should stay here tonight. I'm not that keen to try driving back to Cancun in the dark."

Nelson agreed, saying to me, "The roads are not good at night. I have also been noticing, *Señor* Barnes, that you are feeling uncomfortable. I think you have been in the sun too long. I know what bad burns can do."

It was true. I had been trying to keep my shirt from touching my shoulders too much, a difficult task at the best of times. The skin across my shoulders and neck was feeling dry and tight. And I was feeling extra warm, more that the lingering warmth of the day would justify.

Maria said, "It is an attractive place. Quiet, and comfortable looking."

Nelson said, "If you wish, I can help you. I am well known and respected in the community as a healer. I am not formally licensed, but I have learned many natural healing remedies over the years, and I could help ease the pain. They are the old ways, the Mayan ways, passed down through the generations. It is likely the pain will get worse."

I thanked him for his thought but declined, not wanting to put him to the trouble. He shrugged gracefully, and with a smile excused himself to go and see to the children.

"You should have accepted his offer," she told me. "It *is* going to get worse if you don't do something about it. Don't you start going all macho on me the way Pancho does."

We looked at each other, but did not speak. I saw some indecision in her eyes. She looked about her, at the hotel, at the villas down the beach, at the changing rooms, at the grove, at me. "I don't have a toothbrush."

"That shouldn't be a problem. They probably supply all that stuff in the rooms; it looks like that sort of hotel. And if not, we can always buy what we need."

This seemed to satisfy her. "Alright," she said, "let's see if they have some rooms."

Rooms.

We walked into the main lobby to the desk. As we walked I said, "They'll probably think we're a couple of escaped lovers looking for a place to shack up for a few days."

She dimpled, and dug an elbow in my ribs. It was sharp enough to hurt. Instead, she said, "I like that man. There's something comfortable about him." I nodded. "But," she continued, "you shouldn't ignore the sun. I also know what burns can do. I've seen people whose whole holidays have been ruined by sunburns."

"I can probably buy some cream or something in the hotel. They must have something."

The desk clerk welcomed them, explained the hotel was almost full, but he'd received a cancellation for a suite on the second floor at the front. Would we take it? Maria asked about the sleeping arrangements. He smiled and explained there were two bedrooms separated by a lounge and kitchenette. Each bedroom had its own bathroom. She looked more comfortable.

I saw the look on her face and told the clerk we'd take it. He took an imprint of my credit card. Maria fumbled in her purse for her card, but the clerk told her that he only needed one. He asked about our luggage. I told we had none, and that we had only just decided to stay. Our original plan had been to return to Cancun the same day after seeing Tulum and Xel-Ha, but we'd decided to see them tomorrow. It seemed foolish to drive all the way back, and then return again the next day. This seemed to satisfy him. He'd probably heard similar stories before. He gave us each an electronic key card, and wished us a pleasant stay.

The suite was everything the clerk had described. It was large and airy, and all the rooms had sliding doors opening onto balconies facing the water. With the sun now setting behind the hotel the rooms were in a warm gloom. We explored the suite and saw that each bedroom had a king-sized bed, the ensuite bathrooms were large and well equipped, although in my explorations I saw nothing that looked like salve for burning skin. The kitchenette had enough equipment to make it unnecessary to go down to the dining room for meals, although there was nothing in the way of food except for the makings of coffee and tea. The small bar, however, in the low refrigerator tucked under one counter, was more than full and I treated Maria to a glass of chilled white wine, and I took a long satisfying pull at an icy cold glass of beer.

We took our drinks out on to the balcony and watched the last of the daylight fade over the darkening Caribbean.

There was a knock on the door. I groaned, "Who could that be?" I got up and saw *El Viejo* framed in the door when I opened it. He carried a a small tray holding a few things.

"*Lo siento, Señor*. I am sorry to disturb you, but I saw how uncomfortable you were on the beach. And I heard *la señorita* tell you that you should have accepted my offer. I am very good at helping people with sunburns."

How could I say no? It was kind of him. I asked him to come in. I had taken off my shirt and he sucked in his breath when he saw the state of the burns on my neck and shoulders. He suggested I lie face down on the bed.

As I lay there, I heard him draw a chair up beside me. He sat, and arranged the things he'd brought: a lime, a small bowl partly filled with lukewarm water, and a handful of paper napkins. He took out a small, sharp penknife and sliced open the lime. He squeezed the lime juice into the water, mixing it with a finger. Then he dipped some of the napkins into the mixture, gently squeezed them out, and placed them one by one my burned skin. It felt refreshingly cool. He covered all the affected area.

As he got up he said, "Remain there for at least an hour, *Señor*. If you get chilled, perhaps the *señorita* could cover you with a sheet. I hope you will feel better soon."

He gathered up his things and left.

Maria said, "I've heard of that, but never seen it done. How does it feel?"

"Wonderful. Almost as if there was no burn at all."

"Well, do as he said. Stay there for a while. Later we can go and get something to eat."

******

The dining room was filling up as we came in for dinner, but we managed to find a comfortable table off to one side, yet still be able to look out over the water. Each table was set with clean linens, polished cutlery, salts and peppers and a selection of interesting sauces. A bowl of fresh-cut flowers accompanied by a burning candle were set out on every one. Several diners looked up at us as we passed them on our way to our table. I could see their admiring glances as they caught sight of Maria. Despite having worn the same clothes all day she had managed to make herself look as clean and fresh as if for a new day. I don't know how she did it. I was rumpled. But just seeing her like this made me feel good.

We were just about to order when I spotted Nelson Zengotita making his way through the dining room towards our table. He stopped beside me.

"How are feeling, *Señor*; better? Good. I am glad you decided to stay. You are nice people. I am going home now, but I wanted to ask if you would like me to come with you tomorrow to show you Xel-Ha and Tulum?"

He stopped, and waited expectantly. I looked at Maria with eyebrow raised as if to ask her if she liked the idea. She nodded.

I thanked him for his offer, and for his help upstairs, and told him we'd meet him in the hotel lobby at nine next morning. He smiled and nodded, and left us to our dinner.

"That was nice of him," she said, watching him walk out of the dining room.

"Yes, it was. He seems an interesting person. I think I'd enjoy talking with him."

"It seems you'll have the chance."

"Let's hope so."

The waiter had been standing patiently beside me, and when Zengotita left we gave him our dinner orders. He poured wine and departed. Over the first glasses of wine, Maria asked me, "Are you married?"

"No."

"But I think you've enjoyed the company of women."

"Oh yes. I have no sisters, or brothers, but my mother and I got along well. My father had three sisters. I liked them all; I see them every now and then. In that way I've been fortunate."

"But no woman in your life."

"Not now. Well, not really."

"What does that mean?"

So I told her the full story, from beginning to end. "Four years ago, I met a woman at a party at a friend's home. We discovered we had some interests in common. We started to talk, and eventually we began to see each other. For a while, maybe the first couple of years, we were almost inseparable. It seemed it could be something permanent. But then, things began to change. Small things. The changes were small at first ... almost unnoticeable. She's an interior decorator, one of the better ones in Canada. She owns and runs her own business. It's in Toronto. Suddenly the business got busy, much more quickly than she'd anticipated. It took more of her time. She was meeting some interesting clients, at first locally, then from other parts of the country. They liked the services of her business, and they liked her. She was increasingly in demand. It was good for her business, not so good for our relationship."

"But you continued to see each other?"

I shrugged. "Yes. But, well, the mood had shifted. It wasn't the same any more. We both tried hard to keep it going; we liked each other, loved, perhaps. At least we thought so, on and off."

"And now? How is it now?"

I was about to reply when the waiter brought our meals. He placed them before us with considerable dexterity and skill, assuring us of the excellence of food and the talents employed in the kitchens to prepare it. He made sure our glasses were topped up, and left.

"I'll give you an example," I continued. "When I decided to accept Kevin's invitation to come here, I tried calling Frankie. She was in Vancouver, doing work for a wealthy client. I couldn't reach her. Her mobile was turned off. She's always turning it off, especially if she's in meetings. So, I left a message telling her I was coming here for a while, and asked her to call me. This was over a week ago; I still haven't heard from her."

"Did you try again?"

"What was the point?"

"You didn't see a point?"

"Oh I saw it, alright. It was the one I'd often worked on before … with not much success. I could see that it wasn't working." I stopped for a minute, thinking. Then, "Companionship is important to me. I don't mean being together every minute of every day. No. For me it's knowing that there is a willingness on the part of the other person to share, to be empathetic, to understand instinctively the need to be together just as much as the need sometimes for one's own space. But she doesn't have that. She's very self-centred in many ways. When she talks to me, it's more along the lines of telling me something that is of interest only to her, and it escapes her that it may be of no earthly interest to me. Her conversational skills are sadly lacking … she doesn't know when to stop talking. So with her it becomes more of a monologue than a conversation. It's a wonder she's so successful in business. It used to bother me a bit, even at the beginning. Now it just rankles and I tend to just tune out. So, no, it wasn't working."

She said gently, "We've both been around the course, haven't we? Several times, in fact … at least for me. I like Manuel. He was great fun at the beginning, a real pleasure in fact, after the breakup of my marriage."

"I'm just as happy being here without her. It's a relief, in fact. Yes, I can imagine it was a relief for you, too, when you got back here. A sense of real freedom, perhaps."

"It was. Peter was not a cruel man, but he had devils in him that broke free from time to time. He needed to lash out; he needed to take out his own shortcomings on others." She shrugged philosophically. "I was nearest."

I said, "I think you have other questions."

"Yes. Many. But I'm hungry and our dinner is here. Later. I can ask them later." She paused, then, "I expect you do, too."

I smiled. "I never quiz a lady over dinner."

She gave me a long, quizzical look. "When, then?"

"At a time of mutual convenience. A lady's private life is her own. If she chooses not to share it, that's her affair."

Her quizzical look deepened, then softened into a broad smile of approval. "I don't often meet a gentleman."

I gave her a mock bow. "Thank you, madam."

But then she returned to a conversation we'd had last evening, and asked if I had been a writer all my life.

"No. I've only been writing – well, seriously, I mean – for about fifteen years."

"Seriously?"

"For a living. Fiction. It's what I do now. Before that, I'd had a string of jobs. Some were interesting, most not. But none of them were very satisfying. They were vehicles, only, vehicles to make money. It all seemed such a waste of time."

"So, how did it start? Writing?"

"Mostly by accident. At the time, I was working for a management consulting company. I had got some seniority by then. A part of my work was to help them write sections of the huge reports they did for the clients towards the end of major assignments. We worked in teams. One weekend I had a copy of one of the reports in my apartment. They'd asked me to have a final look through at it before printing fair copies for delivery to the client. It was on a table in my living room. Harry, I told you about Harry," she nodded … "had come over to visit. He spotted the report, and read bits of it. I showed the parts I'd written. I suppose I had an element of pride in wanting him to know it. He looked up at me from his reading. He said, 'This is good. Damned good. It's too good for the clowns you're working for.' Somehow, God knows how, he'd seen something in my work that suggested to him I should be making my living writing."

"Did he ever tell you what it was?"

"No. But he did manage to convince me, over the next few months, that I should take his advice. You have to understand, I was reluctant. I was making a good salary with that company, and I'd heard a lot about poverty-stricken writers."

"So, what happened?"

I smiled. "So, I became a writer. I was getting tired of my job by that time, anyway. Harry suggested I try writing something on the side while I was still working. It seemed an attractive idea, but then I began to think about how busy I already was, and where I'd find the time to do that and write, too. But then, I thought, why not? What have I got to lose? So, one evening I sat down, pulled together a few ideas that had been floating around in my head, and set them to paper. I wrote all night. Before I knew it, the sun was up, and the announcer on the jazz radio station in Toronto was telling me it was seven o'clock in the morning. It came to me then: this was what I wanted to do. I got some coffee, took a shower and changed my clothes, and went to the office. The first thing I did was to write a letter of resignation. My boss exploded when I gave it to him. 'What the hell do you think you're playing at?' He didn't want me to resign, to leave. He'd had plans for me, thinking that I was just the sort of person he could support and promote. I suppose I'd damaged his plans." I shrugged. "Too bad."

"Did you leave right away?"

"No. The accepted practice in Canada is to give two weeks' notice. I wanted to do the right thing. They'd have to find someone else to take my place. It wasn't difficult."

I smiled at her. "That was fifteen years ago. I've never regretted it."

"What happened to what you had written that night?"

"It became my first published novel. It didn't come quite so easily as I make it sound, but it did come. Harry took it around to his publishing contacts. One of them bought it. I have to tell you, Maria, holding that first advance cheque in your hands is a powerful aphrodisiac."

"That was the first. How many since then?"

"Four more. Now I'm working on number six. Or I would be if it wasn't for this business with Kevin and the Avendaño document."

"You're worried about it, aren't you?"

"No. Not worried. Annoyed. There's something strange going on with this whole affair. Kevin's behaving in a way that is entirely inconsistent with what he'd led me to believe at first. And Pancho ... I can't figure him out, either."

"Manuel?"

"Yes. It still bothers me that he and Kevin were together the other evening in Mexico City. They were looking at each other as if they were sharing some secret that they didn't want me to know about. It was almost conspiratorial."

She began to protest, as if to say that she knew him better than me, and that he wasn't like that. I held up a hand.

"And then, the other afternoon, I was in Garibaldi Square. I had just had lunch with Kevin, and he told me he was going to spend the afternoon with some expert in hieroglyphics he'd found. But as I was sitting in the Square, I was surprised to see Kevin and Pancho with another man. I don't know who it was. I had the impression they didn't want me to see them."

"What are you going to do, then?"

"Ignore them. I'm going to enjoy my holiday here in the Yucatán. I'm hoping you will, too."

We made our way through dinner. Towards the end, I reached over and lightly placed my hand on her wrist. I had been admiring the bracelet she was wearing. I tapped it with a finger. It had a delicate, intricate design to it, that looked like an elaborately scrolled "M" set into a filigree of finely spun gold wire. Where the two oblique lines of the 'M' met was set a tiny brilliant diamond.

"This is beautiful."

"Yes. It's from the silver mines in Guanajuato. It's very old. My father gave it to me on my twenty-first birthday."

In the magically intimate way of these things, my hand stayed where it was. Neither of us seemed to notice.

"Old? It looks as though it had been specially made for you."

"It does, doesn't it? But no, it dates from the Conquest times. Father tried to learn its history and provenance, but not much luck. He traced it as far back as the time of Maximilian, but then the trail got so muddled that he lost it. But it doesn't matter: I love it very much. I wear it only on special occasions."

I smiled at her. "Is this a special occasion?"

She looked me straight in the eye. "I think it could be."

My head swam. Again, the little imp on my shoulder was waving a nagging finger at me. 'Watch yourself buddy', it seemed to be cautioning. 'The more impatient they are, the harder they fall!' But right now, the caution was far too faint for me to treat it seriously. It seemed as if this evening, this day in fact, had been the sparkling prelude to a completely new chapter in my life. I wondered if she had had similar thoughts.

When asked, we declined coffee. I had no need for stimulation. She suggested, "Let's walk on the beach."

We rose and made our way out onto an almost deserted beach. The rising full moon painted a long wide river of silver across the water and the whole world in a silvery monochrome glow. There was a gentle breeze blowing in from the water, now countering the day's waning oppressive heat. The sky was full of bright, clear stars.

As we strolled, her hand found its way into mine. We drew closer, hips gently bumping against one another. Occasionally we'd stop to admire the view. I drew her to me and lightly kissed her. Her scent was powerful and I felt rather than heard the gentle chuckle deep in her throat. Her arms tightened around me.

We walked on.

It was one of those magical nights. To a person not afflicted as we were, the night would be ordinary – like countless other nights. The moon shone down, just as it has since before time began. The stars were brilliant specks across the entire arc of the sky, as they had been from before the earliest times. The air a warm breeze, rustling the coconut palm branches, the sand between our toes soft, and the sea made gentle shushing noises as its waves slid back and forth at the edge of the beach. But to us it was a magical night. I'd felt this way only a few times before. It wasn't a new feeling; it was instantly recognizable and welcome. It was as if a soft warm blanket, almost diaphanous, had wrapped us up into our own private cocoon, separating us from the cares and ordinariness of life.

Time passed.

We chatted amiably, saying little of value but knowing every word, every thought we each had served to strengthen the growing bond between us. Our arms were about each other in comfortable companionship, and reaching the rocks at the end of the beach, we turned around and in tacit mutual agreement, headed back to the hotel.

Few saw us as we mounted the stairs to the second floor. It was just as well; I wanted this private moment to be ours alone. Even the desk clerk had his head down, busy with his papers. We approached the door of our suite and I had the card key ready in my hand. We stepped through the door into darkness. She walked in the direction of the bedroom she'd chosen when we first arrived. I caught her hand and pulled her back to me. She folded willingly into my arms and we kissed again, holding each other more tightly.

"Wait," she whispered. "I have to do this."

She pulled away from me and disappeared into her room. I turned to mine, undressed, washed and brushed my teeth, and opened the curtains to let in the ghostly silver light. I got into the king-sized bed. It was large and soft and welcoming. It reminded me of the *letto matrimoniale* that I'd experienced once on a trip to southern Italy. It was large and soft and magnificent, and was filled with unfulfilled promise. I'd liked it so much I decided I wanted one in my own place.

There was a rustle of covers as she slid in beside me. There was the heady, warm perfume of her body. We embraced tightly, holding each other hungrily, luxuriating in that first delicious rush of skin on skin, body against body, warmth on warmth, sweet breath on breath, and the first tentative explorations. It was delicious, exciting, head swimming, and in the sweet silence of the dark night it led, tentatively at first, but with increasing urgency, to honour all the promises this day had been building for us. For those of you who have been here before, there is no need to describe our loving. For those who have not, a book full of words would bring you no closer to understanding. It is enough to tell you that it was blissful and passionate and, for each of us, satisfying beyond our wildest dreams. We spoke no words; none were needed. Inhibitions were flung aside. Here were only passions and the promise of love. Urgencies accelerated; the sudden high vault into ecstasy, and the long, graceful decline into deep, warm depths that ended in sleep.

Chapter 22

It was still dark. The moon had set and a gentle rain was falling. I could hear it pitter-pattering on the roof, just over our heads. I loved the sound of the rain. Even as a child, growing up in a northern land of regularly changing seasons, the rain on the roof while I lay snug in bed brought me a sense of comfort and belonging and knowing that I was safe. Depending on the season, I could distinguish – just from the sound of it – what sort of rain it was, and therefore what tomorrow's weather might be. On hearing it, I would snuggle down deep into the covers, and imagine all the poor people outside struggling their weary ways home to their little hovels. It was all nonsense, of course, the fertile imaginings of an active young mind. My boyhood home was in a comfortable neighbourhood. All the people I knew and saw every day had lives as well managed as our own.

This was a gentle rain, with a soft plinking and splashing as each drop landed, each one almost separately identifiable. But then the rate of fall increased, making a steadier sound. I lay awake, my hands clasped beneath my head, her warm body sleeping peacefully beside me. I stared up into the darkness of the room, thinking about the sudden transformation in our relationship, and pondering – not for the first time – what the immediate future might bring.

It wasn't something I had actively sought, this new magic with Maria. Neither had she, or so I read it. It simply happened, just as the composers of tales and music and countless poets down the centuries have told us. Instant, magnetic, powerful attractions with the potential to be permanent were rare, but not unheard of. In my bones I sensed ours was one of the rare ones.

This attraction to Maria had a similar flavour, yet was much more intense, more directly personal and had all the potential of creating something new and wonderful and permanent. Then I had disturbing images of Frankie standing on one side of the bed, and Pancho on the other. Both were talking to the little imp who had perched again on my shoulder, giving him instructions about all my futures.

I shrugged them all off. I told them they were all interfering with my life. I told them to go to blazes. I told them all this was my affair, and one way or another, each had been partially responsible for Maria and I being here together. Satisfied, I rolled over, placed a gentle arm across her bare belly, and drifted back into sleep.

******

In the early morning, she smiled gently in her sleep and snuggled closer to me and burrowed deeper into the covers. I looked down at her in the soft light. Only her head was outside the covers. Framing it was a mass of lush chestnut hair, *castaña* she called it, splayed out across the pillows. Even in the faint morning light, it sparkled with the lustrous copper highlights she used. She loved to keep her hair clean. Even though all I could see was her head, I could also make out the outlines of her gorgeous, lithe body beneath the covers, and could visualize the small, heart-shaped birthmark under her right cheek that I'd discovered last night.

She stirred, stretched and opened her eyes. I was propped up on one elbow, looking down into those deep brown wells from which shone languid passion, a softer echo of what they'd shown last night. She pulled me down and kissed me. Irresistible waves of desire took over, and although I needed no help, she once again reached down and deftly guided me into her. She panted in my ear, "I want you to come."

******

"Come on, Lazy Bones!" I had drifted off into sleep again, but could feel my arm being tugged in an effort to make me get up. She gave her funny little throaty chuckle as I threw off the covers, delivered her a kiss, and disappeared into the bathroom to shave and shower the sleep out of me. Fortunately, the hotel provided the basic toiletries.

Breakfast over, we found Nelson waiting for us in the lobby. He greeted us with a respectful good morning, and we set off in the car south on the road to explore the mysteries of Tulum and Xel-Ha.

As we drove, I opened the conversation by asking Nelson if he had lived here all his life.

"I was born in this area. My home is not far from here. But for several years I lived and worked in Mexico City. I was the caretaker in a large apartment building."

Even in the week I'd been in Mexico, I found that my Spanish fluency was returning, and now it was easier to follow and participate in most conversations.

"But you came back," I prompted.

"Yes. I liked the city. But my father needed me to help him on his small farm holding, and I came back. I didn't want to leave, but family is important."

It was a lesson I'd been almost too late in learning. My parents and I had been growing much closer in the months before their accident, and their loss was a double blow. I asked him, "Do you have a large family?"

He smiled ruefully. I could see him in the rearview mirror. "I did. Besides my parents, I had two older brothers and a younger sister. But, as you can see, I'm an old man now, and so it is me – me and my sister left."

I could see Maria slowly nodding, as if she, too, were thinking about family, and how important they can be.

He asked us, "Are you on holiday? I think you, *Señor* Barnes, do not live in Mexico."

Maria cut in, "Yes, we're on holiday. I live in the capital, and *Señor* Barnes is a friend from Canada."

"Ah-h-h, Canada," he said. "It is a wonderful country. I was there many years ago. Are you enjoying your visit here?"

I looked over at Maria. "Yes, I am. Very much." A secret smile spread over her face.

"Actually," I continued, "I was invited to come. An old friend from my school asked me to come and help locate an old document. He said it had its roots in traditional Mayan culture. It's supposed to be quite old … more than three hundred years. It's part of the reason I'm here in the Yucatán."

"And your friend thinks he can find this document? Perhaps he is not very sophisticated. But you say you are here at his invitation. Perhaps you think it can be found?"

"He's paying my expenses. So I'm looking on this as an expense paid holiday in the sun. This winter in Toronto has been very cold and snowy."

He nodded.

We drove on, and Nelson told us of how he had come to Xel-Ha first as a little boy, brought by his parents, to swim in the lagoons and dive deep into the caves. They were filled with mysteries in those days.

"But not so much anymore," he continued. "The tourist trade has been very successful, and there has been much development on the site over the past few years. I hope you will enjoy your time there."

In the event, we didn't enjoy it at all. When we arrived, we saw a massive police presence standing there, with firearms at the ready in front of some very businesslike barricades blocking the entrances to the site. Cars were being turned away, drivers being given no explanation and just a curt motion of a policeman's arm to show them the way out.

We were in a line of cars, and our turn came. Nelson told me, "Slow down, don't stop, keep moving, but very slowly." As he said this, he put his head out the window and spoke to the policeman on duty. I half turned around in my seat and divided my attention between driving and what Nelson was doing. At first, the policeman ignored him. Yet his persistence helped a little, but all he could tell us afterwards was that it was a 'drug problem', and that was all he was told by the police. We had to be content with that.

We drove away. Maria said, "Well, we might as well go on to Tulum."

It was another 15 kilometers to Tulum. Nelson explained the historical significance of Tulum. We'd both, in our own times, each been there before, yet it was interesting to hear it all from the perspective of someone who had lived in the area for much of his life, and who viewed the ruins not so much as an historical artifact, but instead as a part of his daily round.

He suggested we head directly for the national park, a large area protected by the Federal Government against excessive development. We'd have a look at the seaside ruins, then lunch in one of the several excellent restaurants established since my previous visit.

As it is with so many popular tourist attractions throughout the world, so it now is with Tulum. Whereas before, on my earlier visit, it was a quiet, almost deserted landscape, today we encountered busloads of visitors, local people selling everything from overpriced T-shirts to "authentic" replicas of the ruins and those who had occupied them centuries before. We also were met first by an official who invited us to pay an entry fee, or view the ruins from kilometers distant.

Perforce, we paid the entry fee. Nelson guided us to the seaside ruins. We parked, got out, and he gave us his best descriptions of the site, the ruins, its history, those who had lived here long before our time, and speculations about why it had all been abandoned. Through it all, as we listened to him, both Maria and I were enchanted by the stunning views.

"You see, *Señor* Barnes and *Señorita* Maria, this whole area is reputed to have been a seaport ... an important one." He waved an expansive arm at the ruins. "These ruins formed only a portion of a much bigger, more thriving community. It wasn't heavily populated, perhaps less than 2,000 people, but through them were traded a number of essential goods ... essential for their wellbeing or for their economy. As you can see, it has easy access to the sea and also to other ports up and down the coast."

He told us the place had been a principal access point for the trade of goods highly prized by the ancient Mayans. Copper artifacts from the Mexican highlands; gold jewelry painstakingly created by local craftsmen; ceramics, incense burners, and objects of flint – all were carried by seafaring canoes and sold up and down the rivers and tributaries of what is now Guatemala, Honduras and Belize. And in return, they imported, for sale inland, salt and textiles, jade and obsidian.

He took us to the three principal buildings still standing on the site, and described for us the protecting wall built to protect Tulum from invasion from inland, a wall hundreds of meters long on the land-facing side, and more than eight meters thick in some places. We admired the frescoes of the Venus deity in the Temple of the Frescoes, and those of the "diving god", whose images appear also in the Temple of the Descending God. And above it all, standing proud on the edge of the land, was El Castillo, the dominant structure built originally as a shrine and a beacon for the homing canoes, but later added to and expanded to the dimensions it is today.

Nelson continued, "Legend tells the story that the shrine was built at just the point where there was a natural break in the barrier reef. It made a perfect landmark for the canoes. From the earliest days of Tulum, it was this fact alone that made it a perfect location, eventually allowing for the broader community to be built up around it."

We climbed to the top of El Castillo and Nelson showed us the serpent motifs carved into the lintels of what had originally been a beam and mortar roof, but was today almost entirely made of stone. And through the two small windows we looked out over the placid waters of the Caribbean.

As we made our careful way back down to ground level he said, "Of course today it has a completely different flavour and feel to the place. We see it as an artifact of the past, overrun by tourists and small tradesmen selling replicas of that past. But the Mayans saw it as it had been formed ... not only a trading port, but perhaps more importantly, a site for the worship of Diving God."

He saw the quizzical look on my face.

"The Diving God? Yes ... sometimes known as the Venus deity, or perhaps more specifically the Bee God. Honey was an important fixture in their diet and this gave it economic importance too. Think of the diving of a bee burrowing deep into the form of a flower to collect the pollen."

"Was it unique to Tulum?" Maria asked.

"No. Archeologists have found similar images in the temples in Coba and Sayil."

We were walking back to the car. "Have you decided where you would like to have lunch?" he asked us.

We looked at each other, and I shrugged.

He nodded. "So let me suggest a place nearby where they won't cheat you and you'll find it quite pleasing. It's a short drive from here; I will guide you, and then leave you to a quiet lunch. I want to see a friend who I think is here today. I will come and meet you at the restaurant later."

"Oh? I was hoping that you would join us for lunch."

"Ah, thank you. I would have enjoyed this. But I think it is important that I see my friend today. There is a small private matter between us."

With that he took us to the place he'd suggested, and we settled gratefully at a comfortable table, out of the sun, with views of the site on one side and the ocean on the other.

It was a languid meal. After the waiter had taken our orders Maria placed her hand over mine, and left it there throughout the entire time. We each managed our meals quite comfortably with one hand. I'm not sure what I ate that day. The strongest memory of that lunch was Maria's deep warm brown eyes gazing languidly at me, and I felt myself sinking deeper and deeper into them, to the point of losing myself completely in the special magic that had formed between us.

We were just finishing when Nelson joined us. He was in a slow, pensive mood, with a quizzical expression on his face.

Without any preamble, he said, "*Señor* Sam, you said you were here on holiday. Yes?"

"Yes, that's right."

"But I think you also mentioned something about an old document."

I looked startled. "Uh, yes. Yes, I did."

"You said you were searching for it, or looking for it, or a friend was look for it. I do not remember which it was."

"Well-l-l, it's a friend who wants to find it. I'm just along for the ride."

"For the ride? I do not know this expression."

"It means I really don't believe he's going to find it, but he asked my help and he's paying my expenses. And since he's paying my expenses, I should at least show him that I'm trying to help."

"Ah-hah. I see. Well, it is possible I know something that could help you." He selected an empty chair from an adjoining table, pulled it over to ours and sat down.

I sat up. "Oh?"

"Yes. What you told me got me thinking. From a few years ago I remembered something a friend told me. I didn't pay much attention to it at the time, but something you said reminded me of it. Some of it I had forgotten. Before I said anything to you I wanted to make sure that what I think I remembered was accurate. It happens that my friend is also a tour guide who works here from time to time. I hoped he would be here today, and so I decided to see him. You will recall that at your kind invitation to join you for lunch I said I needed to meet someone."

I nodded.

"My friend is Mayan, like me. More accurately, he descends from strong Mayan roots, and like me, has lived in this region most of his life. We are about the same age. Our families lived in the same village and he and I grew up seeing each other almost daily."

"What is your friend's name?"

"He goes by the name of Poquito. Most people find it difficult to pronounce our traditional names – his is Tlahuizcalpantecuhtli – and so to make himself more attractive for business, he is as I say a tour guide among other pursuits, he decided a shorter, more familiar name was better."

"That's quite a mouthful," I told him. "Does it mean anything?"

"He told me once that it translates to 'the lord of the star and the dawn', which he thought was amusing, considering he always liked to go to bed early, and sleep late in the mornings."

He stopped, and looked directly at me. He paused, thinking, as if he was making up his mind, deciding about whether to continue. At last, a small smile crossed his face, and he nodded, as if to assure himself he was doing the right thing.

"It's something I haven't paid much attention to. At the time Poquito told me, it seemed an idle topic of gossip, as if he was trying just to pass a slow moment with me while waiting for the next busload of tourists. But, as I said, it was what you said that made me remember about it, and think that perhaps there might be something to it after all.

"We are a poor people, but we don't dwell on the poor part of our lives. We are proud of who we were, what we are, and who we have come from. Our family roots are strong, and we respect those who have come before us. It is in our traditions that we try to learn all we can from the older members of our families."

He paused. Maria and I waited quietly for him to continue.

"This was true of Poquito. He and his grandfather were very close. His grandfather was always telling him stories of how things used to be when he had been a small boy growing up here. Over the years of his boyhood there were many stories. But one in particular was one told him several times. And so, it stayed with him. Much more so than many of the others.

"It was an odd sort of story. It had little to do with his normal life – crops, their animals, family, those sorts of things. Instead, it touched on his work. As a younger man, he had been a labourer, helping to build buildings; sometimes also helping to take them apart or make changes to them. On one such occasion, he had been assigned to help with the renovations of a monastery. It was very old. It had been owned by the Franciscan Order, but they had consolidated their work in Merida and no longer needed the building, and they sold it to a local landowner.

"My grandfather was told to help dismantle the interior walls of what had once been the Abbot's study. They were thick, very thick, perhaps fifty centimeters. Usually it was a crew of two for this work, but that day he was alone – the other man was ill. Towards the end of the afternoon's work he came across a deep hole that had been set or built into one of the walls. It wasn't a big hole, although it had been shaped in the form of a deep square, perhaps twenty centimeters or so on a side, and about forty deep. It was very dry.

"The hole wasn't empty. In it was what looked like an old book. Very old, but in reasonable condition. My grandfather reached in and pulled it out. Bits of dust and old plaster came out with it and fell to the floor. He looked at it. He opened the stiff cover and looked inside. He could not read … at least not very well; he'd never been properly taught. There wasn't much schooling in those days. He set it down on the floor in a corner, and resumed his work on the wall.

"When it was time for him to go home, he was just about to leave when he turned back and remembered the book. He didn't know what it was, but he thought it would make an interesting thing to talk about with his wife. But he was afraid, too. Afraid of being caught with it, accused of stealing. He didn't want that. He was respected in his community, and had no wish to bring shame on himself or his family.

"He was lucky. He was late leaving, and there was no one else about. After carefully looking about him from the doorway of the old monastery he saw that the way back to his home was clear. But to be on the safe side, he covered the book with an old cloth he'd found in another room, and made his way home.

"His wife, my grandmother, showed little interest in the book. She told him to put it on a shelf, but to keep it out of her way. He did."

I said, "Nelson, are you saying that this book could have something to do with what I told you?"

He held up a cautionary hand. "Wait, there is more."

I looked at Maria and shrugged gently. She smiled, and somehow I had the impression that she already knew, or at least suspected, that we'd not yet heard the interesting part. I settled back and listened.

"Over the years, the book stayed in my grandfather's home. He never had any use for it; but he didn't want to throw it out. A simple man he was, but kind, and always willing to help out whenever someone was in need. My grandmother died before him, and he was left with his son, my father, and our family. Eventually my grandfather died, and all of his possessions, including the book, went to my father.

"Our home was small. It was difficult to keep all the things inherited from my grandparents. My parents decided to slowly get rid of many things, including the book. I was sorry to see it go; in a way it had become such a familiar item in our home, that I was so used to seeing it every day in the place where my father had put it when it first arrived. But, well, eventually, it too, went."

"Do you know where it went?" Maria was sitting forward in her chair, listening carefully to Nelson tell his story. Her chin was resting in both hands; both elbows on the table, her eyes strangely aglow.

"Yes, I do. I told you about my friend. He had an interest in the old things. My father knew this, and so he passed it to him."

"So, your friend has it? He gave it to him?" I felt excitement welling up, thinking that maybe, just maybe this was what Kevin and I had come to Mexico to find.

"No. I told you my friend was interested in the old things." He shrugged. "But, like so many of us here, he has not very much money."

"He sold it?" It seemed a logical conclusion.

"Yes."

"To whom? When?"

"Recently. It was a short time ago, perhaps a few weeks. I told you he is a tour guide ... like me. One day he was guiding a group of people. They were from France, Spain, Germany, United States, and Canada. Your country." He looked at me. I nodded.

"The man from Canada and Poquito fell into conversation. His Spanish was much better than that of most of the other people on the bus, so it was natural for them to speak with one another. The man said he was a collector, and was interested in Mayan artifacts. He said that he likes to buy them, when he can, to make sure they are preserved." Nelson paused. "Poquito suspected that perhaps this man was more interested in personal profit. But, anyway, after they talked for a while, and after Poquito had mentioned he owned an old book which had in it what looked like Mayan writing, the man became very excited. He offered to buy it."

I could see what was coming. It gave me no pleasure.

"Poquito needed money. It was a common thing with him, but at the time he needed some even more. He agreed to sell the book. The man offered him five thousand pesos, and he took it."

"He took it," I repeated. I must have sounded disappointed.

"Yes. But you must understand, *Señor* Sam, five thousand pesos is to us a lot of money. For Poquito it was more than half his regular month's income. And he had no need for the book."

"Yes, I see this. But, is Poquito here? Could we talk with him? Perhaps he can remember more about this man."

"I would gladly take you to him, but you remember that I told you I wanted to see a friend. It was Poquito I saw. He told me he was going to Cancun today. People are there he must see. He said he was going to finish soon with the group he was guiding ... they arrived earlier this morning, and then leave." Nelson glanced at the time. "I think by now he will have departed. The daily bus leaves here late afternoon."

It was reasonable, and he said it with the conviction I had learned to read in him. I had to accept it. I looked at Maria. Her eyes mirrored some of the disappointment I felt. But then, I had already begun to wonder at her interest. It seemed that only after we had begun our little trip together here on the Mayan Riviera had she shown any interest in this document at all. Last week, when I arrived, she said she knew nothing about it. I swallowed my suspicions. I looked up at the sky and saw that the angle of the sun had grown smaller. The day was getting on ; we'd been here since lunch.

"Well *Guapa*, I guess we'd better start heading back to Akumal."

She nodded, and then smiled, and in rapid Spanish told Nelson how much she had enjoyed his story, and that she saw how disappointed I was that it had ended this way. I caught only the general gist of what she said.

I signaled the waiter, who had been making impatient noises at us for some time, and paid him. He left with an ironic bow, and as we got to our feet, he was already back at the table busy clearing it, making it ready for the evening trade.

The drive back to Akumal was uneventful. Nelson asked if we could take him to his home and, under the circumstances, I felt it was the decent thing to do. It wasn't very far from our hotel. I stopped the car at his place, and we all got out. He was a courtly man, and he thanked us profusely for the day. I had already paid him his fee, with extra besides to acknowledge his help and the story he had told. It was no fault of his that the outcome was so discouraging. He shook our hands, respectfully, one by one, Maria first. He turned and walked away. We continued on to the hotel.

Chapter 23

The message light on my mobile phone was blinking when we walked into our hotel room. I had left the phone there, carefully hidden, not wanting to be bothered or interrupted while on holiday from frequently useless phone calls. Yet innate prudence had dictated that I at least bring it with me from home. I stared at it, wondering if I should even bother listening to the message. It had been a tiring day; we were both tired, and more on my mind right now was the thought of cool drinks on the balcony and the chance to relax with this wonderful girl who had given herself so willingly to me the night before.

She said, "Will you answer it?" She could sense what I was feeling. It was one of her more appealing qualities, something I'd rarely encountered with Frankie. I shrugged. I suppose it could be important; I'd not had any calls at all since I'd arrived in Mexico.

I looked at her. She came and put her arms around my neck. "Answer it if you must. I'll go and freshen up."

I watched her disappear into her bathroom, picked up the phone and dialed for the message.

It was Harry. He wondered where the hell I was, and would I kindly sober up and call him as soon as possible. 'An emergency', he said.

Over the years I had become used to Harry's high-flown talk and tendency to exaggerate beyond the usual norms. I had been stung more than once by Harry's manufactured emergencies, ones which usually turned out to be something quite ordinary, and that could fit easily into my longer-term schedule. Yet I felt this was different. He'd told me he'd have no need to contact me while I was away, 'so long as', he added darkly, 'you continue writing'. Well, I had done some writing: not as much as I would have at home, but enough to give me some satisfaction. But even if I'd done nothing, he still wouldn't have known about it. So he must want something else.

"Harry? It's Sam. What's up?"

"Where the hell have you been? I've been calling every few hours and all I get is your insipid leave-me-a-message message."

"Settle down, Harry. Just tell me what this is all about."

"I want you to come back to Toronto. Now. You've had enough time for wild-goose chases. I need you to do some work for a change. When can I expect you back here?"

"Before I move an inch, I want you to settle down and tell me what's bugging you. Now."

"That blasted publisher! He's screwed us up royally. He wants to reopen the contract for *"Tomorrow's Generations"*."

He'd named the book I was working on.

"Why? What's his problem?"

"Seeing the nice advance he's given you – us, he thinks he has us over a barrel. In a way, I suppose he might be right. But I'm not going to tell him that. And neither are you."

"Talk, Harry."

He grumbled. By his way of thinking, I should be halfway to the airport by now.

"Jim Farnsworth called me yesterday. You know Jim, I think."

"Yes, Harry," I said patiently, "I know Jim."

"Right. Well, he was his usual obnoxious self. He demanded when you were going to deliver the manuscript you contracted for. I had to remind him that it wasn't due until May, and this was only February. Then he tried to convince me that all of his other authors, yes, he said 'all', managed to get their work in well before their contracted deadlines."

"Yes? And what did you say?"

"In a word, 'bullshit'."

"Good."

"He didn't like that, but he couldn't pursue it when I explained to him that I know many of his other authors. Several of them are mine and I keep very close tabs on their progress, and I know for a fact that I have to chase every one of them for delivery. You happen to be one of the better ones."

"Thanks, Harry." I watched Maria coming back into the room. She came and stood beside me, looking quizzically at me. I nodded, then said into the phone, "So?"

"So then he told me that the contract has to be opened and renegotiated. He said he didn't like the terms, that he wanted to shift publication away from hard copy books to online, and that he wants the royalty structure changed."

"Humph! He doesn't want much, does he? Did you agree to any of this?"

"Are you crazy? Of course not. But he demanded – you know what he's like – that you and I meet with him in his office tomorrow."

"Forget it. Did you tell him I was away?"

"Yes. And then he got really nasty. There's something going on, Sam. I'm not sure what, but it doesn't feel right."

"I agree. Oh, hell! I was just beginning to see some light here on this document I told you about."

"What? Oh, that. You mean you're still chasing rainbows?"

"Come on, Harry, it's not the only reason I came here."

"No. I suppose not. I got a call from Frankie, too. She sounded upset. She tried to reach your phone several times, but only got your voicemail. She even went around and knocked on the door of your house."

Oh great, I thought. "I don't know what she's upset about. I told her I was going away for a while. It's not as if she didn't know."

"Well, you might have some patching up to do when you get back here. Yes, she's back in Toronto."

I looked into Maria's eyes and said slowly to Harry, "I'm not sure I want to bother."

"Do tell."

"It's too long to explain now."

He sighed what sounded like a long-suffering sigh. "Well, it's your life. I'll leave you to deal with your domestic problems. Anyway, how soon can you get back here?"

"He wants me there, too? Why? Can't you handle it?"

"Of course I can handle it myself. But, in a way, I think he's right ... although not for the reasons he may be thinking."

"What's that supposed to mean?"

"I want you there to show him that in no way can he try and twist his argument to make me think you're going to agree with him: to see it his way. If we're there together, in his office, at the same time, sitting across the desk from him, he'll see we're putting up a united front."

"Games!" I said scornfully.

"Yes! Games! You're damn right it's games. But if we don't play it, we're in danger of losing what we've already got. D'you want that?"

"Of course not."

"So, when can you get back here?"

I sighed. "Okay, Harry. I'll see what I can do about getting a flight tomorrow."

Maria didn't look happy.

Harry said, "Call me when you know," and he hung up.

I turned to Maria. I was tired. We were both tired. But content with one another. It had been a long day, and Nelson's story was still very fresh. I had been looking forward to a quiet evening and dinner with Maria, and another night with her in my arms. Even fresher in my mind were the senses of her closeness to me and the powerful, exotic and more than sensual scent she so sparingly used. I felt soured by Harry's call. I reached out and drew her close.

"I wish he hadn't called."

"You're leaving." She said it flatly.

"I have to. It has to do with the book I'm writing. It could become a legal matter. It's the last thing I want."

"It's not about that document Nelson talked about?"

"Oh that. No. That was Harry on the phone. I've told you about him."

"Sam," she hesitated, "mi amor. I'm sorry. I was just beginning to know you. You're very different from Manuel. You are gentle. I like this. You ask me what I want. He tells me what I'm going to get. You ask me what I'd like to do; he tells me what he's planned for us. You make me feel like a real person; not like a kept poodle. You show your emotions, even when you try to suppress them. I wish you could stay. Is there a way you could come back?" Then frustration: "Will I ever see you again? Dammit, can I least know how to contact you?"

We hardly knew each other, and in the part of my mind where suspicions sometimes lived, I wondered if her interest somehow had more to do with the Avendaño document than with me. Perhaps it was just coincidence, a coincidence made by the close juxtaposition of our little holiday here in the sun with the story we'd heard today from Nelson, and with what she knew of the reason I had come to Mexico in the first place. I'd told her about the arrangement with Kevin, and while it's clear she paid it little attention, she was at least aware of it. But now, there she was before me, as eager, hesitant, yet demanding as a June bride.

I took her in my arms. "My love, I'm not leaving you. I must do this. I'll tell you how to contact me. I want to be with you day and night – lips, body, and soul from now until the end of time."

She grabbed me back, and with a ferocity I'd not yet suspected, covered me with kisses.

"Come over here." I walked her over to the little desk in one corner of the room. In the drawer were pads of paper for making notes, and a place holding a couple of ballpoint pens. I took out one of each and wrote down both my phone numbers, landline and mobile, my email address, and the mailing address of my home in Toronto. I folded it gently into her hand. "Here. Keep this safe."

She looked at me for a moment then turned to put it into the bag she was using as a purse. She turned back at me and smiled. "Come," she said quietly, taking my hand. "Can you pour me some wine?"

I did, and while at it got myself an ice-cold beer. The room bar was just about depleted. We took our drinks out onto the balcony and flopped into the comfortable deck chairs. I knew I should be on the phone making arrangements for my return to Toronto, but I needed this quiet interlude with her.

Her soft voice came to me through the gathering evening darkness. "I suppose I might as well go back to Mexico City. There's no point in my staying here now. My friends deserted me; you're leaving. And I've got to get some clean clothes. Look! They're wrinkled, and reek with sweat. And climbing over those ruins today did them no good."

Her hand was resting comfortably in mine. I gave it a squeeze. "You look terrific, and you smell even better."

We decided we'd stay here this night and drive to Cancun in the morning. We'd collect our belongings that we'd each left in our rooms in the hotel there, and check out. I would put her on a plane back to Mexico City, and see what I could do about making return flight arrangements to Toronto. Dinner was an easy, languid meal, and afterward we dragged ourselves back up to the room, and folded ourselves together into a deep, dreamless sleep.

Chapter 24

In Toronto I am instantly at home. It is not my birth city, but after I'd moved here years ago, I knew at once that it will be my home place. There's a feeling about this city I've not experienced anywhere else.

True: other large cities consist of multiple neighbourhoods. They too are filled with a wide range and variety of international restaurants, and have residents from all over the world. Most represent the principle commercial and banking centres for their countries.

Yet, for all that and more, Toronto has its own unique flavour, a character all its own, one that resonated perfectly with me. Masses of trees, tree-lined streets, and both small and large parks. It was not for nothing Toronto had been dubbed 'the city within a park'. It has its own specialty jazz radio station, adding to the city's special ambience. I keep my car radio regularly tuned to it, and I'd come to think of jazz as Toronto's soundtrack.

I opened my bedroom curtains onto a bright, early March morning. In the time I'd been away, the snow had disappeared, except for a few small piles here and there. People were out walking the streets wearing only sweaters or light topcoats. As they passed beneath the windows of my townhouse I could see more smiles than downcast, plodding expressions. But this time of year can be deceiving, and winter's icy blasts are quite capable of unexpectedly returning.

I own a comfortable, although not new, three-story townhouse in midtown Toronto. It is situated perfectly for all of my needs. I could easily walk to most of the shops and services that supplied my normal requirements; there were several very comfortable pubs and coffee shops in the area, and when the occasion called for it, I could get out my car from the adjoining garage and be on the freeways out of town within twenty minutes. Driving in the city had become a purgatory; finding parking even worse, so when I needed to venture farther downtown, reasonably efficient public transit was close at hand.

Last night I had glanced at my phone and saw that I had more than two weeks of accumulated messages. The message light still blinked monotonously this morning. But all that, including the mass of unopened emails on my computer, could wait. There was one call I had made before leaving Mexico. From the airport I called Kevin to tell him I was going.

"Rather abrupt, isn't it?"

I told him, "Perhaps, but I can see that I'm no longer needed here. I have the impression you – and maybe Pancho – can handle things quite well on your own. Besides, I'm needed in Toronto, and I have to get back there."

And so it went, back and forth, until I tired of trying to get him to understand.

I said, "So long, Kevin, they're calling my flight. Bye now."

So there it was: time spent in Mexico but for quite different reasons than had been originally planned. I wondered if I'd ever see Kevin again.

Now, this morning, back here at home, and increasingly fed up with the whole thing, I discovered that available breakfast makings were in short supply in the kitchen and, apart from the two cups of coffee I'd brewed on awakening, I decided to throw on some clothes and seek breakfast in Lin's coffee shop, just a few blocks away. Despite his occasional ribbing, or maybe because of it, I liked going to Lin's. I'd been going there for about ten years. The service was fast and friendly, although on occasion, it edged on the sloppy, the food was always excellent, and he had business smarts enough not to charge for extra coffees – at least not for his regular customers.

Both Lin and the rich aroma of freshly brewed coffee greeted me as I pushed through the door, and he had a cup of my favourite coffee waiting for me as I sat down at a table. Lin was the owner of this place. At one time, he had glowingly told me that he also owned three coffee chain franchises elsewhere in the city, but he preferred to work in this one because of the clientele. I couldn't argue with him about that. This was more than just a simple coffee shop. It was a small but comfortable hole-in-the-wall that served delicious food quickly ('not fast food!' Lin often protested), excellent coffees, and he left his customers in peace to enjoy their stays in their own good time. To add to the pleasure, he mercifully refused to play any sort of loud music, opting instead for a sort of relaxing, formless sort of background music that was there but entirely unobtrusive.

It sounded vaguely Eastern but I could never quite place it. He said, "I haven't seen you for a long time, Sam. You been away?"

"Yes. A couple of weeks in Mexico."

"Mexico! Very nice! You go alone? When you get back?"

"Yes. But I met some nice people there. Last night. Maybe I'll go back again."

"Ah-hah!"

"What's that supposed to mean?"

"It means maybe so we won't be seeing that nice Frankie Giuffrida anymore in here."

"What? Frankie? Now, just hold on, Lin. Don't start jumping to any conclusions. How about earning your money and getting me some breakfast?"

He nodded. But I could see the glint in his eye, as he went back to his kitchen chuckling to himself. I shook my head. It was still too early for me to tackle the Frankie issue, not even to myself.

Much too early. I dug into my breakfast. I wasn't ready to begin the painful process of sorting through my emotions, trying to reconcile how I felt about her, and about Maria. Maria had descended on me like a ton of bricks; her face danced before me, her scent still strong in my nostrils, and the memory of her singing voice rang clear in my ear. The two days we had spent together were a classic example of a 'willows and flowers' interlude, but despite this, I had the underlying suspicion there was more to it than that. Sure, there was a powerful emotional attachment developing. She had shown this in Cancun when I put her on the plane back to her home in Mexico City. She had flung her arms around my neck and insisted, "Call me," and we kissed for much longer than a casual goodbye peck on the cheek would warrant. All this while the gate attendant with the basilisk gaze impatiently tapped her foot, waiting for this final passenger to board the plane. Yet, there was also the hint of something more, and I couldn't shed the idea that it seemed to be centred on the Avendaño document. I'd called her the moment I got home, but there was no answer. I left a message.

And there was another mystery, that document that had taken me to Mexico in the first place. At first, when Kevin had first broached the idea, the whole thing seemed preposterous. Had it not been for the siren call of a tropical sun, at a time when I needed it most, but could not afford the time,

I would have dismissed the whole idea as entirely fanciful, and told Kevin so. On that I had secretly agreed with Harry. But, while there, some odd things had happened. Small things, or events, or something someone had said. Meaningless in and of themselves, yet when taken together seemed to point to something larger; something I couldn't quite put my finger on. It all niggled at the back of my mind, and was just enough to make me want to know more.

Maria had told me about Pancho, his gambling and what she called his shady connections. On occasion, she had hinted darkly at connections to the drug trade. Kevin had also laid his own tale of woe on me, telling of his urgent need to raise sufficient funds to secure the future of his family's property in Scotland. Then Pancho had spoken about his father's political ambitions, and how he was on the verge of declaring himself a candidate to become Mexico City's next mayor. As it is in several countries, being mayor of the capital city is much more than simply being mayor – it is an almost essential stepping stone to the country's presidency.

Then there was the odd moment in Garibaldi Square when it seemed both Kevin and Pancho were doing their best not to let themselves be seen by me. And not hours later, when we met that evening for drinks, Pancho appeared unexpectedly, although I was the only one who was surprised. There, Kevin announced his intentions to delay what had been our intended trip to the Yucatán, because 'he needed to do more research'. In retrospect it proved to be the sheerest kind of sophistry.

And by odd coincidence, added to the mix was Nelson Zengotita, who later told Maria and me his fascinating story of finding an old document.

Finally, there was Maria herself, and her more than casual interest in the Avendaño document.

Unrelated events? Possibly. But they were all swirling around one another, and I was curious enough to want to build a single picture out of them all.

I looked at my watch. It was time to meet Harry. Late yesterday I had called him from Cancun after I'd been able to book my Toronto flight, and he had said, "Great! We're due in Bugger Nut's' office at 10:30, Monday morning." He'd used the same name before with me, although he was careful not to even hint at it when meeting with, or talking to, publisher Jim Farnsworth.

Lin had brought me my breakfast, and I had worked my way through it while pondering these vexing questions. I looked over at him, standing behind the counter, and asked him:

"How much, Lin? Are you going to overcharge me again?"

"It's okay, Sam. I put on your account. You pay me at end of month, okay?"

"Sure. Thanks, Lin." I put a few dollar coins as a tip under my plate, and left to beard Farnsworth in his den.

******

The session with Farnsworth was as difficult and as it was inconclusive. He was characteristically aggressive. He opened with a blunt, "I'm re-opening your contract. I don't like the way it's written, and you've got to accept the changes."

Harry countered with, "Unless you settle down, Jim, and tell us exactly what you have in mind, and are prepared to discuss it sensibly, Sam and I will leave, and we may have to pay a visit to my lawyer."

"You think I'm belligerent? Harry, you don't know the half of it. The company's running out of money. Sales are down. Authors are late in delivering. Bill collectors beat a regular path to my door. Retail stores are closing all over, except for the big chains, and they're murder to deal with. I'm having to reduce staff, and still you want your expensive contract kept as is."

"Yes."

"Is that all? Yes?"

"Look, Jim, all the things you've just told us are not new. They're all common to the publishing industry today. I don't have to tell you that. You knew them when the contract was signed. Yes, you're being squeezed. Worse, the smaller private outlets are being squeezed out of existence. And as for authors being late, well, c'mon now, that's endemic to the trade."

Farnsworth looked at me sourly. "I hear you were travelling instead of writing."

I said, "Yes. I was writing, too."

Harry offered mildly: "Sam's not supposed to deliver until May. What's the rush?"

Farnsworth slumped suddenly in his chair. It was not yet noon on Monday, but he already had the defeated look of someone who had worked a week's worth of fourteen-hour days. He ran a hand through his thatch of graying hair.

"Harry, you know me. We've worked together for a long time. We've had a pretty good working relationship. Sure, sure, we've fought and sometimes fought hard, but this time it's different. I need a concession from you. And you too, Sam." He paused, looking at me.

Harry said, "Keep talking."

"Well, it's like this. We had our regular editorial meeting last Wednesday. One of my editors, Shirley, I think you know her," I nodded, "announced she'd heard that Loft Top are publishing a book that sounds very similar to *Tomorrow's Generations*. She couldn't find out who the author is, but her contact did describe the gist of their book, and sure enough it did sound a lot like yours, Sam."

I must have looked concerned.

"Yes, you would do well to be concerned. Not only does theirs sound like yours, but they're going to publish in June. They're ahead of us. If theirs comes out first, and is successful, think what that'll do to yours. You won't like it. None of us will. I sure as hell won't."

I could see his reasoning. It was difficult not to agree with him.

Harry asked, "So, what do you propose?"

"Instead of publishing hard cover, we publish electronically. We could do that a lot sooner. Exclusively. At least until we see how sales go. As soon I get your manuscript, I can set our people preparing the groundwork for the electronic launch, including all the promotional material. But we'll have to act fast. Besides it'd be a damn-sight cheaper."

Harry and I looked at each other. The question on his face was, Can you deliver sooner than May? I shrugged as if to say, 'I'm not sure. Let me check'. He knew me well enough to read me.

"So?" This, from Farnsworth.

"Jim. We'll let you know. Today's Monday, I'll call you Wednesday morning."

"Not sooner? Time's running out, and I've got a lot do about this. Well, I suppose I have to be satisfied with that. Although I don't know why you can't tell me now," he grumbled. And, as if to add a further sting, he offered, "If we can't work something out, I might have to cancel publication altogether."

"Author's privilege, Jim. You know that."

He stood to shake our hands and walked us out of his office. He still looked haggard, although marginally less so. I suppose he was already thinking we'd agree. But then perhaps he was just hoping. He also knew that what it all amounted to was that the burden of his potential profit now rested squarely on my shoulders.

Suddenly I was angry. Angry at Farnsworth. Angry at the other publishing company and their unnamed writer. Unreasonably angry at Harry for having dragged me all the way back from Mexico – and, let it be said, Maria – for something that could just as easily have been handled by phone. Here they all were, combining and contriving to take control of my life, a situation I had avoided and abhorred for years. I could understand Farnsworth – reading between the lines, and I saw that his whole business could be at risk. Harry I had less patience with; I would have expected him to fight more on my side. I said to him, "I'll see you later. No, I can't stop now. I've got things I must do." I must have been curt with him, because his face fell a bit. He had been hoping, I know him this well, that we'd stop for lunch some place and he'd get me to tell him when I could deliver the manuscript. I wasn't ready for that yet, and I told him so.

I took the subway back to my place. On the walk back from the station I stopped in a nearby deli and filled a shopping bag with sausages, cheeses, pickles, fresh rye bread, a couple of pickled eggs just for the hell of it, and other odds and ends … more than enough to make a comfortable scratch lunch. I also stopped in to replenish my beer supply.

Back home, I built myself the lunch I'd been looking forward to, opened a bottle of beer, and carried the whole package into my study. It was in one of the three bedrooms that came with the house. After settling myself at my desk, and taking a few bites of lunch as well as several satisfying long drafts of dark ale, I instructed the phone to play back all of its waiting messages. Most of them were junk, or redundant reminders of things I already knew about. I deleted them all. The last one, however, was neither. It sounded both mysterious and intriguing.

Without greeting or preamble the attractive female voice announced: "You are invited to our office in Yorkville to discuss with a gentleman a topic of mutual interest." It concluded by giving me detailed instructions of where to find them. There was no name, nor formal signoff, nor request to call back.

I checked the phone's call display for a callback number, but it showed as 'private number'. I played the message again, thinking perhaps I'd missed something the first time through. Nothing new. I shrugged, and turned to a clogged inbox of emails, and dealt quickly with them. There was not enough in any of them to hold my attention for very long, while part of me continued to puzzle over the cryptic phone message. Towards the middle of the afternoon, there was another call from Frankie. Again, I let it go to voicemail. I still wasn't ready to talk to her. When I played it back, her message said, with an emphasis born of impatience that she wanted to "talk" ... her euphemism for an intensive interrogation about our joint future. My emotions were still sufficiently unsettled from my time with Maria that I wanted more time for the welter of emotional storms to subside.

Later that afternoon Harry called. He was anxious to see me that evening. He needed to resolve the issue that Jim Farnsworth had brought up about my new book. I told him I was busy that evening – I wasn't – but I needed time to myself. He didn't like it, but knew he couldn't push me.

"Tomorrow, then. Without fail. I'm busy all day. Six o'clock at The Golden Thumb." It had become our favourite meeting place, the brasserie where we'd had lunch that snowy day when I told him about Kevin's invitation to Mexico.

The rest of the day and evening were devoted to catching up on the mundane but necessary particulars of living, but by noon the next day I had determined to follow up from the call, and so prepared myself to pay the mysterious caller a visit.

Chapter 25

The inner urban community of Yorkville is located in the heart of downtown Toronto. Situated immediately to the north of the city's most brightly fashionable shopping street, it is now an upscale, modern enclave of specialty shops catering to a well-heeled clientele, many of whom live within easy walking distance.

In an earlier time, Yorkville had been known as the spiritual home of the counterculture – hippies, coffee bars, and strumming, upwardly hopeful musicians, several of whom had turned their initially faltering talents into spectacular international careers. It was also a favourite haunt of the after-hours pleasure seekers. It was the mecca for Toronto's counterculture of the 1960s, and in the process, had bred some of the better-known pop musical artists of the twentieth century's closing decades.

Like flies to the honey-pot they came: from all over the country, by plane, train, and bus – mainly bus – seeking fame, fortune, love, and interesting things to smoke. In those long-ago days, a stroll down any of its streets on a hot summer evening after dark revealed a cacophony of musical styles issuing forth from the string of bars along the route. Also clearly seen and heard through the open windows of the grand old, but rather seedy mansions were the athletic gyrations of sweating, eccentrically garbed youthful, and not-so-youthful crowds undulating wildly to the latest dance craze. And not seen, yet sometimes heard, were the occasional pleadings, grunts, satisfying groans, explosive sighs and hurried whispered confidences that arose from behind unkempt hedges inside the low stone walls that separated many of the venerable but now made-over mansions from the street. Most of these places were quite substantial, having been built in an even earlier time to house the large families of the growing merchant class.

However, in more recent times the community has been transformed. It now resembles many of the chic shopping districts of New York, London, Rome, and half a dozen other major cities where the affluent go to spend their dividends. Today its streets are lined with cute clothing boutiques, overpriced gift shops, "be-seen-in" restaurants, multi-million-dollar condos, five-star hotels, and galleries for artists who, thanks to influential patrons, can afford to wait to be noticed.

Finding a parking spot is next to impossible among all the shiny, expensive automobiles parked nose to tail in every available curb lane space. Knowing this, I had taken the subway and was now walking towards the address on Scollard Street I'd been given.

It proved to be a discreet, well-maintained three-story brick building, with a narrow front and a rather closed-in look about it. Snowflakes, which had been threatening all morning, finally began drifting down with suicidal determination, quickly covering the front walk. I opened the main door into the tiny vestibule and faced a solid, locked inner door, and a battery of intercom equipment on the wall beside me. I stamped my feet on the welcome mat to get rid of the snow. The telephone message had said, "Ring code 43". I did. The speaker grill came to life and told me I'd be met.

The inner door opened. It framed a stunningly beautiful young woman. Golden blonde hair framed a lightly tanned, slightly oval face and intelligent blue eyes. She was impeccably tailored, in a navy blue pure wool skirt falling to just above her knees, a tan linen jacket, unbuttoned to reveal a crisp, tight-fitting white linen blouse, and a burnt orange Thai silk scarf knotted at her throat.

Before I could say anything, she flashed a stunning smile at me, and said, "This way, please." She beckoned gracefully with her hand in a gesture that said both 'come with me' and 'pointing towards the elevator'. I followed her deeper into the lobby into the pocket handkerchief-sized elevator. She closed the gate, and said "Three!"

The elevator lifted smoothly off its springs and slid silently up to the third floor while we stood looking at each other. It stopped and the door slid open to reveal a richly furnished anteroom, with several comfortable chairs for waiting. She motioned me to one of them, and disappeared into another room. I sat there, waiting the obligatory five minutes, then she reappeared, and told me:

"DJ will see you now."

DJ? Now where had I heard that name before? I followed her through the door into a large, airy room. It was furnished as, and had the air of, the spacious office suite occupied by the Chairman of the Board of a world-spanning, multi-billion-dollar corporation. Which, as I later found out, I supposed it was – in its own way. Through the picture windows at the end of the office, I could see most of the upper half of the CN Tower. Its top shrouded in a skein of cloud that was rapidly turning from white to gray to black.

The young woman stood to one side while I walked noiselessly over the expanse of ankle deep creamy oyster-coloured carpet. Across the room, a massive mahogany desk was positioned against the south-facing windows. Its leather-inlaid surface was devoid of clutter. It had only a telephone and computer. Standing behind the desk was Dependability Jones, the odd little man I'd first met in the rooftop bar of Mexico's Majestic Hotel.

I looked at him. The original impressions I had made about him in Mexico of being somewhat diminutive and pixyish gave way instead to a clearer understanding of how he now appeared to me. I saw the same man, but what I also saw now was a man of about fifty-five, well dressed, carefully barbered, and as calm and composed as a placid sea at dusk.

I looked over his shoulder out the windows. The sky had now turned a menacing black with the threat of imminent snow. The last feeble rays of sun were being blotted out by the advancing clouds, but before they disappeared, they framed his pure white hair with a halo-like glow. The sound of the rising wind was muffled to a muted hiss by the fortified windows.

"You are surprised to see me, Mr. Barnes."

"This is getting to be a habit. First the terrace of the Majestic and now here. Do you always surprise your guests?" I didn't want to tell him I thought I'd also seen him walking with Kevin in Garibaldi Square.

He eased himself around the desk to shake my hand and motioned me to a chair. I settled myself. His body language spoke of a commanding informality. He wore an air of believing he was in complete control. Facing me, he casually leaned his back against his desk in a "let's-all-be-pals-together" gesture that made it seem as if he was about to address the assembled throng of his employees.

"Did I not explain to you that your time in Mexico could lead to problems for you?"

"You told me. You didn't explain."

The young woman appeared at my elbow and placed hot coffee and cold mineral water on the table beside me. It came on a little silver tray complete with a cut-glass goblet that looked like it had come direct from the Waterford glass works in Ireland; a little jug of fresh coffee cream and a small bowl of cane sugar. She handed another cup to DJ and retreated to the other side of the room. He stirred his coffee thoughtfully, and then sipped it carefully, as though it might still be too hot. He looked over at the young woman.

"Thank you, Lisa."

She smiled and left the room, closing the door silently behind her. I drank some coffee.

He said, "Yes. You are right: I did not explain. Yet I believe I suggested that your enquiries could lead to some interesting difficulties for you, did I not? They have certainly prompted me to revise my plans, and may yet have an influence on my organization."

"And, what is your organization?"

"All in good time. There are, perhaps, some things, that need first explaining."

"Explaining?"

"It is why I asked you to come here today."

"So?" I prompted him.

"There are situations in this world that are not always very clear, or to our liking. Some would call them obscure. Or refer to them with such names as 'hidden agenda', or 'nefarious', or some such. It's sometimes considered to be a game like that of Johari Windows, a tool the behavioural scientists and management instructors sometimes like to use. Deflection is a companion tool; so is downright deceit. Magicians and other like artisans of the deflection trades are no strangers to the device. It is common for them to make the ace of spades disappear while extracting a silver coin from your nose."

"What the hell does all that mean?"

"It means, my dear Mr. Barnes, that you are being taken for a fool."

He had a curious way of speaking, a jerky, somewhat stilted way, as if English was not his first language. The rhythms of syntax and cadence were just different enough to set me off balance, and cause me to listen more intently. He continued:

"Many years ago, when I was a penniless young man in London, I often amused myself by browsing the second-hand book stalls in the many street markets that flourished throughout the city. There was, of course, the huge market in Portobello Road. There were also markets in Swiss Cottage, Camden, Greenwich ... the list is almost endless. Perhaps you know of some of them yourself? A particular favourite was the stretch along Charing Cross Road that used to boast a string of antique bookshops. Alas! No more. They've all been swept away by the tides of modern commercialism. I used to watch people as they strolled by these stands, losing themselves in the little treasures they'd find from time to time. I wondered about this, and asked myself why some people would become so entranced by an old, dusty book. When I looked at them myself, those old books, all I could see were tattered pages, worn bindings, some too far gone to be of any practical use, some with pages torn or missing altogether. It puzzled me. But I was a shy person in those days, and it would have been difficult for me to stop people and ask them about this mystery. Instead, I began to study the books themselves."

"What did you find?'

"At first, nothing. Just old, dusty books. Just as I had believed. As time passed though, it gradually dawned on me that these old books were voices from the past. I don't know how I got this idea, but there it was. I had always liked to read, and in glancing through them, I became fascinated by some of the stories. They told of life as it had been in decades and centuries past. They described events of war, and passion, and commerce, and the doings of kings, princes and nobles completely foreign to the times I lived in. In short, they fascinated me, and I sought to learn more.

"The 'more' led me to other areas of collecting. Yes, by then I had begun to eke out the few spare pennies I had managed to save to buy some of these rare things. For reasons I could not explain, some prices were ridiculously low – low enough to fit even my meager means. But after a while, I began to raise my sights onto other areas – other things that attracted some of the crowds. This led me into the study of old porcelains, and odd candlesticks, and odd bits of clothing strange to the modern eye. And as I studied these things, it began to occur to me that if people wanted these things so badly, why could I not help them get them? At least, that was the thought. I had no idea, then at least, how to go about doing this.

"By chance, one day I encountered a pilgrim soul, a young woman who had as keen an interest in the browsing of old things as I. When I first noticed her, buried deep in the stacks in the basement of a particularly labyrinthine old bookshop, she turned away from me with a very large book open in her hands but clutched close to her breast – as if she was afraid I might forcibly take it from her. I didn't know she was a pilgrim soul at the time. This wasn't revealed to me until later. But I could see, just by her presence in that shop, with no one else there other than myself and the old bibliophile who manned the cash desk upstairs, that her interest seemed at least real."

"Mr. DJ, this is all very interesting, but what has it to do with me?" I was beginning to get impatient.

He held up an admonishing hand. "Patience! I think it's important you know this."

I shrugged, then looked about me for a coffee pot. My cup was empty and I wanted more. The coffee, at least, was proving to be of good value, although I couldn't see where this conversation was going. He saw me look about, reached behind him on his desk to grasp the coffee pot, leaned forward and filled my cup. I nodded my thanks and he continued speaking.

"At first, we just nodded politely to one another. Then, overcoming my shyness, I asked her what was the book she was holding. She hesitated, but seeing I seemed to be no threat either to her or the book, she slowly turned it away from her chest and towards me so I could read the title on the binding. The gold inlay lettering on the binding was worn down almost to obscurity, and in the dusty dim light of the shop was difficult to decipher. The leather binding of that thick book was also badly worn, fading in places and somewhat tattered and frayed. But my eyes were young and what I read was *Religio Medici*. It was by a Sir Thomas Browne. I'd never heard of him until she explained that he had been a seventeenth century doctor of medicine who lived in Norwich, in the east of England. He was apparently one of the great humanist doctors of the age, and not thoroughly besotted only by science. The book was one of a large series. She told me it was one of the great treasures of English literature, and that she had, she simply *had* to have it. I nodded sympathetically, and asked, 'Then why don't you buy it?' She would she said, except that she was five pounds short of the purchase price."

DJ paused. He stared at the wall behind me, but I had the impression he was looking far back into his youth and at that moment when he had met the girl.

"One of my weaknesses, Mr. Barnes, is that I do not like to see women in distress."

"I'd hardly call it a weakness," I offered.

"Well, yes. Perhaps. In any event, she was as downcast as ever I'd seen a downcast person, and it told me I had to do something to help her. I decided to something I'd never done before, and wasn't sure I should be doing, even while I was doing it. I reached in my pocket and pulled out the only five-pound note I had, and said, 'Would you like this?'"

"It was a graceful gesture."

"Yes. To make this short, after a lot of protestations of 'oh, I couldn't possibly do that', and 'are you certain?', and 'I can't imagine what you must think of me', she did accept it. I gave her the money. She marched right upstairs to the old proprietor with the book firmly in hand, and bought it. I was right behind her. I will tell you that I was attracted to her, and I didn't want to lose sight of her. We left the shop together. It had just begun to rain, one of those London midsummer rainstorms that suddenly appear out of nowhere. We stood against the wall, hoping for a bit of shelter. She looked at me, wondering whether to dash off and try to catch a bus, or to stay with me. She stayed. I was wearing a battered old tweed jacket, and I took the book from her and put it under my jacket to protect it against the rain. I still had a little bit of money left and invited her to join me for tea in a small teashop not far away.

"Our conversation in the teashop soon turned to rare books, and other rare things. She told me the *Religio* she'd just bought was actually very rare, and she still had difficulty understanding what it had been doing in that second-hand bookshop, and even more difficulty accepting that it had passed under the proprietor's nose without him wanting to keep it for himself, or demanding a much higher price. Nevertheless, she now owned it.

"I asked her why she wanted it. She told me it was one of a very large set that Dr. Browne had written. She had been slowly collecting the entire set but was missing this one volume. Now her set was complete. She had learned that an entire set could fetch a great deal of money, and while she was mildly interested in the subject matter, she was more interested in making money. Remember, Mr. Barnes, how I described her as a pilgrim soul? Well, when she told me this, I felt a frisson of excitement pass through me. It seemed her thinking and mine were closely aligned. She had told me she wasn't quite sure how to go about selling it, and I suggested I'd like to be able to help her. Her eyes lit up, just as they had done when I offered the five-pound note.

"We agreed to do it. We eventually found a buyer who paid a handsome price. Upon receiving the full purchase price, she said, 'Here's your five pounds back. And also, here is one half of the money. Without you, there would have been no money. Or, it would have taken me much longer, and I didn't want to wait. 'Dependability,' for it was the name she had come to know me by, 'let's do this again. I like you and I think we could work well together.'"

"And did you?"

"Indeed we did! We joined forces. Time passed. We sought out other unusual things. England was a treasure trove for such things. It still is. We built a small business together, and during those years we also saw a lot of each other socially. As time went by, I was growing more interested in her, and was beginning to think in terms of asking her to marry me.

"Then one day she phoned me to tell me she was going away for a few days, perhaps a week, and she'd call me when she got back. At the end of the week she came to see me. I spotted it immediately, a rather large and elaborate engagement ring, its diamond sparkling in the morning sunshine. Her eyes were sparkling too, even while my heart was sinking. I knew what she was going to tell me. She could see it written all over my face. 'Yes,' she said, 'I'm engaged. We're going to married in three months.' What could I do but offer my congratulations and told her I hoped she'd be happy?

"They married. Afterwards we tried to continue the business, but it wasn't the same anymore. The appeal had gone out of it. By then we'd amassed a great deal of money, and I decided I no longer wanted to work with her – nor, let it be said, she with me. I sold her my half of the business, a move that gave me even more money. In the years with her I'd learned a lot about the antique and rare books business, but I was getting restless. I wanted new horizons, new places, new challenges. I chose to come here, to Toronto. Why I made this decision is not relevant."

"Okay, so, you came here. What did you do?"

"As I said, I'd learned a lot in the rare things business. I decided to apply my skills here. But I wanted to create something new – something different from what Angel and I had been doing in London." He saw me about to ask a question. "Angel, yes that was the girl's name. So, yes, what did I do? Shortly after arriving in Toronto, I began a survey of the serious collectors' market in Canada. It was strong, and viable, but it seemed to be missing a focus. It was not easy to put my finger on it at first, but over time I noticed a niche. It was not a niche of specific items; rather, a niche of how to acquire them for future sale. To be sure, I wanted the upper end of the market, known as the carriage trade."

He pointed abruptly to the symbol mounted on the wall facing his desk. I turned to look at what he was pointing at. It was a much larger image of the same motif I'd seen on the business card he'd given me on the Majestic Hotel's rooftop terrace. I took it to be his company's logo.

"Do you see the structure of my logo?" he asked me. "It is a formal square that has been subdivided into sixteen smaller squares."

I could just make out the faint straight lines of the three vertical dividing lines inside the big square, crossed by three similar horizontal lines. All six lines were evenly spaced from one another.

"I call it the Sixteen Square Puzzle. Mr. Barnes, look at it carefully. How many squares do you see?"

I paused for a moment, counting. Then:

"Uh, seventeen. No … wait, there are more. Twenty-two."

"Not bad. But not close, either. Actually, there are thirty. Some have claimed they have seen more."

"Thirty? I don't see that."

"Look again, Mr. Barnes. Look, this time, with your whole heart; your inner being. Cast aside any doubt and trust yourself. Seek the hidden truth."

I took longer this time. Slowly the answer he'd given me revealed itself.

I nodded. "Yes. Yes, I see it now."

"It's not so obvious, is it? But it's there. One only has to dig for it: to have the patience and desire to see."

I turned around again to face him.

"Yes, I see it. But what's it about? Why show it to me?"

"It is a metaphor for how I think and how my company operates. We choose not the obvious, preferring instead to seek out the unusual that is hidden behind the obvious."

"You've lost me."

"Mr. Barnes, anyone can collect art. Or, what they think is art. People who dream of owning great works of art divide into three categories – those who think they see, and those who can't, don't or won't. This latter group will spend money, often great sums, on the most atrocious stuff. If such actions please them, so be it. I consider it to be their folly. There are those who think they believe themselves to be endowed with a skill that far transcends the normal clod who thinks an old work, or even some new ones, picked up in a flea market or the odd gallery here or there will set them on the road to becoming great connoisseurs, privileged to rub shoulders with those who really do know."

"And the third group?"

"A much smaller one. Infinitely smaller. Those with the natural insight, patience, skepticism and innate desire to perceive and look deeply and intrusively beyond the obvious." He stopped and looked at me straight, as if to emphasize his next point.

"I am one of those. In fact, my entire company consists of such people who adhere to this principle. I told you that when I settled here I had come armed with considerable knowledge of the trade. While still in London I had also learned just how many charlatans and fakers there were in this business. I wanted nothing to do with them. I needed to set myself apart, and so I formed my little company for the purpose of working with those few perceivers who knew, who really *knew* what to look for. I gradually assembled a group – a small group – of like-minded people who agreed to work with me, not as employees, but as independent agents. Their task, the task of each of us, was to travel the world seeking unsung works of art that had the potential to attract serious sums in the marketplace."

"You all must be very perceptive to be able to see that potential."

"Oh, we are, we are indeed. Our scope is not just images – paintings, photographs, drawings. No, not at all. We go well beyond those limits. We include everything that can be considered Art. Images, yes. But also sculptures, music, old furniture, poetry, and old manuscripts."

A bell sounded in my head. Old manuscripts. Is this why he has brought me here today?

I asked, "Old manuscripts?"

"Good for you, Mr. Barnes! I knew you would twig to it. You have been looking for an old manuscript in Mexico, is it not?"

"How on earth could you know that?"

"I could say, quite mysteriously, that 'there are ways', to quote an overworked phrase. But in fact, it is not mysterious at all. Let me explain."

"I wish you would. I'd told no one here, except my agent, that I was going to Mexico for that reason."

"Your agent?"

"Yes. I'm a writer. I expect you don't know this."

"… in fact I do."

"Harry Oliver is my agent. He has been for years. Without him I'd have had a more difficult time putting my books on the market."

"Are they so difficult to read?"

"Not at all. Quite readable. But the publishing industry has been going through rough times in recent years, and it doesn't look as though it's going to get any better, certainly not anytime soon. Likely worse."

"But you keep writing."

"Of course. It's my life. I choose to write because I need to write."

"You have now, let me see, five novels in print, and a further one under preparation. Have you not exhausted all your ideas?"

"Exhausted? Far from it. New ideas keep coming all the time. The challenge is in deciding which ones are sellable."

"How do you get your ideas? Where do they come from?"

"To quote a well-known Canadian author, sadly no longer with us, 'Ask a spider where he gets his thread, and you'll know where I get my ideas.'"

"I don't understand."

"They come from within me. Most of them, at any rate. It's the same with most writers. The unconscious mind holds a wealth of knowledge. That's akin to where the spider's thread comes from. He makes it. But I think we're getting off topic. Why is the document I was looking for of interest to you? And why would you tell me this?"

I wasn't yet ready to reveal to him that I'd already had information about the Avendaño document, thanks to the story Zengotita had told Maria and I.

"I know where it is," he said. "Or, more precisely, I expect I know where it should be."

To say I was dumbfounded would be an understatement. I said, "Go on."

"We have similar interests, Mr. Barnes, although at first blush they may not seem so. You went to Mexico to assist a friend in seeking the Avendaño manuscript. My goal was – and is – the same, although our underlying desires, objectives and methods may vary somewhat. You had been told that the search and ultimate recovery of it could lead to significant income for you through your further writings. My interest is to place the document itself on the auction market and to realize a thumping great profit from the sale."

He paused, thinking for a minute. "I'm interested in what you said earlier, Mr. Barnes. You said that your ideas come from within you. You gave me the impression that this is a trait unique to writers."

"No! Oh, no. Not at all. I cannot and do not lay exclusive claim to it. I can't. It is a trait experienced by all creative people ... especially those in the creative arts. Great poetry, beautiful paintings, sculptures in marble, stone, wood and metal that make the heart weep ... all of these, and more spring from the internal source – the subconscious. The same is true, I suppose, of computer software, although this may be stretching a point beyond bearable credulity. So, no, not at all. I'm sorry I gave that impression. It was not intended. But surely you must realise this."

"Thank you. In fact I do. I was about to explain how I knew about your venture in Mexico. As I told you, my company has a number of agents associated with it. We all are very close, and we work on a shared commission basis. Most of the agents live and work in various countries. They are placed in Europe, of course, China, and throughout the Far East, India, and various countries in Latin America including Mexico. Their job is to locate, and open preliminary purchase negotiations with the present owners. They are always on the lookout for, how shall we say, unsung works of art that look as though they have the potential to attract greater value in other markets.

"Whenever one of them finds something of interest, they tell me. Often I will travel to that place to see it for myself. It provides a useful second opinion, and usually my agents are glad of that. I can also assist sometimes in negotiating with the owner to buy it. Besides, it gives me the chance to get out of the office. I did so with respect to the Avendaño book. It is why I was in Mexico.

"Have you ever wondered why it is that people collect old things? Old furniture. Old paintings. Old books. Old coins. Old stamps. Often the older, the better. It is curious, is it not? People are avid collectors. So avid, in fact, that they become aggressive if they see that someone or something is standing in their way of getting what they want."

"Well, no, I haven't."

"Like any other business, the art world is filled with both idealists and pragmatists, as well as those whose souls are more venal than sympathetic. Perhaps you have found this in your own literary corner. The similarities are profound; the motivations familiar. But I believe there is a good deal more to it than the simple desire to own something of value."

"Oh?"

"Yes. Think for a moment of the profound affect that our modern world has on the psyche. And it certainly is attributable to the world we live in today. Consider, for instance, religion. No, I don't mean the bowing and genuflecting. Nor do I refer to the horrible things we see daily on television all done in the name of religion. I despise those whose twisted ideologies result in the killing, maiming and displacement of countless millions. No. Instead, I'm thinking of how the magic of the Scriptures was a permanent presence in the mind of earlier generations. The same is true of the knowledge of mythology, and the classics. How many today speak of these things? How many today can claim an intimate knowledge of them, and make intelligent reference to them in everyday conversation? Ask yourself when you last had a conversation for instance, with someone about Leda and the Swan."

"I'm not sure I ever have."

"These things have lost their grip on a good percentage of the population. They have been all but lost even to the wealthy and educated segments of society. Yes, even to them. The constant striving for personal wealth has replaced the need for the solace of the soul once made possible through the works of the artistic giants of earlier generations.

"Those who collect the works of those giants are the ones who can afford it. But they do it in their own attempt to stop time, to reverse the clock, to seize and hold on to a portion of the past, all in their abiding effort to become one with the past. They seek to attach their names to those portions of the past. Inevitably, such art works end up in museums and other collections. Thus it is the profound hope of such collectors that their names be firmly connected to such collections. And why? To ensure they achieve their own personal form of immortality.

"But there's more to it. A lot more. Not everyone can afford to collect. Yet, those who can't still want their own connection with the past. Whether they get it or not is a separate issue. They go to museums. In fact, they flock to them. Do you know that more people visit museums than attend sporting events? I wonder we aren't told about this by the news media? I suppose it's the vast sums that are spent to promote and hold sporting activities. To the narrowly focused mind, money is an attractive magnet – perhaps in some cases the only one.

"But what are all these people looking for? Those countless millions who flock to museums and art galleries? Some go out of simple curiosity. Many more, the vast majority I contend, seek an enrichment and fulfillment not easily found elsewhere. Yet even when they do go, there is the problem of language. Not spoken language, mark you. It is the language of faith and classical literature. These are the languages of artistic antiquity. These are the languages that are inherent in so many works of art – painting, sculpture, music, literature, you name it, that are at their core, that are the raison d'être for their very existence. And do the people who go to see them understand what those old pieces are saying to them? Perhaps not. And why not? It's from the steady erosion of understanding of the old motivations that stemmed from a broad-based knowledge and acceptance of the Scriptures and the classics. And by the way, this also holds true for those who do collect. Despite their wanting to connect themselves to history and to own something of marketable value, they may well have lost the ability to interpret the old languages."

DJ smiled a gentle smile and gracefully shrugged. He spread his arms wide, as if to acknowledge his understanding of the motivations he spoke of but had no real interest in them himself.

"As for me, and my colleagues, we have only a mild interest in collecting as such, and don't really want to end up actually owning such things. No. Our greater interest is money – making lots of money through the sale of such things. Oh yes, we do like to have nice things around us. Look around you here. You see some of the things I've picked up from time to time. But I tell you this: if someone were to make me an attractive offer for any of it, I'd let it go on the spot. It would have to be *very* attractive, though."

"DJ, as I asked you before, this is all very interesting, I'm sure. But I still don't quite see what any of it has to do with me."

He held up an admonishing hand. "Patience, Mr. Barnes, patience! It would soon become very clear. Let me tell this my own way."

I sighed and settled back in my chair. "Could I have more of that delicious coffee?"

"Of course!" He pushed a control on his desk. The door opened instantly and Lisa, the gorgeous young woman who had met me, came in. "Lisa, Mr. Barnes and I would like more coffee. And more of those excellent biscuits, please."

Lisa smiled, collected the tray with the coffee things, my empty cup and left. Within minutes, she was back with fresh supplies.

"Thank you, Lisa." She flashed a ravishing smile at both of us and quietly closed the door behind her.

DJ picked up the thread of the conversation.

"When we met in Mexico, I was on such a mission. I have two people – agents – in Mexico, and one of them had uncovered information about an old manuscript that was supposed to have something to do with the ancient Mayan language. I was intrigued. We'd never handled anything quite like that before. I did some research into the matter and found that there was a distinct lack of modern knowledge about it."

I perked up. "Did this manuscript have anything to do with an old monk?"

"It did."

"And was it purchased recently in Mexico, in the Yucatán, from an old man who lived there?"

"It was."

"Was the person who bought it your agent?"

"Yes. His name is Stanley Baxter."

"Not a Mexican name."

"No. He's from here. He prefers to spend his winters in Mexico."

"Smart man."

"A matter of opinion, I suppose."

"Why? You like these winters?"

"'Like' is a word I wouldn't normally use in this context. It suggests a willingness to accept, almost completely, winters. No, not like. I would say tolerate vicariously. I travel a great deal, as I've said. Being able to leave, even for a short time, breaks the drudgery of an onslaught of inclemencies."

"This document: what did Baxter do with it?"

"He brought it here to show me."

"Here? It's here? I'm surprised he was able to export it from Mexico. How did he get it out?"

"That's another story for another time. It was here. It's not now."

"Well, where is it?"

"We're not quite certain. We think it went to London. We think it's still there."

"London? You think? You're talking in riddles. What's the story?"

"When Stanley showed it to me, I saw at once how valuable it is. After more than three hundred years it's still in reasonably fine condition, you see. I told him I thought we should have copies made – for backup … insurance, almost. You see, the value is not only in its physical condition, its construction and its age, its contents are also of great value. I know a man in London. He is an expert copyist. I felt certain he could do the work."

"You mean a forgery?"

"No! Not at all! Copies, legal, independently certified copies."

"Right. Copies. So?"

"I rang the man in London. He agreed to do the work. So, I sent Stanley to see him. He took the document with him. He went over there several weeks ago, met with the copyist, and left it with him. The copyist said it would take several weeks. They arranged to meet again to see the finished work. During that period, Stanley spoke occasionally on the phone with the copyist. He wanted to keep track of how the work was going. The copyist kept telling him it was going well, but needed the agreed time. After several of these calls, he began to get quite testy. It seems he didn't want to be constantly interrupted."

"I can agree with that. I hate interruptions. Any artist would. When I'm writing I want to be left alone."

"Yes. Well, on the agreed day, Stanley went back to visit the copyist to see how the work was progressing. The copyist showed him what he'd done. It was still a work in progress, but to Stanley's eyes it seemed finished, perfectly exact replicas of the original. The copyist cautioned him to be patient. He said the curing process was not yet completed, and there were several other small things that still needed attention. Stanley showed some impatience. He wanted to take one copy with him that day, despite what the copyist had told him. The copyist is a perfectionist, and he refused to let it go before he was ready."

"Yes, I can understand that, too. I'm damned if I'm going to release a new manuscript until I'm good and satisfied it's the best I can make it."

DJ nodded. "Several days afterwards, Stanley called on the copyist again. This time, even though the work was still not complete, the copyist agreed to let him take one away – but only overnight. It seemed Stanley was quite anxious to have a chance to read the document, to see what it really contained. He assured the copyist he'd bring it back the next day. This seemed satisfactory to both."

"Wasn't the copyist taking a risk? I mean, isn't it possible Baxter could leave it someplace, or spill something on it, or whatever?"

"In a way, yes. But don't forget, in this case Stanley was – is – the client, acting on my behalf. So the copyist felt the request was reasonable. Stanley phoned me that night. He was excited. He said the copy was spectacular. Yes, that was the word he used – spectacular. It could easily pass, he said, for the original. The cost to the company was well worth it."

I waited.

"The next day, Stanley returned the copy to the copyist, and the man committed to continuing his work."

"And then?"

"And then? Nothing. I haven't heard from Baxter in several weeks."

"Oh."

"Yes, oh. I don't mind telling you I'm getting a more than a little concerned."

"I should think so. What about the documents? You must have talked to the copyist."

"Yes, I have. Twice. He has them. They're safe. He's told me they're now ready for delivery. Have been for several days."

"Well, if they're safe, what's your concern? Yes, I understand about your agent, but still … I get the impression he's able to take care of himself."

"True. But this is not like him. I've known him for years; this is quite out of character."

DJ paused, got up from where he had been leaning against his desk and paced back and forth in front of his office windows. He glanced out at the swirling snow under the heavy, leaden skies, but I got the impression he didn't see it. He seemed deep in thought.

He stopped, turned and looked straight at me. I had the impression he'd made a decision.

"Would you be willing to go to London? To talk to the copyist? I can't go; I've got two critical meetings scheduled for this week, and I'm due to go to Thailand on Sunday for three weeks."

"Why me?"

"Several reasons. You already know about this document ... something about it, anyway. And you do have a vested interest in it. Besides, I know that you have an increasingly ambivalent relationship with your two friends, Mr. Watts and *Señor* Bandilero's son. They, too, have an interest. But I must tell you, Mr. Barnes, that their interests do not fully coincide with yours. I would like to think that yours are more closely aligned with mine. You might almost say that I'm in competition with both of them, as they now are with each other. Or I was up to the time Stanley told me he'd bought the document."

"But now you're not, now that you have the document."

"Yes. I would like to believe so."

This puzzled me. He had it, so why should he feel he still might be in competition with them? I sat quietly, thinking about what he'd said. His mention of my interest in the Avendaño document was accurate – as far as it went. Yes, I suppose I was interested in it, but I had begun to wonder why. If it had any monetary value at all, that money would go only to the current owner able to successfully place it on the auction block. From what he has told me, it seems DJ is now the owner. So, was my interest only intellectual? Well, yes, it was. This whole venture was turning into a story. But the feeling was growing inside me, actually had been for several days, that this was more than just an old document. It was an historical artifact, an important part in the running fabric of Mexico's culture and history, a national treasure. If this proved to be so, I would be quite uncomfortable with it being in private hands at all.

And then there were Kevin and Pancho. Both desperate for money. Kevin had told me at lunch that day in Mexico City about the problems he's been having with keeping his family's estate intact. Maria had been quite clear about Pancho's proclivity for the gaming tables, coupled with his chronic inability to win. Added to which were his, admittedly only implied, associations with the highly lucrative drug trade in Mexico. She seemed to be suggesting he was in financial thrall with them. From what DJ had just said, it seemed he knew a great deal about those two, and I suppose in his mind I could be a more favourable and logical choice. From his comment I supposed that I was in competition with them, too.

I looked up at him. He had been waiting patiently for me. I was also thinking about Harry and Farnsworth. I asked slowly, "What would you want me to do there?"

"Talk to the copyist. Spend time with him, try to find out if he can give any thoughts about Stanley's thinking, demeanor, manner, his whole attitude about this thing. Maybe he said something in passing that could be a clue to what he was thinking or wanting to do or where he might go."

Grudgingly I conceded that this approach might help. "When?"

"Tomorrow, Thursday. The sooner, the better. I talked to the copyist two days ago; he's as puzzled as I am."

"Have you no one else who could go for you?"

"Unfortunately not. The only other agent I have who would have anything of value to contribute to this situation is in Mexico, and she, I believe, is currently unavailable."

I sighed. "Alright. I'll go. If anything, it'll give me another chance to get away from this foul weather for a time."

"You know, Mr. Barnes," he said musingly, "this document has the potential to command a significant price on the auction market. I do not see why you should not benefit from it with your participation."

It was a carrot gracefully offered – a carrot to reinforce my agreement. I looked at him for a long time, then slowly nodded. "Well, let's cross that particular bridge when – if – we get to it." Then the thought occurred to me, quite irrelevantly, that Kevin had still not paid me for my travel expenses – as he had said he would. I was beginning to wonder if he ever would. So, I said to DJ, "Alright. I'll go. Can you make the travel arrangements for me? Thursday will be fine."

He hesitated for a beat, then smiled and said, "Of course. Do you have any preferences?"

"Yes, the morning flight out of Pearson direct to Heathrow, and a small suite in the Draycott hotel just off Sloane Square. The rest I can manage for myself."

His eyebrows rose at my request. Whether from my being able to tell him immediately what I wanted, or from the likely expense of it all, I'd no way of telling. "Very well. Give me your email address, and I'll have the reservations sent to you."

"Yes. Now what is the name of your copyist, and how do I reach him? Do you have a picture of him, by any chance? What sort of person is he?"

"Reginald Binglethorpe. Reginald Sheridan Binglethorpe. If you want to stay on the right side of him you'll remember that he hates being called Reggie. If you want to get on the wrong side of him, that's the best way to do it. No, no picture. He's an odd sort of person. Brilliant in what he does, probably the best copyist in the western world. I can't speak for the East. Takes immense pains, fusses to distraction over every minor detail. He's a big, tall man, about sixty I think. He was married once but it didn't last. Apparently they're still good friends. He prefers living by himself, although I gather he has a cat or two about his home. He lives in, umm, Chelsea? Yes, Chelsea. A little mews house."

I nodded approvingly. "Not bad."

"Yes. But tread easily with him, and you'll get along well. Here: I'll give you his phone number."

He handed me a slip of paper. "Well, if there was nothing else …". I got to my feet.

"Just one small thing. Miss Alvarez is a most attractive young woman, is she not?"

I was startled by this apparent non sequitur, and I must have showed it. Recovering, I said, "Yes. Yes she is."

"I am aware of a liaison that is developing between you and Miss Alvarez, and of your little interlude in going with her last week to Akumal. A return journey for you, I understand. I am also aware of the events that took place while you were there. Also Cancun."

This got my goat.

"Now see here!" I said hotly. I was advancing towards him. "What possible concern is it to you that I went to Akumal? Sure, I've been there before, and yes, I liked it. And who are you to watch and spy on me like this? And yes! Maria is a lovely girl and yes! I'm becoming quite fond of her. But I can't imagine why you should have an interest in her."

He held up his hand to slow me down.

"I apologize if my methods seem somewhat mysterious. But I also fail to understand why your reaction is so aggressive. I have no interest or personal claim on Miss Alvarez, other than the fact that she is my other agent in Mexico."

Before I had the chance to respond, he stuck out his hand for me to shake, and said, "Thank you for coming, Mr. Barnes. I'll see that your reservations are sent to you promptly," and he guided me out of his office.

I shrugged myself into my coat. I needed to get moving as I would be meeting Harry soon. But as I prepared myself to leave, it did seem strange to me that Maria had never said anything about her connection to DJ.

Lisa smiled and said, "I'll escort you out, Mr. Barnes." I followed her to the lone elevator.

Chapter 26

Harry and I had arranged to meet early this evening. He wanted to quiz me about how I was going to finish my book to honour the advanced schedule insisted on by Jim Farnsworth. We were going to meet in the Golden Thumb.

Well, it seems I've committed myself once more. Harry's going to explode. But then again, I'd decided I wanted to see this thing through to the end, and I had the feeling that I would be seeing that end – one way or the other – possibly in London. It was nothing DJ had said. Rather, it was the body of small things that kept accumulating in my mind.

I trudged along through the swirling thickening snow to the nearest subway station. When I'd arrived Sunday the snow had all but disappeared, and now the city was back in the middle of it with this late-winter storm. Not unusual but a damned nuisance. Maria had told me she had been enchanted with the snow. And yes, to be honest, there were times when in the immediate aftermath of a heavy fall it was like a fairyland. I wished she was here now. I wanted to see her, talk to her, have her with me. I needed to call her, hear her voice. I was a little miffed I'd not heard from her. She'd been emphatic about wanting to be able to contact me. I stopped short in the middle of the sidewalk. A stranger, head down against the driving snow and not looking where he'd been walking, bumped into me. Behind me, I heard a muffled curse. I'd better call Frankie. There had already been several messages from her – some anxious or frustrated, others downright demanding. All in good time.

The Golden Thumb was just filling up as I arrived, and found our favourite table, and a waiter materialized beside me.

"What'll it be, Sam? The same?"

"Sure. And how about your special plate of mixed stuff? You know the kinds of things Harry and I like."

"You expecting Harry?"

I nodded, blowing on my hands.

The waiter was back in a few minutes with my glass of 'foaming ale' as I liked to call it, and a plate of mixed cold cuts, cheeses, vegetables and assorted dry biscuits. As I ate, I was thinking about DJ's story of the girl finding the old book, the *Religio Medici*. By one of those odd mental connections, I was reminded of something I'd read years ago by the – now – obscure 2nd century Roman Emperor, Marcus Aurelius. It was his twelve volume *Meditations*. I had none of the Greek in which it had been originally written, but had been given a good English translation of the set by my grandmother one birthday. It was a time when I was not an avid reader of such things, and it sat gathering dust on a lower bookshelf for years. In more recent times, my attitudes have shifted, and one day recently I picked up a volume at random and leafed through it. Several of the Meditations seemed somehow relevant, and one now came unbidden to me. '*Do not act as if thou wert going to live ten thousand years. Death hangs over thee. While thou livest, while it is in thy power, be good.*' Somehow, in the context of the issue with the Avendaño document, this one seemed particularly relevant.

I sorted through the offerings on the plate, selected some, sat back and waited for Harry.

He came thumping in, grumbling and trailing a cloud of snowflakes behind him. "I think it's changing to sleet. It's going to be a hell of a night for getting home."

He sat down and glared at me. "So? What's your decision?"

"Decision?"

"C'mon, Sam. The book. When can you get it finished?"

"You *are* in a bad mood. What's brought that on?" I wasn't going to give in to his bullying.

He slumped in his chair, taking a long pull at the scotch and water the waiter had instantly brought him.

"Oh, hell, Sam. It's been a hell of day. What with that session with Farnsworth this morning, and all the rest of it. That was just the beginning. You may not believe this, but every damn writer I spoke to this afternoon, the ones I could get hold of anyway, all told me they were going to be late on their delivery dates. I know writers are notorious for being late. That's to be expected, but this is beyond the pale. So, I'm hoping against all reason that you, at least, can do me a favour and honour your commitment. I told

Farnsworth I'd call him tomorrow morning. I've got to be able to give him something. It's in our interest just as much as his."

I could see that he was in no mood for playful backchat, and I had no need to needle him. So I said:

"I've worked it out, Harry."

He looked up.

"Yes. Most of it's written, and in pretty good form. While I was in Mexico, I worked out the ending. It had been troubling me for a long time. In fact, I've already pretty well blocked it out. It's maybe another five, six thousand words."

"How long?"

"Farnsworth said that other outfit is due to publish in May. This is now early March. You can have it by the end of March, definite."

He began to relax.

"Yes," I continued. "That'll give Farnsworth and his people enough time to do what they need to get it out by mid-April."

"B-but you said it's still in draft form. What about the editing?"

"Oh, that's okay. You should know me by now. When I say 'pretty good form' it's only because I haven't polished, scraped, honed and pared it down as far as I think it should go. But, I'll tell you this: if you were to read it today, you'd be satisfied. The final, what I call the endgame, like I said, is already blocked out on paper. Most of it's written in my head. It's just a matter of getting that down on paper."

Harry knew from his own experience with me that I was a fast, clean (more or less!) writer. He was looking more relieved by the minute.

"That's good, Sam, very good."

"Yes. I thought that would give you some peace."

"Waiter!" Harry waved at the 'thumb' who'd been serving us, and ordered more drinks. While waiting, we each chewed our way thoughtfully through the plate of snacks.

"Oh, yes. Did I tell you I was going to London?"

"What? When?"

"Thursday morning."

"Why? Does it have anything to do with why you went to Mexico?"

"Yes. I went to see an interesting guy this afternoon. He's in Yorkville. An art dealer, rather an unusual type. I met him in Mexico the day I arrived. I'd just checked into my hotel, and was having a drink on the rooftop patio. Before I knew it, this guy appeared at my table and sat down. He seemed to know who I was. I'd never seen him before. He had sought me out. He asked if he could have a drink, so I got him one. Odd person. He talked a lot, but it was all in riddles. He never said anything that made any sense. Then he got up and left. Just like that. But he did give me his business card. Here, I've got it with me." I fished it out of a pocket and handed it to Harry. "Then, when I arrived home the other night, there was this phone message waiting for me from him … well, one of his people, actually, inviting me to go and see him again today. So I went."

Harry took the card I showed him. "What was he doing in Mexico?"

"It wasn't clear until he told me today. He said he was helping to buy the old document I told you about. But I didn't know it at the time."

"He found it?"

"Yes. Or more accurately, one of his people did. Some guy who lives there all the time. They both came back here, but separately. Then the man who bought it, he's one of the agents of the person I saw today, was asked to go to London to get a couple of copies made."

"Copies? London? Why not here?"

"The best copyist in the world, apparently. Accurately done; legally certified to be true copies. That's the approach they needed to take."

"Sounds intriguing. Who's the copyist?"

"Someone called Reginald Binglethorpe."

"And you're going to see him?"

"Yes. At least, I hope to."

"'Hope to'? Sounds like a damned fool wild-goose chase again. Don't you have anything better to do? Like working on my book?"

"Harry! We've covered that. And since when has it been your book?"

"Just a figure of speech. Well, okay." Grudgingly. "Hm-m-m. Binglethorpe. Binglethorpe." Harry chewed both on a fingernail and on the name a few minutes. Then he snapped his fingers, and exclaimed, "Got it! Reggie Binglethorpe! Yeah, I know him. Well, I know of him. I read a story about him a couple of years ago. It seems to me he was involved with, let me see, wait ... yes, no, yeah, I know what it was. It was the time when old Giulio Sammartini died. Sammartini was the best there was. It was in Italy, he lived there. Trained in the Renaissance styles of manuscripts. He must have been eighty-five, ninety years old. He was still going strong, still taking commissions, turning out impeccable work. Then, one day, ffft!" (Harry snapped his fingers.) "Just like that ... he was gone. That's when Binglethorpe assumed the mantle. Yeah. That was it."

He looked at me. "When are you leaving?"

"Thursday. On the morning flight. It gets me into London at a decent time. The pubs are still open, and I won't have to deal with jet lag so much."

"Trust you to put an emphasis on the pubs," he chuckled.

"First things first, Harry. Always first things first."

"Yeah. Well, you better let me have what you've written so far."

"Well, no, Harry. I'm not going to do that. I told you: it's not ready for delivery yet. I won't let it go until I'm ready for that." I gave him a lopsided smile. "Nice try, though."

Harry and I have had this discussion several times before. With his memory, I'd expect him to remember. And he'd shown me time and again he had an encyclopedic memory. What do they call it? Eidetic? Then I saw him grinning back at me.

"Right. Look, while you're there, can you get me some more of those fabulous cigars? You know, like the ones a friend brought me back from that guy a year ago. You know the kind I mean?"

"Better tell me, so you don't accuse me of screwing up a simple request. How many do you want?"

"How about a case? They come in those nice wooden boxes ... different sizes. Get the biggest."

"Okay. Anything else?"

"Nope. That's it. But do you know where to go for the cigars?"

"Oh, sure. It's the same place where I get my tobacco whenever I'm over there."

"Right. You know London well, don't you?"

"Well enough; I've been there enough times. It's a terrific city. Always something new to do or see."

"Better than Toronto?"

"They're not the same. Two different cities; two different characters. Yet, many similarities, too. It's hard, though, to put your finger just on what makes the differences. They're both big, sprawling. Masses of people from all over the world, foods and cultures of every description. They're both great. But Toronto's my home. It's where I feel I really am 'at home', not only with a nice place to live, but deep inside me, where the idea of 'home' really counts."

Harry nodded. "Yeah, I know what you mean. I feel much the same. There are times when I need to get away, go someplace else, see different things, but I'm always glad when I know I'm headed back here." He glanced out into the darkening evening, made darker by the slanting, driving sheets of sleet. "Snow or no snow."

******

When I got home, I tried calling Binglethorpe at the number DJ had given me. I hoped to arrange a meeting with him. There was no answer, only a voicemail message asking me in the richest voice I'd ever encountered to leave a message and perhaps, at some point, he'd find a moment to call back. If he felt like it. It was the sort of voice reserved for those who wanted to be elevated to the Lords, or who might be looking for a knighthood. I shrugged, thinking this guy would get no farther than an occasional mention in the newspapers, and left a message.

"Mr. Binglethorpe, this is Sam Barnes calling from Toronto. I'm coming to London in a couple of days and would like to meet you. Can you call me back and tell me when I could see you? I got your number from a mutual friend." I left it at that, hoping there would be just enough mystery in my message to intrigue him into returning my call.

I next tried to contact Frankie, but again to no avail, and found that I was getting increasingly annoyed with her. Then I tried Maria. She hadn't called since I'd left her at the airport in Cancun, despite her insistence that we stay in touch, and I was beginning to wonder about her, too. Anyway, I left messages for both, and devoted myself for the rest of the evening to preparing to go to London.

Chapter 27

Just across the road from London's storied Tower, with its long history of many folk terrors, your taxi enters the shadow of Tower Bridge. It drives down a ramp into a secluded, genteel, cobble-stoned enclave filled with expensive low-rise condominiums, smart art galleries, restaurants, provisioners for pleasure boats, two marinas, and several narrow, attractive cobbled lanes. The marinas are home to a variety of well-heeled pleasure craft. Entering from one side of the enclosed, tree-shaded cobble-stoned square, you see on one side the Dickens Inn, busy and noisy with late-evening revelers. On another, a marina, with the tidal waters gently chuckling against the bows of safely moored craft. And on the fourth, you see a row of tastefully designed, cream-coloured townhouses, each looking very much like its neighbour; each in excellent condition.

The taxi drew up in front of one of them. I paid the driver, got out, and the taxi rattled off into the night. I stood in the dark tree-shaded square, looking up at the brightly lit windows in the cream-coloured façade of the house where I was to meet Reginald Binglethorpe. "A house-warming party," he'd said when I phoned him from the airport. "Just a lot of friends come to celebrate Frieda's new home." He didn't explain who Frieda was. I could hear the sounds of laughter and music through the open front windows. From the sounds I guessed the house would be full to overflowing.

I climbed the front steps. As I reached to ring the bell, the door opened and out spilled two men and two young women, all laughing and giggling, being careful not to let their full glasses slosh over their expensive party clothes. The suddenly louder party noise spilled out through the door after them. They pushed past me and ran down the steps into the dark and shaded square. The door was still open. I stepped in and looked about me.

I walked into the large well-lit entrance hall, closing the door behind me. Small light fixtures had been cleverly mounted near the ceiling on all the cream coloured walls and arranged so their light pointed up, but reflected down off the ceiling into the room in a warm, welcoming glow.

On one wall a large gold-framed mirror, strategically placed for a person to fix a hat or adjust a scarf before venturing outside. Beneath the mirror stood an attractive marble-topped table with a huge arrangement of fresh flowers in a large Chinese bowl. Beside it a large wall-mounted coat rack, right now overflowing with an astonishing variety of early springtime outerwear. More coats were piled in an untidy heap on the floor. The opposite wall was empty, leaving enough room for the constant flow of guests moving from the room on the right with the music, to the room opposite on the left. From somewhere else in the house came the tantalizing smells of different foods being prepared. I peeked into the room on the left: it looked like a dining room, but more importantly this is where the main bar had been set up. The hall floor was a checkerboard of white and black tiles. I dropped my coat on the pile on the floor, intending to go into the room with the music and laughter.

A large woman came flowing out of it to meet me. "Hi! I'm Frieda. You must be Sam. Reginald told me you'd be coming." She stuck out her hand. I took it and smiled at her.

Frieda? Of course! This was the 'Frieda' mentioned in the bio Harry had given me. Reginald's ex-wife. She turned and led me through. I admired her full head of lush red hair, which framed her pale oval face, hair that fell in long tresses to just below her shoulders. She was clad in a full-length, kind of wrap-around cobalt blue dress with long sleeves and the sort of collar line that clearly exposed the striking diamond choker she wore about her neck. On a short woman this outfit would have made her look dumpy and dowdy; on Frieda's five foot ten stature it was just right. I'm six feet and she came well up to my eyes. And yes, this was her home.

"Have you lived here long?"

"You like it? No. I moved in just recently; this is a house-warming party."

"Very much. Did you decorate it?"

"I did. I'm in the business, actually. I own my own interior decorating business. Just started a few years ago. It's been busy, busy, busy with new clients ever since. But I thought, this time, I'd like to try my skills out on my own place for a change. Come... we must get you a drink," and she led me into the room with the bar. She had an attractive contralto voice, warm and slightly smoky.

I followed her willingly. The seductive scents of food and sight of the bar had reminded me that I'd not eaten very much on the plane, and was still hungry. But first things first.

The barman gave me a glass of the dark bitter beer I'd asked for. I looked at Frieda enquiringly. She said, "No thanks; I'm trying to keep a reasonably clear head this evening. Come, I want you to meet some of my guests."

Among the music and the dancing, I was introduced to a bewildering array of pleasant men and women, all of whom seemed to be close friends of Frieda's. It was clear from their high spirits and general demeanour that the party had been well under way for several hours, and showed little sign of slowing down. I smiled and nodded and chatted amiably with each of them as the introductions were made, while Frieda and I drifted from group to group, adroitly missing the still-dancing couples. With those I didn't meet I exchanged vague smiles. The room was warm, and the air close despite the large open front windows that let in some fresh air.

"Are you hungry?" she asked and without waiting for an answer walked me towards the back of the house into a room where buffet tables had been set up. Even at this late hour they were still groaning with an astonishing array of hot and cold foods. She must have seen the look on my face.

She waved at the tables. "Help yourself. I must go and speak with the cooks for a minute, but I'll come back to bring you up to Reggie."

Reggie? The bio Harry gave me said he insisted on being called Reginald. DJ had said as much. He hated 'Reggie'. It seemed he makes quite a point of it.

I took a plate from the pile and selected a few things from various delicious-smelling serving dishes. I wasn't overly hungry, but needed something to satisfy the gaps left by a less than adequate reheated meal the airline had provided. It was all attractively arranged and displayed, and certainly more than enough to satisfy anyone. I wondered if Frieda had catered it all. It seemed likely after I'd caught several glimpses of the smartly dressed waiters and the waitresses in dark dresses with white collars and clean white aprons.

I was able to find a quiet corner to eat. It wasn't easy. I disliked wandering about a crowded room with a plate of food – too easy to drop or spill something, and too cumbersome to manage the fork to eat while holding the plate with a full drink balanced on one edge of it.

Frieda seemed a pleasant person. About forty-five, I would have thought. Energetic, kindly, thoughtful, very much at ease with herself and in control of her surroundings. Pleasant voice. I could see by the way the serving staff deferred to her that she commanded the respect that goes well beyond the fact that she was paying their wages. I liked her.

She approached me. "Ah! There you are. I thought we'd lost you." She pointed to my empty plate, "Have you had enough?"

"Yes, thanks. It was delicious."

"Oh, good. This is a new catering service. They've only just recently opened in this area, and I thought I'd give them a try. So … shall we go and find Reggie?"

"Lead on." 'Reggie', again.

From the outside, these houses seemed quite narrow, compact and introspective. It was a different story inside: the house gave a sense of spaciousness and depth. The cream coloured walls and the lush pale gold broadloom everywhere except the front hall contributed to this sense of openness and freedom. The heavy brocade curtains on the floor-to-ceiling windows added elements of comfort, solidity and permanence. Even with all the guests milling about, the house still felt very comfortable.

Frieda motioned me up the wide staircase. People were sitting on several stairs, alone or in couples, chatting away but beginning to show that stage in the evening when a party has reached its peak and beginning to settle down into those who feel they must leave, and the more dedicated ones determined to mine every last bit of value from free food and well-stocked bars.

Upstairs, we entered a large room. The floor-to-ceiling window design I'd seen downstairs was repeated here. These were covered in lush, red damask curtains, now closed against the night. The floor was covered with the same light gold broadloom. The room was furnished mainly with clusters of easy chairs and small tables and lit with a combination of table lamps and standing lamps, all of them on now. Opposite the windows were built-in bookcases, and set in the corner formed by the bookcases was a comfortable wing chair, table and table lamp.

A small cluster of guests had gathered about a tall, portly man seated in the wing chair. He was clothed in an elaborate bright red knee-length frock coat, creamy-white knee britches, and powdered wig. My first thought was that the Count Almaviva had stepped out of the last act of "The Marriage of

Figaro". From the coat's shoulders came the dull gleam of a handful of epaulettes. The coat would have done justice to any eighteenth century general, but instead he rather reminded me of someone taking a break from rehearsals for "The Pirates of Penzance" and had just stepped outside for a smoke. Its row of gold-plated buttons led the eye down to his spotless cream britches. His crossed legs displayed white cotton stockings, and shiny brown buckle shoes. His round florid face was topped with a thick unruly mass of white curls that had crept out from under the wig, and his bright blue eyes gleamed with merriment and gave the impression of harbouring a joke which no one else was allowed to share. I looked around at some of the other guests. All seemed to be dressed normally – 'normally', that is, for this sort of party. It certainly wasn't a fancy dress party. I'd not seen any other guests in fancy dress.

He was talking animatedly, his body still but his face and full voice alive with the amusing story he was recounting. Occasional chuckles and titters floated out from the group, more frequent as he neared the end of the story. Frieda nudged me forward into the group. Spotting me coming towards him, Reginald paused in mid-sentence.

"So," he boomed, "you're the writer fellow who's been telephoning me." He reached out a hand to welcome me into its midst. With a broad, ebullient gesture he pushed me gently into an empty chair opposite to await the finish of his story. As I sat, he continued with his story to the others. A short time later an explosion of laughter burst out, members of the group swaying in merriment. Still laughing, he waved them gently away.

Waiting for him to finish gave me the chance to study him. I immediately agreed with what Harry had said about Reginald being a 'raconteur par excellence'. He had found a copy of Reginald's bio in his files. It told me that Reginald was fifty-eight, divorced, owned a mews cottage in Chelsea, and lived alone. He was a bon vivant, a reasonable cook, enjoyed entertaining at home and in the better restaurants, had eccentric personal tastes, was a skilled copyist usually much in demand, politically neutral, and 'comfortable', bio-speak for a private income.

He looked at me. "Your glass is empty."

"Yes."

"Well, we'd better do something about it." He heaved himself out of his chair and dragged me up out of mine. He led me into the next room where the upstairs bar had been set up. His voice boomed out, "Fill this man's glass, and mine, too."

The white-coated young man behind the bar jumped to obey.

Our glasses filled, Binglethorpe led me over to a quiet alcove at the front of the house. We sat in comfortable chairs right up against the heavy damask curtains. But one curtain had not been thoroughly closed, and through the narrow opening I could see the windows that looked down into the open square. Pools of soft light puddled the square, evidence of the streetlights barely showing through the leaves of the tall trees.

As he settled into his chair I was still getting used to his flamboyant costume, and wondered if I should risk rudeness by asking him about it. Instead, my eye caught a glimpse of the pin he wore on his chest. I'd never seen anything like it.

"What is that pin you're wearing?"

"You like it? It was a wedding present from Frieda. She likes to visit the Silver Vaults. One day she spotted it in the window of one of the shops. She went right in and bought it. She presented it to me on our honeymoon while sailing the Greek isles."

It was about three inches long, and had at its top end what appeared to be a cluster of three feathers, each made from what looked like diamonds. He said it was known as a Royal Presentation stick pin, dating from the 1860s. Men wore full, elaborately-furled neckties in those days, and stick pins were used to help keep the ties from spilling out and overflowing the wide collars of otherwise impeccably dressed gentlemen.

"Why 'Royal Presentation'?" I asked.

"It was a conceit of the Prince of Wales of the time. He'd have them made up and gave them as gifts to favoured personal friends."

"Are those diamonds at the top?"

"Indeed they are. They're set into a pattern called The Prince of Wales Feathers."

I sipped my drink and nodded. It was interesting, but I was now beginning to feel the effects of the long flight, and didn't pursue it. I can never sleep on planes, certainly not on those overnight flights. But this had been the daytime flight when everyone else was awake. Even so, I really wasn't up to strenuous conversation right now. I'd only come here because it seemed the surest way of connecting with Binglethorpe. And now that I'd met him I was feeling I'd like to go back to my hotel and get some sleep. Maybe I could arrange to meet him tomorrow.

He noticed me beginning to slump, and nodded knowingly. "You must be tired."

I stifled a yawn. "I am. But I was wondering if we could talk about Father Avendaño and his document."

"Yes, of course. But can I suggest we not do it here? There are too many ears for my taste. Why don't you come around to my office tomorrow?"

It seemed a reasonable suggestion; so I agreed. He fished into an inner pocket in his frock coat and handed me a business card.

"Here," he said. "This is my address. Any taxi will find it."

I glanced at the card. He was quite central. I looked up at him.

"You're in a nice part of town."

"You know it?"

"Not very well, but I've walked around there. So, no problem about finding it. I'll take the Tube. What time should I come?'

"Shall we say eleven o'clock?"

"Fine." With that, I got up and prepared to leave. Then I turned back to him: "Do you think I could call for a taxi?"

"Of course." He got up. "Here. Let's find Frieda. She'll do it for you."

Shortly afterwards, a taxi pulled up to the door, I said my goodnights to Frieda and Reginald, and left. It felt as though they were bowing me out into the night; I suppose I must have made a good impression on them, but could not see why.

Chapter 28

London is well-known for its mews cottages. They can be found in various parts of the city. Many of them are clustered in the depths of Chelsea, that urban enclave sandwiched between the King's Road and the river. What used to be the long-ago barns and stables of larger homes have long since been converted into serviceable, practical and very private little homes. These are the sorts of properties that make real estate agents sit up and take special notice when a prospective client contacts their office looking for one.

Most of them are situated side-by-side, down obscure but attractive cobbled lanes. They form long picturesque rows, with their neat window boxes, flowering vines, and Grecian-style urns guarding their front doors, many filled with well-trimmed greenery.

Now though, in this early spring, after last night's chilling rain, it all still looked rather forlorn and washed out and sad.

"Only, of course now with spring more or less on the way, it's just beginning to lose the look of shriveled flowers and bare branches," Reginald told me as he took my hat and coat and hung them up in his tiny cupboard.

I nodded while looking past him into the interior of his home. The house had a comfortable, compact feeling. It reminded me of the elaborate dollhouses I'd seen displayed in a specialty shop window in Toronto. Everything neat and tidy: cut down to scale, all flowery and chintzy and solidly well mannered. It was just the sort of home I would have expected Reginald to have.

He led me through into his 'parlour', as he called it, but to me it looked like a normal living room, although rather low ceilinged. There was the flicker of a bushy gray tail as a cat quickly disappeared into another part of the house. There was an open fireplace on one wall, its flames cheerfully licking around the perfumed spruce logs he must have placed on the fire just before I arrived. The fireplace wasn't an Adam, but from its attempt to look old, I supposed it might well have passed for one. One of the less elaborate ones. In front of the fireplace two large, overstuffed upholstered easy chairs flanked an equally comfortable looking two-seater sofa. All were covered in the same expensive flowered chintzes, similar to what I'd seen once when strolling through Peter Jones, the large department store not so many miles from where I was now standing. The large Anatolian carpet had a woolen pile thick enough to muffle any footstep. I thought it might have been a court carpet from the Hereke factory. It was large enough to reach out to conceal almost all of the highly polished pine floor that peeped around the edges on each of its four sides. Potted tropical greenery reached towards the off-white ceiling from planters in various corners of the room, though it was not big enough to conceal the built-in bookcases on either side of the fireplace. A polished round mahogany table and four matching chairs stood by the windows that overlooked a small courtyard at the back. I imagine this is where he ate most of his meals. A tall, dark rosewood drinks cabinet stood in the corner beside the doorway to the small kitchen.

"What would you like to drink?" He seemed rather agitated but was trying hard to hide it. I decided to ignore it.

"It's a bit early for me. Could I have some coffee?"

"Yes, of course."

He disappeared into the kitchen. As I sat down in one of the armchairs, I could hear him clattering about making coffee. To make conversation, I said,

"Frieda seems a nice person."

"Yes." I thought he sounded rather non-committal. He stuck his head around the corner of the kitchen opening. "We thought it would work … our marriage, I mean. But Frieda's a very strong-willed person. I am too, for that matter. And our interests were quite different. We could see early on that it wasn't going to work. So, we came to an amicable agreement." He disappeared back into the kitchen, and said no more.

When he returned with the coffee he sat down on the sofa opposite me, and said, "So, now you have come to learn about Avendaño."

"Yes. Harry Oliver told me you might know something about this man."

"Oh? Who is Harry Oliver?"

"You don't know him?"

"No. Should I?"

"Well, he seems to know something about you. I thought that since he told me about you, it stood to reason you'd know him."

"Apparently not."

"Mr. Binglethorpe, as I told you last night I'm a writer … a novelist. Harry is my agent in Toronto. He's also a relation, as well as a personal friend. In other years, he'd done some writing himself … for a small country newspaper. One time he did a story about the differences between forgers and professional copyists. There were references to you in his files. He has an admirable memory, and when he and I met the other day, he remembered about you right away. But I had also supposed that while he was writing his story and doing the research, there would have been some contact between the two of you."

He raised a hand in minor protest. "Please, call me Reginald."

I nodded.

"No, I've had no contact with him. I wonder where he got his material?"

"I don't know."

"Ah well. In any event I hope he told the truth about my skills, and put me in a good light."

"Mr. Bingl…er, Reginald, I've known Harry a long time. He's an honest man."

"Well!! That's refreshing! In my business people are not widely known for their honesty or forthrightness. Perhaps I should like to meet this Harry of yours sometime."

"Harry's a man of eclectic tastes and interests."

"This is an odd business that I'm in," Reginald continued. "It's all too easy for careless people to call me a forger, which is something I most certainly am not. And I have the certificates and credentials to prove it." His voice hardened. "But still, there are those who don't want to listen – or who won't. They prefer mischief to facts; ideology to truth; their own view of life to the realities of the world. Why, I can't say. A problem with human nature, I suppose."

I nodded. "Perhaps you could tell me a bit about your work." I *did* want to know more about Avendaño, but I didn't want to deflect him from this other important subject. All in good time..

He brightened. "But, of course, my boy! I'd be delighted." He drank some coffee. "I don't know how much you know about me. I am a member of the Royal Society. My professional training was many years ago at the Royal College of Art." He gave a discreet cough. "If I may be permitted a small moment of personal pride, I will tell you that I graduated with some of the highest honours ever awarded an arts student. They loved my work. In fact, examples of my early works are still on display in their Students' Gallery." He gave himself a quiet, modest smile.

I asked, "What are they of?"

He held up a finger in tacit warning. "Nothing too extraordinary. My masters at the school didn't want me producing works that someone could come along and take away with them without approval, hoping to make a killing in the nefarious markets. No, no! My early works were copies of copies; copies already so widely available in the public domain and accepted by the public that no one would bother giving them a second glance."

He picked up his mug of coffee and blew on it. "The purpose of my work is straightforward enough. I make copies of well-known works of art – always under contract. In the usually accepted sense, this means paintings. Most would prefer to hang something on their walls that has the look, feel and texture of a painted picture, instead of a mere framed photograph. I satisfy this desire. And I am well paid for it."

"But isn't that forgery?"

A pained look darkened his face and he raised his eyebrows as if in mock despair at my naivety. "My *dear* boy!! Forgery? Not at all! I run an honest business. Consider the many copies of the Mona Lisa that still hang today on buyers' walls. They were made in the 16th and 17th centuries – when copying famous artworks was a thriving business. No. For each commission I provide the client with two verifiable proofs of genuine copy. One is a small addition to the work itself, one which I make exclusively known only to the buyer. I take pains to point these facts out to him while at the same time comparing my work to the original. He can readily see what I show him."

"And the other?"

"A signed, independently notarized certification confirming a legitimate, contracted-for copy."

"You seem to have covered yourself well."

"Those earlier copyists could do no more. And so I should. The art world is slippery enough without actively inviting trouble. For instance, I won't do works of French origin."

"Oh? Why not?"

"The French authorities are very touchy about people copying the works of their native sons, especially the dead ones. Anyone buying a copy, no matter how legitimate it may seem, no matter how much they might have paid for it, runs the risk of the having the work destroyed – deliberately. This is a certainty when and if the buyer decides to send the work for authentication by the authorized committee for the artist concerned. A lot of it has to do with the principle of protecting the artist's heirs. They deem the copy as being an infringement on the artist's work."

"Destroy the painting? Seems a bit extreme, don't you think?"

"I do. But that's the way it is. The owner can sue but he won't get anywhere. He'll just be sending good money after bad. The French law is among some of the strictest in the world. They have a right to destroy the work under something called 'the moral law of the artist'.' There was a case last year about a Marc Chagall painting. Perhaps you read about it."

"Hmmm, no, I don't think so."

Reginald continued: "Never mind. Well, I won't expose a client to that sort of business. While I said my work was straightforward enough, it really doesn't explain any of the complexities I face in every new commission. But I overcome them. It is why I typically do much better than my competition."

"Competition? Do you have much?"

He bristled. "Charlatans, all! They can't hold a candle to my work!"

"Yes, Harry did mention something about the mantle passing to you when Signor Sammartini died."

A look of gentle respect filled his face. "I studied under him," Binglethorpe said quietly. "He was like a god to me; he could do things with paints that I did not know were possible. He was arrogant in his mastery of the subject, yet oddly gentle with me. He must have seen the talent in me; I can only assume so. I loved that old man. It was a love built on respect for his talent, yes, but even more on his ability to draw me out, to teach, to show, to demonstrate, to explain. He gave freely of himself, yet was jealous of his position in the art world. He knew there were countless others intent on diminishing his reputation. Jealousy again. He constantly fought against those forces, and was usually successful in protecting himself. Yes, he was a god to me." He paused, then brightened.

"And yes, he did tell me I was the best he had ever tutored. I was flattered, of course. But also wary. I knew of others in the field who were well regarded, whose names and works were treated with great respect. But, when Giulio died, those others suddenly did not seem so good; it seemed that the industry, such as it is, was turning to me."

I nodded. "And they still feel this way?"

He shrugged good-naturedly. "Yes. But as I told you, there are rivalries, professional jealousies, attempts to one-up me. I take it all in my stride. For I know, I *know* I am the best!"

I let it go. Instead, I wanted to know about the Avendaño document, so I asked him, "But the Avendaño document isn't a painting. You said you did paintings."

"That damn book! It's one of my more unusual commissions. Not exactly in my usual line of country. I only took Jones's commission because he's brought me business before. But it has been a challenge for me."

"Oh?"

"Oh, yes!" he said with considerable feeling.

"You mean it's difficult?"

"Yes! And in more ways than one."

"How so? You called it a book. You mean copying a book was difficult?"

He looked slightly offended. "Difficult? Oh that! No, not at all. It was just a matter of finding and assembling the materials. That was a minor challenge, and not an insurmountable one. Just about everything I was able to find right here in London. Then, while I still assembling the materials, I'd also had the opportunity to examine the original. I saw at once how straightforward my work would be. The construction was not complex. So, no. But, it was that wretched man that DJ sent over here to me."

"Man?"

"His agent. The man who brought me the book to copy. So, DJ described him to me. Stanley Baxter. I'd never met him before. Bright red hair falling over his eyes; splotchy freckles across his pale white face, a leer instead of an honest smile; a handshake like a cold, dead fish. A most unpleasant person. I knew from the beginning we'd not get along. He was demanding; overbearing; insisting I work in a certain way. I had to tell him in no uncertain terms that he was quite wrong, that I had no intention of following his instructions – that I would work according to my own rules to meet the commitment I'd made to DJ. He didn't like that. No, not at all. We had words, I don't mind telling you. Serious words. It was very vexatious for me. I had to give myself a stiff drink after he'd left."

"How long did he stay?"

"Too long."

"No, but how long?"

"I don't really know. It felt like ages." He paused. "In retrospect, I don't suppose it was more than half an hour or so. He'd told me what he wanted me to do. Four copies; not the two that DJ had ordered. I told him that's not what DJ had requested. He said that he'd talked with DJ and they'd changed their minds about the number of copies. He said it with an air that made me suspect he wasn't quite telling me the truth. I don't think he'd cleared it with DJ at all. But, I shrugged, and told him I'd need to reconfirm this with DJ before starting work. His manner changed – quite dramatically. It was a mixture of rage, anger, sheepishness, slyness, coyness and, it seemed, a desire to try and get me on his side. He oozed false charm. He said, 'No. Don't talk to DJ. Do the two for him, as he requested. But I want two for myself.'

"'Why?'" I asked. 'For friends, as gifts. They're both interested in these sorts of antiquities.' I could see all the time he was hedging."

"But," I offered, "this could be a valuable object. It could be worth a lot of money. I thought DJ's interest was to put the original on the auction market; he only wanted the copies to show as sales examples, to create some prior interest before the original went to auction."

"Exactly," said Reginald. "Its potential value is enormous. I can only hazard a guess at thousands and thousands, possibly hundreds of thousands. I'd actually heard half a million."

"Dollars?"

"Pounds."

I thought for a moment. Then, "Why do you suppose Baxter wanted extra copies?"

"Judging by his obsequious manner, I'd hazard a guess that he wants to pick up a little something extra for himself."

"Are you going to make the copies for him?"

"I'm not inclined to; I suppose I might. I've been working on the ones for DJ so far. But then again, I'm not sure."

"Why not?"

"Well, there are the ethics of it for one thing. Baxter's not my client. Also, much of it has to do with payment of my fee. At first, Baxter said nothing to me about his paying me; he said I should talk to DJ about it. Then later he suggested he would be working at ensuring my fee would be paid. He talked about how he was going to talk to some people about showing them the copies he wanted me to make for him."

"Sounds like a scam to me," I offered.

"It does rather, doesn't it?"

"Has he been in contact with you lately?"

"That's just it. This was all a couple of weeks ago. Then, after we'd argued, I told him we'd better just communicate by phone, so I could report progress on DJ's copies to him. He agreed. Reluctantly, I thought. He called regularly after that, every few days. Then, out of the blue, he appeared on my doorstep again."

"When was that?"

"Yesterday."

"Did he explain why he was there?"

"He was a different person this time. Not demanding. Agreeable, polite, smiling almost to the point of obsequiousness. He asked if he might take away one of my copies. He said it was to show someone who might be interested in buying the original. I thought the request a bit strange but, since he was acting as DJ's agent, I agreed to let him have one. I also decided to contact DJ to tell him of this."

"And did you?"

"No, damn it all. I've been frightfully busy since then, and haven't got around to it yet."

I pondered this. Then: "Do you know if the document is genuine? It seems to me this would be important to establish, given that DJ wants to place it in open auction."

"Yes. The issue of provenance. It was the first thing I thought of. DJ had told me that it would be almost impossible to prove provenance. The story he got from Baxter was that the old Mayan had had the book in his family's possession for decades ... centuries. But the old man had no idea who had made it, or what the circumstances of its manufacture had been. All Baxter could do was try to confirm ownership. He brought a letter to that effect. Still, it left us all on somewhat shaky ground. Not a very comfortable position to be in, is it?"

"No. So, what did you do?"

"There's another aspect to this; rather an important one. At least, I feel that it is."

I looked at him. "Oh?"

"Yes. Do you know what paleography is?"

"I've heard the word, but that's about all."

"Then let me explain. In its own stuffy way, the dictionary defines it as the study of ancient forms of writing, including the determination of origin and date. Decipherment is also a central issue. The subject is also of peripheral interest to philologists – those people interested in the study of language. Taken broadly, it's all rather interconnected. In my own experience, I've expanded this to include documents of any kind that are more than a hundred years old. This is a rather arbitrary determination on my part, but I've been told by those in a position to know it's not too far off the mark. It can be any sort of old written material. The subject is as much a science as it is an art. One of its purposes is to establish whether or not a given document is genuine, authentic. There are various techniques available to the paleographer for this."

"You mean, carbon dating?"

"Well, yes, there is that. Even though carbon dating is not an expensive business, it does require access to the right sort of people with the right sort of equipment. It also requires the irrevocable destruction of a piece of the document. A small portion to be sure, but something nonetheless. No. I've dabbled in paleography for several years. But I'm sure you know that a little knowledge can be dangerous. I knew just enough about the subject to know I didn't know enough. Not for something like this. As it happens, I know an expert in the field. He's a professor of archeology at London University. He's also a member of the Royal Academy. He has thirty years of solid experience. He spent a number of years attached to the Universidad Iberoamericana in Mexico City. He has written widely on the subject of old documents, a particular hobby of his. I approached him, and asked if he'd be interested in having a look at this document. He was very interested, so much so that he was keen to start work on it right away. We met one afternoon, here – I wouldn't let the document out of this house – and he pored over it. He also knows a good deal about seventeenth century Mexico, an added bonus. So, he was able to subject the document to various tests, none of which would cost DJ a penny. I felt it was an appropriate thing for me to do."

I said: "But surely he'd want a fee?"

"Oh, he did. I paid him from the fee DJ agreed to pay me. It wasn't a lot, considering."

He paused, thinking. Then shrugged and smiled thinly. "I suppose though, DJ will want to obtain other expert opinions as well. If he can."

I thought this last was an odd thing to say.

"What do you mean?"

"Oh," he gave a weak smile and waved a dismissive hand. "Nothing. Just an idle thought."

I still though it odd, but did not press him. "What were the tests?"

"Oh. It's a matter of what they call internal and external evidence. Comparing the manner in which the text is written to other sources created at about the same time and location. Examining the materials that were used to produce the document and comparing them in the same way. For instance, how does the written Latin align with the Latin that was commonly spoken at the time? Does it contain words or phrases, or colloquialisms that conform to the times in which the document is claimed to have been created? Or consider the ink that was used, and the writing instrument that was used. Research would be needed to first identify what these materials actually were at the time. The next step would be to compare, chemically if necessary, the materials used in the document with what the research had revealed. And so it goes. The wood used in the outside covers. The goatskins used to cover the wooden covers. The method of treating the skins before usage. Even the perceived age of the document. Yes, it's all quite an involved process."

I nodded in understanding. "And was your friend able to reveal anything of interest?"

"Professor Simpkins, a most thoughtful and thorough man. We've had several good times together at Academy functions. Yes; after several days of study he said he was ninety-five percent convinced the document is genuine. He was certain enough to feel compelled to write me a letter confirming his analysis. He said this document reminded him of another book he'd examined. It came from a slightly later time, about 1730. It was beautifully hand painted, every page, and covered in goatskin. He'd looked up the auction price, which came in at close to half a million pounds. Personally, I think the Avendaño book has greater historical significance, and therefore could be worth a lot more."

I gave a slow whistle. I was beginning to see why people like Kevin, Pancho and DJ had such an interest in the Avendaño book.

"But I don't understand. Why is such a high value placed on these things? They're old, and probably not in very good shape."

"But that's just it, my boy. It's the age in them that makes the attraction. It's also quite possible this is the one of its kind in existence. Unique. And there is something else."

"What?"

"Have you ever wondered why people collect things? Especially old things?"

"Well, no. I've always taken it for granted that some people like to collect stuff."

"Yes, yes. But it's a good deal more than that. I have a theory."

"What?"

"Certainly, the money is a factor, often the most important visible one. The most obviously apparent one. But I wonder how many collectors realize that they're responding to an inherent cultural draw ... a need, almost. Inherent in each one of us is the impulse to connect with the past. Not just the amorphous past, but the people and their many activities of years, centuries, ago."

"You may be right. DJ said much the same thing to me. Only he put it in different terms."

"How did he express it?"

I recounted the gist of that part of the conversation I'd with DJ that snowy afternoon in his office.

Reginald nodded, rather sagely I thought, but seemed no longer interested in pursuing the notion.

I asked: "Are you satisfied with your friend's assessment?"

"Absolutely."

I pondered this, wondering about the other five percent. Instead, I asked: "Can I see what you've done for DJ?"

"Mr. Barnes, what is your interest in this document?"

I had been wondering when he would get around to asking me this. If our roles had been reversed, it would have been one of the first things I'd have asked him. But I said,

"Purely intellectual. At least, that's the way I see it now."

I could see he was puzzled by this. Here was a man who dealt in the treacheries of the art world. It was this experience that caused him suspicions beyond a mature person's normal skepticism. He had said it himself; his world was filled with charlatans, and perforce he was obliged to navigate his way carefully through them all if he had any hope of retaining his own carefully-built professional integrity. "I don't understand."

"It's simple enough. An old friend contacted me several weeks ago. He told me of his interest in locating an ancient Mayan document in Mexico. He asked for my help, and in exchange would make it easy for me to write the story for future sale. Once I got to Mexico, and met him there, the whole scenario had shifted away from any beneficial involvement for me, and more towards his complete ownership of the project."

"Some friend!" Reginald interjected.

"Yes. I suspect it was his motive right from the beginning. Why he needed to involve me remains a mystery. In any event, there I was on the ground, and his subversive attempts at screwing me made me determined to see what I could do on my own. Besides, I was in a place that had nothing to do with the foul winter I'd been experiencing at home. I did some nosing around and one day, more by accident than design, stumbled across a man who claimed to know a good deal about the document, although not much about Avendaño. As luck would have it, later that same day I was called back home to deal with an issue my publisher had raised, one which my agent, Harry Oliver, felt I should be on hand to help resolve.

"I took care of that problem, but in the meantime DJ had asked to see me. Did I tell you I'd first met him only a few weeks ago? It was in Mexico City. He approached me… I still don't know why. Anyway, he asked me to go see him in his office. This was Tuesday, two days ago. I went to see him, not sure what to expect. He told me a lot about his business and how he conducts it. During the course of the conversation, he mentioned one of his people had actually found the document in Mexico and had brought it back to Toronto. The two of them subsequently decided that copies should be made. I assume they contacted you for this, or DJ did anyway. The rest I suspect you already know."

"Most of it, yes. But you haven't answered my question. Why are you here about the document?"

"Oh that. Simple. DJ decided he needed someone to come here to find out more about what was happening with your work."

"Humph! He could have called me."

"Yes. Well, anyway, he couldn't come himself: other commitments. I understand he's travelling right now. And he had no one else in his group he could send. I think he asked me to come almost on the spur of the moment. I suppose he felt he could trust me to give him a true report. I don't know why he felt this way."

"You didn't ask him?"

"No. By that time we were discussing flight schedules and hotel bookings. And to tell the truth, I'm involved enough in this whole business already that I want to see it through to the end. I wanted to come. Besides, I like London."

"Most commendable," he said, somewhat wryly I thought. Then, "Do you know London well?"

"Well enough. I used to live here when I was younger. And I've come back often enough over the years."

He nodded, and drained the rest of his coffee. He heaved himself out of his chair. "Well, then. Come upstairs with me. Let's go and see what all the fuss is about."

With that, he led me up to his combination office and studio. On entering, I saw a large, open, well-lit room that seemed to take up the entire second floor. In the middle stood a large worktable. Lining the perimeter walls were shelves and counters, and built into them were cabinets and cupboards designed, I supposed, to house all his files and work tools. Mounted high on one wall was an air-cleaning unit.

This was a much more utilitarian room. It contrasted starkly with the comfortable, cocoon-like atmosphere we'd been sitting in downstairs. Under the carefully placed ceiling lights, I saw the wide variety of tools and materials that were scattered in cheerful abandon about the counters and his worktable. Yet I also suspected he knew exactly where each item was, and could put his hands on any one without a moment's thought. He had struck me as a man thoroughly set in his ways.

He beckoned me over to the big central table. It was crowded with an impressive array of specialized supplies and tools. Only a small space on the edge was left for working. It was near where he stood.

"Surprised?" he asked.

"Astonished. Do you need all this to copy the document?"

"Most of it, yes, although some it's for other projects I'm working on." He waved at the cupboards under a window. "And more in there, for this project. But come: let me show you the work I've done for DJ."

Near his elbow were what looked like two books, each about two inches thick and measuring roughly the size and shape of a typical telephone directory. He paused a moment, studying them, then pulled one towards him to show me. It was closed. He tapped the top cover. It sounded woody.

"Yes," he said. "The covers are wood and tightly bound in goatskin. You can see where I've had to damage the sewing around the edges and there in one corner to reflect the damage done over the years to the original."

I looked closely, and saw what looked like gut stitching that had been worn away. I wondered how he did it.

He lifted the cover to expose the contents. With both hands, he lifted the whole book, raised it high over his head, and took away one hand. The contents cascaded to the floor. They were not in separate pages, as I had been imagining, but it was one continuous, fan-folded sheet. He called it accordion-style folding.

"You see how he made it?" explained Reginald. "The material is known as Amati paper, very expensive, and quite hard to come by. It's

253

made from the bark of fig trees. They carve it carefully from the tree, stretch it out in the sun to dry, and then afterwards coat it both sides with a thin layer of paste from limes. This toughens the bark, and makes it easier to write on. This process was developed in medieval times, and used extensively into later centuries until the printing press finally came into its own. Although I have to say that books made this way, from these materials, were not in common circulation. No, indeed, they were intended only as tributes to those in power, political as well as religious leaders. From Avendaño's perspective, it was the perfect material. He had been granted permission by his bishop to make the book in the first place. This meant that he would be obliged to present a copy to his bishop as a tribute to His Grace's generosity."

"Generosity?"

"Generosity of spirit. More likely political expedience. But the generosity of showing a willingness to grant Avendaño leave to work on the book, in addition to his regular duties of converting the native Mayans."

Carefully, he refolded the entire book and laid it on the table, leaving the front cover open. He invited me to look through the book, page by page. If it had been an ordinary book, it would have contained less than one hundred pages. As I leafed through them, it became much more clear what the book actually contained. On the left side of each page was a column containing the now familiar symbols of the high Mayan hieroglyphic language. On the right side, in a second column with the texts carefully lined up against each symbol, was its Latin translation. Ever since I'd first heard about this book, or document as I'd been thinking about it all along, I'd never been entirely clear what it was or what it contained. It had been variously described to me as a 'treatise', a 'compendium', a 'dictionary', and a 'grammar'. Now that I had it in my hands, or at least what Reginald claimed was a true copy, it was obvious that it was at once both a dictionary and a grammar.

Some of the writing was hard to make out. It had been what looked like being painted on the pages with a sort of brush or feather with a not too fine point. The instrument's point seemed to fray quite often and needed to be sharpened or fine-tuned with a sharp knife. There were blotches of ink dotted here and there in the writing, making it even more difficult to read. The script, or font as we would think of it today, combined both thick and thin brushstrokes, and reminded me of the curiously shaped runic writing so familiar to readers of modern fantasy novels. The Latin was of the seventeenth century, making it a challenge to read. Despite this, I could see that in most of the entries opposite the Mayan symbols there was what appeared to be a direct translation, as well as some text that could be either a longer definition, or instructions for grammatical usage.

I turned to him, feeling the joint emotions of amazement and respect. "This is an extraordinary work of art." He beamed at this. "And do you mean to say you've done all this by hand? In the few weeks since you got the original? It's amazing."

He assumed an air of quiet pride. "Yes. It's true. The longest part was copying the hieroglyphics. They have to be rendered just so, or else their meaning can be lost – or mean something entirely different. I had the original open all the time, being careful not to get any gesso or ink on it. Now that would have been a true problem."

"Can I see the original? I'm curious to see the differences between it and what it is here."

His face fell. Again I saw the agitation return that I'd noticed earlier. It was if his whole manner, his whole being had crumpled inside him, and now he seemed just a tired old man with nothing to live for.

"Oh, my dear boy! Didn't I explain? I can't find it. I don't have it. It's missing. I still can't believe it. It's gone!"

The shock of his words hit me like a tidal wave. I had been anticipating so much to see the actual document that this news had even more devastation. "Gone? What do you mean, gone? It can't have. Don't you have it here, somewhere? Maybe you've just misplaced it." Then, more thoughtfully: "How could this have happened? Are you sure it's missing?"

"I'm positive. As to how, I can only speculate it was that wretched man again. He came to see me two days ago. We were upstairs, right here in my workroom. As I told you, he had told me he wanted to take one of my copies to show to an auction dealer. I don't know which one. He claimed DJ had asked him to do this. While he was there, I had already wrapped up a copy in preparation to lend it to him. But just then, I heard a knocking on my front door, and so I went downstairs to see who it was. I was back in than ten minutes, but on the way back upstairs I met him coming down. He said he was late for an appointment and had to leave. I showed him to the door, and closed it behind him.

"I had several other things to do that day, and again yesterday, and then Frieda's party last night. I was out of the house for a good deal of that time. It wasn't until earlier this morning, just before you arrived, actually, that I thought I'd have another look at the original. It was only then I discovered it was missing, that one of my copies had been put in its place. I was keeping the original in a cupboard, here, under the table. It wasn't supposed to be very secure; I just didn't want it to be too obvious."

There didn't seem much to be said after that. His dismay, plainly visible, was no greater than mine. We both felt loss. His feeling of loss was acute, while mine was only marginally less so. He had accepted a commission which he could not now fulfill. Worse, he was now technically in breach of contract – a problem for anyone doing serious business. As for me, I had been curious, interested, to see and touch the original document. I'd been living with this notion for several weeks, and it had been gradually growing on me. Now the opportunity had been snatched away. My feeling of loss was born of disappointment.

Beyond that, I had discovered that in the short time I'd known him, I liked Reginald. I'd not been sure when I first met him last evening at Frieda's, but now I was feeling that in him was something of a kindred spirit. I suppose it happened when he told me of how he structures his commissions, and goes about doing his business. It seemed very crisp and businesslike. I began to think I'd like to try to help him recover from this loss.

I saw plainly what I suspected when I first arrived – his agitation was now painted all over his face, and his body language told more clearly than words how stressed and upset he was. At the door, my coat on, I reached out to shake his hand to thank him for his hospitality. I told him:

"This is a bad thing for all of us. Maybe you'd better tell DJ. In the meantime, let me help. Maybe I can think of something. Perhaps the two of us working together might prove a better chance of getting it back."

He nodded wanly. "I'd appreciate it. Nothing like it has ever happened to me. But I just don't know how you could help."

"Neither do I, right now. But let me at least give it a try."

"But what can you do?"

"I'm not sure – yet. We're both upset right now. Perhaps when I think about it more calmly, something will occur to me. I'll let you know."

Morosely shaking his head, he said: "I don't what you can do."

As I walked out the door, I repeated: "Neither do I. But you never know."

He closed the door behind me.

Chapter 29

It had stopped raining. An insipid watery sun worked hard to show itself through the clouds. It was just after the noon hour; there were several good pubs within easy walking distance from Reginald's home. I quickly found one I'd been in before.

I paid for a pint of bitter at the bar and settled into a comfortable chair at one of the several empty tables. Most of the lunch crowd had gone back to work. I took a long satisfying drink, then pulled the tablet out of my bag. After it woke up, I saw there was an email from Maria. It looked like a long one. Finally! I thought. Maybe she'll tell me why she's been so silent since I left Mexico. I began to read.

'Dear Sam:

'It's been awful. And I feel awful. I've been wanting to write to you for days. I no sooner got back home than I discovered my father had suffered a heart attack and was already in the hospital. I've been with him just about constantly since then. He's holding his own, but the doctors say it's still too soon to predict any outcome from this. All I can do is sit with him, hold his hand, and try to be the daughter to him I've always wanted to be. I've never liked hospitals; they make me feel very uncomfortable. I don't know why. But I've been told there are many people like this, who have an unreasoning fear of disease, medicine, death, and all the trappings and procedures that make up the professional medical community. So I suppose I am just one more like that. Despite this, I owe more to my father than I do to my fears, and so I stay with him as much as I can during the visiting hours, and when he is even remotely conscious to know I am there.

'But there has been another problem, one that in its own way is just as serious. A friend told me that Manuel has got himself into trouble … serious trouble. It has something to do with the people he's been dealing with. I was afraid something would happen to him, and now it has. He was badly beaten a few nights ago. Something about drugs and money he was supposed to have paid to them. I don't know all the details. And do you know what? I'm not sure I want to know. He and I have been together for several years, but as you know, or I guess you suspected, we've been drifting apart in recent months, and it's been mainly because of his activities. I know he needs money … lots of it, but I've told him many times he was playing a dangerous game. So now he, too, is in hospital here in Mexico City, a different hospital from where my father is. I suppose I should go to see him, but again, I'm not sure I really want to. I'm a compassionate person (as you well know!!) but there are some things I'm not sure I can bring myself to do.

'All this to say I'm so sorry I've not been in touch with you before now. I feel awful that I've been so silent. Our days together last week are a joyous, happy memory for me, and the passion we shared was exquisite. Is that the right word? I feel it is. You have made me feel whole again, Sam, and I am more than grateful for it. I've only told you a portion about me, as you have with me, and there are other aspects of my life I feel I want to share with you. I look forward to the time when we can be together again for me to do this.'

I was surprised and softened by the intensity of her words, her emotions. I was still trying to come to terms with how I felt about her – and not to mention my increasingly ambivalent feelings about Frankie. Whom, I recalled, I had not yet heard from since before I went to Mexico more than two weeks ago. Perhaps she was trying to tell me something. Perhaps Frankie was sending me a message that was loud and clear, and perhaps I was too dull not to be hearing it. Frankie and I had had long silences before, and maybe this was just one more, prompted by whatever influences were pressing on her. But then, perhaps I just didn't care as much anymore. I shrugged, took another long pull at my drink, and returned to Maria's letter.

'When I met you the day you arrived in Mexico I had little idea our lives would become so entwined. Nor, I suspect, did you. Although, on second thought, perhaps you did. I could feel it when you took my hand. I liked it then. I like it even more today. You have been good for me, Sam. Good to me, and good for me. I'm experiencing a sense of freedom I've not felt for years, not since the time I left that man in England, the one whom I married. I told you about him: but it's a chapter of my life I'd sooner forget and put behind me for good. I'm also feeling a release from Manuel. Yes! I know he's been a good friend of yours. And, no! I don't want to do anything that would harm your friendship. But he and I have had our own issues, none of which have anything to do with you. It is happening, Sam. I know it.'

Which, I reflected, left the ball firmly in my court. It was a sensation I'm not sure I was ready for. Suddenly it seemed all the relationships were unraveling. Me from Frankie. Maria from Pancho. Me from Kevin. And also, it seemed, me from Pancho. Vacuums were being created and, as we all know, nature abhors a vacuum.

But how would it, they, be filled? Despite my ambivalence, I knew I wanted to see Maria again. And from the tone of her letter, it was evident she wanted to see me. This was reinforced by what she wrote next:

'But what I also wanted to tell you is that I am coming to Toronto. Some people I know there have asked me to come. They said there was some urgency about my being there. But it will depend on how my father is doing. I won't leave him until I am more sure that he will recover. Right now it's too uncertain, but I'm hoping that by this time next week the doctors will be able to give me a better idea of how he's doing. So once I know more, I'll write you again and give you the details about my travels.

'Sam, I *do* want to come. I'm so excited at the prospect of seeing you again. Oh Sam, I want to see you so much. I hope you do, too.

'Love you. I mean it.

Maria.'

That's right, I thought. And I think I know who those people are. Or, at least one of them. This was more than simple coincidence. It was DJ who had told me that Maria was one of his agents. She had been with me that day when we'd heard the story from Nelson Zengotita about how the Avendaño document had been kept, recovered and sold. In DJ's office he had told me about how one of his people had bought the document, and carried it to Toronto. Now Maria tells me she's been asked to go there, too. It all was beginning to fit. Or so I conjectured.

I drained my glass and had the bartender give me another. While he poured it, I glanced over the lunch menu and told him what I wanted. He nodded, and handed me the full glass. I paid for both and returned to my seat.

So now, I was faced a small dilemma. Reginald had asked my help to recover the original document. DJ had asked me to trace Baxter. Both were, I assumed, still here in London. But Maria could well be in Toronto in a few days' time. I wanted to do both, but was not sure how much time I'd need to remain in London to help track down the book – if indeed I ever could!! I had only the vaguest idea of where to start. It was to speak to DJ, but I was less than clear what he could tell me, or do for me while sitting in his Toronto office. No, wait. He told me he had to travel: to Thailand, and he'd be away for several weeks. He was likely there now. He would, however, be available by email.

Then there was the news about Pancho. It was shocking. The tone of Maria's letter made it serious. I knew I should contact him. But again, ambivalence intervened. The last time I'd seen him was that late afternoon with Kevin. I knew they were both up to something, and that they didn't want me to know about it. Pancho had disappointed me. Kevin too, for that matter. There was as yet no proof, other than their conspiratorial behaviour. I felt released from obligation to either of them, which had made the trip to the Yucatán all the sweeter.

And yet, and yet. Pancho was still my friend. I owed him at least the human gesture. He was in hospital, suffering from who knew what sorts of injuries. I resolved to ask Maria for his contact information in hospital.

Taking another bite out my sandwich, I pulled the tablet towards me and replied to Maria's letter.

My Dear,

I'm so sorry to learn about the troubles you've been having, and especially about your father and Pancho. When the time is right, please tell your father that I am saddened by the news, but that I am encouraged that – as you say – he is holding his own. Tell him I wish him a speedy and complete recovery. Also, may I ask you to relay to him my sincere thanks for his grace and hospitality for the time he gave me when I visited him last week. He's a kind man, and I'm sure he went out of his way to make me feel welcome.

Could you give me contact details so I can write to Pancho? I understand fully your feelings about hospitals; I've not experienced it, but I empathize with those who do. I know it's not pleasant. I'm in England right now and think at the least I should send him an email. Even if I were in Mexico, I'm not sure I would go to visit him. At least, not until he was released back home.

I'm delighted you're coming to Toronto. You say it could be as soon as next week. This is wonderful! And yes, I understand it depends on your father's progress. I think of you often. The few days we spent together are a bright memory at a time when my life was becoming more complicated. I don't know how long I'll have to be here, but I don't think it'll be too long. I think I should be finished what I'm doing here in a few days, and then I can fly back to Toronto and hope to be there in time to greet you.

I look forward to it very much.

Love ... I mean it, too!

Sam.

I looked over what I'd written before sending it. On the re-reading, it seemed rather cool and flat, and did not disguise my ambivalence towards Pancho. It certainly went nowhere near conveying the flood of emotion I felt when I'd read that I would soon see her again. It was one of those heart-stopping moments that seem to colour the rest of the day. And with her news, my day had suddenly become a lot brighter.

I'd known it from the moment I first saw her. There was an immediate connection between us. It struck me like a thunderbolt. Win, lose, or draw: I knew she was the one whom I would defend against all competition. How did I know these things? How could I be so certain? Words were inadequate to describe this assurance. It defied all logic. Yet in my bones, in my very inner being – in that dark, warm, secret place where each of us lives, I know, I *know* that she was the one. The one with whom I would gladly share all my worldly goods.

I was in love with her. It's a confession I'd not been sure I could make to myself, given my innate independence, a state I'd guarded jealously for years. Where had this come from, I wondered? Not only that, my feelings now were in stark contrast to what I felt whenever I thought of Frankie. With her it was a different sort of relationship, and despite the years we'd known each other, there still was that indefinable distance I could never quite understand or overcome.

Yet, cautious soul that I am, I also knew I'd best be somewhat careful at this stage. It's one thing to have soul-searching face to face conversations with a special person. It's another matter entirely to send a soulless message across the Internet. It's far too easy to misinterpret an email – no matter how carefully it's written. Besides, my Spanish is not yet good enough for written thoughts, and I perforce must use English. Conversely, Maria's English, while much better than my Spanish, still had not yet gained the authority of confidence inherent in a native speaker. At this early stage, I wanted no misunderstandings, and hoped fervently my message would go through 'clean' to her.

I clicked 'send', watched the message disappear, and wondered how long it would be before she replied.

Now, another message – this time to DJ. I'd need to take care how I composed it. I had no intention of telling him about the missing document, nor of Reginald's suspicions that Baxter might have taken it. Yes, DJ would need to know, but I'd prefer that the news come from Reginald. I thought for a few moments, then wrote:

Hello DJ,

I've just finished a most interesting meeting with Reginald Binglethorpe. He showed me the results of the work you asked him to do, and I must tell you I am astonished with the high quality of it. I'm sure you will be pleased. I'd like to talk to Stanley Baxter, as I have some questions about the provenance of the document you and I discussed. Reginald gave me his mobile phone number and as soon as it's convenient, I'd like to meet him here in London. Finally, I expect to be back in Toronto sometime next week.

I hope your trip is proving successful, and I look forward to meeting you again once we're both back home.

Regards,

Sam Barnes.

Which, by a round turn, brought me right up against the issue I'd been pondering since Reginald told me about the missing document: whether and if I could make contact with Stanley Baxter, and what I would say to him if I ever did.

I pulled my mobile from a pocket and dialed the number Reginald gave me. It rang several times, then went to voice mail. I cancelled the call without leaving a message. I felt I'd have more luck if I contacted him cold, instead of giving him advance notice through voicemail.

I still hadn't worked out what I would say to him. Or how he would react. What was clear though was the need to recover the stolen (yes, I had begun to think of it as stolen) Avendaño document. This man, Baxter, had no legal right to it. He had been entrusted by DJ to carry it to London, and place it in Binglethorpe's hands. That is where his commission should have ended. Instead, he gone beyond the brief DJ gave him. Twice, in fact. Having Binglethorpe make two additional copies, regardless of how he intended to pay for it – if he ever intended to, was a move that could well weaken DJ's chances of making good profit from selling the original. It might even ruin them altogether. And stealing the book from Reginald was beyond the pale. While I had no particular interest, one way or the other, in protecting DJ's interests, I was nevertheless offended by this man's actions, and I'd feel better to see things put right.

I gave a casual wave to the bartender as I left. The sun had broken through the clouds and I decided to walk. There was a hint of spring in the air and, while it was too soon for the blossoms to emblazon the fruit trees in the parks, the first crop of spring bulbs, daffodils, narcissi and tulips was already in full bloom. Even the grass had shed much of its patina of dull winter brown and was returning to the more welcoming warm weather greens.

Here I was, in the middle of one of the world's great cities: a city I'd fallen in love with as a teenager and had never got over it. I might as well be taking advantage of it now that I'm here. I had little else to do, other than contacting Baxter. Until I'd done that, my time was my own and I decided to make the most of it.

I'd been strolling my way through Kensington Gardens and Hyde Park, stopping briefly to pay homage to a childhood memory at the Peter Pan statue. Now I was nearing busy Marble Arch corner, with the choice of walking along Oxford Street, dense with traffic and the ant scurry of the afternoon shopping hordes, or taking a brief walk along Oxford Street then cutting through the side streets to the nearby Wallace Collection in Manchester Square. Once before I'd visited that impressive collection of French eighteenth century arts, most of it from the court of Louis XIV. But on that occasion, my time had been limited and I'd resolved to return as soon as I could. Being in an introspective mood, I opted for the Wallace Collection.

To get there, I needed to walk a short distance along Oxford Street before turning off at the corner anchored by the massive bulk of Selfridge's department store. As I strolled along, dodging hordes of pedestrians, I took in the scenes of street life. In the doorway of a clothing store, a cluster of three teenage girls, each with her hair dyed in pastel shades. One girl sported predominantly green hair with yellow streaks. A second had red and green streaks, while a third was in purple and orange streaks. A fourth, just joining the trio, had her hair cut so short her skull was showing through. In the street was the usual jam of traffic: two rows of red double-decker buses, eastbound and westbound, groaning and rattling their way, nose to tail like families of elephants crossing the veldt. An endless stream of taxis, their diesel engines grinding slowly along, decked out in all their modern multi-coloured hues, stopping frequently at the many pedestrian crosswalks to let the hordes of shoppers cross. A street busker, with a piano keyboard slung from his neck, working his way through a tune, while his companion fingered his way plaintively in clarinet accompaniment. A wizened little man, in grey ski jacket and red Tam O'Shanter wool cap, selling roasted chestnuts from his blazing brazier, the nuts packed in little brown bags.

Farther along I glanced into the large picture window of a busy coffee shop. Two middle aged men huddled at their table in dark conspiracy over their coffee cups. An older, careworn woman, a restaurant employee, steadily removing the large filled plastic garbage bags from the receptacles the customers used, and replacing them with fresh ones. Alone at another table, an older man in flowing white hair and dark glasses sat munching his way through a hamburger and soft drink. Three dust-stained outdoor construction workers, prominent in their fluorescent traffic vests, were taking a welcome break from the cold and damp. A homeless person, in loosely patched and tattered overcoat, furtively huddled in a distant corner of the restaurant, carefully nursing his coffee, using the cup to warm his chilled hands.

I was approaching Selfridge's, the impressive department store that anchored this end of Oxford Street. I looked at the corner of the building and stopped. Someone bumped into my back, and cursed quietly. "Sorry," I muttered, automatically. But my eyes were fixed on a familiar figure standing beside the department store, window-shopping through the large plate-glass windows.

'No,' I thought. 'It can't be.' As I drew closer, I found that it indeed was. I crossed the street and stopped beside him.

"Hello, Harry. What on earth are you doing here?"

He turned to look at me, an impish grin lighting up his face. "Oh, good. There you are. Surprised?"

"That's putting it mildly. Yes. And there *you* are. But I don't understand why. You might at least have called me to let me know. Where are you staying?"

"Call, and warn you I was coming over? Not a chance. I decided I'd better buy my cigars myself: I didn't want you screwing up what I asked you to get. I'm not staying anywhere. At least, not yet. I just arrived this morning. Been walking about, just enjoying being here. Where are you staying? Maybe they could give me a room."

I told him where I was staying, and suggested we both go there soon to get him checked in. "But I think I'd better call them now to let them know."

"Okay."

I called the hotel and requested a room for Harry on the same floor as my own. Within minutes, they gave me a confirmation, but asked that Harry be there before 6pm to sign the register. I conveyed this request to him.

He waved his hand airily. "Oh, sure. That's no problem. Let's go get the cigars now, and then we can have a glass or two before going to the hotel."

"I had planned to go the Wallace Collection today. It's not far from here."

"Sam, my boy, I didn't come all the way over here just to go and look at old furniture. We'll go get my cigars."

And with that, he started walking in the direction he thought the cigar shop was. I reached out a long arm and pulled him up short. "Where are you going?"

"I told you. The cigar shop."

"That's not the way." I pointed. "That is."

"Oh. Oh well, I suppose you do know your way around here."

"Harry, it doesn't become you one bit to act the hillbilly. I know you've been here before."

He smirked. "Just testing."

"Oh sure. C'mon, stop playing the fool."

I did indeed know where the shop was. "It's a long walk. We'd better take transportation."

"A cab?" He sounded doubtful.

"In this traffic, it'd be midnight before we got there. No, we'd best take the Tube."

"Okay."

It's the same shop where for years I've bought pipe tobacco whenever I was in London. Before me, my father had had his supply shipped to him each month. He once took me there, and to my young child's senses it revealed a new world of wonders of essences and aromas. The shop was low-ceilinged. The shelves in glass cases ranged along two walls groaned under the weight of identical glass jars, each with its own unique tobacco mixture. In an adjoining smaller room, fitted with humidity controls, were cases of cigars. The tobaccos came from all over the world: Virginia, Turkey, Syria, China, and more. It was like entering an ancient spice shop. The medley of aromas was intoxicating and seductive. The tobacconist, Edward Covington, a man with a scrawny neck encased in a high white collar, used his large but oddly delicate hands to mix the special unique blends demanded by each of his many regular customers. A finely-tuned copper balance scale held the place of honour on the polished wooden counter, and on the scale, the tobaccos were carefully measured out, according to each client's personal recipe. Along a third wall stood a floor to ceiling glass case, filled with displays of expensive pipes and smoking accessories.

Covington's was located in the eastern reaches of the City, that square mile of London that is the mecca of the money men drawn from the four corners of the globe. It is housed on the lower floor of a 17th Century church reputed, although never quite proven, to have been designed by Christopher Wren. The arrival of the shop in the church dated from the time when the ecclesiastical authorities had come face to face with the hard realities of falling revenues, and perforce admitted among themselves they must consider drastic changes if the ancient building was to be kept in even reasonable repair. In those distant days, smoking was still socially acceptable. Today, not so much. But then it was an easy choice to invite the proprietor of a popular tobacco shop, whose lease on premises in a different part of the City was about to expire, to relocate to their basement.

It proved a great success. Sales increased. Loyal patrons found their way to the new location. This pleased the church elders. Their contract with the shop stipulated that, in addition to the nominal monthly rent, a defined percentage of all sales would accrue regularly to the church. Perhaps they imagined that this might even have a positive affect on attendance at their Sunday services.

Even today, with the downturn in popularity of smoking, sales had managed to hold steady, supported by a loyal clientele who had seen the decline in convenient, comfortable smoke shops, and realized that there was still at least one stalwart who continued to buck the downward trend.

Harry's eyes bulged when we entered. He moved silently from case to case, studying the contents and relishing the flavours in the shop's atmosphere. Once he'd completed a full circuit of the room, he eased himself into the walk-in humidor to commune with the cigars on display.

Edward Covington stood behind his counter, silently watching Harry as he made his way about the displays. He turned to me. "Mr. Barnes. So good to see you again. Will it be your usual recipe?"

"Please, Mr. Covington. A pound this time."

"Very good, sir. And what about the other gentleman? What would he like?"

"Harry. Come and meet Mr. Covington."

Harry emerged from the cigar room, his face aglow. I introduced the two men, and they entered into a thoughtful discussion about the various merits and drawbacks of all of the cigars available in the shop. Throughout this exchange, Mr. Covington, with the skill born of long practice, continued preparing my recipe for me.

"Yes," he was saying to Harry, reaching for a glass jar on one of the high shelves, "we received a new shipment from Havana last week. They're beautifully made. It's the same brand I sold to Mr. Barnes last year. Were they for you? Did you see them in there?"

"They were terrific. No, I didn't. Where are they?"

"If you can manage to wait a few minutes while I finish Mr. Barnes's order, I'll take you in there."

"Sure, sure. Take your time."

We spent the remainder of a congenial hour in that inviting environment. The combined perfumes of all the tobaccos in that showroom was heady, and the display of antique pipes was fascinating. It was more than just a shop; it was a museum and emporium in the finest traditions. We each reveled in it, ambling about, looking at all the fascinating things in the cases, but by the end of the hour we'd seen enough. We collected our purchases and bid Mr. Covington a pleasant good afternoon. I thought I saw him breath a discreet sigh of relief at that, guessing that he probably wanted to close up shop and go home.

It had begun to rain again; a slow, drenching, chilly drizzle of the kind that guaranteed you would be quickly soaked to the skin if you stood out in it long enough. We promptly searched out a nearby pub, and joined the other late afternoon drinkers.

We settled at an empty table, and I said: "Okay, Harry. Now suppose you tell me the real reason you're in London?"

"Well, Sam, I'll tell you. I've been wanting, needing actually, to come over here for some time. And why? It's to meet some Brit publishers. They have access to markets that we don't in Canada, and I want to expand some of the offerings of some of the writers I have in my stable."

"Am I one of them?"

"Sure! Or, you would be if you'd finish that damned book."

"What about the others that are still in print?"

"Oh, sure," he waved his hand airily. "We'll cover those, too."

"If you can." I suppose I sounded dubious.

He clapped a hand on my shoulder. "Don't worry, my boy. I have great powers of persuasion."

I nodded. "When are you going to see them?"

"I've got all the meetings set up for tomorrow. Three of them. All in the same afternoon. That way, I can get back to Toronto the next day. My flight's already booked."

"I think I'll be staying for a while. I'm meeting with a private detective tomorrow morning. I'm still trying to find out what's happened to the Avendaño book. It must be still here in London. DJ in Toronto told me about him. He asked me to make contact. I don't know what good it will do, but I'd still like to try." I drank some beer. "Why don't you come with me? I don't know if it would help, but I don't see the harm in it."

He shrugged, as if to say, Well, why not? "Okay. What time are you going to see him?"

"Eleven. I don't know how much we'll learn, but I doubt the meeting will last more than an hour. Maybe less."

"Sure."

"He's supposed to be very good. I've never heard of him, but DJ told me he has a crack team of experts working for him. Computer technicians. History buffs. Several with fine arts degrees."

"Sounds high-powered."

"I s'pose."

The bar was filling up now, noisier and more crowded with that warm, frenetic chatter that comes at the end the work day. We looked at each other as if to agree we should leave. Harry already had a couple of scotches in him and was beginning to nod off. Jet lag catching up with him. "C'mon, let's get out of here."

It was still raining. We flagged a taxi and had the driver take us to the hotel.

Chapter 30

Promptly at eleven the next morning, we were ushered into the inner sanctum of Billy Strange, Private Investigator. He was speaking energetically on the phone as we entered and waved us to the two chairs in front of his cluttered desk.

The Strange Agency is housed in a nondescript low-rise office building just off the Strand, not far from the Law Courts. He finds it convenient, he said, when one of his clients is being prosecuted. He may be called to give evidence. The agency occupies a full floor in the building. Its open space is filled with portable cubicles, each self-contained and occupied by an even mix of young men and women, all of whom are minor geniuses in their respective chosen fields of detection, security, computer technology, and fine arts. Billy Strange occupies a tiny corner office with glass walls, making it possible for him to monitor the activities of his staff.

Strange was a thin wizened little man, and by his voice as he spoke on the phone, I took him to be a cockney, that breed of irrepressible English born within the sound of East London's Bow bells. He appeared ancient, but let on to us later that he was "just 40". I took him at his word. As we entered, his head was enveloped in a smog of cigarette smoke, and even as we watched him on the phone, he deftly lit a new cigarette from the glowing stub end of the old one. Squashing out the last of it, his manner suggested he wouldn't be too much longer on the phone.

While we waited for him to finish his phone call, he used a hand to flap away some of the pall of grey smoke around his head, making it easier to see him more clearly. He had pale yellow hair that was too long for neatness. It lapped over his shirt collar at the back, and had an unruly curl in front. He was clean-shaven, revealing a thin, bony face that was not wearing very well. He wore what appeared to be an inexpensive black serge suit that hung on him at odd places, and made me think it had been cut by an inexperienced butcher. His white shirt was in need of laundering, and when he shifted position in his chair, the shirt revealed a somewhat frayed collar at the back. His electric blue tie was of the sort that suggested he bought ties by the dozen at one of those deep discount clothing shops. By contrast, when he stood up later to see us out, I noticed his black shoes were polished to a guardsman's mirror finish, and looked as though they had been handmade on a bespoke last, carved to his specific measurements. He gave the overall impression of an energetic ferret.

He finished his call, and half stood to lean across the desk to shake our hands. The initial courtesies over, he waved us back into our chairs and launched into a short marketing spiel extolling the high and varied virtues of his agency. Harry and I glanced at each other, bemused, then sat back and let the information flow over us. When we had reached the point where we felt we could just about take no more, Strange shifted gears to discuss the Avendaño book.

"Mr. Jones has given me my brief. We spoke on the phone yesterday, and he followed up with a written contract by email. We've agreed the scope and payment arrangements. He states his objective is to recover the document. He is less clear about what should be done about Baxter. The brief remains rather sketchy on this point. He gave me the general outline of what's transpired, but I'm sure there's more to it all. So, Mr. Barnes, what more can you tell me of this problem?"

I gave him of the gist of my meeting in Toronto with DJ. I recited the details of my conversation with Reginald Binglethorpe yesterday, giving it to him in chapter and verse. I concluded by favouring him with the benefit of my own thoughts: "I don't know this Baxter. There's no proof that he did take the book; I have this only as hearsay from Binglethorpe. And, even if he did take it, I don't know why. Right now, it's all speculation."

He frowned over this for several minutes, then proceeded to read us the benefit of his experience. "The secondary art auction market in London operates within a limited scope, although more are trying to break into it. But this should not be taken to mean it's not important. It is also very busy. The principal players are here, and in the main are well known to us. Dealers from all over Europe and the South Americas come regularly to buy. Often for reasons nefarious. They know they'd be more successful in getting a better price. That market is also highly lucrative, sometimes more so than the major houses. Great amounts change hands with considerable regularity. Frequently valuable pieces make their way into private collections, where they stay hidden for many years."

He paused to light another cigarette from the depleted butt of one that had just dropped an inch of ash on his jacket. Carelessly brushing away the ash, he continued, "Your man Baxter is now known to us. It is only a matter of time before we land him, and the book. And, by the way, Mr. Barnes, it is clear that he did take the book when he bought it from that old man in Mexico. If he took it then, he felt a sense of ownership. He carried it to Toronto. From his viewpoint, it has only been lent to Binglethorpe. Why would he not want to reclaim it as his own?"

"Because he turned it over to DJ in Toronto, at DJ's behest. Because it was the same DJ who used him as agent to bring it over here. He was just the messenger. Now it's DJ who uses me as agent to try to get it back."

"Quite so. But he may not have seen it that way. No. Mr. Barnes, while it may not be supported in law, there is sufficient circumstantial evidence to suggest he now has the book. That's the basis we're working on. We hope eventually to have firmed up the evidence so that it *would* be legally supported – should we decide to take it to the courts."

It was clear the Strange Agency was staffed with competent, accomplished people. We must have looked suitably impressed.

Harry asked, "How did you manage to get on to him?"

Strange pointed through his glass wall to his employees in the cubicles. "Two of my staff have already interviewed the key players I mentioned. They are very accomplished interviewers. Beyond those, we have his phone number and a description. But Baxter is stubborn, and not readily amenable to revealing the location of the book. Now we know his intentions, and can find him again when we need to. He still believes he can sell the book for a thumping good price. Our objective is to disabuse him of this notion."

"And recover the book," I offered.

"Yes."

"Can you succeed?" Harry again.

"Of course! We haven't lost a client yet."

It was a weak joke, but I took this to mean that DJ would get his book back. Although how this would be accomplished, and what he intended to do with it remained less obvious. Yes, I know he'd told me he wanted to put it up at auction, and perhaps this was still his intent. But the more I thought about it, the more ambivalent I was beginning to feel about the whole idea of selling what was, after all, an important cultural treasure. I was beginning to think that it should, in fact, be turned over to the cultural people in Mexico.

As if he was reading my mind, Strange offered a parting thought. "Incidentally, Mr. Barnes, DJ asked me to mention to you that the Mexican authorities are interested in speaking with you."

"To me? What do they want?"

"It seems they think you might know something about the Avendaño book."

"Who are these authorities?"

"I'm told they belong to a department of government ... Mexican government. The Department of Heritage was mentioned, but I'm not sure if that's correct."

"Oh, yes? And how do they plan to meet with me?"

"Again, I'm told that a couple of men from that department will be going to Toronto next week – to see you, among some other things. Some sort of conference, I understand."

"Don't know what I can tell them, but I've no objection to meeting them."

"Splendid. Perhaps I should let Mr. Jones know."

"Never mind. I'll talk to him myself. I'm returning to Toronto tomorrow."

Harry must have looked surprised. I turned to him. "It's okay, Harry. I can't do anything more here. This meeting with Mr. Strange has convinced me of that. I'll book the same flight you're on."

Chapter 31

The usual pile of mail waited for my return. One envelope had familiar handwriting. I slit it open and sighed when I read the opening paragraph. It was inevitable. I had been thinking that it would be only a matter of time, so her letter today came as no surprise.

'Dear Sam,

'I've tried to think of the right way to tell you this, but each time I started to write it just wasn't coming out right. I've tried to contact you by phone; you never answered. I considered sending you this by email, then decided you would be more certain to get it if I sent it by hard copy mail So, here it is. Vancouver is a lovely city, and I've decided to move me and my business here. I've written to all my employees to tell them, and we're sorting out all the issues about moving, both for the business and for them. Some want to stay in Toronto; others show some interest in coming out here.'

Out here. Interesting. It means she's still in Vancouver.

'But moving the business is not the only reason. I've met a man here who is everything I ever dreamed of. He is wonderful!!! And I can't imagine my life without him. Those times when I came back to Toronto were terrible for me; very hard. Hard for many reasons but mainly because I couldn't talk about him – or us.'

I assumed the "us" meant she and this guy.

'I've known for some time that things were not right between you and I. This goes back to even before I met Gustavo. Often, when we were together, you suddenly weren't there for me. I could see you and talk to you, and you talked to me – but you weren't there.

'When we first met, I felt as though all my birthdays, Christmases and the joys of new spring times were happening all at once. The joy I felt was unbounded. Our separations were torture, and I couldn't wait to be with you again. I'd never felt that way before, even though I'd known several other men. You seemed to me all the strengths of character and integrity and forthrightness that I'd been seeking all my life.

'It lasted well. But, what happened, Sam? Why did it fall apart? I've searched within me and have not found very much to describe or account for what has happened to us. So, while I hate to say, I can only conclude that the failings – most of them anyway – must have been yours.'

Looking at it logically I suppose it made a certain sense. But she was only partially right. Relationships depend on the combined strengths of both parties. True, the actions of one can often outweigh the balance, enough to cause the split. Yet those same actions often have their sources in the other person. One doesn't usually cause the split unilaterally. The latter day equivalent of death by a thousand cuts.

'I know I've led an interesting life. My father trained me to be independent; it was that independence that has contributed much to my success in my business. I know you were glad for me, and supportive of me, and not too demanding for the times I had to travel away for my business. And you must also know that I appreciated your support, very much. Possibly more than you ever suspected.'

And so it continued for another three pages. She asked if she could come to get the personal things she'd often left at my place, and wanted to know when I could get my own things I'd left at hers. She hoped this did not come as too much of a blow to me, but she also suspected that it wouldn't hurt me too much – if at all.

'You will always be a dear friend. But my heart belongs in another place. Will we ever be fully friends again? I would like to think it, but you must provide the answer. If I have hurt you, I am sorry. Sometimes our dreams match with reality, but most often not.

'Fondly. Yes, my Dear, fondly. It used to be 'love', but I can't bring myself to say it any more.

'Francesca.'

So there it was, as clean and soulless as she could make it. I had loved Frankie, or imagined I did, but she had a way about her that put her in that band of like-minded women who want to castrate their men, and keep them safely bridled for the duration. I am not that man; I recoil at the very thought of it. And, even early on, it had given me good reason to evaluate the possibility of any future relationship with her.

All of which made the prospect of a future with Maria so much the sweeter. No demanding vine, she. Rather a woman secure with self-confidence to her very core, yet with the grace and empathy to understand and accept her partner's need for independence. She, like I, knew how to spell all the words, thus paving the way for a smooth, unburdened relationship.

Reflecting on Frankie's letter I thought, at least she is fulsome. Some men are turned off with a simple 'we're through', sometimes with an exclamation mark for added emphasis. Others are given a paragraph or two explaining she's inadequate to the tasks of the relationship. But in Frankie's case, I had the benefit of a three-page screed in which I learned more about my shortcomings than I'd ever expected. She treated me to vivid descriptions of my own inadequacies, ones that had contributed to the inevitable breakdown of our relationship. Yet, try as I might, I could find little evidence in her letter of her own failings. But then, I already knew about them.

When I looked at what she had said in a different light, I could understand, and possibly even accept, her point of view about my failings. And yet ... and yet ... fair's fair: yes, even in love and war. Well, love anyway. We'd started off well. At first we were an enthusiastically passionate duo. We couldn't get enough of each other. It lasted for two years. Nights, weekends away, extended trips to exotic foreign climes, snacks by the fire at midnight, picnics in the parks, wine tastings, plays, concerts and the odd sporting event: all helped towards cementing a relationship that had started in fire and only soared from there.

But after a while cracks appeared in the cement of our bonding. It seemed all our activities, no matter what they were, weren't enough to hold it together. The activities – all of them – were not to blame: they still held their own allure. But the excitement of being with her doing them had withered. It was no longer *fun*.

Early in our relationship, I came to the conclusion that she was inherently selfish: that the entire world revolved around her. This was borne out by just about everything she did or said. She almost always spoke in the first person about events, or matters concerning us. She almost always talked about how such things would affect her, giving hardly a thought to how such things might affect us, or other people – all depending on the context of the conversation. At first I thought I could live with it, and deal with it in my own way ... mainly by just ignoring it, asserting all the while my own independence. At first I imagined I could try to teach her –

yes, teach her to see things another way, to be more empathetic, to imagine how things seemed to other people. But it was a hopeless cause. More, over time it just wore me down, one small event at a time – like the death of a thousand cuts.

I came to the realization that she would never change. It was becoming more clear that this was an inherent attribute of her character. She, of course, would never admit it was a flaw. But to me, to the way I had been brought up to respect the views of others, and yes, to be empathetic, I saw it as a flaw – and a serious one at that. I saw it on the matter of being interrupted when I was working, writing. I hated being interrupted. It was just what I had told Binglethorpe: interruptions broke my train of thought; they shattered the careful delicate structures of thoughts, the cloud capp'd towers, I had so painstakingly built up in my mind during a writing session. And for what? Some insignificant, trivial question that could just as easily have waited until I was finished writing for the day. Some silly thing that simply *had* to be asked right now, because she might 'forget' to ask it later. Why the hell couldn't she just write it down, and hold it till later?

So yes, I could see it coming. It had been gradually growing for a while. I wanted to deny it, but like the proverbial elephant in the room, it could not be ignored. It started subtly enough, as these things often do. We were having dinner, a most enjoyable one. Over the coffee and liqueurs she abruptly wasn't there. I had come to be used to her moods, her sudden chameleon shifts in internal focus. But this was different. I could not describe it, although I felt it. She knew I felt it but did nothing to correct it. She did come back, but much distracted. It was then the coffee turned sour in my stomach, and the brandy lost its appeal. We struggled our way through the rest of it, and I breathed a silent sigh of relief when she announced she wanted to go home. We parted shortly afterward, she to her place, and me, more puzzled than angry, to mine. It was more than a week before we spoke again.

I saw this letter of Frankie's as rather ironic. Not so much in what she said, although that was certainly a part of it, but the fact of it ... the length of it. Frankie was a woman who didn't like surprises. It was one of the odder aspects of her character that I'd had to come to terms with during our time together. She hated being surprised, even for the more pleasant things in life. She always wanted to know well in advance what I'd planned for her birthdays. For her first one after we'd met, I told her that morning I'd planned a full day of fun events, followed by a special dinner, topped by a late evening theatre event. She exploded when I told her that morning when I arrived at her place to collect her. We spent the next two hours shouting at each other: she complaining she'd had no time to prepare ... her hair in a mess .... No proper clothing to wear .... Other things she'd wanted to do ... nails .... Any excuse she could muster. I was nonplussed, chagrined, upset and becoming more than a little angry at her outbursts. They were completely unjustified. Explanations were futile, and attempts at reasoning fell on deaf ears.

I had, quite naturally I felt, expected her to be pleased, possibly thrilled, that something nice had been planned for her. I had seen no reason why she couldn't be flexible enough to be able to fall in with the plans that had been made for that same evening – for her. It came as a complete surprise to me that she exploded into a white-hot heat, damning me from head to toe by her manner, and complete shift in attitude towards me. It ended by her being tight-lipped, an iron black thundercloud painted across her face, and only the shortest of answers to my attempts to get her to see reason. Hah! What a joke – on me. The only reason she saw was that she had been inconvenienced. I gave up and walked out the door. We didn't speak for days afterwards. All I know is I knew what I felt – damned uncomfortable, asking myself a bunch of questions I never thought I'd need to ask. Whose fault was it? Who had made the wrong move? I leave it to you to decide.

In the end, I concluded we were both right ... and both wrong. But by that time the damage had been done, with little chance of recovery. I walked out, leaving the gift bag of presents I'd specially selected for her on the living room floor.

The cracks had long since been appearing; they only continued to widen. Now, here was her letter. Based on all that had come before, I supposed it was inevitable. How did I feel about it? Not angry. Not upset. Neither up, nor down. Empty, perhaps. Twinges of regret for what might have been. But perhaps now I could openly accept what I had been unconsciously trying to convince myself of, that it had been over long before now. Maybe I should have taken the first brave step and talked to her. Except in recent weeks she has been singularly uncommunicative, and I've been chasing around the world looking for a book on an errand Harry had labeled a wild-goose chase. It seemed I was right, and had begun to prove him wrong. And perhaps he was beginning to see it, too.

I shrugged. There was little I could do about it. She'd made her decision. What I would do would be to wish her well, and put the whole thing behind me. To tell the truth, it was a relief from the tension that had been building for too long. I would write back. Acknowledge receipt of her news, tell her I wished her well. I bore her no malice; we had had some good times, and for a while at least, we did have a relationship that seemed to be working – despite the periodic sessions of strife that set me off balance for days. I owed her that, at least. Today, I thought. I'll write her this evening. It was Saturday, not much was happening and it looked like I'd have the rest of the day to myself.

I opened my email to see if anything new had come in. There was a message from Maria. It bubbled over with excitement and concluded with, "I'm coming to Toronto. Next week. My flight arrives Pearson at 15:30, next Tuesday. Please meet me."

With those final few short words, there was the same instant lift I'd had in that first electric moment when I'd seen her stepping out of Pancho's car at the Mexico City airport. The same pressing need to see her again. The same seductive scent that had been so powerful for me during the nights we had spent together.

Chapter 32

I left home early on Tuesday afternoon, and drove to the airport. I didn't want anything to prevent my meeting her flight on time. Toronto traffic is notoriously congested, and there was no way I was going to allow it or anything else to stop me. It was good to get out again; I'd spent the last couple of days trying to get the book finished, as I'd told Jim Farnsworth and Harry I would. I'd just about succeeded.

I planted myself squarely outside the international arrivals gates, and waited. Shortly after, the doors opened and a trickle of arriving passengers came through. They closed. They burst open again and her lithe figure leapt into my arms. I held her tightly, and kissed her, savouring the luscious wonder of her, and of the miracle of clean, healthy, lively girl gradually molding her body tightly with mine.

We stood there, kissing, for seeming ages, oblivious to the swirl and crush of arriving passengers, clouds of baggage on trolleys, and all the friends and relatives who had come to meet their flight.

Finally, I came up for air, leaned back a touch, and gazed at her. "I am *so glad* you're here." She dimpled, kissed me back, and leaned down to pick up the small hand luggage she'd dropped at her feet. "Come," she gave me a whisper just loud enough to be heard above the chattering hubbub around us. With one arm around her I use the other to push, awkwardly, the trolley that carried her two suitcases. We headed towards the parking area where I'd left my car.

"Oh, here, I almost forgot. These are for you," and I handed her the huge bouquet of fresh-cut flowers and funny 'Welcome' balloon I'd bought on my way out to the airport.

"Sam!" she cried out in delighted pleasure. "They're beautiful. Thank you, so much. I love them. Quick! Let's get them to a place where I can put them in water."

"Suits me."

As I maneuvered the car out of the parking garage, she turned to me. "My father thinks the book should be returned to Mexico. So do I. He said he would help to make it easy for everyone."

"If it can be found."

"What do you mean?"

"The last I heard Stanley Baxter has it. He's trying to sell it on his own."

"Stanley Baxter?"

"Yes. A lot's been happening since I got back from Mexico. I'd better bring you up to date. But tell me, how is your father? Is he getting any better? I imagine so, since you're here."

"He *is* getting better. The hospital told him he could go home in two weeks. They don't see any reason why not. He's a strong man, and they're pleased with his progress. He told me there was no point in my waiting for then. He knows how much I wanted to see you, and he sends his best wishes."

"That's good of him. And I'm glad he's recovering, not only for his sake but yours, too. Your letter sounded very worried."

"Well, I *was* worried. The heart attack came as a horrible shock. He's always been so healthy."

"I'm glad you came. I've been wanting to see you ... very much. I didn't realize how much until I feared that you'd have to stay and take care of your father, and not be able to come here at all."

She held my right hand, and I was forced (forced? I loved it!) to drive with my left hand. She laid both our hands in her lap, on the same short black leather skirt I'd first seen her in. Then I felt her mood shift. "I'm so glad your government gave up that stupid requirement for Mexicans to have visas to come here. I was rushed enough as it was. A need to get a visa might have ruined my chances of making my flight."

"Yeah. The new government has had to undo a lot of the damage done to the country by the previous crowd. They were a disaster, and I refused to even consider voting for them, Sweetheart. I hated what they were doing. Canada's good reputation in the world had plunged during the years that crowd was in office. We used to be held in high regard, and I like to see that we are finally regaining that reputation. We couldn't under the old lot."

"You voted them out?"

"Certainly. Thank god enough people who felt the way I do finally got off their backsides and voted. For a long time that was a problem we faced here ... too many people were too damned lazy to vote. They'd give you all the excuses in the book – my one vote doesn't do any good; I don't know who to vote for; I don't know what the issues are; it's too hard to get to a polling place. Cripes! They made me sick! If they don't know what the issues are, or who to vote for, it's their own damned fault. They're too lazy to pick up a newspaper and *inform themselves*. Companies are required by law to give each employee four hours from work so they can vote. By law! And still people didn't take advantage of it. It's no wonder this country was in the mess it was in! But we're finally! pulling out of it. I did all I could to convince all the people I've known, not many but enough, to be sure they had a clear understanding of all the issues during the last election campaign, and then make absolutely certain they cast a ballot. And I kept trying to get them to convince all the people *they* knew to do the same thing. But I'll never tell them who to vote for: that's their business." I paused. "Well, thankfully, it seemed to have worked."

She pressed my hand between hers, and then patted it. "Settle down, Sam. I can understand how you feel. You love your country, as I do mine, and it's hard to watch it being damaged."

"Well, it was. But it's gradually getting better. More the way we used to be."

"Good."

"Yes. For a long time there were far too many people here and across the country who believed the sun shone brightly from that Prime Minister's backside. They finally realized it just wasn't so, and they defeated him at the next election."

She chuckled. "I don't know that expression; I'd never heard it before. But I think I know what it means."

"Right." I took a deep breath. "Anyway, you didn't need to get a visa, and you did make your flight, and you did arrive here as you told me, and I did meet you, and here you are now sitting beside me driving into town, and I'm the happiest man in the world."

"Will you take me to my hotel, first?"

"Hotel? The most beautiful girl in the world comes all this way to visit me, and she wants to stay in a *hotel*? Not a bit of it. Cancel it. You're staying with me. Which hotel is it?"

"With you? Are you sure? Do you have the space?"

"The answer's yes, to all three."

She had leaned forward in surprise, then she settled back into her seat. "Well, good, that's settled. As long as you're sure you can manage to have me there." She paused. "We'll have to let my hotel know."

"I'll do that. Which one is it?"

She named it; it was centrally located. I nodded. "We can stop there on the way to my place."

"Alright. Do you live very far?"

"No. I have a wonderful townhouse in midtown. It's very comfortable. You'll like it. Lots of space, a library and music room combined, a good sized kitchen, two bedrooms, one I use as an office, laundry, dishwasher, and one of the things I really like about it, it's within walking distance of all my favourite places. The place is in something of a mess; not very tidy. I've barely been there these past few weeks. And I must introduce you to Harry."

"It sounds wonderful. Harry? Oh, yes, I remember you mentioned him. Does he live close to you?"

"No. He's in a different part of town. But that's okay; we see each other enough."

"Now, Sam, tell me. What about the book? I'm curious to know what's been happening since I saw you last."

"Ah, yes, the book. Do you know, that damned book has taken over my life recently? It seems I've thought of little else. But two good things have come from it. Two trips to places I enjoy – Mexico and London. Three, actually. Three good things: I met you."

She squeezed my hand.

"Yes. I just got back from London on Saturday."

"Why did you go there?"

"DJ sent me. You know, Mr. Dependability Jones, master art broker, and key silent denizen of the international art world. I had no idea you knew him." I glanced over at her.

She ignored this. "Why did he send you?"

"I was in his office last week. He had invited me. After a long conversation about his business, he suggested I go on his behalf to London. We'd talked a lot by then. It had been an interesting meeting, and he told me a lot about the way his operation works. Did I tell you that I'd met him once before?"

"No."

"It was in Mexico, the day I arrived. I was sitting in the rooftop bar at the Majestic, enjoying a cold glass of beer, when this character appeared out of nowhere, and sat down at my table. He damn near demanded that I order a drink for him."

"And did you?"

"Yes."

"Why?"

"He intrigued me. I was curious to know more about him."

"Oh?"

"Sure. It was his manner. He seemed, I don't know, otherworldly. He spoke in riddles half the time. But, yes, at the end, just before he left, he told me, warned me, actually, to be careful. He advised me to return home at once. I had no idea what he meant. Besides, I had just arrived. I was in a place I happened to like. I wasn't going to up and go just on the word of a complete stranger. And a rather odd one at that." I paused, thinking. "So, anyway, after I left you to come back home, I got a call from him; well, somebody in his office, inviting me to go and meet him. I didn't know who or what to expect, so when I arrived I was surprised to see him. He was quite hospitable; his manner was different from what I'd remembered from the first time. More polished, if that was possible, and certainly more professional and down to earth."

"Why do you say, 'if that was possible'?"

"That day in Mexico, he was as sharply dressed as anyone I'd ever met." I recited the image still sharp in my mind's eye. "Seersucker jacket, light blue; canary yellow, sharply pressed fitted trousers; white socks; pure white yachting shoes; cream coloured Sea Island cotton shirt, obviously made for him, and a new Panama hat. And his manner was one to fit that costume perfectly; it's as if he'd lived in it all his life. I didn't see how he could better it."

She chuckled, "Yes, that's DJ, alright."

"So you do know him."

"Oh, yes, I've known him for several years. Through my father. He got me to work for him several years ago, shortly after I returned from England."

"Work for him? Doing what?"

"You must know by now how he works ... how his business operates. Yes, he's based here in Toronto. Behind the scenes he has a dozen or so backers, all very wealthy, all interested in collecting or trading in unusual art works; anything to do with the artistic world, actually. To help him do this, he has established a network of agents, he calls them spotters, in many different countries. I'm one of his agents in Mexico."

"And Baxter's another one. How many are there of you in Mexico?"

"As far as I know, we're the only two. But I don't know him very well. Hardly at all. I met him once. It was just last year, only after I'd learned there was another of DJ's agents in Mexico. I didn't like him. He was rude, pushy, and he made a number of disparaging remarks about me."

"I'll kill him for that." This made me angry; how could anyone say negative things about this gorgeous creature sitting beside me, this most wonderful girl in the world? And I'd never even met the man. Even so I was beginning to dislike him.

She laughed. "No. You don't need to do that," squeezing my hand again. "Just don't have much to do with him."

"That's a promise easy to keep. And yet, this is the guy who seems to be right at the heart of this whole Avendaño book business. What does Jones think of him?"

"Well, he's not very happy. He told me it's just sheer luck that Baxter had been in Tulum just before us. I don't know why he went there, and neither does DJ."

"You've spoken to DJ?"

"Yes. He called me after Baxter had phoned him to tell him he had bought the book, and would be bringing it to Toronto to show it to DJ. He said he needed to remain in Mexico a few more days before leaving for Toronto. DJ called me. He asked me to contact Baxter because he hoped I could do something to make sure the book was protected. He didn't say what that could be. He felt two people working to protect it was better than one. I tried contacting Baxter several times. But he never answered, nor called me back even after I'd left several messages."

"Yes, I've had the same experience. He's a hard man to get hold of."

We were approaching the hotel Maria had booked. I found a parking space nearby, a minor miracle, and we entered the lobby. She explained to the clerk she wanted to cancel her reservation. He smiled and assured her there would be no problem, and thanked her for letting them know. We went back to the car.

As we made our way to my place, I said, "I don't understand why you didn't tell me about all this: this business with Baxter and DJ."

"Oh." I've learned that some English women are masters at the sliding descending diphthong, that overly expressive tone of voice that showed a certain doubt yet also suggested an absolute assurance, a steely resolve. Maria must have learned it, too, during her time in England. I did find it attractive, but it also signalled that she was going to tell me more of this odd relationship I was just now learning about.

"DJ is a very complex man. He's almost paranoid about keeping secrets to himself, especially ones that concern his business. It's a tough world and business he's in; he prizes trade secrets that have the potential to increase his wealth, and that of his partners. He impresses this attitude on each of his agents, not only when he first engages them but constantly. It becomes a way of life for each one of us."

"And you didn't feel any compulsion to tell me about it?"

"How could I? Now, please, Sam, don't be upset. So much has happened so quickly that I'm only now beginning to see things more clearly. At first, I imagined you wanted the book all for yourself; you and your friend, Kevin. Then, somehow, Manuel became interested in it, too, and I was beginning to think that he and Kevin wanted you to be kept completely separate from it all. Now, I see that that is true. It was you DJ trusted to go to England to try to find Baxter. That told me a lot. Frankly, I don't think Manuel and Kevin are behaving very honestly."

We were at a stop light. I leaned over and kissed her on the cheek. She smiled, wanly, I thought. "Never mind, dear, it's alright. We can get it sorted out. I hope."

I turned into my street. I parked the car, handed her out, lifted her bags from the trunk, and we entered my home.

She stopped in the entrance foyer as I closed the door behind us. She gave bright squeals of pleasure as she looked about her. "Sam! It's beautiful! I had no idea. It looks so wonderful, so comfortable."

I grabbed her and pressed her against the wall, and held her tightly, kissing her passionately, madly, abandoning all reason. Her response was equally enthusiastic.

******

I've not told you much about my place, mainly because I didn't think you would be interested. Nor did I think it would add much to the story. But now I was seeing it afresh, this time through her eyes. And I could also sense that she was composing herself, almost as if she was preparing herself to tell me something important. She walked about the house, carefully seeing each room in detail: picking things up and putting them down, admiring, examining, questioning. I could tell from her body language she was beginning to feel quite at home. You've no idea how much pleasure I took from this.

It's not one of those places that are all glass and chrome and black leather and tiny bright lights. None of those things had any appeal. Most decorators today seem to think those characteristics are mandatory for a bachelor's home; even Frankie had tried to foist them on me when I first bought this place, and had asked her to think about how it should be decorated. She was still quite new in her decorating business. But when she told me what she thought, I put my foot down and told her flatly, no thanks. I wanted comfort in my place, and not feel I had strayed into an airport lounge or some avante garde bar. She didn't like it. She walked out in a huff. I went ahead and had the place done up the way *I* wanted it.

Tough.

We'd been through both bedrooms. The smaller one I had equipped as a functioning office, but with a sofa and pull-out single bed so it could double as a guest room. When she saw the king-sized *letto matrimoniale* bed in the master bedroom, she asked, "Is that for us?" I nodded. She teased, "I'll bet you've had lots of girls there." "Sure, thousands." She caught my mood, hugged my arm, and said, "Never mind." She whispered, "I know it's for us."

She stood in the middle of the en suite bathroom, admiring the oversized shower stall. I was quite proud it. It was my own design, with three shower heads at different locations, a seat stretching the length of one wall, a couple of little shelves here and there for soaps and such, with the entire interior covered in those wonderful handmade finely crafted tiles that are the specialty of Puebla, a Spanish colonial city about 100 kilometers east of Mexico City. I'd visited there one day, and on a whim had bought a large supply of tiles on the spot, and arranged for them to be shipped home. The pleasure that day was in the browsing and making selections from the wide varieties of designs, colours and sizes on vivid display. It cost me a fortune, but looking again at the artisans' designs, outlined in natural blues, reds, yellows and greens, I was once more reminded of why I had done it.

She ran a comb through hair while standing in front of the good sized mirror, and I could see how the very efficient lights I'd had installed for shaving complemented her colouring in a way that was very attractive.

After we'd entered the kitchen to get some welcome drinks, she exclaimed, "I'll enjoy cooking here." It was another feature of the house I enjoyed, with its gas stove, convection oven, built-in refrigerator and freezer, adequate coffee pot, and a whole range of good quality pots, pans, electric equipment, and cooking utensils adequate for the challenge of even the most complex of recipes. She also admired the plentiful shelving spaces.

We'd moved into the living room. I'd lit the fire against the chill of the evening, and the Modern Jazz Quartet was playing softly in the background. We were sitting close together on one of the sofas I'd had covered in deep brown soft corduroy. She sipped from her drink and set it down on the small table beside her. She turned to me, a clear air of determination about her

"Sam, I think the book should go back to Mexico. It's not right that it's been taken out of the country the way it was. It belongs to the country. Not to you, not to DJ, not to this Baxter, and certainly not to any private collector."

She sat back and folded her arms across her chest.

"This might come as a surprise to you, but I happen to agree with you. I've had this feeling for some time."

She sat forward again. "You do?"

"Yes, I do. I've felt it ever since the day that Nelson Zengotita told us the story about how his friend had sold it. Even then I had the odd feeling his friend had been tricked. Besides, I'm getting sick of this whole business. It's not what I imagined when Kevin first contacted me."

She nodded. "I talked with my father before I left. He told me some people from the Heritage Department wanted to speak with you. He also said he'd be willing to help get the book back."

"That's interesting. I was told the same thing by the detective in London. I wonder how he knew. What could your father do?"

"I don't know. But they will be coming here this week, on Thursday, I think. Will you meet them? My father? Oh. Well, I'm sure you know he's very well connected in the government."

"Oh sure I'll meet them, although I don't know what I can tell them. But I'll answer their questions. Well, yes, I did gather that. As I told you, he gave me a lot of his time, he was very generous, but I could tell that he wielded a considerable amount of influence."

"Alright. They said they'd send you an email. Did you see anything yet from them?"

"No. I'll check in a while. Who gave them my email address?"

"I did. After I spoke with my father, and he said he would help, he must have contacted the Heritage people. He called me later and asked how they could get in touch with you."

I was getting a little rankled that others were pulling strings about me behind my back, making decisions affecting me, almost trying to control me. And I told her so. I didn't want to cause any friction between us, with her so freshly here, but I also needed to let her know that I'd make my own decisions.

"Sam, I'm sorry. I thought it was the right thing to do."

"Well, okay. I'll meet with these people if they want to see me. I see no reason not to cooperate with them. But I think DJ should be there, too. Didn't you tell me he'd come back to Toronto sooner than planned? I'll call him and suggest it. But I'd like you to call him, too, and insist on it."

"Alright."

I got up to put more wood on the fire, and then extended a hand to her. "Come, let's get you settled."

Chapter 33

Maria had spoken to DJ. She told me afterwards that their conversation had been long and, at times, difficult. Her purpose was to convince DJ that the book should be returned. He held out during most of the conversation, because he saw the book as being essentially at the heart of a standard business deal, where he had access to a valuable asset which he was intent on exchanging for cash – considerable amounts of cash. But towards the end, Maria simply got fed up and threatened to break away from DJ's organization. This made him think: he didn't want to lose her, especially now that Baxter's services to him seemed in doubt. She had proven valuable to him on other projects. Finally he appeared to have given in, albeit reluctantly.

Armed with this knowledge, I called DJ shortly afterwards. He was less than the cordial self he had been with me in our earlier meetings, but he agreed to meet me next day in the lobby of the hotel where the two Mexicans were staying. I told him that I'd learned they were in Toronto for a weeklong international conference hosted by the Royal Ontario Museum. It was something to do with the growing threat to the safekeeping of historical artifacts.

******

"Good afternoon, *Señor* Barnes. Thank you for agreeing to meet with us. And who is this gentleman with you?" We were met at the door of the hotel suite housing the two Mexicans whom we'd arranged to meet.

I introduced DJ as the person who might have some additional knowledge about the book.

"Ah, yes! We have heard of *Señor* Jones, and had been wondering if we would be able to speak with him as well."

We all shook hands, and DJ gave them a tight smile.

"Let us all set down and be comfortable." Alba waved to the chair and sofa setting by the windows. "Perhaps in a little while I could order some refreshments. But for now, let us begin our little conversation."

As we settled ourselves, I gave myself a moment to study them both. *Señor* Alba was tall, thin, somewhat stooped, had a cloud of snow white hair that covered his head and did much to frame a face that appeared to be on the wrong side of sixty. He reminded me of a tenured university science professor. I learned later that that is exactly what he is, with a career specialty in paleontology. His companion, *Señor* Zamora, was much younger, perhaps mid-thirties, had an air of implicit toughness about him, and gave the impression of a young man who had successfully endured both basic and advanced police training, and who might well have advanced into detective ranks. He was neatly dressed in a well-cut dark suit, with a crisp white shirt and discreetly patterned tie. My instincts told me to be careful of both of them, but especially Zamora.

It was the younger *Señor* Zamora who opened the conversation. "As you know, we are with the Department of Heritage in Mexico City. It is a part of the Mexican Government. We are both connected to the section that specializes in the security and protection of our country's cultural heritage. Our mandate is to ensure that all artifacts of a historic cultural nature that belong to Mexico, stay in Mexico. Yet, when we learn that such artifacts have been removed from the country without the proper authority, it is also our mandate to find them and bring them back.

"Do you know the story of the burning of the library at Alexandria? It's ancient history now, but still relevant. Some sources suggest it was accidental: Caesar's legions burning his fleet in Alexandra harbour, and the fire spread to the library. Or, perhaps it was Queen Zenobia's revolt in the 3rd century that caused the library's destruction. Others have suggested the Muslim overthrow of the city in the 7th century, that caused all non-Muslim artifacts to be destroyed. Whatever the cause the result was the same. The greatest, most extensive collection of precious books and knowledge throughout the then known world. Burned! Obliterated! All destroyed beyond any hope of recovery. Thousands, hundreds of thousands of volumes, gone: stolen from all the peoples of the world and all the centuries that have come afterwards.

"Closer to our own time, not long after the American invasion of Iraq in the early 1990s, there was the ransacking of the museums in Baghdad and the criminal theft of thousands of priceless historical objects. Many, most of them actually, are still missing. They are still out there, being peddled on the black market. Many will probably disappear into private hands, lost more or less forever to the collective benefit of the broader public. In even more recent times, there has been the near absolute destruction of Homs, of its precious and architectural sites, most of them irreplaceable, all due to the vicious civil war which still rages today in Syria. Madness!

"We have no desire to see such things happen in Mexico. All such treasures are the property of all humanity, and in our case, we are the custodians of history – in all of its forms – that are, or have taken place, in Mexico. We are a proud people, *señores*, with a proud history; and now, with a President and Administration taking a renewed interest in our history we, *Señor* Alba and I, are charged to ensure the security of such treasures. And we take such a charge very, very seriously.

"Father Avendaño's book is one of them."

I looked at him and nodded, as if expecting him to continue. DJ said, "That's most commendable."

He continued: "Yes. The reason we wished to speak with you, *Señor* Barnes, is because we have learned that you have recently taken an interest in Father Avendaño's book. We wonder if you could explain to us your involvement with it."

"Certainly," I said. "I first learned of this book about a month ago, when a friend I'd known years ago wrote and invited me to join him in the search for it. At first I thought it was a crazy idea, and didn't want anything to do with it. But as time passed, the whole notion began to grow on me, and it gradually became more attractive. And there was another factor."

"Which was?"

"I don't know if you gentlemen have ever spent a winter in Canada, or in this city."

They both shook their heads, and Zamora said, "Alas, we have not."

"You're lucky. However, unless you happen to enjoy the prospect of endless stretches of long, bitterly cold nights, and gray overcast days, and the occasional blinding snowstorm, I'd recommend against it. This past winter has been a particularly difficult one. You need only to glance out a window to see it's not over yet, although what you see is nowhere near as difficult as it has been."

"And your point, *Señor*?"

"My point is that I'd had it with winter, especially this winter. I needed a break from it, and a return trip to Mexico – I'd been there before and liked it – was especially appealing."

"Yes? So you went to Mexico. And welcome you were. We always welcome visitors from abroad. But I think you really went there to meet your friend, so you could both find the Avendaño book and sell it. Is this not the case?"

"I'll tell you, *Señor* Zamora, that I had little faith in our being able to find it. A document not seen or heard of for a few hundred years? That no one knew where it was, or even if it ever existed? No. As I said, I was there to take advantage of a break from our notoriously uncomfortable climate. I have been working on writing a book in recent months, and I felt a change of location would help move it along. I was getting stale, and actually needed a change. That my expenses were going to be covered by my friend certainly helped in my decision to go."

"Your expenses? You mean, your travel expenses?"

"Yes. Didn't I explain? My friend had told me he would cover all the expenses of the search for the book, including my travel costs. I suppose he felt he had enough evidence that he could recover all the costs once he'd sold the book."

"Did you see this evidence?"

"No."

"Why not?"

"After I arrived, it soon became obvious that he was becoming evasive. I thought it strange, and challenged him on it – several times. But it was for nothing, and eventually we drifted apart. I had begun to see that he had little interest in working with me, although for the life of me, I couldn't figure it out."

"Did this not seem strange to you?"

"I told you it did."

"And you didn't pursue it?"

"I told you I did. Have you not been listening? But after several attempts, I gave it up, and decided to enjoy the holiday that he had given me."

"Do you know what he has been doing since you parted company?"

"No. Suspicions, yes. But no evidence."

"What do you suspect?"

"I have another friend in Mexico. He lives there. He is the son of *Señor* Bandilero. Perhaps you know him? I've known the family for several years."

"We know of *Señor* Bandilero, but have never met him. I understand he has political ambitions. And you believe there is a connection between your two friends?"

"I believe there might be. I also suspect they may have decided to work together, leaving me out of it, to find the Avendaño book."

"Why would they do that, do you suppose?"

"Again, I can only guess. But consider this: I know they each are facing serious money problems. They each have large debts, for which they're being dunned regularly. I am fortunate enough not to have such problems, but I know what it can do to a person's thinking. I don't think they bear me any ill will; rather they're desperate to find a way out of their problems, and this perhaps had clouded their thinking."

Señor Zamora nodded, and glanced at his partner, who shifted gears and took up the thread of the conversation. "*Señor* Jones, they call you DJ, do they not?"

"They do." DJ's answer was measured and cool.

"Do you know a man called Stanley Baxter?"

"Yes, I do."

"What is the nature of your relationship with him?"

"I run a business here in Toronto, a business that specializes in the purchase and sale, *legal* purchase and sale I might add, of art works of all types. My organization reaches into many countries, Mexico among them. My partners and I agreed years ago that we would engage agents, or 'spotters' in all countries other than Canada, agents who would remain alert to artistic items that might be coming available on the market. Stanley Baxter is one of our agents. Because he had chosen to live in Mexico, he has proven to be of some value to us."

"Why is that?"

"Because he's there on the spot; he's there all the time. He was one of our original agents."

"Were you aware that *Señor* Baxter had managed to acquire the Avendaño book?"

"I wasn't; at least not until he phoned me a few weeks ago and told me he'd managed to do it. I was, of course delighted that he had. I told him to bring it to me here as soon as he could."

"Are you not aware that the export of historical treasures is closely monitored, and requires proper authorization including an export license?"

DJ's answer was testy. "Of course I am. That's standard in this business. Don't insult me, gentlemen. He told me he would need time to make those arrangements."

"*Señor* Jones, we have no reason or desire to insult you. We merely wish to establish the truth of this rather sorry situation. And, of course, it is our intention to recover the book."

Zamora took over the questioning again. "*Señor* Jones, we know there was an export license obtained. We also know the book was indeed brought here to Toronto. And we have more recently learned the book is now in London. I'm sure you know these things, too. But I wonder if you know the license was obtained through false pretenses, and therefore the book was exported illegally?"

"Illegally? How so?"

"It seems your man, Baxter, was aware of, or came into contact with – it doesn't really matter which – a man in Mexico City who was able to make a quite credible copy of the Avendaño book. The copy was then used as display to the authorities, and on the strength of it being a copy they agreed to issue the license. It was only after the license was issued that the original was substituted for the copy when *Señor* Baxter was preparing to leave Mexico to come here. In short, he brought the original with him."

"But why would he want an export license for a copy? And why a copy?"

"Well now, you see how clever he tried to be. He insisted to the copyist that the copy be as authentic-looking as possible. He made it worth his while to take the extra trouble and time. When he applied for the license, he showed the copy to the authorities, explaining it was a copy, but because it appeared so authentic, he needed a license to show that he was acting legally – even though it was only a copy. But, he absolutely needed the license when the time came for him to pass through departing Immigration at the airport."

That crafty devil, I thought. So that's how he did it. I said. "You gentlemen are well informed."

"Yes, *Señor* Barnes. And it gets more interesting, yet. We wondered how Baxter knew of the copyist. It was an idle thought that occurred to us, but we did not pay much attention to it until we learned that a certain Manuel Bandilero had helped Baxter."

"Pancho?!"

"*Si*. Your friend, Pancho Bandilero, although why you call him with the name of an outlaw, we are not certain."

"Oh, that. It's a nickname I gave him when we first met; with that big, black mustache of his he reminded me of the old pictures of Pancho Villa I'd seen. But how do you know that Pancho was involved with Baxter?"

"Ah. Another interesting connection. The Mexican Reconstruction Board is represented in our Department. Our Director was in a discussion with *Señor* Echeverria, and during the conversation he mentioned the matter of the Avendaño book. It seems his daughter had said something to him about it. He thought it important enough to offer his services to help with the book's recovery to Mexico. The Director told us about it just before we left to come here."

Great, I thought. Now Maria could be under suspicion. But DJ cut in, "*Señorita* Alvarez is another of my agents in Mexico. She, too, has been valuable for my business: more so, in fact, than Baxter. After Baxter told me he had purchased the book, I called Maria and asked her to contact Baxter so that she, too, could see it and confirm it. I had also had it in mind that she might be able to help safeguard it while Baxter was preparing himself to come here. That must have been what she told her father. She is actually now here in Toronto, if you would like to speak with her."

"I see. Well, yes, it does meet with a certain amount of credibility."

"*Señor* Zamora, I have no reason to be other than frank with you."

This seemed to embarrass him, and he coughed slightly to cover it. "No, no, I don't think that will be necessary. You gentlemen have been quite open with us on this very disturbing matter. But, *Señor* Jones, there is another point which puzzles us. We told you that we have learned that the book is in London. It seems very odd, do you not think, especially since you did have this precious work in your possession."

"Odd? Not at all. I told you I am a businessman, a far cry I think from the world which both of you inhabit. Since, yes, I did have the book, it was also clear I had a clear, valuable and marketable asset. I also believed I had it quite legally. Since its value was obvious, even without a detailed scientific analysis, I wanted to capitalize on it. You spoke earlier of a copy being made in Mexico. I wanted copies; clear, verifiable, excellent and legal copies. Not forgeries: copies. There is only one man in the world who is capable of such excellence. He is in London."

"Could you not ask him to come here?"

"You are a scientist, Sir. Would you travel to a distant place to undertake a detailed analysis of a valuable work without all of your equipment, tools and reference works? I think not."

Señor Zamora conceded the point. DJ continued: "No. I know Binglethorpe somewhat. He is a genius, but a touchy and at times an irascible one. No, it was better for the book to go to London. I sent Baxter with it."

"You sent Baxter?" They were both incredulous.

"Why not? At the time he was the obvious choice. I was preparing a business trip to the Far East and could not afford the time to take it myself. None of my other colleagues was available. I thought I could trust Baxter." He paused, thinking. Then, "At least, I thought I could."

"What do you mean?"

"A couple of weeks after he got there, I lost touch with him. I called Binglethorpe, and he was beside himself. He hadn't heard from Baxter in the time that had been promised, and he was getting increasingly upset and worried. By then I was getting close to the time when I had to leave on my trip. This was just last week. It was fortunate I had arranged to meet with Mr. Barnes, here. I told him about the situation, and asked if he would be willing to go over and talk to Binglethorpe and see if he could find any way to locate Baxter." DJ glanced at me, and smiled. "Sam agreed to go."

They turned to me. "And did you find him?"

I shifted in my chair. "No. I met with Binglethorpe last Thursday. DJ had told me about his agitation. It was nothing compared to what I saw when I went to his studio. He was beside himself; close to tears, not thinking clearly."

"Why?"

"He told me the book that had been left in his care had been stolen. He used the word 'missing', but it seemed obvious from what else he told me it had been stolen. He had just discovered the loss the morning I met him."

"What did you do?"

"Not much. I had little to work on. All I had was a mobile phone number for Baxter, and a quick glimpse of one of the copies Binglethorpe had made. It was a masterpiece. I didn't even know what Baxter looked like. So with that, and the suspicion that he was still in London, I agreed to try to help find him. But I knew it would be almost hopeless."

"Knowing that, why did you agree?"

"I suppose I felt an obligation to DJ here, since I had agreed to go on his behalf to meet Binglethorpe. And remember, I've been involved on the periphery of this whole business of the Avendaño book for several weeks – almost a month. I was getting more curious about the whole thing, and I just wanted to see a finish to it. If there was going to be a finish."

"Most commendable," Zamora said, echoing DJ's earlier dry comment. "But, in fact, you could do nothing."

"That's right. Fortunately, DJ called me the same day, after I'd seen Binglethorpe. He told me he'd engaged the services of a private detective in London, and would I go to see him? I said I would."

"And what did you learn?"

"That Baxter had already been in touch with the major auction houses in London, and they had refused to touch it. Something about lack of provenance."

"Yes, they made the right decision. Obtaining provenance, verifiable proof of ownership of historic works of art, can often be very difficult and time-consuming. So, did they find Baxter? Or the book?"

"Not quite," DJ cut in. "I spoke with the detective earlier today. He tells me Baxter has been trying the black, underground market. Apparently some interest has already been shown."

"To buy it? But we'd never see it again!" The two men were horrified. Both their faces registered considerable dismay. They shook their heads in almost woeful surrender.

What they didn't know is what DJ had told me before coming to this meeting. That Baxter had been completely unsuccessful in his attempts to sell the book, that he and DJ had spoken on the phone, and DJ had convinced Baxter to return the book to Binglethorpe. DJ also told me, but not Baxter – yet – that as soon as the book had been returned, he was going to turn Baxter loose from his organization. Baxter could take one of Binglethorpe's copies, but DJ would be canceling Baxter's connection to his company. DJ confirmed to me that the book had been returned, and is now safely back in Binglethorpe's possession.

DJ looked at the two Mexicans. "Gentlemen, it is clear we have all been put to a considerable disadvantage through Baxter's activities. But I do feel a certain sense of responsibility for a lot of what has happened. So, I would like to redouble my efforts to find the book, even though I have already been put to considerable expense and such efforts would likely incur more."

The two men, *Señores* Alba and Zamora, looked at each other and, as if an unspoken agreement had passed between them, the older man replied: "*Señor* Jones, we appreciate your attitude and willingness to help. We appreciate that you understand the Avendaño book is a priceless artifact that does, indeed, belong to the Mexican people. You will be interested to know that we have been authorized to offer a reward for its safe recovery, a reward in the amount of $100,000 US."

DJ and I said nothing. What more could be said? It was enough to know that the money was effectively ours, and it would be only a matter of time before we could actually collect it. We stood, and DJ said, "Gentlemen, we thank you for a most interesting discussion. I, we, will certainly do our best to recover this valuable artifact for you."

We all shook hands, and DJ and I left their suite. We parted on the sidewalk outside the hotel's main door. Just before he walked away, DJ said, "I'm going to call Binglethorpe, and get him over here as soon as possible. I don't want to take any more risks with that book." Then he added, somewhat wistfully, "But I still think that book is worth a lot more."

Chapter 34

I still hadn't spoken yet to Pancho. The pressure was building in me to do it. It had been a week since Maria first told me of his injuries, but a week filled with enough to keep me more than preoccupied. That said, I did feel some guilt in not calling him before now. I felt the obligation to do so, an obligation to clear the air with him. He was still my friend, after all, despite, or maybe because of Maria's concerns about his dealings with Mexico's drug culture. And now the news that he'd been directly involved in helping to spirit the Avendaño book out of the country. Then too there was the growing bond between Maria and myself. I hadn't planned it – who does? But it was happening, and to be honest, I welcomed it. I suppose part of it was the 'rebound syndrome' from Frankie's departure from my life, but more important, Maria was proving to be just what I needed, and long had been looking for. Even without speaking to him, I knew that Pancho would be unhappy about this; it would be like a red rag waved before his macho tendencies. Ah, hell! It had all become a big sorry mess in the friendship he and I had enjoyed for years and, if nothing else, I wanted him to understand.

There was no time like the present. I had come back home after leaving the meeting with the two Mexicans, feeling somewhat elated that it had finished the way it did, although somewhat niggled by DJ's parting comment. At this stage it was hard to tell who had won, if indeed 'winning' was to be an objective. I suppose the real winners would be the Mexican people, their cultural fabric strengthened by this one small but important thread in it. DJ had gone back to his office; Maria was out shopping for the heavier clothing she discovered she needed after arriving here. I was alone at home.

I glanced at the time; it was late afternoon, and if I had any feeling for hospital routines, it would be in the hour before the kitchen staff came around with the evening meal service. He would likely be alone. I picked up the phone and dialed the number of Pancho's hospital room.

"Oh, it's you." His voice sounded slightly blurred. I suppose it was from the medications they were giving him.

"Yes, Pancho, it's me. How are you feeling?"

"How should I be feeling? I've got two broken bones, a sore kidney, bruises everywhere, it hurts like the very hell each time I breathe, and you've stolen my girl from me. And you ask me how I'm feeling."

He was not his usual ebullient self. I knew these moods; they were fortunately few and far between. But when they did appear, they plunged him wallowing into deep despair, so deep it seemed he would never emerge.

"Pancho, how did it happen?"

"You really want to know? How did you know?"

"Yes," I said patiently, "I really want to know. I wouldn't be calling you if I didn't. Maria told me."

"Maria? Yes, she would do that. She came to see me shortly after the – the accident."

"From what I heard, it was no accident. Do you want to tell me about it?"

"No. It wasn't an accident. They beat me, Sam, they beat me so much I thought I wouldn't survive."

"Why?"

"I owe them money. A lot. I couldn't pay them. They kept threatening me; it got worse and worse. I thought I could; I promised them – several times."

"Couldn't you talk to your father? He's always struck me as being a reasonable person."

"I couldn't. It was bad enough they knew who I was – his son. I didn't want to get him involved. It would ruin his chances at election."

"Election? How much money? Who are these people?"

"Stop! ... Please, stop."

"Pancho, I think you'd better tell me the story."

He paused; he groaned – I suppose it was because of his injuries, but maybe part of it was the trouble he was in.

"Sam, you know I like to gamble. The cards, the wheel, the horses … games of chance. The riskier, the more exciting, the more challenging. When the trust fund my father had set up for me was finally turned over to me, I had access to all the money I needed. It gave me the freedom I'd not had before. What had been the odd game here and there became a habit… more nights out, more afternoons at the races. More. More. And then the luck, my luck changed. Instead of the big winnings, I started losing. It continued, and didn't stop. It wasn't long before I had to borrow to cover my losses. And that got expensive. But I couldn't stop." He gave a rueful laugh which ended in a fit of violent coughing. Recovering, he continued: "The people I borrowed from seemed okay at first. But it wasn't long before I realized it was drug money they were lending me. I had to keep on playing; I kept hoping I'd start to win again so I could pay them off. As each loan came due with them, I had to borrow more – to pay them, and also to cover my new losses. After a while, they started to get suspicious. It was getting ugly. They kept demanding; I kept promising … It went on and on."

Another coughing fit. "Well, I suppose you can guess what happened. I'd had a hell of a fight with Maria; she walked out. I was in a mood that didn't care very much. I was due to meet the people a couple of days later. It was late at night, they were waiting for me. There were three of them. I'd never felt anything like it. Kicking, punching, some kind of club … it was dark, I couldn't see. They left me lying there. The next thing I knew I was here in the hospital. I suppose whoever found me looked through my pockets and found my identification. I still had my phone; it has all my contacts, so I suppose they called my parents … Maria, too."

"Jesus, Pancho, I thought you were smarter. This is terrible."

"Thanks for nothing."

"So what are you going to do?"

"I've already done it. You know that old book you were looking for? It's going to be sold. It's worth a lot of money. After it's sold, I'm going to get a piece of the money, enough to get out of trouble."

My heart sank. Should I tell him? I knew I had to. He would find out anyway, and if he found out from someone else and then learned that I'd known and not told him, our friendship – which had become very shaky – would be in ruins. I didn't want that. I took a deep breath.

"Pancho, it's not going to be sold. The book is being returned to Mexico. It can't be sold. The man you've been working with, Stanley

Baxter, has already tried to sell it. No luck. But even without that, it's a national treasure of your country. It belongs in Mexico, not in somebody's private collection."

There was a long silence from the hospital room. For a moment I thought he'd fallen asleep. Then, "Why did you take Maria?"

"Pancho, I didn't take Maria from you," I said quietly.

"No?" Bitterly.

"No!" Emphatically. "It was her decision, made of her own free will. You need to understand this."

"All I understand is that she's now distant from me. It's been like this, growing, since the day you arrived."

"Have you talked with her about it?"

"No. Why should I? She's not interested. *I'm* not interested." Pause. "I loved her." Wistfully.

"Not enough, Pancho. You didn't love her enough. Or maybe you loved her too much. Either way, I think you loved you more than her. She tried … she tried to tell you. Your lifestyle. The people you were dealing with. She couldn't hack it any longer. You must have seen this coming; I'm sure you must."

"No, Sam. No! I didn't."

"Pancho, we've been friends for a long time… years. I've valued your friendship. I still do. But do you really think that I would deliberately take your girl from you? No! Don't you realize what you were doing to her? She told me once about her life in England, about that guy she was married to before. Marriage is supposed to provide stability to people; not upset; not uncertainty. That's what she had with him – upset, stress. That was the life she was living, and she hated it. Didn't she ever tell you about it? She must have. In the end she couldn't take it anymore. She ran from it. You must have known that! And then what? She went from one sour relationship to one that she thought was a good one … with you. But it turned sour, too."

"No, Sam, no!!"

"Yes, Pancho, yes. I love her, Pancho. I've told her that, and God help me, she loves me, too. She's told me. I want her. I can give her the stability she needs … she wants. She sees this, and wants to make it work this time. For her, it's the last time."

"You? A writer? What kind of stability can you give her?"

"I don't have the money you have, Pancho, nor that sort of money in my family. But I don't have your problems, either. I'm comfortable. You've never been here, so you don't now how I live. I own my own home, and car, and last year I bought a place in Nova Scotia, which is a great place to escape to from the city for a few weeks. Yes, I'm a writer. But against all the odds, I'm a successful one. And I mean to keep on being successful."

There was a long sigh from him. Then a longer silence. Then, "Alright, Sam. You win."

"Win? What kind of talk is that? There's no winning, there's no losing. This isn't some goddam game of chance, Pancho. It's not some zero sum game where there are those who come out ahead, and others are left behind. You're a good man, Pancho. You always have been, and you always will be. But you need to pull yourself together. Get yourself well, and when you're better, I want you to come here and visit me. You'll like it. No, it's not Mexico City, but it's one of the finest places in Canada. And you'll be welcome. I've plenty of space, so you don't need to feel crushed."

"Thank you, Sam. It's a nice thought."

And he hung up.

The phone buzzed in my ear until I slowly replaced the receiver.

******

There was a knock on the front door. It was Maria back from her shopping. She took one look at me, and said, "What's wrong?"

"I've just finished speaking to Pancho. It wasn't the best of conversations. But at least I think we understand each other."

"Were you talking about me?"

"Yes. Part of the time, anyway."

"And what about me?"

"I told him I loved you and wanted to give you a good, stable, happy life."

She put down the shopping bags she'd brought with her. She lowered herself into a chair, and looked up at me. "I'm sorry for Manuel."

"Do you still love him?"

"Yes. No. Not the way I used to. It's all changed. No, Sam, not because of you. Well, not all. But you know the way I've been feeling about him. I told you. It was no good. I've known for a long time it was never going to work. I tried to tell him, to make him see. It was no good."

I reached down to take her hand and slowly draw her up to me. I held her tightly. She was shivering in my arms. I stroked her hair, her back, her arms, and just held her. The shivering got worse, then slowly began to subside.

"Would you like a drink?"

"Yes. Please. Scotch."

I crossed the room to the bar table that was set up permanently against one wall. I poured her a stiff scotch and handed it to her. She sipped at it, then drank a large gulp, greedily. She sat down again.

She looked up at me with a small smile. "Thanks."

"Don't mention it." I sat down on the arm of her chair. "I also told him we were going to try to get the Avendaño book back to where it belongs. He didn't like it. Did you know he's got serious money problems?"

She nodded. "Yes. Well, not exactly, but I suspected something like it. Did he say how much?"

"No. And I didn't ask. But it does sound serious. He was really dejected when I told him the book was not going to be sold. He had been counting on it to get him out of his problems."

"Why did you tell him?"

"I had to. He was going to find out sooner or later. It was better the news came from a friend."

"Yes, I suppose you are right."

"I know I am."

She was about to speak when we were interrupted by the telephone. It was Harry. "Sam, Jones just called. He said you're going to return the book." Harry sounded as though he was giving me some new information.

"That's right, Harry. We decided it yesterday. It seems the right thing to do."

His voice fell. "Oh." Then: "He also told me he's bringing Binglethorpe to Toronto. I'd like to meet him. Hey! I've got a terrific idea. Why don't we all get together for a dinner? Welcome Binglethorpe. Meet everybody. I hear Maria's here, too."

"Yes, she is. She's right here beside me."

"She's with you? You work fast. I wish you'd worked as fast on your writing."

"Knock it off, Harry. You'll get it when I told you. But yeah, the dinner sounds like a good idea. Do you want to set it up?"

"Sure. Who do you want there?"

"You, Maria, DJ, Binglethorpe, me. That should do it."

"Okay, five. I know just the spot."

"I thought you might."

One of the things I haven't told you about Harry is that he is a member of an exclusive dinner club. Has been for years. They meet every few months. I've had some memorable meals with him, as his guest, and it was obvious that he was the right person for this event.

"Okay, I'll get on it. I'll call you back," and he hung up.

An hour later, he called back. "It's all set up. My Uncle's Retreat. Saturday evening, seven thirty."

"Great. What about DJ? Can he make it?"

"Oh, sure. He said it was a good idea. But he wasn't sure about Binglethorpe. He said he might be too tired from his flight, or some such nonsense. I told him to handcuff him and drag him along, come hell or high water. He's invited. I want to meet him."

"Thanks, Harry. We'll be there."

I finished the call and turned to Maria to tell her about the dinner.

"That's good," she said. "I'd hoped we could agree about the book."

Chapter 35

Like any large modern city, Toronto has its share of restaurants. Restaurants to suit any schedule, from fast food to leisurely dining; and any taste, from hot and spicy to bland and mediocre, with all the international flavours and styles in between. The city is home to immigrants from all over the world, and is much the richer for it. For they have brought with them not only their traditions and languages, but also their skills and knowledge of the particular brands of cookery native to their countries. It is one of the many reasons I've felt so much at home in this city, and have come to regard it as 'my own' and 'my home'. I have sampled my share of them, but am always open to trying a new one.

Harry had an even better knowledge of the city's restaurant scene. His dining club membership had given him entrée to an impressive selection of the finer establishments throughout the city, ones he was able to recite with great pleasure and a certain amount of proprietorial glee at the slightest provocation. However, for this evening, he had outdone even himself.

My Uncle's Retreat is not easy to find. The owners made this conscious decision at the beginning. Over the years it has proved to be the right one. It is not in the Entertainment District, nor is it within aural range of the many nightclubs that typically party into the small hours of each morning. Instead it is tucked away in a discreet corner of one of the many narrow lanes, only some of them named, that can be found in the city's downtown core.

The air had turned cold again; a damp, raw, searching cold, with just enough wind to bite right through all the layers on your body and deep into the bone. A late winter storm threatened, with promise of more snow before morning.

You park your car in a nearby busy public parking lot. Then, bundled against the cold wind, walk down Uncle's Lane. You walk quietly through the early evening gloom past closed garage doors and silent, narrow gardens, still brown and introspective and winter burned. You stop before a heavy, green painted door sporting a knocker in the form of a stylized sommelier's cup, with a door latch shaped as a large black iron ring, reminiscent of what might have been found on the heavy, dark, oaken door of the entrance to an eighteenth century coffee house. A gentle tapping of the knocker results in a small window high up in the door sliding open, and you are carefully examined to ensure you have the right credentials to enter this discreet establishment.

Inside you and your party are greeted as long-lost family and escorted to a sheltered alcove on one side of the dining area. The alcove comfortably holds your reserved table – a table which proves to be massive: round, wooden and polished. There is plenty of elbow room, and it is big enough to comfortably fit the five upholstered chairs, each designed to accommodate even the most well-fed patron.

The chairs are pulled out from the table by the two polished waiters assigned for the evening to our party. Heavy, crisp, snow-white damask napkins are flourished, leather-bound menus presented, and the pair stand ready with pads and pens poised to take careful note of our individual orders.

Maria ducked slightly as she slipped gracefully into the low alcove to take the chair facing across the intimate dining room to the fire that was sending occasional puffs of perfumed wood smoke into the air. With her back to the alcove wall, the candles on the table, augmented by the discreet lighting in the room and the flickering flames from the fireplace, her face was illuminated with a warm glow, and my heart skipped a beat once more at the thought that this beautiful woman had so willingly given herself to me.

The rest of us arranged ourselves: me beside Maria, Harry on her other side, with DJ and Binglethorpe facing us.

DJ turned to Harry. "Sam told me you wanted to meet Reginald." He waved towards Binglethorpe. "Here he is – in person. Reginald, Harry Oliver, a man who knew about you even before I did."

Among the other introductions, Harry and Binglethorpe reached across the table to shake hands. "You've just arrived from London, is that right? I'm glad you could make it this evening. Mr. Jones wasn't sure that you would."

Reginald let out a loud guffaw. "Oh, that! Not at all, my dear fellow! A slight misunderstanding. You know how it can be on those long distance trunk calls." He pulled a huge silk magenta handkerchief from a pocket and wiped his face. He was wearing the same bright red, high collared frock coat and white britches I'd first seen on him at Frieda Mainwaring's party. He turned to me, "Have you ever wondered how Mozart is so often able to tug at the heartstrings? He puts his whole humanity into his music. Consider the middle movement of his 16th piano concerto, or the Contessa singing her heart out with 'Porgi Amor' in the *Marriage of Figaro,* or the tenor, um, what's-his-name, lusting after Tamina in *The Magic Flute.* Sheer magic, I tell you!"

"Well, I have. Sort of. But, jazz is my weakness."

"Jazz? Jazz! It's a music for cretins. It has no soul. It's not actually a music at all. It is a discordant noise. It grates the ear, causes dyspepsia and forces a civilized man to drink." He looked at me with sorrowful pity in his eyes. "But despite all that, young Sam, I like you; despite this deplorable weakness in your training. I suppose it's because you live here in this vile climate. Yes, that must be it."

I patted his arm. "It's alright, Reggie, not all of us can have your talents."

"I detest," he said through clenched teeth, "being called Reggie."

"Sorry. Of course, I knew that. But you don't really expect me to accept being so casually called a cretin, do you?"

DJ stepped in. "It seems our Sam has been instrumental in bringing us all together. I understand you had asked him to help you locate Baxter and the book."

Reginald shook his head mournfully. "Indeed I did, but that was ages ago."

I said, "A long time? It was only last week."

"Ah, yes, my young friend, but surely you must know a great deal can happen in the space of a week. And it appears that so much has."

DJ said, "Yes."

Maria turned to Harry. "Mr. Oliver, this is a delightful place. How did you happen to know of it?"

I said, "Harry belongs to this exclusive club that specializes in ensuring its members are well fed, well lubricated; are able to do it often enough, and in quiet discreet comfort; well away from annoying noisy people who think a hamburger and French fries constitute fine dining."

Harry chuckled. "Close enough. But Maria, my dear, you must call me Harry. I reserve Mr. Oliver for bill collectors and some of my more disagreeable clients." He glanced over at me. "Fortunately, Sam over there is not one of them. Despite his youth, he still has the presence of mind to remember what I drink whenever we meet at the Golden Thumb."

"The Golden Thumb?" She was perplexed. "What is that?"

I explained, "It's a bar he and I like to use."

"What an odd name. I should like to see it."

"I'll take you."

She leaned closer, saying quietly, "Do you know what I'd really like to do? I'd like to go skating. Do you remember I told you once it's something I've always wanted to do? Could we do it?"

I thought for a minute. "Sure. But we'd better do it soon, though. The ice won't hold much longer. There already have been some warm days." I thought for a minute. "What about this evening? After dinner? The rink at City Hall should still be okay; it's pretty cold tonight, and there's talk of more snow."

She put her hand on my arm. "Oh yes, Sam, it sounds lovely. Yes, let's. Let's do it."

"It's a date. They should still be renting skates. I hope we can get a pair to fit you."

We smiled conspiratorially at each other. I glanced across the table.

Harry was saying to DJ, "And you say they want to *pay* to get the book back?"

"Yes."

"They must want it awfully badly to pay that kind of money."

"Well, they do. There's a principle involved, a critical one, so it's not so much the money. The money is there only to reinforce the principle."

"What principle?"

"Sovereign protection of historical treasures. It was clear when we met them the other day. They were nervous, anxious even. They claim it's a vital link connecting the ancient Maya traditions to today. The only one, in fact. They're astounded it's been found by a complete stranger, and in a place where it's been sitting under their noses for several hundred years.

They think … they're hoping, it could shed vital new light on why the old civilization collapsed. Help fill in some of the missing details." He paused for a moment, then, "But they were very worried when they learned somebody was actually trying to sell it. They feared it would be gone forever and they'd never get it back."

Harry nodded. "Sure. But, do you have the book? What are you going to do with the money?"

DJ looked thoughtful, "I assume that's why we're all here this evening. To discuss this. Yes, I have the book. Reginald brought it with him. It's locked in the safe in my office."

Harry said, almost under his breath, "That's going to be some discussion!"

******

The wines had been presented, tasted, approved, and poured. The soup savoured; the fish enjoyed, the meat course admired and discussed. Now the cheeses and fruits were before us, accompanied by coffee, brandy and liqueurs, and cigars for those who wanted them. I puffed contentedly on my pipe while Maria sat serenely beside me, her cool placid exterior masking a smoldering passion underneath. I could feel the heat from her body even without touching her.

"Well," DJ said finally, "let's get to it." He glanced at his watch, carefully removed an inch of cigar ash, shifted in his chair and looked around the table.

Harry opened the conversation. "Well now, we've enjoyed a fine meal and time together. It's been my great pleasure to have you all here as my guests. In the past few hours we have come to know each other somewhat better. The Club is honoured to have been host to you fine gentlemen; one of whom pounced so mysteriously on Sam in Mexico City, the other who has just joined us all the way from London. The Club is graced beyond its wildest imaginings with Maria's presence, a young lady who by all accounts and appearances appears to have captured my nephew's heart."

Maria blushed. I gave a tight smile, thinking: Harry, you and I are going to have a little discussion about not letting cats out of the bag before they're hatched.

He continued: "As your unofficial host here this evening, I have chosen to assume the position of discussion leader and, if necessary, mediator. I am aware that there are still serious issues before us. I am also aware, or at least have sensed from our time here this evening, that there still remain some differences of opinion. It is my hope, as I think it is all of yours, that when we leave this warm ambience, we can all do so in a mood of collective agreement and mutual courtesy and cordiality.

"This table is round. I selected it on purpose. I did not want to give the impression that any one of us would automatically hold a position of power, authority or control over the rest. That was never the intent. Thus a question of precedence need not arise. Instead, we are here as equals, with a mutual interest in the Avendaño document. While our individual interests may vary from one another, yet they all seem to focus on doing what seems best … what is right. Each of us has our own ideas, yet based on what I've gleaned here this evening from my various conversations with you, we share a common cause. All we need do now is bring them together to find the right direction to go in."

I took the pipe from my mouth and stared at Harry, then quickly looked away. Never, I thought, never have I known Harry to be so eloquent. I was impressed.

Reginald put down his glass and applauded. "I've never heard a finer description of solipsism. Oh, well done, sir!"

DJ looked sourly at him. "We *are* trying to be serious here, Reginald."

"Oh, don't I know it. Yes. It's a fine speech, a flamboyant speech, an opening that this gathering is hardly worthy of. And what does it give us?" He reached for a bottle and refilled his glass. Taking a long swallow, he continued, "It opens doors. It opens vistas mysterious, it creates visions of things unseen. It enables. It protrudes into places disguised against unwanted and strange intrusions. Look! Look at DJ over there," he waved his arm expansively, "sitting smug and complacent, as if he has already secured formal group agreement about Avendaño's book. He knows there is tension here: it palpitates about the table, no matter how controlled you each otherwise try to appear. He sees the look of uncertainty so clearly obvious on young Sam's face, a look mirrored so engagingly on Maria's lovely countenance. They know; they both *know* what is the right thing to do, yet they have no interest in creating dissent or adding to the already palpable tension."

DJ cut into Reginald's mid-flow. "Thank you, Reggie."

Reginald stopped abruptly, and looked about him at the rest of us. He seemed somewhat bewildered. He'd certainly enjoyed the wines, and I had the impression he'd just realized where he was.

Harry said, "Well, yes, it's true – there is a variance of opinion. Perhaps, DJ, you could let us know your own views."

"One way and another," replied DJ, "I've gone to a good deal of trouble about this book. A lot of money has been spent; and promises have been made. My partners have begun to ask questions about when I'm going to complete this deal."

Harry asked, "What are you expecting from the book?"

DJ's response was swift and sure. "A sale at auction for the best possible price."

I had to cut in. "But you can't," I protested. "You said you'd agree to give it back in exchange for their money."

"Sam, I never told them I would. Perhaps they managed to get that impression, but I never actually said it to them. Perhaps you got it, too."

"Well, DJ, I'm not sure I can agree with that. You and I were both present, we both heard the same words spoken. I came away with the distinct impression that if you returned the book to them they'd pay the reward. I thought you did, too."

"I've done a lot of thinking about it since then. I think we should tell them we'll do the return, and while they're still here in the city, do the exchange. I think they said they'd be leaving tomorrow afternoon. I could call them and set up a quick meeting for tomorrow morning. I'll give them one of Reginald's excellent copies instead."

There was a chorus of protests.

"But you can't!"

"It'll never work."

"Don't be greedy."

"They'll detect a fraud."

"My copies are good, but they're not *that* good."

"I don't want to be a part of this."

I held up my hand. "They own it, DJ. They already own it. Even though you may have possession of it right now, they *own* it."

"Well, now, that's open to debate. They haven't paid for it yet. It's in my safe, in my possession. If this were to go to law, I believe I'm in a reasonably strong position."

Harry took his cigar from his mouth and said, "Better think again. That book was spirited out of the country, using means that were close to fraudulent, if not totally so. By a man acting under your direction, I might add. I'm not so sure you'd have any kind of case at all. You'd likely end up with egg all over your face … or worse. Do you really want to be a guest of the Crown for several years? Or of Mexico? I'm told it's bad enough here; you don't want to even consider a Mexican jail."

"Jail? What are you talking about? This is a simple commercial transaction."

Harry said, "A commercial transaction already tainted. And, by the sound of it, to be tainted even more. The border security people might take a dim view of it if they ever got to hear about it."

Maria's face – dismay.

Reginald – bewilderment mixed with concern. He quickly poured another glass.

Harry – simmering anger against fraudulent double-dealing.

Me – I wasn't damn well going to let him get away with it. "No, DJ, no! I won't let you do it."

"No? How would you propose to prevent me?"

"Simple. I've got *Señor* Alba's phone number; I can call him tonight and advise him to contact the RCMP. This is an international matter; no local police force would dare touch it."

Harry said to DJ, "You're as bad as your man, Baxter. Didn't you just tell me you'd ended your association with him? Now you want to use his own methods."

DJ seemed unfazed by the barrage of criticism. "I did get rid of him. He's gone. He owed me money, but I choose not to press for collection. I have no wish to have anything more to do with him." He looked around the table. "I had been hoping that we could have had a rational conversation about my idea. I see that is not possible. So, if you will all excuse me …" He threw down his napkin and prepared to rise from his seat. Maria got up suddenly, walked around the table and put her hand on DJ's shoulder. He stopped.

"*Estimado Señor*," she said softly, her tone conciliatory. "Please! Stay with us. Don't leave. You are an important part of this group. Yes, you have an idea that differs from the rest of us, but perhaps we can spend a few more minutes to talk about it ... and them. Perhaps we can find an agreeable solution. Perhaps you will tell us what you hoped to gain from it."

He looked up at her and smiled. "Well, perhaps there is still room for discussion." He looked around at us all. "What am I hoping to gain? Money, of course. Money to recover my expenses and to make a healthy profit besides. But more, much more than simple money. A certain prestige in the marketplace, a prestige that would come from owning a truly unique historical item that would do wonders for my collection, and my business. The Mexicans will have the book; not the original, granted, but they'll have the information they seek, and that is as much of its value as is its antiquity. The information."

Harry took off his glasses, polished them, and putting them back on, said, "I think we should all take a step back and think this through. All of our interests are involved ... one way or another. DJ, you stand to lose whatever profit you might have realized from the sale of the book... and yes, the prestige you mentioned. Although I have trouble accepting honest professional prestige gained through fraudulent means. Sam, you still would have the chance to gain from telling this story. Reginald, your income is secure – DJ assured me this evening your fees for making the copies will be honoured, as I am sure, he has already committed to you."

Reginald nodded, "Yes, he's told me that."

Harry continued, "Maria, in a way, you stand the most to gain, and perhaps also the most to lose. This book, this Avendaño manuscript, is a national treasure of Mexico. Rightfully it belongs to the Mexican people. By being here with us this evening, you are the de facto representative of the people. Whether or not they will ever know it, your desire to return the book will always be to your credit. Besides, did not your father help in this matter? I thought I'd heard he was somewhat instrumental in making sure the two gentlemen from Mexico met with Sam and Mr. Jones. I believe he also guaranteed the reward funds."

"Yes," she said, "it is true. My father did agree to help, and yes, he did these things."

I said, "I think we'd be better off deciding what to do with the reward money instead of going on about the book. As far as I'm concerned the book – the original – must be returned. I'm sure you have all been thinking about the money all evening." Heads around the table nodded. "So let me start with an opening bid. In one way, those funds belong to all of us – collectively and individually. One hundred thousand dollars is a lot of money. Going just to one of us would only cause dissension and more conflict. Do we want that? I don't think so. I agree with Harry, even though he hasn't actually said it. I've known him a long time, and there are times when I know what he's saying without him actually saying it. I think this discussion should be about what to do with the money."

DJ said wryly, "You are very fortunate."

"You, DJ: would you consider a percentage of the money, as well as the copy that Reginald made? If it is as good as he says…"

Sotto voce from Reginald, "They are. Masterpieces, both!"

"… then I'm sure you could command a quite respectable price for it."

DJ turned to Reginald. "I'd like to see it. Didn't you bring it with you?"

"I thought it better not to. It's in a safe place."

"Is it in your home? Better make sure Baxter doesn't get wind of that."

"No, it's not. And Baxter's already got his copy. Even if it was, he'd have no way to find it. But never mind: I've put them in a place not another soul can get at."

DJ said, "If it's in your home, a determined person will find it."

"I won't argue the point, DJ. I just told you: it's not in my home. Take it from me: it's safe."

"Alright," DJ dismissed it. He looked across the table at Maria. "*Señorita* Alvarez, what are your views? About the money."

I had to remember that Maria was one of DJ's agents in Mexico. I saw that his question could be a test of her loyalties, now that she and I had become so close. She knew I wanted to return the book. As for the money? Sure, I wanted money. Who doesn't? But I had no legitimate claim to any of it. Besides, I was not so hard up that I needed to be greedy. I looked at her knowingly. We'd already had a brief conversation about this whole issue. She looked long at me for a minute, then turned back to DJ.

"The best thing," she said, "would be to refuse the money. Just return the book."

"Impossible. I've gone to too much trouble. And expense."

"Well, what, then?"

At this point Harry interjected. "This is pointless. We're getting nowhere. I've got a suggestion, and I'd like each of you to comment on it. One way or another, we've each been involved in this issue. It's getting late and we're not getting anywhere. Okay. There seems to be a general agreement that the book – the original should be returned. I know, I know, DJ, you don't like this. But really, it's the best way. And I'm sure each of us, even you, will feel easier for it.

"But this leaves us still with the question of the money. I've heard two suggestions. One is to refuse it; the other divide it evenly amongst the five of us. Isn't that really what you were suggesting, Sam?"

I shrugged. "I'm not sure what I was suggesting. Well, maybe that was it. But I don't need to hold to it." I looked at Maria. "You know, it occurs to me, Maria, that your Dad would feel more comfortable if we did keep the money."

She looked doubtful. "Why?"

"Because I think he went to a good deal of trouble to convince whoever it was to put the money up in the first place. If it were returned, it would impact him, and maybe not in a way that he'd appreciate."

She looked at me for a long time, then said quietly, "It was the President who approved it."

I nodded. "I suspected something of the sort. I remember from the day I had lunch with him. He told me even though the President had appointed him to the Chairman's job, the two didn't have very much to do with one another. In fact, he even said they often could not agree on some important matters."

"He used his agency's own money. But he felt because this was of such national importance, he thought it wise to discuss it with the President. The President was delighted at the news, and agreed to the whole plan."

"Well, then, all the more reason to not embarrass your father. I liked him, and I wouldn't want to make life difficult for him."

She sighed, and nodded. "Alright. I want to say something. To all of you." She rummaged in her purse and pulled out a sheet of paper. "Before I left Mexico, I had dinner with my father. He gave me this."

She unfolded the paper and held it up for us all to see. "This is a letter. It is signed by my father. For those of you who don't know it, he is the

Chairman of the Mexican Reconstruction Board. It's a very influential position, and as I mentioned, it has an immediate connection to our President. The letter is addressed to *Señor* Jones, here, and it states that the sum of one hundred thousand American dollars will be paid in exchange for the return of the Avendaño book. The letter also states that it is accompanied by a bank draft for that amount." She paused. "The draft is made out in my name."

A chorus of questions. "In your name? How? Why? What's that for? Where is the draft?"

"Be calm, my friends," she replied. "My father told me that I was the one he trusted. Since I was coming to Toronto anyway, it made sense for me to carry the funds with me – in this form. As to where it is, it, too, is safe." She smiled. "You wouldn't expect me to carry it around with me, would you?" Her tone sobered, and she turned to me. "I agree with Sam. It would be an embarrassment for my father to have the money returned. Even if he never said anything to the President, he would eventually hear of it. There were enough clerical and other people involved in releasing the funds, and who would also be involved in receiving them back, so that word would eventually filter through to the President. So, reluctantly, I agree the money should not be refused. But then, we still have the question of what to do with it."

Harry said, "Well, I think where this is leading is that the funds could be divided equally among the five of us."

There was a long silence. Then, Reginald cleared his throat and, surprisingly said, "I've been thinking. The suggestion to have twenty percent of a hundred thousand dollars is tempting; immediately tempting beyond all dreams and notions of the treasures of Ind and the Arabees. But is this really the best use of such money, this windfall, this unexpected manna from the skies? I don't think so. Besides, I should have no claim on any of it. I was hired under contract by Master Jones here to undertake a task for him. I have fulfilled that task, and now expect to be paid against the delivery of my work. That was the agreement, and so it shall stand. However, in today's world, sums that are truly useful don't begin until at least many, many more thousands of pounds, or dollars, and twenty is nowhere near the mark. Far from it. But a hundred? Well, now, this is a different story. A story with meat on the bones, with a fervent message buried deep in its bowels, a device suitable for making a real impact. Twenty thousand? Poof!" he snapped his fingers. "It would be squandered in no time on things frivolous, trifling, and of no moment. So! I suggest something different. I suggest the money be used, in total, to assist in future research projects, projects designed to uncover even more of Mexico's vibrant and valuable historical heritage. There must be some sort of organization here in Canada that does this sort of thing, is there not?"

There was another long silence around the table. I struck a match and tried to light the dottle in the bottom of my pipe. Reginald poured himself what appeared to be yet another reviving glass of wine and looked around expectantly. Harry looked thoughtful; DJ doubtful. Maria's face lit up as if she couldn't believe what we'd all just heard. To my way of thinking, Reginald has suddenly proved himself another sort of genius. The first was when I was in his studio when he showed me the copies of the book he'd made. The copies were magnificent. But will he, can he, be taken seriously? Will they?

I said, "You know, it's actually not a bad idea. I think we should take it seriously." Maria squeezed my hand.

Harry looked over at DJ to see him butting out the end of his cigar in an ashtray, and making it clear he had something important to say. "I'm impressed with Reginald's idea. So impressed in fact, that I'd like to recommend acceptance."

"What has made you change your mind?" asked Harry. "Ten minutes ago you wanted nothing but money and some prestige."

"Both true. But for me, the prestige is more than the money. Yes, I would be out the expenses I've been put to. But if we can agree that I will keep the other copy Reginald has made, and use it as I see fit, then we can proceed with his suggestion."

"You're paying for them," Harry said, almost dismissively, but to general agreement. "But what about the prestige thing?"

"Ah, well, this is what I would like to put forward. It happens I am well acquainted with the person in the Royal Ontario Museum who has responsibility for all out-of-country digs. I thought I'd talk to him and see if he would be interested in what we've been discussing here. I have a feeling he would be. And, if I could do a deal with him, I'm sure he would not be averse to making it widely known that I had been instrumental in augmenting his typically meager budget."

"It's not exactly what you had hoped for though, is it?"

"No. Not exactly. But there are some other matters between he and I, ongoing matters not associated with this issue at all, that I've been assisting him with. This could be, to coin a phrase, the icing on the cake."

"You'd be satisfied with that?"

"Yes."

"Fine. Wonderful, in fact." A look of welcome relief on Harry's face. "Then all we need do is work out the details. Would you, DJ, arrange to meet with the Mexican gentlemen tomorrow, to give them the book? How they get it out of the country is their problem. And would you also talk to your friend at the ROM? Perhaps, after you two have come to agreement, you can ask Maria to help turn over the funds to him."

"Yes, I'll do both."

"Well, then, it seems we have at last come to a mutual agreement … just as I predicted. Excellent. Well done, everyone. Now, let me call for another bottle so we can confirm our agreement in the best possible way."

Harry raised a hand to signal one of the waiters. I drained my glass, looked at Maria, who nodded. I rose, and said, "Thank you, Harry, but I think we've had our fill for this evening." I took her hand. "Maria and I are going skating."

Chapter 36

Toronto City Hall at night is one of the 'must-see' views in the city. The two curved towers, with their arms outstretched, are welcoming at any time. Floodlit at night, as they are this evening, they form a ghostly backdrop to the large open public square before them. Often the floodlights were coloured – sometimes green, sometimes blue or red. This evening they were subdued mauve, light blues and vibrant orange. Anchoring the other end of the square is the skating rink, surmounted by graceful arches and bordered with concession booths selling hot chocolate, coffee, and skate rentals.

It had just begun to snow as we arrived; gentle white snowflakes glittering in the reflected light as they floated to earth. We stopped at the skate rental booth. They had skates available for each of us. I paid, and we carried the skates over to a bench at rink's edge to change. I helped tie her laces, tightening them just enough to be comfortable, yet give her balance.

I took her hand and pulled her to her feet. She gave a small cry of alarm as she wobbled a bit, but held her balance. She took my arm and we made our way gingerly out onto the ice. It was hard and smooth. A clean, fast surface, now gradually covering with the new snow. A skating party was just breaking up. Most of the group were already off the ice and preparing to leave. It was just as well. I hadn't been on skates for a while, so was in no hurry to go flying across the ice and run the risk of hitting someone. It seemed we would have the rink pretty much to ourselves.

"I liked your Harry. He is everything you said he would be."

"Yes, Harry's a good guy. He's a true friend. I'm lucky to have him both as relative and agent. He'll not take nonsense from anyone."

She asked, "Will he do it?"

"Who?"

"*Señor* Jones."

"I don't know. I don't know him very well, if at all. You probably know him better. I've only met him three times. But, well, he seemed sincere this evening. So if that's anything to go by, I guess he will."

We managed our way across the ice. She was gaining confidence; mine was returning. After a while she said, "I'd like to try it alone."

"You're sure?"

"Yes." She stood for a minute with an uncertain look on her face, then determination took over and she slowly glided away from me. Then she came back, a small triumphant smile lighting her face. She, I, and the ice around us were bathed in a gentle greenish glow from all the lamps in the overhead arches. They had been dimmed to match the mood of the declining evening.

We skated, sometimes arm-in-arm, sometimes alone. It was exhilarating after the heavy dinner and intense discussion. There was little wind, but the cold still intensified. Snowflakes sparkled in the glow from the overhead lights as they floated down around and about us. They gathered in constantly changing patterns on the ice as we stepped and sailed and swirled across it. Time gently passed. Somewhere from a nearby clock tower the midnight hour chimed. We were alone on the ice. We might well have been alone in the whole, wide world. She stopped and came over to me.

She said, "Can you hear it? Listen." I could just make it out, but even so it was immediately familiar. The unmistakable rhythms of the Modern Jazz Quartet's "Skating in Central Park".

"I was hoping I'd hear it again," she said.

"It's perfect," I said with a sly smile.

"Did you have something to do with it?"

"I might have."

"Tell me."

"We were getting the skates. You turned away so you could look at the ice and admire City Hall and all the buildings around here. I whispered to the man and asked him to play it."

She threw her arms around me and hugged me tight. "Thank you, thank you, *mi amor*. You remembered. It's beautiful. I love it. I love you." She kissed me with more passion than ever before.

I said, "Come, my love, it's cold and it's late. Let's go home."

******

In the end, it all worked out. Maria and I fell into a pattern of easy domesticity. I put the finishing touches on the manuscript I've been working on. When I delivered it to Harry two weeks before the deadline imposed by Jim Farnsworth, he glanced at it, then set it aside. "Hmph! I didn't think you'd do it, what with your chasing around the world instead of working!"

Maria liked working with DJ's group of art dealers. With Baxter no longer in the picture, DJ asked her to assume full control of the liaison between the group and what he had identified as a growing market in Mexican artifacts. With the lessons of the Avendaño book now thoroughly learned, he saw there was a greater need to ensure that all matters were handled transparently, and he realized Maria's connections would ensure this. We never did find out what happened to Baxter.

I was still troubled about Pancho; I wanted no misunderstandings between us. He had been, and as far as I was concerned, still was a good friend. I liked him, and so Maria and I were planning a trip to Mexico City before it got too hot there to try and smooth over any bumpy spots still in our friendship. I've spoken with Pancho a couple of times since the dinner meeting, and am happy to tell you he's not only healing from his injuries, but has decided to turn his energies, time and considerable intellect to supporting his father's friend in his bid for the Presidency of Mexico. I still would like him to visit us, and perhaps we'll take a few weeks at my new seaside place in Nova Scotia. He said he'd need to think about it.

Pancho also told me that he'd had one brief conversation with Kevin Watts, that will-o-the-wisp antiquarian hunter. Kevin had visited Pancho in hospital, and Pancho, who had got it from both Maria and me, told him of the decisions we'd made about the Avendaño book. Shortly afterwards, Kevin returned to England, in black despondency to a most uncertain financial future. He still hasn't paid me the expenses reimbursements he had promised, and I don't suppose he ever will. That said, I do feel a certain obligation to Kevin. He had, after all, given me an interesting few weeks through his original invitation and, though he had not foreseen it, gave me Maria besides. I felt I owed him something for it all, and if I ever get around to writing the story of Avendaño book, I'll make sure he benefits from some of the proceeds from any book sales. It had been, after all, his idea.

The morning after our joint dinner, DJ met with the two Mexican gentlemen, and in a small ceremony, handed over the precious Avendaño book. They accepted it graciously and, though they tried to mask it, with considerable relief. That afternoon, they boarded their scheduled flight to return home. I never did learn how they managed to remove it from the country. Perhaps one of them had wrapped it up in his soiled shirts and buried it deep in his suitcase. DJ told me afterwards he was just as glad it had turned out this way. In his words, "The book was just too hot for him to handle." He also told me that he and Reginald were flying to London on Monday, as he wanted Reginald to place the two copies directly into his hands. He also suggested that Reginald might be persuaded to make additional copies.

And me? I've long had considerable respect for the world's great religions. Although I've never immersed myself very deeply in any of them, I am more than aware of the positive influences they can have on great populations. That they also can be frequently twisted out of shape by those who are intent on causing trouble is not in question. But where I often see their value is in their influences on intellectual learning, the creation of great works of lasting artistic merit, and on the cultivation of men and women whose interests extend far beyond the rigorous disciplines required of their faith.

Father Andres de Avendaño was such a man. From the few accounts I've read of his life, his intellect soared over that of his monkish colleagues. He was learned, scholarly even, curious about the world around him, adventurous – willing and able to bring together opposing factions, and get them to work in harmony. From all this sprang the published work you have been reading about.

I would have liked to have known him. I think we could have been friends.

THE END